STRIVERS ROW

During the 1920s and 1930s, around the time of the Harlem Renaissance, more than a quarter of a million African-Americans settled in Harlem, creating what was described at the time as "a cosmopolitan Negro capital which exert[ed] an influence over Negroes everywhere."

Nowhere was this more evident than on West 138th and 139th Streets between what are now Adam Clayton Powell and Frederick Douglass Boulevards, two blocks that came to be known as Strivers Row. These blocks attracted many of Harlem's African-American doctors, lawyers, and entertainers, among them Eubie Blake, Noble Sissle, and W. C. Handy, who were themselves striving to achieve America's middle-class dream.

With its mission of publishing quality African-American literature, Strivers Row emulates those "strivers," capturing that same spirit of hope, creativity, and promise.

NO MORE MR. NICE GUY

NO MORE
MR. NICE GUY

· ·

C. KELLY ROBINSON

VILLARD · NEW YORK

VILLARD BOOKS is a registered trademark of Random House, Inc. Strivers Row and colophon are trademarks of Random House, Inc.

Library of Congress Cataloging-in-Publication Data is available.

ISBN 0-375-76047-4

Villard Books website address: www.villard.com
Printed in the United States of America

9 8 7 6 5 4 3 2

First Edition

Book design by Jo Anne Metsch

*In memory of Grandpa and Grandma Robbie
and Mom and Dad Alford
With love, Chet Jr.*

Check it out, I've got about ten minutes before I run to the FedEx of-fice and mail this final copy to Random House, so forgive me for being brief! If I leave anyone out, charge it to my head and not my heart. After giving thanks to God the order goes as follows:

To my family: my wife, Kyra, for years of support and for obsessing over the title of *No More Mr. Nice Guy* (smile); my parents, Chester and Sherry, for unconditional love; my brothers, Russ and Barrett, for making big money so you can take care of me someday (you think I'm kidding?); my sister, Shelli; and my niece, Alexis, for letting me see life in a fresh light through your precious little eyes. To my cousin Tony Alford, thanks for using your powers of persuasion on behalf of *Between Brothers*. You da man! To all of you and my aunts, uncles, cousins, and in-laws, I love you.

To my friends: the life of a writer can get pretty solitary at times, but I thank everyone from Howard University, Washington University, St. Louis, Dayton, and beyond who has supported me and kept in touch despite my being hard to catch these past few years. You all know who you are and I hope to be a better friend as we move forward.

To the professionals: Melody Guy (thanks for helping develop the final title—whew, that was hard work!), Brian McLendon, Janet Wygal, and the entire Villard/Strivers Row family; Elaine Koster, Peggy Hicks, Smith & Polk Public Relations, Pageturner.net, and Tina McCray. Once I do the writing, you make so much happen.

To the authors: If I try a complete list I'm bound to forget someone. All the authors from the African American Book Club Summit, it was an honor and a privilege to cruise the Caribbean with you and develop lasting friendships. Thank you Tracy Price-Thompson, Tajuana Butler, William July, and Timm McCann for supporting *Between Brothers* with your "brand names." Thanks to Brandon Massey, Parry Brown, Vincent Alexandria, Lolita Files, Edwardo Jackson, Eric Pete, Marcus Majors, Travis Hunter, William Fredrick Cooper, Tonya Marie Evans, Brian Egeston, Victor McGlotkin, and everyone else who has provided encouragement, feedback, and networking opportunities.

Last but not least, thank you to every reader, book club, journalist, and bookseller who supported *Between Brothers*. If I have not met you, I hope to have the pleasure as I continue down this road.

Sincerely,
C. Kelly

NO MORE MR. NICE GUY

CHAPTER 1

IF YOU CAN'T BEAT 'EM JOIN 'EM

Early May

MITCHELL

The night I decided to become a Dog, Nikki Coleman reached over our table and slit my chest wide open. As her razor-sharp nails took root, she gripped four smooth fingers around my heart. Gaining the traction she needed, she skillfully maneuvered the still-beating, pulpy mass from its place and let it thud onto the red tablecloth at Luigi's Fine Dining. A veteran of these attacks, I swayed to and fro on my side of the mahogany booth, awaiting the death blow. I knew I wouldn't be disappointed.

Nikki thought she knew how to let a brother down easy. As my heart flopped around on the table, she said, "Mitchell, you are so sweet. I'm enjoying our friendship, too." Her wide eyes beaming with detached warmth, Nikki smiled at me like a nurse comforting a dying patient. "Thanks for sharing that with me."

Thanks for sharing that with me? As I processed Nikki's response, my brain began to spin like a pig roasting on a spit. What was she talking about, *Thanks for sharing that with me*? I'd spent many hard-earned dollars taking this woman to restaurants, theaters, symphonies, and comedy clubs throughout the Windy City. God only knows how many gallons of gas I'd used up. The drive from my pad in Hyde Park to her overpriced digs in downtown Lincoln Park could be a real killer. I had probably spent close to fifteen hundred bucks on Nikki, and only tonight, after three months of sexless friendship, had I laid my feelings for her on the line. Nothing overblown, just the truth: I was interested in being more than friends. *Thanks for sharing that with me.* The words stabbed at my every nerve. What the hell kind of response was that?

Even in that moment of agony, my eyes rested on the curves of Nikki's fleshy lips as she smiled innocently. "Mitchell, are you okay?"

Before I knew what was happening, the words escaped my mouth. "Did you, uh, understand me, Nikki? I just said I've been infatuated with you for years, and after getting to really know you, I have real feelings for you. *I want to make you happy.*" Aware my voice was a bit louder than necessary, I leaned forward and placed my elbows on the tablecloth. "I didn't tell you how I felt so I could be patted on the head."

The woman of my dreams had taken a sudden interest in the details of the tablecloth. "Mitchell, just let me —"

"Could you ever feel the way I do? Yes or no. I deserve a real answer."

The sudden arch of Nikki's back told me she wasn't expecting this. A woman of her quality probably broke a new heart every day. I suppose that's why I never had the courage to rap to her back when we were classmates at Martin Luther King High. I could tell I had thrown Nikki off, but she was struggling to keep her cool. She mussed the edges of her hairdo and looked at me suspiciously. "I — don't know what you want, Mitchell. I just thanked you for your honesty."

"A thank-you isn't going to cut it, Nikki," I said. "How do you feel about what I told you? Do you even care?" I refused to break eye contact with her, despite the fact that I felt a good pitch hike building up in my throat. I never was good at hiding my emotions.

Nikki glanced around the room, seemingly hoping we'd be interrupted by our waiter. She managed to keep a crisp, sweet air to her voice. "Mitchell, this is really not the time or place for this discussion. Besides, I'm not ready for anything serious right now."

My mind whirred in frustration at the familiar sentence. I get this type of bull from women all the time. Always in the wrong place at the wrong time. If you're me, the woman says she needs a break from relationships right now. But if you're a brother who's been with every woman in town and treats them all like trash, the same woman suddenly makes room in her schedule.

I wasn't buying what Nikki was selling. I think she expected me to meekly accept her verbal pat on the head. She probably even figured we would end the evening in a civil fashion, like two grown adults. She was mistaken. "Okay, sister, no hard feelings. It's cool." Knowing full well that our dessert had yet to be delivered, I decided to fast forward through our date. "So, how do we split this bill? I can pay for the appetizers, but you'll need to handle your own entrée, drinks, and half the bottle of Chablis."

It took every ounce of my manhood not to crack up *hard* at Nikki's reaction. Beautiful as she was, shock was not a look this woman wore well. Her jaw plunged into her firm, buxom chest. Her right eye twitched violently and looked ready to drop from its socket. I swear her hairdo frayed and melted around the edges.

"Is this a joke?"

I told her no.

"You're out of your mind, Mitchell. *You* invited me out tonight."

"Yes," I replied in a cool tenor, "but that took place under a separate set of circumstances. You knew when you stepped out that door how you felt about me." Shifting in my seat and staring Nikki down, I leaned in again. "Based on your condescending reaction, I'm guessing I never had a shot with you."

Nikki waved a hand dismissively. "Mitchell, has it ever occurred to you that maybe I haven't thought about it?"

I was having none of it. "Please, Nikki. You were morally obligated to dis and dismiss me a long time ago, sister. You know how many other women I could have been pursuing these past weeks?"

"You're a damn fool, do you know that?" She grabbed her sequined purse. It was clear she was ready to go.

I decided to discard any remnants of shame. "You got that right, I am a fool. I'm a fool for thinking we'd ever be more than buddies. Nikki, buddies don't buy each other extravagant, expensive meals. You better be glad I got those Milos tickets for free, otherwise you'd really be in debt." I extended my right palm as she reached for the coatrack behind our booth. "Now pay up."

That line got me an eyeful of ice water and a string of four letter words. Nikki had completely changed personalities now. "Like it's *my* fault nobody wants your dull ass!" As she struggled into her black wrap, she slammed three twenties onto the table, threw her maroon Coach bag over her shoulder, and stepped. *Better her than me,* I thought; *at least she can hail a cab in this city.* I'd be kickin' it solo in my Accord tonight.

The first few minutes after Nikki stormed off into the cool night air, I was a little embarrassed by the stares and snickers of couples at the surrounding tables. When a red-nosed man in a loud aqua suit caught me staring back at him, he stopped laughing long enough to apologize. "Tough break, bub. I hope you drove tonight!" As he slapped a meaty palm against his knee, I turned back to Nikki's empty seat. I accepted a pile of napkins from my waiter and began to dab at the plaid pattern of my tailored suit. It took just two minutes for my embarrassment to turn to a feeling of liberation. I faced up to the ugly truth: I didn't seem to be the type of man most women wanted. Now, finally, I was going to do something about it. Settling back into my seat, I asked the waiter to bring the Italian ices Nikki and I had ordered for dessert and began to construct a battle plan.

"Sir," the waiter asked, "you still want me to bring *both* desserts?" I guess he figured Nikki wasn't coming back.

"My good man," I said, stuffing a twenty into his hand, "bring 'em both, along with another glass of the house wine."

When he brought the ices, I downed them in minutes. Dessert never tasted so good.

Four hours later I walked through the door of my apartment and joined my older brother, Marvin, on the L-shaped leather couch in our living room. I packed my mouth with a wad of strawberry Bubblicious and tried to explain the evening's disaster. A former star wide receiver at Ohio State, Marvin has massive shoulders that shuddered in amusement as he lounged on the other end of the couch. "My little brother, I think it's safe to say you pushed a bit too hard. God don't like ugly, Mitchell."

I turned over onto my stomach and buried my head in one of the puffy cushions. *He'll never understand*, I told myself. As much as people think Marvin and I are two peas in a pod, we couldn't be more different when it comes to our attitudes about women. Marvin's already been married and seen a woman bear what he thought was his child. It may not have lasted forever, but he knows what it is to experience a long-term romance. Sometimes I wonder if I'll ever taste such pleasures.

Even though I knew he would never get it, I tried to educate him. "Marvin, what you're hearing is raw emotion. I am a *good* man, can't nobody tell me different. For years I've been cutting these sisters a break. *'Sorry, Mitchell, you're just not my type.' 'Sorry, Mitchell, I already have a boyfriend.' 'Sorry, Mitchell, I'm not ready for another relationship right now.'* You know what? I'm through taking the blame for the way these women treat me. They got the problem, not me."

Fiddling with the remote control of our Sony wide-screen, Marvin got up and paced the floor of the dimly lit room. "You know what? It's too late for one of your anti-Oprah, woman-bashing rants. I've gotta be on a plane to D.C. in the morning." He tossed me the remote and stood over me with a look of concern on his face. "Bottom line, Mitchell, are you okay? It's almost two in the A.M. Get some rest. So what if one sister rejected you? There are other fish in the sea." He leaned over and popped me on the shoulder before turning toward his bedroom.

As my arm throbbed, I resisted the urge to whimper like a schoolgirl. My brother always forgets I'm not quite at his fitness level. At six feet tall and 190, I'm at least ten pounds heavier and three inches thicker than I was as a baseball star at Georgetown. I bit my lip in pain and yelled, "Oh, there's fish out there, but most of them aren't worth catching!"

Marvin turned back suddenly and gripped me in a headlock. "Mitchell, you need to stop running sisters down! Have some patience, man. You'll get your woman one day. In the meantime, just treat the sisters right. It'll come back to you someday, trust me."

Once Marvin finished his little sermon, he released me from his grip. Catching my breath, I lay back against the couch and chuckled in disgust. Like Marvin had to preach to *me* about respecting sisters.

Who did he think he was talking to? I, Mitchell J. Stone, have always respected women, always played by the rules. From Ms. Tasha Parker, who was kind enough to relieve me of my virginity, to Ms. Carmen Usher, the last serious relationship I had, I have always been the perfect gentleman. I've never slept around, never forced unsafe sex on anyone. I've never sullied a girl's reputation in locker rooms teeming with sexcapade stories. And I've never, ever, had more than one partner at a time. I am the ultimate good man, nice guy, Mr. Right, you name it. I am the man you could take home to Mama.

Even in high school and college, I learned this was nothing to be proud of. I was no fool; I could see the brothers who got over were those with the slickest raps and the baddest reputations. And I wasn't in that club. So I endured my romantic life and took it as it came. A couple of girlfriends sophomore year at MLK, baseball and basketball groupies who just wanted to be on my arm for the exposure. Getting picked up by Tasha at a party junior year and learning the temporary joys of sex. Pulling some reasonably attractive dates for proms, turnabout dances, and homecomings, although they rarely returned my calls afterward. My teens and early twenties were an occasionally thrilling, largely disappointing experience where dating was concerned. But I endured those hodgepodge years by clinging to a bold prediction my father made the day I left home for college.

After calling me into his office den and offering me one of his fat Cuban cigars, he handed me an industrial-supply pack of Trojan condoms, the same size and brand I had seen him plop into Marvin's lap two years earlier. My father, a moody journalist of limited words on his bad days, sat before me with that box and probed my eyes like a concerned physician. "Mitchell, you're going to need these." He held up an ebony hand as I tried to protest. "I know you haven't been as lucky as you like with women, but you need to watch out—you're going to get up there on campus, and eventually things will change."

Even at seventeen, I was already a cynic. "Yeah, right, Dad. Whatever."

"Ah, ah—women don't like what's good for them when they're young, son." He lowered his gold wire-rimmed frames and peered at me in a way that demanded my respect. "Pay attention. This is serious stuff. When they're your age, girls want someone who offers danger. Someone who sends a chill up their spine and strikes a little fear into their heart. Personally, I don't think they can help it." I tried not to tune out my father's stiff East Coast accent completely. I'd already heard his academic hypotheses about why women went for "bad men" more times than I could count. I didn't ask him to expand. "One day, son, usually as they near graduation from college, something changes." He grinned at me like a kid with a secret.

I kept eye contact with my father and tried to keep a straight face. I decided not to remind him for the umpteenth time: Times Had Changed.

"Mitchell, at some point women start thinking about how to find a man who brings home the bacon. Someone who'll be a good father to his kids, or to the kids she may already have by Joe Blow. They learn they need a clean-cut, responsible straight-arrow who works hard, cares for his family, and limits his romantic yearnings to his wife." He ran a hand over the shiny slope of his bald head. "That's where you'll come in. When women you know reach that stage, they'll be beating down your door. And that's when you'll need these," he said, patting the box of Trojans.

That was eleven years ago, and my father's predictions have yet to come true. In fact, I only recently threw out the remainder of that Trojan pack, when I came across it while cleaning out my folks' attic. The number of condoms that were left is a secret I'm taking to the grave. Sure, there've been a few women in my life since then, but I always end up in the same place: the Friend Zone.

I had hoped that Nikki Coleman was going to change all that. I ran into Nikki three months ago at Trinity United Methodist Church, the church my mother forced me to attend until I was sixteen. Marvin had convinced me to make a rare appearance, in order to see him sing a solo with the young-adult choir at that week's Sunday-morning service. As I melted into the plump velvety cushions lining the pews, I felt a tentative tap on my right shoulder.

Oh, great, I thought. I was sure it was someone like Mrs. Griggs, the most senior citizen of the church and a grouch who always tried to embarrass me by asking me who I was. Or else it was some Holy Joe like Don Parsons, a childhood friend who thought he'd found God and liked to judge anyone who didn't see things his way.

When I reluctantly turned around, my heart almost stopped. Nicole Coleman, the woman who broke more hearts among the discriminating brothers at MLK High than any other woman in our class. The woman who had accompanied me to the top of MLK's academic heap—I was valedictorian; she was salutatorian. We had every college-prep course you could name together, co-led the National Honor Society, and even had a few friends in common.

But I always knew what Nikki was where I was concerned: a dream. I didn't have the flavor of the superstar jocks, pretty boys, and roughnecks who competed for her attention. Seeing the talent of the field she had before her, I graciously excused myself from the fray and took my place as a benign, emasculated "friend." But this was a new day and a new me, and Nikki Coleman had taken the initiative to approach *me.*

Even though Marvin was in the middle of his solo, crooning the lyrics to "No Ways Tired," I kept my back to him for what felt like minutes as I admired Nikki's style and whispered a "what's up" in her direction. Tall for a woman, she still had the same Coke-bottle profile: long legs, trim waistline, perky but unobtrusive breasts, and that rich maple complexion that seemed to call my name. Her hair, the color of ebony with copper-toned highlights, was cut into a stylish layered bob. Her eyes, two pearls of cocoa brown, danced with ambition, intelligence, and bold sensuality. She was fine! I was back in high school all over again, hooked.

After service, I broke away from my family and met up with Nikki at the rear of the sanctuary. "Say, stranger," I said, "what's up?" I had become so accustomed to rejection by then, I was almost free of the self-consciousness that normally plagued me. As far as looks go, my only concern, as always, was the size of my ears. I consider myself a reasonably handsome guy, but I've always known my ears are abnormally small. *Like two little brown quarters*, a nameless playground bully taunted when I was in the fourth grade.

That day at the church, Nikki crossed her arms over her beige Donna Karan suit and smiled like she'd received a very pleasant surprise. It turned out that her uncle was a member of Trinity and had invited her to attend. When she told me that she remembered hearing me talk about Trinity in high school, I felt like doing back flips of joy. If she remembered a little detail like that, I had to have been on her mind at some point! I immediately turned off my Platonic Friend mind-set and switched over to Man in Hot Pursuit, though I attempted to mask it by talking with her about work.

Nikki and I both work for Empire Records. Headquartered in a fifty-floor skyscraper just off the Gold Coast in downtown, Empire is divided into six separate record labels. Nikki's an associate director in the corporate promotions department, while I'm doing time as a financial analyst at Evans Entertainment, Empire's R&B label. The funny thing is, we had hardly seen each other in our time working at Empire. The last time we had really hung out was at our five-year high school reunion.

That day at Trinity, by the time we were done comparing notes on the financial troubles at Empire, which had everyone worried about layoffs, Nikki and I realized we were enjoying each other's company. As the conversation flowed freely and I felt my sap rise, I filled with more hope than I'd allowed myself in a long, long time.

The next few months unfolded like a movie script, at least compared with some of my other dating experiences. I knew Nikki had broken up with her first love, Barry Roberts, and there was no sign of other men in her life (which, of course, meant absolutely nothing). We wore out each other's phone lines several times a week, clashing swords over the ins and outs of affirmative action and Prop. 209, the contributions of gangster rappers to the black community, man sharing (a concept I facetiously advocated), and our various theories on the success or failure of every artist on Empire Records' roster. We worked out at each other's fitness clubs a few times, admiring each other's stamina on the StairMaster, NordicTrack, and stationary bikes. Nikki even tolerated my collection of *Hits of the 80s* CDs, which is all I play when I cruise around in my ride. I knew we were meant to be when she sang along with me on DeBarge's "Rhythm of the Night." Most girls rip the CD out and threaten to pitch it when that selection comes on.

Each weekend, as we exposed each other to our favorite haunts in Chicago, I dared to think that my father's prediction was finally coming true. My years of chivalry, monogamy, and occasional loneliness were paying off. This Nice Guy was going to get his girl.

After three months of buying Nikki dinner and movie and theater tickets—I decided it was time to put up or shut up. My boss, Stephon Evans, better known as "Babyface Jr.," gave me two free tickets to the Milos show at McCormick Place. Milos, a jazzy brother around my age, is the best-selling artist on Evans Entertainment's roster. Perks that juicy don't usually trickle down to us bean counters, but Stephon owed me a favor for saving him $55,000 in studio-construction costs. He was right on time, too: I hooked everything up for Nikki that night.

The concert went smoothly, and even though I sensed that Nikki enjoyed Milos's presence onstage more than my company, I remained optimistic. It was time, I naïvely thought, to move. From the concert it was on to Luigi's, where the night ended with the ice water thrown in my face. What can I say? With women I had a perfect record: Rejection, 18; Mitchell Stone, 0.

It's been a full six hours since Nikki broke my heart. As I leave the past behind and stare blankly into my TV screen, I realize MTV is having a Janet Jackson marathon. Right now they're showing "If," that old video where Janet whips her unbelievably toned body into too many positions to count. Before I give in and unzip my pants all the way, I reach for the remote and cut the boob tube off. When your appetite is wet for steak, ground beef just won't do. No sense fooling around. It's time to figure out how to deal with my women problems.

I turned twenty-eight in February, meaning I've been trying to win girls' hearts for fifteen years now. Fifteen years, at least at my age, is a pretty long time. Fifteen years that haven't exactly paid off yet. Women pay me about as much respect as Rodney Dangerfield. I'm not exactly a spring chicken anymore, either. A few blinks of an eye, and I'll be thirty. I should not have to end up alone, or settle for someone I don't love, just to have a partner.

As a nice guy, I clearly can't compete with the men my black queens most want: the Dogs, Players, Roughnecks, Casanovas, and Ladies' Men. Mitchell J. Stone, however, ain't about to take defeat lying down. I can stay on the path to nowhere, or I can carve my own. If Bill Clinton, my political hero, could reinvent himself at will to survive, why shouldn't I be able to do the same, in order to give my sisters what they want? I can't beat the Players out there, so I'm joining them.

I suppose the devil will be in the details. Adopting the ways of the mysterious, sexually charged, hot-tempered Hound will be hard work, but as a pragmatist, I'm up for the challenge. As I flick the living room lights off and head toward my own room, I am filled with a sudden sensation of peace. I'm gonna sleep good.

This should be one of my last nights alone.

CHAPTER 2

THE WEAKER SEX

Early May

NIKKI

t was 11:13 in the morning, and I was knee-deep in sexual harassment. Colin Lee, Empire Records' vice president of promotions, was tripping.

A reed-thin, basketball-height Brit, he sat behind the glass desk in his office and eyed me smugly. Just above him hung a portrait of his father, Earl Lee, a distant cousin of the British royals and a 40 percent owner of Empire Records. The evil smile on Colin's face was almost as frightening as his father's.

I had always heard that Colin had a roving eye, but somehow I had managed to stay out of his line of fire. Until now. He leaned back in his high-backed leather chair and filed his nails as I stepped across the threshold of his office. "Nikki, my dear, do come in and have a seat." His cold blue eyes swept over my neck, breasts, and legs as I slid into the middle chair opposite his desk.

Determined to protect my career without sacrificing my pride, I crossed my legs and put on a phony smile. "So, Colin, what did you need—"

He stopped me cold with a simple stare, laid his silver nail file on the desktop, and stood. Smoothing the fabric of his navy worsted suit, he strode to the wall-length window behind him. He turned his back to me and basked in the panoramic view of Lake Shore Drive and Grant Park. As the room brightened with sunlight, I started to boil with anger. Colin was planning something; I had an ominous feeling.

"Nikki," he finally said, "I have some important news for you. But first I feel I must remind you of my track record. How many blacks work in Empire's promotions department?"

I scrunched my nose in confusion. "Six." *What*, I thought, *does this have to do with anything?*

"You're right," Colin said, "there are six black employees in the promotions department now. Before I came aboard, there were none. Would you say that opportunities for minorities have improved under my watch?"

What did he want me to say? I was not about to bow down and call him the Great White Hope, if that's what he was after. "Colin, you have opened quite a few doors for my people, I'll give you that."

He turned and stepped to within inches of my chair. Now the boy was all up in my personal space. He leaned against the desk and folded his arms smugly. "Nikki, love, I'm no bleeding-heart liberal. Whether it's Britain or the States, handouts only harm those who receive them. I'm simply a fair man—I've always believed in giving minorities the chance to succeed. My point is, I take care of you. And in return, I need a little favor."

I wasn't sure where he was headed, but the pounding in my chest told me it was nowhere good. I gave him a chance to back out, before he crossed the line. "What sort of favor do you need, Colin?" I narrowed my eyes as if I was really concerned. "Are we having another problem with the promoters for Whitestone's tour?" Whitestone is Empire's biggest heavy-metal band. The guys were all assholes, but I'd ridden the success of their promotional campaigns onto Empire's fast track.

"Nikki, this isn't about business." Colin placed a freckled hand on my right shoulder. I decided he had five seconds to move it. It was

gone before I could decide whether to pop him one or just send a
knee straight to the groin. "Nikki," he said, "I have to make a confession, my dear. I . . ."—he snapped his fingers, searching casually for
a word—"I am *affected* by you. I think we need to deal with this.
That's why I called you here."

I tried to ignore the burning pain in my chest. "Colin, I don't think
this discussion is proper—"

"Humor me, Nikki. Understand something. If I can't have women
who affect me, well, it tends to distract me from accomplishing my
work. You've heard, have you not, how often we men tend to have
sexual thoughts?"

"I think the question is when *don't* you have sexual thoughts."

Colin found my response a bit too funny. When he was finished
laughing in his annoying, hacking manner, he folded his arms again
and looked me up and down as if I had just stepped off the center-
fold of *Playboy*. He seemed to be damn near hyperventilating as he
bathed me in breath that smelled like a spoiled ham sandwich.
"Well," he said, "you best believe I'm no better than the average man,
Nikki. I'm sorry, but the problem is that I'm attracted to you. You
should have seen this dream I had about you last night." He kicked
his right foot out and rubbed his chin, and I watched my dreams of a
career at Empire began to vanish. How was I going to respond to a
statement like that?

I shoved my chair back toward Colin's office door and leapt from
my seat, the metal tips of the chair scraping into the marble floor. But
Colin just continued talking like all was well.

"The problem is, I don't know how much longer I can focus on my
work, if I have to keep dreaming about you."

I turned toward the door and locked my hands against my hips. I
had heard about Colin's flirtations before; most women at Empire
are too timid to speak up about it. Not me. "Colin, I'm leaving before
we both regret it. You are *not* talking to me like this." I turned back to
him, maintaining eye contact as I spoke. If he thought I was going to
roll over and just accept his little game, he had another thing coming. Didn't he know black women are the strongest creatures this
planet's seen?

He flopped back into his seat and eyed me as I stood a few feet from his open door. I knew his secretary, Martha, was standing just outside, looking on with the eye for detail that would soon feed the company grapevine.

As I neared the doorway, Colin called out to me. "Nikki, you're just a bit too high-strung. Would you please have a bloody seat and let me straighten this out?"

After my Date from Hell with Mitchell Stone on Friday, I was in no mood for male nonsense. I could feel and hear the rasp in my voice. That always happened when I was ready to explode. "So what exactly is this about, Colin? And you better make some sense, quick." As I twisted my neck, I felt myself slip into sistah-speak. The gloves were off; if Colin wanted to act ghetto, I could show him the real thing.

"Nikki," he said as I returned to my seat, "I just wanted you to hear this from me. I'm attracted to you, but I realize this is improper. The only solution is to have you transferred to one of the divisions' promotion departments."

"What!" I couldn't help but leap out of my chair again. "You can't!"

Leaning forward against his desk, Colin smudged the glass desktop with his sweaty fingers. "Listen, love, you needn't make this difficult. I'm trying to avert any harassment or unfair treatment here. If you stay under my supervision, I can't be held accountable for what may happen." His nose started to redden, and it was dripping with sweat. Clearly Colin had some major personal issues. "You see," he said, "I have a history of this sort of thing, and—well, let's just say Dear Old Dad won't stand for it anymore. So I must be proactive, and get you far away from me as quickly as possible."

I headed for the door, full blast. There would be no turning back now. "That's fine, Colin. You be proactive and try to transfer me. I'll be proactive and get myself an attorney." My forehead was on fire. As I stomped past Martha, who was lying in wait outside the door, my head swam in disbelief. This had not happened. *I could lose my job! Why*, I asked myself, *did I lose my cool so quickly?* It's not like I was some sheltered little girl. I had been hit on and harassed by men in every setting imaginable: nightclubs throughout Chicago; Bulls and Bears games; the sidewalks of Hyde Park, where I attended college; the offices of more than a few professors and high school guidance counselors; even on the job, although usually it was by one of the artists I worked with, not someone in management.

Normally I know how to figure out where men are coming from, so I can cool the situation off before it goes too far. Most of the tore-up brothers who try to come at me know they'll never land me; they just want a smile, a wave, an acknowledgment that a fine woman deems them worthy of some attention. The professors and counselors are usually just middle-aged men trying to drown the depression of feeling over-the-hill. A few flattering words and the faking of a few skeletons in my closet (such as an abusive, alcoholic boyfriend who stalks all of my lovers) normally gets them off my back. So I usually know how to give men what they want, even when I have nothing to offer them. It's a gift that's won me more than a few promotions, as well as a few boyfriends.

So why had I lost it with Colin? I knew I did nothing wrong, but I also knew I could have handled this without putting my job on the line. As I stepped onto an elevator crowded with people headed downstairs for lunch, I decided to forgo the social hour. I was so upset, I resorted to one of my classic coping mechanisms, licking my lips like some goofy dog. I needed some privacy.

As I crossed the plush beige carpet of the lobby, my assistant, Sylvia, opened the glass door that separated our department from the outside world. "Nikki, we need to get ready for your three o'clock with James Martin. We promised Mr. Lee we'd get him in for that presentation this week!"

My mind was too crowded to think about that washed-up soul singer. I looked at Sylvia as she let the door shut and turned to face me. A couple of years older than me, probably knocking on thirty, Sylvia is a pretty little woman who could have been a model for *Vogue* or *Cosmopolitan* in her younger years. She's worked at Empire Records for six years, and word is she has her eye on making it into corporate management someday. The girl's read a few too many stories of women who started out in the secretarial pool and wound up in the executive suite. Somehow, I don't have the heart to tell her she'll have to get a degree, one from a real college at that, if she's ever going to be somebody at Empire. Maybe I've never bothered because her gossipy comments about my sex life, my weight, and my faulty-ass father have all made their way back to my burning ears. Sylvia serves me well to my face, but I can't trust her as far as I could throw her. I'll admit, though, I could probably throw her pretty far.

I tried to keep my voice stern, so I wouldn't sound like a woman whose career was falling apart. "Sylvia, please clear my schedule until three. I'll meet with Mr. Martin, but that's it for today. Something's come up."

Crossing her arms over her white pantsuit, Sylvia eyed me with anticipation and tried to sound concerned. "What's wrong?"

I walked past my cube-shaped office and headed to the conference room at the end of the hall. "No time to talk now. Later."

The next minute, I was hidden safely within the soundproof conference room. I reached for the phone and dialed up my girl Leslie Forbes on speakerphone. I slid out of my high heels and put a burning hand to my forehead as she answered the phone.

"This is Leslie." Leslie always sounded like a woman in command. With three crisp words, she reminded me that unlike most women I knew, she was in full control of her destiny, at least where her professional life was concerned. The girl was making her father's holding company richer with each passing day.

"Hey, girl," I said, "it's Nikki." Without getting up from my cushy seat, I slipped out of my pinstriped jacket. All I needed was a tall glass of zinfandel.

"What's up, Ms. Coleman? Didn't expect to hear from you so early. You all right?"

With most people I couldn't have been so blunt. But this was Leslie, so I got right to the point. "Leslie, why are men so weak?"

"You're asking the wrong person that question, sister girl. You know I haven't swung that way since my freshman year at Brown."

"No, uh, that's why you should be best equipped to answer that question. What tipped you off that they weren't worth all the effort?"

Before Leslie could respond, she was interrupted; I could hear the frantic shouts of her office employees in the background. It sounded like they all wanted a piece of their boss lady. Leslie sighed. "Hold on, girl." She yelled back at the mob of voices, which just set them off again. Whatever news they were delivering, it wasn't good. Leslie sounded pissed. I could see the scene in my mind: Leslie, tall and bulky in her favorite leather pantsuit, seated at a massive teakwood desk in an apartment-sized office. She was probably surrounded by inventory samples, financial statements, and bankbooks. I guessed she was yelling at either her controller or her marketing manager. Probably both.

"Oh come on," she shouted, "not the Homewood branch again! That place has caused one headache too many. Mark, you tell Sarah I said they hire one more person who rips off the inventory, I close the muthafucka down! Except don't curse at her." I heard her office door slam shut. "Sorry, girl. We had another case of employee theft. Apparently no teenage hoochie in Homewood can work at our shop without helping herself to free shampoo and conditioner. Thank God for insurance!" Her crisis hadn't taken her mind off my welfare. "So what happened, girlfriend?"

I recounted my experience in Colin's office, blow by blow. Jomo Hayes, my Part-Time Lover, would have cut me off halfway through; men can be so impatient. But my girl Leslie sopped up every sordid detail. When I finished, I was more pissed than I was when I burst out of Colin's office. "I don't know whether to quit, or sue his British ass off!"

Leslie groaned. "Girl, you need to get some more informed opinions on this one. Me, I'd step, but I can't relate to *having* to work for a living." Leslie is as honest a person as I'll ever know. Even though she's built Leslie's House of Style into the largest black hair-and-beauty salon chain in all of Chicago, she knows she has it good. She had great ideas like a lot of us, but most of us don't have a father who leaves behind a fat trust to fund your business ventures. Franklin Forbes was an Australian of old money and few scruples. She put his money to work in ways he never would have dreamed, but Les knows she's no expert on dealing with adversity. "Have you talked to your mom yet?"

"She doesn't need to be burdened with this crap," I said. "Her blood pressure's sky-high these days. My father is trippin' again—wait, that's another story, another day. Forget I said anything. No, I haven't told her."

Leslie cleared her throat. "I shouldn't even fix my mouth to speak it, Goddess help me. But what about Barry? His law practice is booming, you know."

The mention of that name took me into another world. I stared aimlessly at the swarming goldfish in the small aquarium across the room. Barry Roberts. The one and only love of my life. Barry wasn't my first lover; that would be Chuck Spencer, a.k.a. Lowball, the eighteen-year-old dopeslinger who taught me all the positions over the course of twenty-three afternoons in his grandmother's basement. That was ninth grade, one year before Barry came along.

Barry wasn't my first, and I can't even say he was the best; that honor definitely belongs to Jomo. But none of that really mattered. Barry was the one I connected with in my innermost being, my thoughts, my heart. He was the one who could anticipate my every sentence and meet my needs before I could even articulate them. He was also the most pretty man I've ever dated: tall and solidly built, with soft curly hair that fit his oval head like a frame and a wardrobe purchased exclusively from stores on the Magnificent Mile. Every woman's dream, at least before light-skinned brothers went out of style. When he got his "best friend" pregnant in my sophomore year of college, shock was an impossible reaction. There had never been any question that women threw it at Barry nonstop; the miracle, in my desperate imagination, had been that he was man enough to be faithful.

I didn't really need Leslie to bring Barry up just then. As if I didn't have enough mess to deal with. Barry was just another reminder that my search for Mr. Right had been off the tracks for far too long. "Leslie, why are you going there? You know I don't need Barry in my life right now."

"Oh," Leslie said, "and you *do* need someone like Jomo? Okay, Nikki, whatever. Had your weekly HIV test yet?"

Leslie knew she wasn't right. I had told her about the HIV test I took last year, and she hadn't let me live it down since. "Leslie, I'm still clean, as always. Why you gotta go there? I told you about that in confidence—"

"Forget I said anything, girl. You don't need me tripping. On a more pleasant note, what happened on your outing with young Mitchell Stone? You were pretty coy yesterday."

Leslie's question provided some much needed comic relief. "Oh, you'll like this, Les. I've been nice enough to spend some of every weekend with this Negro for the last few months, right? You know, just kickin' it."

"Yeah, I thought it sounded like things were working out well. Thought you might be kicking Jomo to the curb and making a go of it with ol' Mitchell."

I didn't even try to fight the chuckle that built up in my throat. "Uh, no. Come on, Les, this is Mitchell Stone we're talking about."

"And?"

I buried my head in my hands. Leslie had been out of the game a bit too long. There are two types of men: those who make you want to hop into bed, and those who don't. Mitchell has never quite fit into Class Number One. I'm very selective about who I sleep with, but the one thing you can bet on is when I give it up to a guy, it's because my body demands I do so. Now, if the brother has no job, more than one gold tooth, a Jheri-curl, cuttin' breath, multiple babies, or an abusive streak, then those bodily demands are denied. But Nikki Coleman doesn't give pity sex.

Not that giving Mitchell some was always out of the question. I remember seeing him for the first time, sophomore year at MLK. He was playing a pickup basketball game with Barry and a few other shorties. His brother, Marvin, was already a legend for his football exploits, and known for being fine, too, despite being a religious nerd. I remember thinking Mitchell looked a lot like his brother. They had the same height, broad shoulders, rich caramel complexions, and wide eyes that demanded the attention of any admirer. That said, Mitchell fell a little short of Marvin's photogenic quality. He was handsome but imperfect: lips and nose a little too big, ears almost nonexistent. Regardless, I was a bit intrigued, enough to ask my girl Angie Wright about him as we sat by the court that day. I only remember one thing between the time I asked and the time I lost interest—she told me he was a straight-A student. I was already being run down by my friends for being a bookworm back then; I was not adding to that by dating another egghead.

I tried to make the picture clear for Leslie. "Leslie, I downgraded Mitchell back to friend status after our fourth date, you know that. The times we went out, we never did *anything* physical. He treated me like a porcelain doll, like he couldn't breathe on me, much less touch me."

Leslie's voice dropped an octave. "What," she asked, sounding confused, "he didn't have any moves? He was stiff?"

"No, he seemed to be comfortable with his body. He's not a nerd or anything; he just didn't have that 'way' about him. You know, like the way Barry has that fluid ease about his walk that screams, 'I Am the Man'? Or the way Jomo, whatever you may think about him, moves with a hard, macho flair that *tells* you he can throw down in the bedroom!" I realized I was chuckling a bit too much for the workplace. God forbid Colin might be having my conversations taped. "Les, Mitchell was just too much of a gentleman. A woman likes to feel she can drive a man out of his mind."

"Nikki, he was Most Likely to Succeed at MLK, not Most Desirable Male. You expected him to paw your gear off on the first date?"

"Well, it makes a girl wonder. You know, now I think I understand those gay rumors Shelly Bivins tried to spread about him senior year." I paused, realizing I was on sensitive ground. "Not that there's anything wrong with being gay, but I know Mitchell was upset with Shelly over that. But when he acts like he's too good to go for a goodnight kiss, what's a girl to think?"

Leslie sighed in what sounded like resignation. "So you wrote him off a long time ago. What was the big deal about the other night then?"

I recounted the experience, the way Mitchell orchestrated Friday night like some staged production: the Milos concert, the boat ride on the Chicago River, dinner at Luigi's. Leslie oohed and ahhed at every step, like she didn't know I'd been treated to these antics by more brothers than I can count. By the time I detailed Mitchell's profession of love and his sudden loss of good sense, she almost dropped her phone.

"Girl, you have driven a good man to his knees! Not now, Mark." I heard her office door slam shut again. "Whoo! So Mitchell *is* losing his mind."

"What do you mean?"

"Well, my cousin O'Dell said Mitchell reserved his entire restaurant for tomorrow night. Told O'Dell the restaurant would only be open to a select group of brothers. Most of them are folk O'Dell knows—Tony Gooden, Malik Samuels, Bobby Wynn, Brian Winands . . ."

I was confused. Leslie had just named some of the most heartless, shallow players we attended high school with. With the exception of Tony, these men were responsible for a total of twelve illegitimate babies. "I know Mitchell used to be tight with Tony, but what's he doing with those other losers?"

"That's what O'Dell's trying to figure. All Mitchell said was he's looking for an instructor. Is that strange or what?"

A voice on the other side of the conference-room door called out for me. "Nikki!" It was Sylvia. Reality began to creep its way back into my brain. "Leslie, I've gotta go. You hear what that nut's up to, I'd like to know. I need a good laugh these days."

"Call me tonight, girl."

"All right. Later." I slipped my feet back into my heels and opened the door. Sylvia whirled into the room, her hands a blur as she ran down all my phone messages from the last thirty minutes. I let them all float in one ear and out the other, until she mentioned James Martin again. Apparently he was coming in early, so he could make another meeting with a rival label across town. I went over the list of materials we needed for the meeting and reviewed my draft of the promotional plan. If James Martin really thought another company would be better prepared to get him back on the charts, he was a bigger fool than my father.

I rushed back to my office and hit the speakerphone to order a bagel and salad from the café downstairs before throwing myself into another proposal draft. I had to push my encounter with Colin to the side until I had time to make a clear-headed decision about my next step. I knew that I was going to have to raise some hell, but I would wait until I got off work to figure out how. There was only one problem: I had a burning, sinking feeling I was going to start by calling attorney Barry Roberts, Esq.

. . . .

CHAPTER 3

THE DOG POUND

MITCHELL

t was six-thirty Tuesday evening, and I was trying to keep Marvin out of my business. He had just returned from his trip to D.C., where he made the rounds at *Meet the Press*, *This Week with Sam and Cokie*, Howard University, and Capitol Hill. Marvin's something of a local celebrity, and his local TV appearances have won him national recognition. He makes trips all over the country now, networking on behalf of his law firm, Wilder & Thorpe, and serving as the poster child for Black Republicans. If I hear him blame all of Black America's problems on fornication one more time, I'm gonna be sick to my stomach.

That hadn't stopped Marvin from trying to infect me with his wisdom, of course. As I finished brushing my hair in front of the bathroom mirror, he eyed me judgmentally from the living room couch.

"Mitchell," he said, "I guess you're going to have to learn your lesson the hard way." He sighed like a parent addressing a six-year-old child. "Do you really think turning yourself into a Ladies' Man will help you find a good woman? Is that what you think the good sisters out there want?"

I tucked a navy blue rugby into my slacks and gave him a wide smile. "Brother man, don't knock it until you've tried it."

Marvin walked over to the doorway of the bathroom. "Don't do this, Mitchell. Be true to yourself. We both know you were raised better than this."

"Marvin, please." I tried to ignore my anger as I leaned over the sink and glimpsed the top of my head. My spongy mass of finely graded curls, the sole evidence of the drop of Choctaw Indian in the Stone bloodline, was shiny and well groomed. I'd always gotten compliments on my hair, but I knew those days were coming to an end. When I looked close enough, I noticed that a tad more light hopped off the mirror from the top of my head than from anywhere else. Thinning hair is a family tradition. Any Stone male who makes it past thirty with more than an inch on top is blessed. Dad is bald as a baby's bottom, and Marvin, six months shy of thirty, is already cutting his hair without a guard. Pretty soon he'll look like Isaac Hayes. Not me, though. As I'd been doing for the last three months, I retrieved my trusty can of Kiwi black shoe polish from behind the mirror. A few dollops in the right places, and voilà—the doughnut hole forming atop my head was gone.

By the time I finished touching up my fade, I was ready to address Marvin's criticisms. "Big brother," I said as I shrugged my way into a faded bomber jacket, "you have some nerve saying I was raised better than that. If I wanna try being a Ladies' Man, who are you to judge? You don't see me calling you a failure 'cause you couldn't keep your marriage together."

As I grabbed my car keys from the closet, Marvin blocked my path to the door. I quickly realized I had stepped over a very thin line. There was a good possibility I was not going to make it to my appointment alive.

"Mitchell," Marvin said as he pinned me against the door, "get out of here, now. If I respond to that crack, you won't live to see twenty-nine." I responded by ducking under his arm and scrambling out the door while I still could. *What was I thinking?*

Twenty minutes later I climbed out of my ride and stepped hard into O'Dell's Chicken & Waffle Shack. Located a few blocks from the heart of the Loop, up the street from the fifties-style Mickey D's and Ed Debevic's, O'Dell's had a prime location for an up-and-coming soul-food joint. My boy O'Dell Reese, a hanging partner from my days at MLK High, opened the place last summer. As I knocked on the wooden door, O'Dell peered through the glass pane. Short and thick, O'Dell looks like an athletic version of Eddie Murphy in *The Nutty Professor.* Now he was dressed in a tattered Levi's shirt, Wrangler jeans, and clunky Timberland boots; his only attempt at looking like a chef was the large white apron wrapped around his pudgy waistline.

"Mitchell, what up, man?" O'Dell's voice was still flavored by a hint of his parents' Louisville upbringing. He pulled me inside the restaurant and wrapped me in a quick bear hug, suffocating me with the smell of fried potatoes, Miller Lite, and Michael Jordan cologne. O'Dell and I saw each other only a few times a year, so I never quite got around to telling him to tone down his greetings.

I wrestled myself from his hug and clapped him on the shoulder. "I'm chillin', man. Is everything ready?"

Fingering his short 'fro, O'Dell frowned, wrinkling his impressive beard. "What'd you do, boy? Something's different about you."

It took me a second to figure it out. "What, this?" I tapped my chin, which was covered with a well-groomed goatee. It was a look I hadn't tried since my teenage-rebellion years.

O'Dell grinned mischievously. "Well, it's not as sharp as mine, but it's a start. So when you gon' tell me what this night is about? You must have one hell of a bash planned."

I decided to sidestep his question. "O'Dell, I told you, man, just mind the store for me." I reached into my jacket pocket and removed my suede wallet. I unzipped the sucker and handed him a check for five hundred dollars. "I know it's not a full night's take, but it should get you close, huh?"

O'Dell gripped the check eagerly. "Hey, man, what are friends for?" O'Dell had been pretty tight-lipped about how the place was doing, which meant he was still losing money, so I wasn't offended that he took the check. Now that the weather was starting to warm up, despite Lake Michigan's constant chilly breezes, traffic would be picking up, and hopefully the Shack would break into the black. In the meantime, I was all for helping a brother out. O'Dell slipped the check into his right jeans pocket and yanked his head back toward the bar, a waist-high, one-hundred-yard stretch of wood topped with a slick varnish. It wasn't pretty, but it was homey enough for anyone in the mood for soul food and brew. "I'm gonna slip back and finish the last batch of ribs and wings, Money," O'Dell said. "You mind watching the door? You can let your guests in and—"

"O'Dell!" We were interrupted by the insistent voice of Lyssa, O'Dell's junior-high sweetheart and mother of their four kids. The oldest twin boys, now six, were already too cool to stay home with their grandparents. I could hear them frolicking in the kitchen with Lyssa and the hired help. O'Dell had himself a true family business. But I could see it didn't come free. "O'Dell Reese, Jr.," Lyssa yelled, "get your behind down here right this minute! I can't watch these kids and do all your work for you! These ribs are burning!"

"The love of my life calls," O'Dell said, rolling his eyes not so playfully. His smile was wide, but his droopy eyes told the real story: O'Dell was a brother burdened with wife and children, the two central pillars of manhood. As I watched my boy trudge off to do Lyssa's bidding, I reconsidered: maybe being a male version of an old maid wasn't so bad after all.

I stood alone in the middle of the lobby and inhaled the cedar scent of the floorboards. Slowly, I traipsed toward the back of the restaurant to the Grub House, the main room and center of action at O'Dell's. The cedar-paneled walls were covered with an array of sports paraphernalia, Greek-letter organization symbols, black-college sweatshirts and gear, and numerous photos of O'Dell and Lyssa with celebrities ranging from Scottie Pippen to *Ebony* publisher John H. Johnson.

Obeying my instructions, O'Dell had organized his two largest round tables, each of which seated six, in the middle of the Grub House floor. I took a seat at the far table and leaned back, tilting the wooden chair at a thirty-degree angle. My Dog Pound would be arriving shortly.

I was glad that O'Dell had his hands full in the kitchen. I wasn't eager to tell him he was not one of the guests of honor this evening. When you want to master an art, you go to the best. I needed to learn how to be a Casanova from a true master, and O'Dell wasn't quite as accomplished as my guests of honor. Lyssa wasn't the only woman he'd ever boned, of course, but it was always obvious that once he'd hit those skins, O'Dell was no good for anyone else. Sure, he talked all the typical trash, whenever they had their little weeklong separations in our days at MLK. *I don't need that trick, yo. It's plenty of better-looking honeys just waitin' on a brother.* O'Dell was right, he could have done better, but he never did. He'd mess with a girl here or there during their breakups, then go crawling back to his "baby." But today you couldn't tell O'Dell he wasn't the most skilled Player who ever lived in his single days. We all play along with him, in the way the family of the terminally ill agree to any silly or wishful statement, but we know the boy's a stone-cold perpetrator. There was nothing O'Dell could do for me tonight, except serve up a hot meal.

Amidst the noise of whizzing cars and blaring horns outside, the guests began flowing in shortly after eight. As a trio of waiters and waitresses, kids in their teens and early twenties, emerged from the kitchen, I steeled my nerves and headed back out to the lobby. There was no turning back now.

Within minutes I was making my rounds through the Grub House. Guy's "Groove Me" blared over the speakers, and the hired help scurried back and forth with mugs full of suds.

The first brother I ran into was my boy Malik Samuels. Malik and I were running buddies in junior high, playing side by side on the basketball team at St. Mary's and collaborating on a couple of big science-fair projects. At MLK our friendship survived on the strength of our shared time on the bench of the varsity basketball team. Malik was always suffering with one knee injury or another, and I was always suffering from a lack of talent.

"Gotta tell you, Mitch," Malik said as he patted down his immaculate fade and checked his look in the mirror over the bar, "you freaked me out with this invitation. I *had* to come out and see what this was about." Dressed in a tailored olive sport coat and baggy Guess jeans that draped his lanky frame, Malik still had the easy style that always drew women like flies. He had been the first guy I knew who perfected the acts of adolescent romance: French kissing, fondling, and driving downtown. His expertise was so legendary by seventh grade that girls black and white were taking a number to meet with him in the band room after school. I still have him to thank for my early understanding of the female anatomy. I remember envying Malik on a level I had previously reserved only for my father; here was a guy doing things I could only dream of. How did he know where to put everything, where to touch, where to probe, without doing something stupid or embarrassing? Malik had been as cool to me at that time as Michael Jackson himself. A Thriller of women.

I continued to make my rounds, popping into the various cliques that form when you put a group of competitive brothers together. I spotted my boy Trey Benton, tonight's only Caucasian guest. I was still five feet from him when he yelled at the top of his lungs. "Stoney, what up, Boyeee!" His head shaved bald and his face covered by long sideburns and a bushy goatee, Trey probably looked more frightful to most white people than did any of us brothers in the room. As always, he was dressed like a white Tupac, sporting an oversized jean jacket, denim pants that exposed a large sheath of his plaid boxer shorts, and a pair of Air Jordans with fluorescent laces. Folks tended to either love Trey or hate him, viewing him either as a wanna-be or a "down homie." Judging by the number of high-yellow kids he had running around town, it was clear plenty of sisters thought he was down. "Stoney," he said, hugging me close, "how's the boy who pulled me through honors calc?"

"I'm good, baby, I'm good." I clapped him on the shoulder as I pulled away. "How's Jeanine?"

Chewing on his lip, Trey broke eye contact and fondled the Bud Lite in his hand. "Yo, she buggin', I'm gonna have to kick her to the curb. It's all right, though. There's always plenty more where she came from. Ya know how it is!"

I had absolutely no idea how that was; if I'd been able to land so much as one good woman with the ease he did, I wouldn't have been at O'Dell's that night. I rolled with his crack anyway and continued through the crowd. Every type of brother was up in the place. Natty dressers. Pretty boys who looked like crosses between a DeBarge, Gregory Abbott, and Ginuwine. Big-time jocks who were still built like solid rock. Homely brothers with wack gear but the charisma of ten men. They all had one thing in common: more women than they could handle.

I was about to start the meeting when I was yanked back toward the bar by my former best friend, Tony Gooden. In his first year as deputy mayor of Chicago, Tony's huge ego had swelled to frightening proportions. I guess being top aide to the mayor of a major city can do that to you. Tony and I hadn't hung out much since high school, partly because I knew he hadn't handled local fame and influence very well. Most people insisted he'd turned into quite the asshole. But I was touched that Tony, who fancied himself Chicago's Most Eligible Bachelor, thought enough of me to bless us with his presence tonight.

He leaned toward me and smiled. "You know I couldn't miss this, man. Free grub *and* free networking? They're the engine of commerce and politics. That's what I *do*." Leaning against the bar, Tony loosened his red power tie casually. "Now, explain this business to me." He plopped his invitation, a piece of beige stationery with red lettering, onto the varnished countertop. I tried not to flush in embarrassment as I read the now familiar words:

Fellow Brothers (and Trey),
You can ask ten people the definition of success and get ten different answers. My personal definition of success is a willingness to pay whatever price is required to reach your goal. My brother, if you have received this letter, it says something very powerful

about you. It says that I, Mitchell Stone, your friend and brother, deem you worthy of assisting me in my latest goal. It means that you have exhibited characteristics that assure that you can train me in a life or death mission.

If you are interested in hearing more, please join me on May 12 at 7 PM for an evening of FREE FOOD (WINGS, RIBS, & FRIES) AND BEER at O'Dell's Chicken & Waffle Shack. We'll trip, we'll grub, and then we'll discuss my plans and the role you might play in them. God bless, As-salaamalaikaum, and etc.

Your boy,
Mitchell Stone

As I smirked at the self-important tone of my own words, Tony eyed me impatiently. "You gonna explain this, Mitchell? What the hell are you talking about?" He paused and leaned in toward me. "You're selling some of that Amway shit, aren't you?"

"If I'm going to have to explain this to you," I replied, "I may as well explain it to everyone."

Five minutes later I had calmed everyone down. I hopped up onto the little platform stage at the front of the room and started speaking over the strains of Bobby Brown's "My Prerogative." "Brothers, I'm here tonight to do something I never thought I would. You all know I've never been a star on the football field of romance."

"There's a news flash," Bobby Wynn taunted from the back of the room. Once an asshole, always an asshole.

"Well, brothers, I've finally tired of being passed over by the sisters for the likes of you. I'm selling out, there's no need sugarcoating it. That's my purpose tonight, to find the Dog who can best teach me his tricks. Take a look around, brothers." I paused as the men looked around, eyeing each other with reservation in some cases, amusement in most others. "I think we're breaking a record tonight. Have there ever been this many Players in one place?" I paused and pointed out Malik Samuels. "Malik, you're used to being the guy who's had the most women in any given room, at any given time. Am I right?"

"What? I—well, yeah, now that you mention it." Malik crossed his arms. I could tell I had caught him off guard.

I felt a wicked smile creep across my face. "Take another look around, man. You think you're still the top Player in *this* room?"

Malik's eyes flitted confidently over the crowd, until he locked onto Bobby Wynn. A star quarterback in our MLK days and an unrepentant Ho, Bobby has kids by two of the same women Malik has knocked up in recent years. "Damn." Malik's confidence was clearly shaken.

I seized the opportunity. "Let's take someone else. Tony, you got a late start compared with a lot of these guys, but since you've been in the mayor's office, you think anyone here's matched your rate of pulling?"

Tony took one look at Bobby, Malik, Trey, and Brian Winands before shrugging. "I wouldn't even wager on that one. But hey, there's more than enough booty around town to share, right, fellas?"

The restaurant rocked with arrogant laughter. I calmed the brothers down and proceeded to walk them through my desire to become one of them.

As I stood there before my prospective instructors, I remembered that Tony is not your average Dog. When he and I first met freshman year, he was a short, skinny, baby-faced goof with an overpriced wardrobe. It took him a while to grow into his looks; today he resembles a black Michael J. Fox.

It was always obvious, though, that Tony had Player in his blood. His father, Dr. Wayne Gooden, was a dean at a local community college but was well known for his dashing style: an S-curled head courtesy of Lustre, flashy double-breasted suits with gold cuff links and ties more appropriate for a nightclub, and a shiny red Jaguar. Dr. Gooden got around, politically and socially, so Tony's eventual blossoming should have been a given. Whether he'd ever admit it or not, though, Tony's transformation was hard work. I actually had the nerve to pity him throughout our junior and senior years of high school. The boy spent every waking minute either chasing ass or trying to pretend he had landed some. At first it wasn't pretty. Some of the very brothers here tonight had laughed in Tony's face as he accosted girl after girl in hallways, at football games, and at dances and parties around town.

Then senior year Tony got his break: he discovered the fertile ground of the moderately attractive female. These were the girls that he would never have considered dating publicly. The girls who had a decent butt, nice breasts, or long legs but a jacked-up face. The ones who were the constant subject of "brown bag" jokes. When somebody like Bobby Wynn used the term he was joking. Tony took it to heart. That boy got more practice sex with so-so girls than anyone I've known. By the time winter of our senior year rolled around, he was experienced and confident enough to move to the big leagues. I watched in amazement as the women on his arm became more and more attractive and, to a limited extent, more intelligent. He even made a competitive run at Nikki Coleman, although he fell short at the last minute. Even though I continued to cling to the hope that I'd find more happiness than Tony by just being myself, I had to give him limited props even back then. That night at O'Dell's, I realized he had been right all along.

Recalling Tony's evolution helped clarify my choice for a Ladies' Man instructor. As I wound down my talk, it all made sense now. Most of these other brothers were getting over on uncommonly good looks or body builds, ungodly amounts of comic genius, or an elusive roughneck quality that I'd never be able to affect. Tony Gooden was the best example of what I could become: reasonably attractive, charming, and witty enough to give women exactly what they wanted, whether it was good for them or not.

When midnight rolled around, the guys' pagers started blowing up. Nervous wives. Jealous girlfriends. Booty calls. Mistresses. These men were in demand. Lyssa walked into the midst of the Grub House floor and encouraged us to find our coats and get to steppin'. "Y'all ain't got to go home, and I know you whores ain't going home anyway, but you got to get the hell out of here! Good night, people!" As she waved with fake sweetness in her wrist, O'Dell materialized behind her, smoothing things over by shaking hands and slapping backs. "Y'all gonna have to come back and see our full menu! You're gonna love our black-eyed peas. . . ."

After thanking O'Dell and Lyssa and dropping a few more twenties as their tip, I hopped into my Accord and was on Lake Shore Drive in minutes. I left the windows down so I could suck in the breezy air and the faint saltiness of Michigan. Now that the winter season was officially behind us for a few months, I could revel in the beauty of my Windy City. I couldn't imagine living anywhere else. People complained about the cost of living, about crime, about the inconvenience of getting around, but in my mind, no price was too high.

No price was too high when it came to my love life, either. I'd be lying to say I was completely comfortable with my planned transformation. Player does not run deep in my family lines. Oh, we hear legends of second cousins and great-grandfathers who left trails of bastards from town to town, but not very often. Most Stone men have been Do Right Men—loving fathers and at least primarily faithful husbands.

Until this week, I had lived in fear of hurting or offending any woman I dated. I always put them first, tried to treat them right. But I had been reminded time and again that that's not what many sisters want. I knew what they wanted now, and I was ready to start serving it up. Maybe then, if only then, I would finally get a sister like Nikki Coleman to pay me some attention.

CHAPTER 4

LIZARDS

Mid-May

T

N I K K I

he moment I dreaded arrived shortly before lunchtime today. Barry Roberts, the man who still owned a small piece of my heart, was seated across from me. Toggling his gold-trimmed Dwayne Wayne goggles, he leaned over the slick marble face of the table separating us. I wondered if he realized that his voice, after all these years, was still full of sex. "You're sure he didn't give you any other alternatives, Nikki?"

The question didn't exactly boost my confidence. "What do you mean? Who wanted to hear about alternatives when I'd been told he was transferring me because of *his* weakness? He had no right to let sexual attraction affect my career. Isn't that the very definition of sexual harassment?"

Barry started tapping the table with one of his feet and put a hand to his mouth. He looked like one of those impossibly handsome professionals who populate your average soap opera. I wondered how his other female clients could even take him seriously. "Let me get this straight," he said. "This transfer he had planned, did he tell you, or did he have reason to believe, that this would constitute a promotion?"

"He made no claim like that whatsoever, Barry. He was almost sheepish about it, in fact. He *knew* he was doing me no favors. Transferring me from the headquarters to a division is a demotion, everybody knows it."

"And he's that arrogant, to think he could get away with telling you exactly *why* he was transferring you?" Barry's eyes sparkled with disbelief. I could read his thoughts. He probably thought Colin was a world-class fool. Like Colin, Barry has lived with a mantle of privilege his whole life, but he knows how to protect it. I think one of the first things his parents taught him was how to hide his motivations from everyone: employees, friends, and lovers. Shaking his head, Barry looked at me and bit his lower lip. "How old is this gentleman?"

"Rumor has it he turned thirty-eight last month."

"Hmm. Close to middle age. He's single, right?"

I recrossed my legs and wondered if I was still looking as cute as I did when I left work. "Divorced. No kids, supposedly."

"Middle-aged, divorced. How's this guy been doing on his job?"

"Empire Records has been in better shape," I said, "if that's what you mean. Colin's father is rumored to be shopping the company on the market."

Barry rose from his seat and walked over to the window, which provided a bird's-eye view of Buckingham Fountain. Rays of sunlight shimmered against the streams of blue water gushing from the fountain. "Nikki," Barry said, "I think you've walked into a potential gold mine. When I first heard Colin Lee was taking over your division, I had some concerns. Lee's notorious for his lack of couth. I think he's really done it this time. To tell you that his lack of control over his sexual desires was going to hamper your career, it's like he was handing you a winning lottery ticket."

I raised my hand, feeling caution creep up my spine. "Barry, I'm not so worried about the money as much as the principle here." Barry's firm specializes in corporate finance; I was only looking at him for this case because I knew he did some civil work pro bono, his version of community service. So I was a little unnerved by his sudden focus on the money issue. "Barry, I want to send a message here: no woman should have to suffer for a man's inability to control his little gerbil. That's not our problem."

Laughing, Barry unbuttoned his navy pinstriped jacket. I was a little surprised to see the way his white oxford billowed over his waistline. Barry was still pretty, but he was carrying a few extra layers now. If I was petty, I would have felt vindicated by his mushiness. Unfortunately, I was too big a person for that. I preferred to think of Barry's gut as a badge of courage, earned through the fires of marriage and fatherhood.

He flashed the smile that used to turn my knees into butter. "Some things never change. Nikki Coleman still wants to change the world. More power to you, my sister." He planted his feet far apart and crossed his arms crisply. "I would be honored to represent you, Nik."

"I'd appreciate it. I know a few other attorneys, but I wouldn't know what I was getting. How much will you charge in fees—"

Barry stretched out his right hand insistently. "No charge for friends, Nik." *Please.* The only people Barry didn't bill for every possible hour were the low-income clients he represents as a hobby. I wondered if I should take his offer as a show of pity.

"Barry, trust me, Empire has been very good to me lately. I can afford to pay you." I resisted the temptation to tell him I was on schedule to make eighty-three grand this year, before bonuses. I knew he'd just dwarf it by throwing out his own six-figure take.

"Nikki, we're not together anymore." Barry came and stood over my chair. He even had the nerve to put his hands on my shoulders. "You don't have to be threatened by my offer to help. There are no strings attached."

I peered over my shoulder and frowned at him. "What would Sarah say about this?" Sarah is Mrs. Roberts, but only because she got knocked up with Barry's son, Joshua, while he and I were still dating. Saying Sarah's name was a big mistake. It just reopened the door to the night my hopes for lifelong romance vanished into thin air.

I had been out kicking it with my girls Rochelle and Lovina, sorority sisters who are now practicing attorneys in D.C. Rochelle had just split with her boyfriend, a local drug lord, and Lovina and I were both in long-distance relationships. We'd been out late hanging at Water Tower Mall and a few clubs, and we stumbled into our cramped University of Chicago dorm room a little after one in the morning. I made my usual call to my mother to make sure she was in safely and collapsed onto my bed without changing out of my silk pantsuit. While Lovina passed out on her own bed and Rochelle turned on the TV so she could trip off *It's Showtime at the Apollo*, I melted into my covers. Then the phone rang, an insistent, early-morning ring that made all of us a little antsy.

"Nikki, it's for you." Rochelle jerked her head at me, telling me I'd have to get my lazy butt up and answer the phone myself, she wasn't bringing it to me. I answered cautiously. Barry rarely called me this late at night, and I knew my mama was okay. Who was this? "Hello?"

"Hey, girl." I knew the voice immediately. My girl Angie Wright, the Third Musketeer after Leslie and me. Without thinking it would ever matter, I'd always taken comfort in the fact that Angie was attending Spelman, right across the street from Barry's Morehouse stomping grounds. Like me, Angie was a sophomore, so she couldn't quite hang with Barry's senior crowd, but she knew enough people to keep informal tabs on him. "Nikki, I don't know what to say . . ." The fiercest, most proud woman I knew, Angie freaked me out when she started whimpering all of a sudden. "Nikki, you know I'm your girl, right?"

As I braced myself for Angie's news, Rochelle joined me on my bed. She had read the fear on my face. I could feel my heart thumping with nervous anticipation. "Angie, what's going on? Holding back is just making this harder for both of us."

"Nikki, I'm sorry. I couldn't let this go on. It's not my place, but you need to find this out for yourself." She paused, probably biting her lip the way she always did when making a tough call. "I want you to call this number and ask for Barry. Just do it! You have to make your own conclusions, okay? I can't say any more."

I was on my feet now, pushing out of my heels and throwing my jacket onto the floor. "Angie, what's the phone number?" A wave of placid anger began to wash over me.

Three minutes later I dialed the mysterious number. As Rochelle and I held hands anxiously, the phone rang once, twice, three times. Four. Rochelle leaned against my shoulder like a child outside a cage at the zoo. "No one's picking up?" She looked more upset than me. "Maybe Angie's playin' with your head, girl. You said she has a weird sense of humor, right?"

"Not like this." I pressed the receiver of the phone so deep into my left ear, I was afraid I'd give myself a permanent welt. Some trick was going to answer this phone, and I was going to have to figure out how to deal with it. Five more rings passed. Just as I moved to place the phone back into its cradle, the ringing stopped.

"Uhh, hello?" The woman's voice was flighty, almost airy with radiant satisfaction. This was a sister who'd just had her pipes cleaned, but good. She'd probably picked up out of concern the caller was a distraught relative or friend.

I glared straight ahead and forced myself to speak. "Hi. May I speak to Barry Roberts." It was a declaration, not a request.

The trick sighed impatiently. "Um, well, okay." I heard the phone travel a bumpy path from the woman's hand over to her probable bedmate.

My heart cracked into pieces when I heard that voice answer. Barry sounded the way he always sounded after a rowdy time in the sack. "H-hello?"

I had two choices that night: crumple into a heap or make the most of this. "Hey!" I yelled. "Guess who this is!" The words were barely out of my mouth before they were drowned out by a loud dial tone. Not even Barry was cool enough to talk his way out of that one.

I didn't crumple into a heap that night, though I did treat myself to a good cry and a late-night trip to the Cheesecake Factory with my girls. And when Barry flew home the next weekend trying to make his case, he only made it worse. He actually thought revealing the fact that he'd been seeing Sarah, a yellow-toned sister with blood bluer than his own, for two years would make me feel better. That last night before I sent him back to Atlanta a free man, he dropped what he thought was his final ace.

"She's carrying my child, Nikki. That's the only reason I was there that night. I'd broken it off months ago, before she started harassing me about her health. Sometimes I sit up with her, you know, helping her with morning sickness—"

"Barry," I yelled, "get the hell out of town and out of my life! You lying, conniving piece of shit! This woman has your baby, and you don't even share that? You are so fired!" I remember that day as vividly as yesterday, standing on the sidewalk in front of my dorm and slapping his cheek with every ounce of strength I had left. I was hurt, and not just by his cheating. This trick was having his child? That had been my ultimate dream for the last three years. Now this cheating whore had been blessed with his baby? I'm not religious now and wasn't then, but if I had been, that cruel fact would have driven me away from belief in a higher power.

Except for a few one-night stands, I didn't date for the next couple years. I'd had other cheating boyfriends before. I guess before Barry, it was almost what I expected from men. But with Barry, it had been different. It was the closest I'd ever come to understanding how a happily married woman feels, one who so adores and respects her man, the mere thought of him with someone else tugs at her sanity. Do you ever recover from pain like that?

By the time I snapped out of my trip into the past, I realized I was back in the main lobby of Barry's law office. A skinny white secretary with stringy blond hair was tapping away at her computer and eyeing us suspiciously as Barry extended his hand. "Nik, thanks for thinking of me. I'm really touched you sought me out. I'm going to touch base with a couple classmates who specialize in harassment law and get the filing and discovery processes under way. Don't worry, we'll make this right." He gripped my right hand with both of his. "I'll be in touch."

What exactly is he thinking, I wondered. Was he turned on by this, the return of the ex-girlfriend who did things in bed that Sarah could never do? Was I a sitting target for a brother fighting off an early midlife crisis? I didn't know what to think. Maybe Barry was just a well-adjusted, mature family man concerned for an old friend. "Thank you, Barry," I said as I shook his hand. "I'll be waiting on your call." I tried to smile without looking too inviting. "See you later."

Questioning my sanity, I stepped off the elevator and walked out onto Wacker Drive. It was just two blocks to the Sears Tower, where my mother was standing outside the main entrance, her arms crossed and her right foot tapping lazily. As always, Mama was the picture of piety, fitting for a social worker who has devoted her life to propping up the bruised psyches of battered and abused children. Dressed in a flowing white Egyptian number sparkling with bronze buttons and designs, she looked ready for a Kwanzaa celebration. I shook my head at this radiant, plump little woman. How many times had I told her she doesn't need to draw attention to herself when she rides the L train downtown? Fighting my way through a rowdy crowd of white teenagers who looked like they were on the run from their chaperone, I finally reached my mama. I reached over and hugged her, feeling her familiar warmth and smelling the buzz of her Chanel. "How's my mama today?"

Stepping back, she fixed her hands in the form of a square, as if to frame me in a picture. "My child is fine, can't nobody tell me my child ain't fine." Ever the cheerleader, my mother has always drilled my intelligence and my beauty into my head, repeating her observations like they're indisputable facts. This used to annoy me, until I met girls like Rhonda Tippin, who dropped out of school to prove her mother's constant reminders of how "no-good" she was. I know I'm blessed to have Ms. Ebony Taylor as my mother. She grabbed my hand as we headed around the corner to Ricci's for lunch. "Now, tell me how this meeting went. You're determined to put your legal future into the hands of Fickle Pickle?" Mama has insisted on referring to Barry by this name since the night I told her about his affair.

As we entered the dark lobby of Ricci's and confirmed our reservation with the snotty hostess, I summarized my meeting. "Barry's going to do some investigative work, seeing what other stories are out there about Colin's behavior. He's confident they'll be able to build up a good-enough case. He thinks Colin may agree to settle."

My mother peeked at me over her menu. "Is that what you want? To settle and walk away with a bunch of money?"

My mother was forgetting whose child I was. "You raised me better, Mama. I told Barry I'm not worried about money so much. I just want my job intact, and I want Colin to learn a lesson from this. But I think that can be accomplished with a settlement."

Mama flicked a roll of braids out of her right eye. "Nikki, you're a grown woman. We don't have to spend time on that unpleasantness now. I just want you to watch yourself here. You realize you're surrounded by lizards on every side right now?" She leaned forward and counted off the names. "Colin. Barry." She twisted her nose as if she had sniffed a whiff of skunk. "And Jomo. Ever think it's time for some housecleaning?"

"Mama, you left out one lizard: Gene." I didn't need anyone, even my mother, criticizing the men in my life, so I injected the unpleasant subject of my father to get her off track. Parenthood is a funny thing: when you make a baby with an asshole, can you ever make amends for it? Mama's decision to lie down with a married man looking for a quick bang cursed me with something a girl least needs: an absentee, irresponsible father. I'll always love my mother more than anyone on the face of this planet, but sometimes I doubt I'll ever stop wondering, *what the hell was she thinking?*

My mother's eyes were on the tablecloth. "I seem to recall, my child, that my pastor back in Tennessee used to say something about how chil'ren should respect their elders. You better recognize, child." Her eyes leapt off the table and back into my view. The message was clear: *No matter how big you get or how much money you make, you will always be my child. Always.* "Now, a more pleasant subject. Your father, speak of the devil, finally got his pension funds released."

I wasn't sure what to make of her announcement. I thought I had been the only connection between my parents for the last several years. I hadn't seen them hold a civil conversation since I was fourteen years old. "How did you hear this?"

"Bessie Ann, my bingo partner from that church across the street from the house, is good friends with Gene's wife. And no, Jennifer isn't aware that Bessie Ann knows me." Jennifer is Gene's wife. "Anyway, Jennifer calls Bessie up this morning bragging that Warren Motors finally closed Gene's old plant and freed up the workers' pension assets. Get this." She shooed away the approaching waiter, who slung two glasses of ice water onto the table and scurried away. "Jennifer *claims* his investments have done so well that his take is over five hundred thousand dollars."

"How in the world did he accumulate that much, Mama? His ass isn't old enough to be retired in the first place. He's barely fifty years old."

"I think if we found out, we'd have to be killed, baby. Don't forget your father was head of the union at that plant for fifteen years. Who knows what deals he cut to get his fund padded?"

"So when do we get our piece?"

The creases in my mother's brow gave me the answer before she could attempt to fake the funk. "He promised he'd give me money to put down on a new house, Nikki. He *promised*."

"Which means shit coming from his ass." My mother agreed I could stop pretending to have a clean mouth the night she caught me riding Lowball bareback in the shower. I still remember her booming, frantic lecture, which was followed by an emergency run to Planned Parenthood. *No more secrets!*

"Nikki, don't count him out just yet. He knows he never held up his end with your expenses while you were growing up. And he knows I need his help to get out of that godforsaken neighborhood."

As we ordered our meals, I flirted with hiring a roughneck type to strike some sense into my father. The only show of responsibility Gene Coleman had ever made toward me was the dubious privilege of his last name. Sure, he would drop by the house every few months and send money at erratic and unexpected times, but the man had lived most of my life in denial. My half-sisters, Tisha and Tia, first greeted me by punching and kicking me until I was a bloody, sniffling bag of eight-year-old bones. Now that we're adults, we're a tad more civil toward each other, but that's not saying much. I still run into Coleman cousins, aunts, and uncles who have forgotten I existed. They all say the same thing. *Gee, uh, I'm trying to think of the last time your daddy mentioned you. It's been so long . . .* Sometimes I wonder if they have any more couth than he does.

After all Gene's failed to do for me, he's crazy if he thinks I'll let him get away without helping Mama. The house she's living in, the one she reared me in, is falling apart. Worse yet, it's down to being one of a handful of homes left on a block rife with crack houses. I tried to get her to move in with me when I started at Empire, but she refused so she could stay near the Rosewood Community Center, which she runs. It wasn't until she witnessed a carjacking on her street three months ago that she got serious about moving. I've already given her three thousand toward a down payment but I'm bone dry now. Lincoln Park rent is running me close to a thousand a month, and after hooking up my wardrobe, paying on my University of Chicago loans, and stashing a portion in my Lexus savings fund, my checks are spent. Gene promised me once that he would make up for his failure to be a father to me by always providing Mama and me with financial help when we needed it. I've managed to do without his help up until now, but it's time for him to step in and do his part. If he doesn't, I'll do whatever it takes to make him regret it. This is my mama we're talking about.

After Mama and I finished lunch, I walked her to the L stop before heading back to the office. The day rolled by as I walked through my tasks like a robot. Life at the office was pretty awkward. I e-mailed Colin a note saying that I had retained legal counsel and was assessing my options. He e-mailed back and encouraged me to take my time thinking things through. His tone was apologetic, but then he had to go and get cute. *You need to be very careful here, Nikki. You don't want to be the man who yells "Fire" in a crowded theater, making a racket for nothing. If you want a future in this industry, remember, no one likes a tattletale.* Was this asshole serious? I printed the message out and slapped it into my briefcase.

Plaintiff's Exhibit A.

CHAPTER 5

BAD HABITS

B

NIKKI

y the time I got home from work, I was ready to chill out. My legs felt heavy, my mouth was dry, and my hair felt ready to fall into my lap. The weight of my potential lawsuit, seeing Barry again, and worrying about my parents was starting to feel like too much. I was one big ball of tension. Standing in the kitchen, I started to unbutton my blouse and checked the time. It was six-thirty, and I was supposed to meet Jomo at 911's preview party at eight. 911, a hot group with a name that was now awkward, was Evans Entertainment's newest act. Jomo played some of the keyboards and bass guitar on their project, so he got a few free passes. Which he expected to translate into a pass into my pants, I'm sure. Well, he had another thing coming. I was going to be strong tonight. I had already made the first step in the right direction by not going out with him tonight. Of course I knew he'd be calling before the night was through.

As I sat in a hot bath full of Victoria's Secret apple-

scented bubbles, I let every muscle in my body relax and allowed
Jomo to enter my thoughts again. Physically he is nothing short of
a vision: a lean hulk of a man with a head full of orange dreadlocks
and the attitude to match. He knows how to show off that figure, too.
I'll never forget the day we met in Empire's lobby. He was wearing a
pair of form-fitting Calvin Klein jeans and a tight T-shirt. Everything
about him, from the way he moved to the way he talked, told me immediately that this was not some inept, little-dick man trying to front
for some action. This was a man for whom certain things, clearly
music and sex, came naturally. The man was musical, cultural, and
fine. That was all I needed.

We went out three times before I surrendered the goods. I'd always
heard three was the minimum number of dates you should have before giving it up, and this was definitely a time to make do with the
minimum. We treated sex like a daily marathon for the next month,
before I started to tire of Jomo's insistence on leaving in the middle
of every night, along with his reluctance to ever have me over to his
place. I wasn't really disappointed by then, I had just wised up. Unfortunately, downgrading Jomo from potential Mr. Right status wasn't
enough to keep him out of my bed. He's been over here a couple of
times a week for the last three months, including the time I was semi-
dating Mitchell Stone.

Toweling off from my bath, I jumped a little when the phone rang.
I wrapped the towel around my damp body and grabbed my cordless.
"Coleman residence."

It was Jomo. "Where are you? Nikki, it's getting late. The party's
still jumpin', but Stephon Evans ain't tryin' to let folks stay up in here
all night. You only got a couple more hours to get down here—"

"Jomo, I'm not coming. I'm tired, babe. I just spent all day fighting
off my hound of a boss and trying to figure out how to knock some
sense into my father. I just need some downtime, okay?"

"Nikki, you sound stressed. And you and I both know Daddy's got
the number-one remedy for that right here." I imagined Jomo fondling his groin, never mind the fact he was probably standing in the
middle of a crowded room, using a public pay phone. So fine, but so
little couth.

"If your remedy came without a price, Jomo, maybe I'd invite you over tonight. Sorry, your timing's off. Like the song said, 'Maybe we can try again'—later."

Jomo laughed. "I'm hurt. Guess I'll have to soothe my fragile ego with the heat of another woman's arms. You don't mind, do you?"

"Jomo, I'd be disappointed if you didn't." He could really be an ass sometimes. I knew he whored around, but I didn't need it thrown in my face. "I have to go."

"Hey, hold up. I met a dude says he knows you. Works for Evans Entertainment, some type of accountant or something. You know a Mitchell Stone?"

"Stone?" *Oh, God*, I thought.

"Said he went to high school with you. Guess he didn't make much of an impression."

"Jomo, I know Mitchell Stone." There was absolutely no need for those two to know each other. But I decided to play along. "Tell him I said hi. I haven't seen him around in a while."

"All right. I think he was hoping you'd show up, too. Though he seemed a little, uh, worried about the fact that I knew you."

"Jomo, the way your rep precedes you, I'm sure he would be suspicious of how I know you."

"No, he's wondering if I *know* you, girl, in the biblical sense of the word. Don't worry, I decided to keep your pristine rep in sparkling shape. I played it cool, you know, the 'She's a good friend' angle. I don't think he has a clue I've had any more action from you than he's had himself."

Like I really cared. "Whatever, Jomo. Look, have fun tonight. And if you decide to do a girl bareback, please let me know. I need all the help I can to resist you the next time you try to get some."

"Oh, now—"

I hung up before he could get indignant with me, as if every word wasn't true. Feeling thirsty, I finished changing into my strawberry negligee and laid my copy of Rosalyn McMillan's *Knowing* on my oak nightstand. As I walked into the kitchen and poured myself a tall glass of Evian, I listened to the call of my body. I knew Jomo would probably come calling eventually. He'd been hot for me all week. The question was, would I be strong enough to turn him away?

I wish I could say the answer was yes. By eleven o'clock, Jomo and I were buck naked on my living room couch. Jomo, to his credit, had already sent me to the moutaintop twice and by then had me spread-eagled on the couch as he plunged deep, rounding third, and nearing home plate. As we panted, groaned, and moaned like savages, the phone rang. My hands glued to the back of Jomo's neck, I realized I'd made a big mistake. I never made love without turning off my ringer and muting my machine! "Jomo, get up!"

"What the—I'm about to get my groove on here, baby!" Sweat dripping into his eyes, Jomo continued to pump like an uncontrollable beast. He was going nowhere until he had finished his business.

Four rings later, Mitchell's voice boomed through the apartment as Jomo and I continued our warm, sticky dance. *Um, hi, Nikki—this is Mitchell, Mitchell Stone . . . Look, I know you're busy and all, but I've left you a couple of messages this week, and . . . well, I'd just like to hear from you.*

"Oh, damn, man, get on with it!" Jomo cried out in agony as his chest swelled and he grew unbelievably harder within me. Apparently he didn't appreciate the interruption, either.

"Shut up, Jomo, I may as well hear what he has to say," I panted. My ears tuned into Mitchell's voice, I whipped my hips up with enough force to break Jomo in half.

Well, give me a call sometime. I'm, uh, not calling anymore. I did enjoy our dates, though, so stay in touch. Bye.

"Nikki—Uhhhh!" Jomo's eyes bugged out like a cartoon character's and his mouth filled with slobber as he crossed home plate. As he collapsed onto me, smothering me in Jovan Musk, I couldn't help laughing. Jomo and Mitchell had hung up on me, almost in sync.

While Jomo grabbed a shower, I considered returning Mitchell's call, but I just couldn't. He had really pissed me off the other night, fronting me just because I wasn't willing to lie and say I find him exciting and sexy. It wasn't my fault he's a Nice Guy. He may think he's not appreciated, but he has no idea what some of my sisters out here go through. Plenty of women want to settle down with a safe, clean-cut type. Somewhere there's a woman looking for a good husband and father figure, and that woman will worship the ground Mitchell Stone walks on. But that girl ain't me.

Jomo emerged from the shower, a massive do-rag wrapped around his dreads. "I gotta run," he said as he hopped into a pair of snug jeans. "Take it easy."

"Nice doing business with you," I said. I couldn't resist the urge to mock my Part-Time Lover's habit of coming and going. "So where does your wife think you've been all this time?"

Standing in front of my full-length mirror, Jomo paused as he smoothed out his cotton rugby shirt. "What in hell you talkin' about, girl?"

"Jomo, do you really expect me to believe you never have me over because you live in a funky house full of broke musicians? I know you're hiding a wife and kids somewhere."

"You couldn't be more off track. Jomo Hayes is a rolling stone. Look, if you wanna see my place and get grossed out, you're welcome." He took a seat beside me on my four-poster bed and snapped up his boots. "I'll even fix you a meal in my little kitchen, okay? You set the date, girlfriend."

"I'll take a raincheck. Bye, Jomo." I reached up and kissed him quickly. If truth be told, it was just a diversion to avoid an awkward silence that might tempt me to wait for the phrase *I love you*. I hadn't been that stupid in a long, long time.

CHAPTER 6

UNCA MITCH

MITCHELL

any men, sick with heartbreak their macho exteriors must
deny, take solace from a handy shot glass, a frothy beer
mug, or a conveniently packaged high. Tonight I resorted
to a simpler, less controversial method: Natasha Parker,
the lady who helped herself to my virginity a little more
than a decade ago.

The day after I'd left that pitiful message on Nikki's answering machine, I drove a few blocks west to Tasha's
apartment near Fifty-fifth and Garfield. I let myself in
with the key she gave me the week after she moved in
and slipped past her daughter's room to the doorway of
the master bedroom. She was waiting for me, smiling
and dressed only in a pair of chocolate lace bikini panties
and a matching sheer bra. The air was thick with the
smell of fresh flowers and a laser beam of Chanel No. 5.

There wasn't much need for conversation; we'd been
on the phone for ninety minutes before I'd hopped into
my ride. Shaking her head and returning to her copy of

Eric Jerome Dickey's latest novel, she pretended to ignore me as I stripped out of my shirt and slacks.

She looked at me curiously as I crossed her thick, crème-colored carpet. "Can I help you?"

"Oh, but yes." I climbed into the canopy bed with nothing on but the family jewels.

We talked first, but only for so long. As I ran my hands over Tasha's firm breasts and slid my fingers to her back, unhooking the bra, Nikki Coleman started to take a backseat in the theater of my mind. As my nature rose firm and fast, my journey away from love's difficulties was only beginning.

After I had run my lips over the curves of her chest, the simmering surface of her smooth stomach, and the insides of her long, tan thighs, Tasha turned me onto my back and returned the favor. Nearly three months out of practice, after naïvely "saving" myself for Nikki, I had to slow her down several times to avoid being a two-minute brother. After Tasha had nearly worn me out and wrapped me in a Trojan, I grabbed her long legs, climbed on top, and slowly entered my only "lover-friend." As I moved into place, our eyes locked, and I felt a bead of sweat break out on my forehead.

The ride was smooth, slow, and damn good, but no words were spoken. I don't know why Tasha's always silent, but for me the math is easy. Passion will make you say some stupid things, and we respect each other too much to lie. We're medicating, plain and simple: some folks do it with greasy French fries and Häagen-Dazs, we do it with each other's bodies. As Tasha looked me in the eye and gyrated intensely I responded in kind, manipulating her into positions she'd introduced me to years earlier. Before I knew it, the treatment had run its course, as our bodies spasmed and the air whispered with our muted cries.

Around 9 A.M., the blare of Tasha's alarm clock and the pungent smell of burnt incense jerked me from peaceful slumber. Tasha was sorting dirty clothes into three neat piles: whites, brights, and darks. As I watched her in motion, I noticed she was wearing the silk teddy I had bought for her birthday last year. She was seeing someone else at the time—I think his name was Lester. Only I would be fool enough to buy lingerie I'd probably never enjoy firsthand. It didn't matter, of course—Tasha and I both knew I'd see her in it eventually. We have sort of a codependency thing going. We're constantly unlucky in love, so we made a pact years ago to always be there for each other in a sexual pinch. If I had a nickel for every night I've spent at her place after a disappointing date or an unreturned phone call, I could retire.

"Look who's up." Tasha stood at the foot of her king-sized bed with hands on hips. "How long until you leave?" She smiled playfully, but I caught the undertone. She wanted me to spend the day with her. We were just friends, but I suppose doing the Wild Thing made us a little more serious than your average platonic friendship. Life would have been so simple if we could have fallen all the way in love.

I smiled at her. "Come on, Tasha. I cuddled, I spent the night. I'll even fix breakfast." I climbed out of bed and searched the room for my plaid boxers. Her room was full of fresh flowers—cobalt blue vases bulging with lilies, snapdragons, and red carnations dotted her dresser, armoire, and night table. "We have this discussion every time. You wouldn't keep a man from God's house on a Sunday morning, would you?"

"Since when do you step up in church, on Sunday or otherwise? Is Marvin singing again, or has he finally decided to go all the way and become a preacher?"

As I slid into my warm boxers, which I had apparently tossed into Tasha's fake cactus in the rush of passion, I rolled with her crack. "Marvin may be off his rocker, but I don't think even he's crazy enough to preach."

Tasha scooped up a pile of whites and opened the creaky wooden door of her bedroom. She had her long hair pinned up into a bun now, bringing order to the mass of curls I'd dug my fingers into the night before. She paused and looked up at me again. "How *is* Marvin these days?"

I waved her off. "Ah, he's getting by." My mind flashed back to

Tuesday night. I hadn't told Tasha about that argument with Marvin, because I was still sorting it out myself. I knew better than to throw his ex-wife and her child into Marvin's face.

Marvin has lived through a humiliation few men could handle. He and Angela were high school sweethearts. Angela, the shapely cheerleading captain with powerful thighs, was the perfect physical complement to a hunky boy like Marvin. More amazing, she was every bit as square as he was, keeping her legs closed until the day they walked the aisle. They had a storybook wedding, the month after their graduations from college. Angela's father, the Right Reverend Matthew Pierce, hooked the ceremony up. The finest foods, the most elegant outfits, including the tuxedo with tails I wore as best man. The wedding was so live, I almost got religion watching them say their vows. A couple of years later, the storybook marriage got even better when Angela became pregnant. When Marvin III was born, you would have thought Jesus had come back. I even got swept up in it. Not knowing any better at the time, I looked at the little cherub Marvin brought home from the hospital and swore he had my eyes, Marvin's nose, my mom's bone structure, and my father's moody personality. My nephew.

Marvin III was six months old when he was hospitalized with leukemia. He was in and out of the hospital for testing and chemotherapy over the next couple of months, and everyone noticed that while Marvin was a pillar of strength, Angela was a walking wreck. Most everybody figured her fragility was due to maternal concern.

One day at the hospital I was stunned to see Tim Dinwiddie, a friend of Angela's, come rushing into Marvin III's room. Something about his frantic nature, the way he looked at little Marvin, set off an alarm inside me. When Angela shuffled Tim out into the hallway and they had a war of words, I knew what was up. By the time I caught up with Tim, near the main lobby, he broke out on me big-time. "Look, kid, they're gonna have to get that boy's blood type eventually. If little Marvin ever needs bone marrow, he may need me—that could be my son!" The look in his eyes chilled me more than the menace in his body language. "Like it or not, I deserve to be here!" As I stood there with my mouth wide open and feet rooted to the carpet, Tim rushed through the crowded exit.

I dreaded the thought of telling Marvin the truth. Out of love, I gave Angela two days to tell him before I would. The next thing I knew, Marvin was ordering every blood test under the sun, despite the fact that Marvin III had come through his chemotherapy and his leukemia had gone into remission. When little Marvin's blood type turned out to be AA, compared with Marvin's BB, we were all devastated. After years of turning away football groupies and saving himself for a lifelong marriage, my devoutly Christian brother filed for divorce two weeks after receiving the test results. To this day, Angela claims he never considered counseling or anything. The damage to his faith in her, and maybe in himself, was too great.

Replaying that terrible time in Marvin's life reminded me again how cruel romance can be. Three years after the divorce, Marvin was still trying to bury his pain by traveling the country as a champion of the religious right. As I sat on Tasha's bed and thought of it, I realized how insensitive my crack about his divorce had been. *I've got to clean that up,* I reminded myself.

Not that I didn't have my own problems. I had wound up at Tasha's last night after Nikki refused to return my phone messages, again! What was she doing that she couldn't answer the damn phone or at least call a brother back? I was so tired of being taken for granted. It wasn't like I had managed to get her out of my mind yet. But that was another point altogether. I hadn't called Nikki to beg my way back into her life; I knew there would be no need for that, once I was a well-established Ladies' Man. I just figured, while I was still Mitchell Stone, Nice Guy, I should call and see how things were going on her job.

Rumors were running rampant around Empire Records about Nikki and her boss, Colin Lee. Nobody at Evans Entertainment was buying the rumors that she was actually messing with Lee, but everybody was curious. I decided there was no point torturing myself over Nikki's troubles, though. If she wanted me, she knew how to find me.

"Unca Mitch!" A miniature version of Tasha, a toffee-colored little cherub with saggy cheeks, yelled to me from the doorway of the bedroom. Maya, my five-year-old goddaughter, is a light in my life but also a perplexing little creature. How many times has she awakened to find "Unca Mitch" standing in her mommy's bedroom, half naked and still horny? I knew from behavioral-science electives in college that this was definitely not healthy. Tasha is usually careful to shield Maya from her social life, but she's always made an exception with me, believing that the "Uncle" tag is a sufficient emotional guardrail. Uncle *is* a long way from Daddy. Maya's daddy, Jason Raines, is with the army in Germany, and has been since the month Maya was born. He writes occasionally and sends money when he can, so Tasha has allowed Maya to at least know her daddy is alive, not some mythic soldier killed in combat. Maya knows I'm not her daddy and never will be.

"How's my favorite darlin'?" I picked Maya up, slung her over my shoulder, and headed into the kitchen to help Tasha prepare breakfast. We fried up smoked sausage and cooked a dozen pancakes, and I made one of my famous suicide omelets. I threw some of everything into the frying pan to concoct my little egg creation: mozzarella cheese, sliced tomatoes, green pepper, sliced carrots, fried chicken pieces, and a dash of Sylvia's soul-food seasoning. Half an hour later we were seated at the oak-grain table in the breakfast nook, Tasha and I enjoying our omelets while Maya slurped loudly on a glass of milk.

"So what else are you doing after church and family time?" Tasha's eyes flashed with skepticism as she washed a bite of omelet down with some Minute Maid.

I responded by crossing my eyes at Maya, who ripped off a peal of laughter. "Gee," I said, "I thought I only saw one child sitting at this table."

"Oh, excuse me, Mitchell, am I being too nosy now? Excuse me, I can't ask my best male friend how he's spending his day. What in the—" Tasha glanced at Maya. I saw the weight of parenthood clamp hold of her, forcing her to censor herself. "What in the *world* was I thinking?"

"Look, Tasha, if you wanna ask me something, just come on out with it." I braced myself, hoping my intuition about what she'd say was wrong.

Tasha sliced into her first pancake. "I heard about your little Dog party this week. You weren't going to mention that to me?"

Damn. "What's to mention?"

"Mitchell, you just held a party for some of the most trifling, disrespectful, deadbeat-daddy Negroes in Chicago—"

I fixed her with a judgmental stare. "Uh, hold up, Miss Thing. If memory serves, a certain female has danced between the sheets with at least two of those very same Negroes." I figured Maya had no idea what I'd just said, but it was clear her mommy got the point.

"Hold *up*, Mitchell." In an instant, Tasha put on the phoniest mommy smile in the book. "Maya, baby, why don't you take your plate into the living room? You can watch your *Sesame Street* tape!" As Maya yelped in glee and leapt from her chair, Tasha turned back to me. The smile was gone. "Now, look here, nigger. Yes," she said, seeing the horror on my face, "you made me go there. What other type of asshole would disrespect me in front of my little girl?"

"Tasha, come on—"

"Listen to me, Mitchell. This is not about me." As she calmed down, the peaceful look that edged onto her face reminded me of the real Tasha, the dedicated English teacher and devoted mother I admired so much. "Mitchell, this is about you. Why did you tell those guys you wanted to be like them? Half of them thought you'd lost your mind, and the rest are probably stupid enough to try to teach you a few things."

I leaned back against my chair and crossed my arms. "Tasha, how many times have we argued about why I can't find Ms. Right?"

Tasha clapped both hands against her head. She seemed to be seriously concerned about me; why, I couldn't figure out. "You think you have to become a Dog to get the right woman's attention? Doesn't that sound a little ass-backwards to you?"

I glanced at Tasha's clock. "I really need to get going if I'm going to make church on time." I got up from the table and kissed her on the cheek. The sweet taste of her skin transported me back to the days of our first encounter, when she waltzed up to me at an MLK football game and asked for *my* number. My luck with women was so dismal that my boys O'Dell and Tony were more shocked than I was. I mean, Tasha was—and still is—fine!

Tasha and I talked on the phone day in and day out for the next two months before we went out. She was a junior at Hyde Park Academy, a former cheerleader who dropped from the squad when her dad's death sent her into a rebellious frenzy. She'd already experimented with things I considered off-limits: pot, every brand and proof concentration of alcohol, even LSD. And Home Girl definitely knew her way around a mattress: I later found out she was juggling two other brothers at the same time we were "talking."

Even in retrospect, though, our first night together was still pretty special. I don't really know why I hadn't had sex before that night. I guess opportunity, time, and privacy had never quite converged in the way I needed them to, until then. It was almost like an exchange—she had opened up to me about her father, and the way his death had robbed her of the chance to heal some old wounds. He was a Vietnam vet who'd piloted for the army, and while he'd clearly loved and provided for her, he'd been distant. She'd held some grudges, and by the night he drove his car into a shallow lake, they hadn't had a conversation in weeks.

I guess none of the *other* guys she was seeing had taken interest in her pain, so when I did it opened up the physical floodgates: a kiss became a tongue-thrusting mouth meld, a fondle became an excuse to remove clothes, and the next thing I knew I was kicking in Tasha's bedroom door. She spent that night and several more teaching me the dips, valleys, and peaks of her body.

I owe Tasha to this day for whatever skills I have as a lover. I guess that's why I felt obligated to explain my actions to her this morning.

"Will you do me a favor?" I draped an arm over her shoulder as she finished her breakfast. "Trust me? We're supposed to be there for each other. You don't have to approve of what I'm trying to become. But I would expect you to understand why I'm willing to try this."

Shrugging out of my hug, she stood and crossed her arms. "You know what, Mitchell? You're exactly right. You do this. I hope it makes you happy."

There was a finality to her voice that bothered me. I knew Tasha wasn't jealous of the women who would likely flock to me once I became a Dog; as a friend, she really thought she was looking out for my best interests. I waved my arms around in confusion. "Are we, are we cool here?"

Tasha gave me a half smile. "We're cool. I'll see you once you've gotten your sowing of oats behind you."

"What?! Tasha, need we start on how many oats you helped sow back in the day? Of all the hypocritical, double-standard—"

Tasha went to the sink and started rinsing her plate. "Mitchell, I'm a single mother with a child to protect. Being a Dog, Player, whatever you call it, is not easy work. You're playing with fire. I've been with enough Dogs to know. If you hurt yourself or someone else, I don't want me or my baby to be in the way. Bye! Call me when you're a real man again."

"I'll call you all right. But I'll be a man with the woman of his choice on his arm." With that, I rolled through the living room and tickled Maya into submission before going upstairs to shower and get dressed. It was clear Tasha and I wouldn't be agreeing anytime soon.

Several hours later, as I rode home with my family from church, I had almost put my argument with Tasha out of my mind. I leaned against the leather backseat of my father's Avalon and surveyed the wide-open spaces outside. Rolling fields of corn, soon to be mowed over to make way for yet another upper-middle-class subdivision, made a pleasant border to my parents' plat. Sycamore Woods is an enclave of brick five-bedroom homes, all built within the last two years. For the Homewood area, Mom and Dad got a pretty good deal. I'm sure it helped that the developer is my mother's third cousin. I swear my mother's family has a hand in every type of business. I don't think Mom's paid market price for anything since the seventies.

As my father whisked the car into the driveway, my sister Deniece wailed away on Pastor Willis's antics at the morning's service. Her voice, soft but commanding, was heavy with laughter. "Mom, say what you want, but that preacher man needs some help! He's losing it! Have you ever seen *anything* like that?"

Striding into the kitchen to check the chicken she left simmering in the Crock-Pot, my mother refused to accept reality. "Pastor knew what he was doing. It was about time he made his point, showing up these showboaters! I'll bet people will think about what they put in the offering plate from now on!"

"Well, I would hope so, Mom." I followed her into the kitchen, unable to contain my amazement—and my amusement—any longer. "Mom, the man stopped five different members before they made it down the aisle with their offering and opened their envelopes in front of the whole church!"

Deniece laughed. "Poor Mrs. Tyson! When Pastor read the amount of her check out loud and said there was no way that represented ten percent of her weekly paycheck, she looked ready to faint!"

"I tell you," I said, "I've never seen anything like it. The man called people out left and right! Mom, is he that hard up for money?"

My mother, on the other hand, didn't care to discuss Pastor's antics. She ignored Deniece and me until she had changed into her favorite Adidas sweat suit and returned to the kitchen. "Mitchell," she said as I helped her prepare a salad over the kitchen sink, "you can criticize Pastor Willis when you reactivate your membership. As long as you insist on living apart from the church, you have no right to judge."

A grin on his face, my father ambled up and took a seat at the island in the middle of the spacious kitchen. "Susan, leave my boy alone." I like that, the way my father always defends me from my mother's self-righteous attacks. My father and I don't have a whole lot in common. I have his bone structure and his miniature ears, but my height, athleticism, and occasionally outgoing personality are inherited from my mother's family tree.

In addition to the physical differences, I lack my father's emotional intensity. I've always been a hard worker, but I've never pushed myself for perfection the way he always has with his writing. With the exception of one embarrassing affair when I was in junior high, my father has always walked the narrow path of the committed family man and the consumed professional. He compartmentalizes his life and plans everything to the nth degree.

By comparison I've always been laid-back. There have even been times through the years when Dad's asked how I could be his son, like the day I refused to study for my SATs. What was the point of studying for a test designed to measure my comprehensive knowledge? Either I was gonna know stuff or I wouldn't. We fought tooth and nail over that one, and even when I got a 1,410, he refused to see the wisdom of my ways. Despite our differences, though, I have to give it to my dad; he looks out for his baby son.

He leaned against the counter and expanded his defense of me. "Mitchell has had two examples in his life where church is concerned, Susan. You who go, and I who don't. He's old enough to make his own decisions about church. 'Nuff said."

"Fine, Father Stone," my mother replied. "One day the Lord will bring you both to your senses."

"Oh, Lord, she's preaching again." I walked up behind my mother and tickled her shoulders, hoping to distract her. It worked.

Half an hour later, we sat down at the marble-topped table in the dining room, which looks out on coral-rock steps that lead down to my parents' kidney-shaped pool. My nostrils filled with the smells of collard greens, pork chops, mashed potatoes, macaroni and cheese, and cinnamon apples. Mom and Deniece had done it again. I looked at them across the table. Where Marvin and I look like our father spit us out, Deniece looks like my mother with Dad's ebony complexion. They're beautiful women, not knockouts but the type of Phylicia Rashad/Debbie Allen women who make the world go 'round. My mother is vice president of finance at Walker Hair Care, a family-owned manufacturer of hair products run by my uncle Grady. Deniece is the business manager for my father's newspaper, the *Illinois Observer*. These are career women who still believe in tearing up a kitchen when they can make time. Both are examples of the quality type of woman I hope to win over and settle down with, once I've established my reputation as a Player. Something's got to change my luck with women.

Full of conflict and loving reassurance, our dinner conversation for the next ninety minutes covered the same ground as every Sunday. Pastor Willis and his crazy antics. My father's plans to increase coverage of the latest scandal in the mayor's office. Marvin's invitation to address the graduating class at Oral Roberts University, one we all demanded he reject. Deniece's planned reunion with her estranged husband, Willie, an event no one knew how to react to. My recent raise at work, one that finally got me past the sixty-thousand mark, was another topic. As always, dinnertime was rife with controversy, jokes, demands, defensive posturing, and warm looks of unconditional love. Then Marvin shattered it all.

"Mitchell, why don't you tell everyone about your little party this week?" He kept his eyes on his plate and his fork poised inches from his lips.

I shoveled a fork deep into my peach cobbler, my eyes glued to the plate. "I don't know what you're talking about."

Marvin placed his elbows on the table, something I knew he'd never do when dining with Rush Limbaugh. He swept his eyes around the table like a little kid with a secret. "Mitchell's trying a new tactic with the ladies."

Before I knew it, Marvin dragged me kicking and screaming into a defense of my plans. My father was deafeningly silent, which I took as a tacit show of support. My mother, on the other hand, started pulling out Scriptures. Deniece told me to "just be myself." Marvin was holding his stomach and rocking with laughter.

I got up from the table. I didn't have time for this. "Look, y'all, if you love me, you'll respect my choices. I'm going to try this, like it or not. I never asked for anyone's approval."

My mother pointed a fork at me judgmentally. "Mitchell, don't let rejection make you give up on the real you. Weren't you the one always insisting that *Dog* is a ridiculous term?"

I paced the dining room as I replied. "Mom, I'll admit, I always thought women who used that word were ghetto. I thought it was a throwaway term, something used by people who couldn't express themselves clearly. But ghetto or not, I've come to realize the term fits. Think about it." The room grew silent at the sound of my conviction. "Real canines, regardless of how many positive traits they possess, are all characterized by the inability to control their most base desires. That's why you see the scrappy little cocker spaniel humping his girlfriend in full view of children in the park, or the parched Doberman quenching his thirst in his owner's toilet, never mind that he's been taught better."

My mother was not amused. "Mitchell, watch your language."

"Don't you see? Dogs just do what comes natural. In that sense, any man who does what comes natural, which often means following the call of his manhood, could be classified as a Dog. And that's clearly what women want." My voice hiked up into high-C range as I finished making my point.

The conversation turned into a two-way, me and Mom. My father got up, grabbed a newspaper from the kitchen, and headed for the bathroom. Cutting her eyes at him, my mother tried to talk some sense into me. "Mitchell, your problem is that you haven't taken enough chances with women. You don't need to be some whore to accomplish that. That's always been the problem with you Stone men. Think you're God's gift, like the exact woman you want should come to you." She paused as Marvin looked at her like he'd been slapped in the face. I knew they'd be having their own conversation later. "Mitchell, just start asking girls out. It's that simple. A catch like you, they'll be on you in no time."

I glanced at my watch. "Mom, you gave me that same speech when I graduated Georgetown, remember? You swore I'd be married with children by the time I was twenty-five. Well, guess what? That ship has sailed. Desperate times call for desperate measures. I'm outta here." I crossed over to her side of the table and planted pecks on both her and Deniece. "Marvin, I'll see you tonight." As I walked out to the foyer, I shouted in the direction of the locked bathroom door off the hallway. "Dad, take it easy!" I heard his muffled response as I grabbed my jacket from the closet. My family could mock me all they wanted, but I was betting Mom would get off my case when I brought home the wife and grandchildren she'd been expecting for the last couple years.

Why else did she think I was trying to become a Dog in the first place?

CHAPTER 7

CLASS IS NOW IN SESSION

MITCHELL

pulled out of my parents' driveway and stopped at my apartment, where I changed out of my suit and tie and into a pair of khakis and a fresh rugby. I also made sure to touch up the top of my fade with a little more black shoe polish. No Hair Club for Men for me.

I had agreed to meet Tony Gooden, the instructor of my "How to Be a Dog" course, at Comiskey Park for my first class. The Sunday-afternoon Sox game against the California Angels gave us an opportunity to chill in the mayor's stadium box and catch up on our recent exploits.

Tony had stayed around town to attend Northwestern while I was off in D.C., so he was more plugged in to what our MLK classmates were up to these days. Along the way, he was careful to name-drop a list of twelve sisters from MLK whom he had supposedly "nailed" within the last year. His coup de grâce, a rumor I'd heard but not yet believed, was his recent engagement to Juanita Collier, a long-legged, Nubian model who got her start doing ads for Saks and some other high-rent department stores. According to Tony, she'd just been signed to do *Sports Illustrated*'s swimsuit issue. The woman is something to behold, in a Naomi Campbell sort of way, and somehow Tony had managed to pull her. They had even reached the shacking-up stage. Tony's ability to land a catch like Juanita confirmed he was the right man for the job: teaching me how to be the ultimate Ladies' Man, in as little time as possible.

As much as I respected Tony's accomplishments, I was still pissed by the time we sat down to eat at Comiskey's Stadium Club. Frank Thomas had already hit three home runs, pushing the Sox's lead to 6–1. The game was irrelevant now, so Tony began his diagnosis of me, the hapless student. I knew I was the one who'd asked him to train me in the ways of Dogism, but the boy was quick to press my nerves. The day's lesson was just a bit much. It all began when he started in on my apparently unimpressive sexual track record.

"You're kidding me, right, man?" Tony looked at me like I had a beanpole growing out of my right ear. Seemingly checking himself, he lowered his tone before continuing. "You've only been with *four* women? A twenty-eight-year-old man? You're leaving a few out, right? You know, the one-night stands, the ones you did doggy-style . . ."

I held up four fingers. "Four, Tony. F-o-u-r. Count 'em, you're a smart boy, Mr. Deputy Mayor."

"Damn, exactly when did you become aware that sex existed? You *do* need my help."

"My limited exploits have been by choice, man. Women flirt with me, I'm just selective. Some of the sister-girl temps at work make eyes at me all the time—I even got propositioned by one of our rap artists last year."

This actually impressed my foolish friend. "Who? One of the famous ones?"

"You know Saucy Sheryl, the one who—"

"Do I know Saucy Sheryl? Hell, yeah, that girl is fine. Full of back, tightly stacked, and all that. Why wouldn't you hit that?" Tony reduced the intensity in his eyes and looked at me wearily. "Oh, yeah, I forgot. You're Mitchell Stone. O.N.G.—Original Nice Guy."

I shook my head. "Sheryl wasn't about nothin', man. She just wanted a night of passion, I could see it in her eyes. And she already has a man and two babies, at the ripe old age of twenty-two. What'm I gonna do with that?"

"Hmph," Tony said. "If I recall, Tasha Parker has a little girl. That doesn't stop you from taggin' that at whim."

I wasn't even going to ask how he knew about that. The grapevine was no joke. "What Tasha and I do, as two consenting adults with no current love interests in our lives, is our business, Tony. You can step off that subject right now."

"All right, to the business at hand." He whipped out a miniature Franklin planner and poised a gold-tipped Cross pen overhead. "Who *have* you slept with?"

"Like I'm gonna tell you. Tony, you're supposed to help me deal with my sexual future, not my *past*, fool."

"Mitchell, those who don't know their sexual past are doomed to repeat it. Give it up." I listed off the names of my partners—Tasha, Carmen, Monisse, and Holly. Tony raised an amused eyebrow. "*Holly*, huh?"

"Don't ask."

Tony smirked. "That's all right—more about white women later. All right, now, who would you *like* to have slept with? Pay attention— this is important, because in order to make up some believable stories, you've got to base them on sincere fantasies."

"What the hell is going on here?" My patience was gone. "You're supposed to help me figure out how to land these women, Tony, not tell me to fantasize about them! I've been doing that my whole life!"

Tony grinned slyly at the blond, busty waitress who brought our drinks, before responding. It was clear from the smirk on her tanned face that she was trying to keep from laughing at my tirade, which had been plenty loud enough for her to hear. I knew Tony would make something out of it. "You'll have to excuse my friend here, Becky. He's wound a bit too tight. I'm here to teach him how to please a woman, treat her the way she dreams of being treated. Maybe we can discuss how I do that sometime." He slid the oily words out of his mouth, along with a welcoming wink.

Becky looked ready to fall for it. "Oh, I don't know about mixing business with pleasure, Tony." They had exchanged names when we first sat down. "But I could make exceptions. . . ." She smiled at us both before walking away. It was clear the smile thrown at me was only for the purposes of her tip.

"Listen to me, Mitchell," Tony said as Becky slinked off, "do you want to be a Dog or not? Dogs, like it or not, get much love. That means a string, a trail, a marathon path of past lovers, partners, one-night stands, you name it! If you want a woman to believe you're in that club, you've got to have stories to tell! What woman will see you as a challenge when all you have to offer is a drunken one-night stand, a three-month college relationship, a workplace fling, and a sick friend/lover thing with Tasha? They'll see that, and keep right on stepping." He clapped his hands. "Wake up!"

"I'm not following you, brother. I'm gonna pull a woman like Nikki Coleman by telling her a bunch of pornographic stories—which is exactly what they'll be, given my history, *stories*—and she'll fall head over heels for me?"

Tapping his finger against the lacquered wood of the table, Tony sighed as if dealing with a disobedient child. "No, Mitchell, you're not following me, not one damn bit. No Ladies' Man focuses all his efforts on one woman; if he did, she wouldn't want him. Haven't you figured out that much? The appeal is when she has to work to get your attention, or at least to get you to put her at the front of your line. But first you got to have a past that explains why you have a line of women in the first place. This is what we're going to do: we'll list out fifteen women, all of them fictional, but we'll base their profiles on women you've known. That'll make them ring true. Then we'll construct a story around how you pulled each and every one of them into your bed, her bed, or some less traditional place." He paused in sudden thought. "Matter of fact, most of your stories should involve somewhere other than the bedroom—even women who aren't freaks like the thought of being with a man who can handle himself in *any* situation, know what I'm sayin'?"

I couldn't have been more confused if I'd tried. I snapped my fingers impatiently. "Tony, the point. Please."

"The point is, we're gonna work together to spread these little stories of ours all around Chi-town. We should get some help, too. You'll need to get Tasha, your sister, and your female friends to play along, whether they realize it or not. And we'll have a few of my boys play a role, too."

"I don't know if I like this." I started to massage my temples. *What was I doing?*

"Mitchell, trust me. First step's always the hardest. Remember the first time we stepped on the baseball diamond freshman year, trying to prove we could make varsity squad early? You were obviously scared the way your knees knocked and your eyes looked ready to pop. Well, you know what? I never told you, but I was frightened, too. Couldn't imagine how we were going to outhit, outfield those juniors and seniors. But we did it, didn't we? By the first real game, I don't think we even remembered how impossible making the team had seemed."

"And?"

"And it's the same with this. You can't imagine taking such a savvy step to improve your love life. You don't think you can do it. Well, *I* believe in you, Mitchell. *I* know you can do this. You, too, can be a Dog. Now stand up and say it with me!" Hoisting his Bud Ice in the air, Tony stood and laughed loudly as Becky, who had arrived again, tittered like a schoolgirl.

I stayed in my seat and cut my eyes at the both of them. "You, sir, can go to hell."

Tony slipped his right arm over Becky's shoulder and saluted me before taking another swig of his beer. "I don't *even* think so. Now stop pouting, we got work to do, as soon as I get Becky's phone number, that is. You've got a reputation to build!"

Like it or not, I was on my way.

IGGIN' ME

Late May

My girlfriends and I are what you might call testosterone-impaired. Except for my visits from Jomo, I have no romance in my life, and Angie and Leslie have even less. So since it was a Friday and spring was in full force, I grabbed Leslie and Angie for a long lunch at Navy Pier. We single girls enjoy our time together so much, we were able to ignore the glaring sun and focus on the cool breezes blowing in off Lake Michigan. Once we ordered our entrées, Leslie started entertaining us with her latest complaints about her employees at Leslie's House of Style.

"How did Michael Jackson say it in 'Wanna Be Startin' Somethin' '? *If you can't feed your baby, then don't have a baby!* Hee Hee!" She shook her head wearily as we applauded her impression. "Do these fools so much as think before they lie down anymore? I mean, are there any *females* over the age of sixteen without children these days? Present company excluded, of course."

Angie, who's a political journalist with the *Tribune*, shook her baby dreads and smiled at Leslie. "All right, Les. Lay it on us. What did one of your trifling employees do now?"

Leslie smoothed her silk blouse and crossed her arms. "Girl, it's not any one person. I'm just sick and tired of people backing out of work so they can take care of kids they can't afford! Do you know I had to close the Oak Park branch all last weekend because *both* of my store managers' kids were sick?"

I took a sip of my virgin strawberry daiquiri. Considering I was about to have my first discovery session with Colin and his attorneys, I really felt like banging back a margarita. "Leslie," I asked, "these girls didn't have anyone else to watch their kids while they came in to work?"

Leslie chewed on her lip and cut her eyes at me. "One's a girl, one's a guy. Neither of them married, or even still seeing the parent of their little crumb-snatchers. Supposedly neither of them can afford day care, and they don't trust anyone else to baby-sit."

Angie smiled mischievously. "Apparently, girlfriend, you ain't paying your people well enough. Why don't you hire nannies for all of 'em? You know you got the money, Forbes."

Leslie's eyes filled with self-righteous anger. "You know what, later for that! I am a woman, a strong, independent sister who believes in helping my folks out. I give my people flextime, full fringe benefits, merit-based raises, and profit-sharing incentives. But dammit, I think I've hit my limit. I had my controller count up the total number of employees with children last week. Can you believe it accounts for seventy-two percent of our employee base? And the average age of these fools is only twenty-two!"

"Leslie, no one can force you to hire people with children," I said. "Granted, you wouldn't want to let the EEOC catch wind of your discrimination. But for real, the facts are that neither teen pregnancy nor single parenthood is unusual anymore. Hell, *we're* the oddballs, not everyone else."

"That's a crying shame, if that's the case," Angie said. "We should be the model for young sisters coming behind us—we all have our education, careers, and financial base *set*, free of the influence of any man. *Now* we can make the choice to get a man and start a family if we want. If all sisters followed our path, the community would have a lot less problems."

"Just one problem with your theory," Leslie said with a crooked grin splitting her face. "Some of us may never wind up with the hubby and two-point-two kids. Some of us are quite happy being man-free."

"I have a feeling we'll all follow our own path," I said. I was hoping to get off the track we'd started down. Angie claims to have gone almost a year without having a man. Leslie, of course, for much longer. I don't know if I believe Angie; granted, she hasn't trusted a man since her fiancé, Bruce, eloped with the stripper he screwed the night of his bachelor party. But I have a feeling she still calls one brother or another for the occasional tune-up.

Leslie's needs are a little different. I think she finally got tired of being ignored. It seemed men both black and white passed her over, whether because of her weight, her self-described "mulatto" features, or her scathing wit. Many late nights after she'd been dissed again at clubs where men hopped on me like white on rice, I reassured her that her time would come. I remember the night I even told her that she could always "settle" for a white man — it was good enough for her mother, after all. There's someone for everyone, and I still believe the man is out there who will love Leslie for all she is. Until he comes along, though, Leslie has resorted to her own measures. I know she's been spotted at some gay bars over the years, and she even talks casually now about some of her gay friends. Personally, I never ask questions, and I don't let her give me any details. I'll never judge anything my girl does in private, but that's exactly how I let her keep it.

About the time we started to wonder where the hell our waiter had disappeared to, Angie asked the question I least felt like answering. "Speaking of following our own paths," she said, "how goes the story of Nikki Does Jomo?" She patted my hand playfully as the waiter finally arrived with our salads. "I'm bad, I know I'm bad, always getting in your business."

I don't know if it was stress over the lawsuit, but I was feeling a little annoyed. "You're right you're bad, Angie. Why the sudden interest in my bedtime stories? I remember when we agreed to keep certain things off-limits." I ran my tongue over my lips. "I'm not a sideshow, you know."

Leslie smirked. "Nikki, baby, we just jealous. You got two sisters here who haven't been served since Jordan left the Bulls for good. We gotta live through somebody."

"I don't get it," I said. "Honest to God, I don't know how you two go as long without it as you have."

"It's real easy when nobody's offering," Leslie said.

"Please, Leslie," I said, "you can't tell me you don't have men of all hues trying to push up, especially with the power you wield at House of Style?"

"Oh, I may get a few flirts on occasion," she said with a laugh, "but they know they're pissin' in the wind. I don't exactly follow a 'don't ask, don't tell' policy with my love life, you know."

I snapped my fingers at her. "So you wouldn't take any, even if it was served up on a silver platter?"

"Depends on the day of the week." Leslie frowned suddenly. "Come on, Nikki, you're gonna get me depressed. You know I've never had many men step to me. But if a candy bar like Jomo offered me a bite, yeah, I'd help myself for old times' sake. But I bet I'd still say, like Ray Parker, Jr., 'Girls Are More Fun.' "

"Leslie!" Angie's reproof echoed my thoughts. "The subject on the table is whether we, as lusty and attractive women, miss the presence of a man in our bedroom. And I will unashamedly say, Hell yeah!"

Angie's admission stirred my curiosity. "What is it that changed everything about sex for us?"

"Changed everything how?" Angie asked, picking the carrot slices out of her salad.

"Well, you remember what sex was like when we were in high school?"

Leslie eyed me suspiciously. "Uh, you mean junior high for some of us, don't you?"

"The exact year we took our first steps isn't the point here, Leslie. Do you *remember* what sex was like in those days?"

Angie waved a hand and speared a pickle. "Sex back then was the way my mama always told me it would be. Something to be endured."

Leslie yelped in empathy. "Lying there while he whips out his stuff and passes Go before you've even pulled out all your Monopoly pieces! Waiting and wondering when it'll be over, all the while hoping you won't get pregnant or catch HIV? That's what I remember."

"You know," I said, "I still can't look Lowball Spencer in the eye when I see him around town. It's been almost twelve years since I last slept with him, and I still feel like he thinks he owns me. The way his eyes grope me, the way he stares through me." I shuddered involuntarily. "All I ever was to him was a vehicle, you know? Something to get him off. I still can't remember why I slept with him in the first place. I damn sure hope it wasn't for love."

"That doesn't take a genius," Angie said. "I'm sure it was the same reason I let Kelvin Dewitt be my first—put up or shut up. You know I didn't realize I'd been date-raped until that term was invented back in the late eighties? All those nights he spent badgering me to give it up, threatening to go do someone else if I didn't ante up. By the time he took what he wanted, he'd made me think it was all my idea. The more I think about it, the more pissed-off I get." Angie stopped and stared off into space. There was no need to say anything else.

"Let's lighten this mood," Leslie said. "Apparently things took a turn for you two. What was it that tripped the switch, you know, that turned screwin' into making love, this *thing* you feel you can't live without?" I think Leslie was into the occasional one-night stand in her secret life, but my girl was relatively chaste.

I smiled at my naïve friend. "You *have* been out of the game too long. When I figure out why one man does it for me in bed while another can't do what I could do for myself, I'll let you know. Some brothers have it, some don't."

"What about Mitchell Stone?" Angie asked. "Does he have it, Nikki?" Angie loves to talk about Mitchell. She had a crush on him back in junior high, and they even dated for a few months in eighth grade. Apparently it was just one of those empty, puppy-love type of things. When I first went out with Mitchell back in February, Angie thought it was the coolest thing. I took that as proof that Mitchell never stirred any embers in her heart. Angie didn't want Mitchell, but she thought any other woman who wouldn't have him was out of her mind. "Is Mitchell even in the running anymore?" she asked.

"Girl," I said, "I downgraded Mitchell to permanent-friend status a while ago. Where you been?"

"Excuse me, I just thought you might want a backup. I wouldn't exactly call Jomo reliable."

"Well, I called Mitchell last week and never got a call back. I'll see him when I see him, simple as that." I was a little hurt Mitchell never called me back the other day. It was almost like he knew what I was doing with Jomo that last time he called. I knew I was being paranoid. Just because Mitchell was on the warpath against sisters didn't mean he thought the worst of me. Did it? I figured he'd come around eventually, and we'd be good buddies again. All in time.

By the time I finished tripping with the girls and strolled back to the office, it was almost two o'clock. I thanked God it was Friday; that was my only hope of getting through this meeting with Colin and Barry. Barry surprised me when he scheduled the meeting on Colin's home turf at Empire's offices, but he promised it would work to our advantage. I didn't even kid myself; I had no idea what to expect.

After I dropped off my purse and freshened up in the ladies' room, I met Barry in the reception area outside Colin's office. He was dressed in a very expensive, taut navy blue suit, drawing glances of interest from female executives and other passersby. "Hey, Boo," he said, "how are you?" His use of my old nickname threw me a little bit, but I brushed it aside.

As we crossed the threshold and entered the conference room, Colin rose from his seat at the head of the large table and stepped in front of a pudgy little man in a brown Brooks Brothers suit. "Barry, how the hell are you?" He pumped Barry's hand like a political candidate and patted the right shoulder of the little man. "This is my attorney, Jack Hamm. Not much to look at, but mark my words, he's the best." He winked knowingly at Barry.

"Mr. Hamm, your reputation precedes you." Barry slapped Colin on the back and gripped Mr. Hamm in a firm handshake. His back arched in regal pride, he met Colin's gaze. "Colin, you been getting out to the club much lately? My father and I haven't seen you on the racquetball court in a while."

As we took our seats, Colin and Barry carried on their own conversation, swapping names of their fellow club members, all of whom are among Chicago's Rich and Famous. Even five years after Barry and I split up, I found myself marveling at the way he carried himself with Colin. Most people at Empire Records lived in fear of Colin. I always have. Not that I've ever shown it, of course, but I've never been truly comfortable with my white superiors at work. I do have quite a few white friends at my level and below, but when you're dealing with someone who determines the if, when, and how much of your paycheck, it's a little difficult to erase the reality of slavery and racism from your mind.

Barry, however, was completely free of that baggage. He wasn't just surviving his interaction with Colin, he was enjoying every minute of it. Maybe that had something to do with his parents, Bahamian immigrants who came to the States believing they could take the country by storm.

Once the social hour was over, Hamm and Barry started going back and forth about how to deal with the "situation" Colin had caused. Barry leaned over his notes, calm passion spurring his words. "We want what's best for Empire Records, Colin. And what is best for Empire is for Nikki Coleman, this proven and highly valuable employee of yours, to feel that her right to an equal-opportunity, harassment-free workplace is being respected."

Hamm, a fidgety tan-faced man with a pug nose, clicked his teeth loudly before responding. His accent was straight outta Brooklyn. "What you got here, Barry, is nothing but hearsay—he said, she said. Now I could get into an argument over whose testimony would get more respect from a jury, but—"

"Jack, let's be respectful here," Barry said, patting my hand. I tried to ignore the spike of warmth that his touch caused. "We're both representing clients with upstanding reputations here. If you want to get technical, Colin would be more exposed than Nikki. Come on." He eyed Hamm conspiratorially. "You and I both know when sexual matters are involved, a man is guilty until proven innocent. It's in your best interest to settle our concerns now before we have to file formally."

I tried not to laugh at Barry's argument. It sounded smooth, but we both knew it was bull. Juries may favor a female's word in the *average* sexual-harassment case, but this was a black female subordinate charging a wealthy British millionaire. All I needed was a few asshole jurists trying to get back at Johnnie Cochran for playing the race card, and Colin would walk away untouched. We were the ones who needed a settlement.

Barry winced slightly as I pinched his knee under the table. He knew I didn't want him to overdramatize things. "Jack, Colin," he continued, "all we want is a signed contract protecting Nikki's employment at Empire Records." He slid two copies of the text across the table. "I've drawn this up as a first draft. The major points are as follows: first, Colin pays Nikki two hundred thousand dollars for her pain and suffering and goes on record with an apology to Nikki for any 'offensive comments that she feels compromised the equal-opportunity policies of Empire Records'; second, Colin promises to employ Nikki in her present position as associate director of corporate promotions for the next eighteen months, unless she chooses to request a transfer elsewhere; and finally, Colin promises, under threat of breach of contract, to keep all these terms confidential. If any of the terms float back to Nikki, you and Empire will be liable."

The grin on Hamm's face as he read the fine print told me he was concerned but not horrified. I could tell he wouldn't mind signing right now in order to save Colin's ass. But as an attorney, he had to show out first. Forty minutes passed while I watched the clock and let Barry, Colin, and Hamm argue the finer points. I knew what I was holding out for, and in what order: an apology, job security, and money.

Finally, Hamm grabbed a pen in his spongy hand and began making a final flip through the contract. "With the revisions we discussed, I think it may work. Colin—" He stopped when he realized Colin was staring at me.

"Nikki," Colin said, "I just can't get over how irresistible you are." He took a beat before turning to Barry. "You must have really enjoyed yourself, my man."

"What?" I said, in the most even voice possible.

Colin folded his hands together and smiled like he knew some dirty little secret. "Pretty novel concept, hey, love? I guess you spent most of high school and college paying Barry's legal fees in advance. Why should you be different? What you're doing is a practice as old as time itself." He winked knowingly.

My forehead felt like a warming oven. "Barry, what is going on here?" I felt my tongue lapping across my lips. Something was *very* wrong.

Hamm rustled his papers. "Look, folks, let's keep personal business out of this. We got ourselves an agreement here. Barry and I can iron out the details over the phone—"

I stopped Hamm's desperate attempt to escape with an outstretched palm. "Excuse me, *I'm* not done. Barry, I want to know what it is Colin thinks he's talking about."

Barry tossed his glasses onto the table and started shaking his head back and forth. "Nikki, sometimes you're best off ignoring silly comments." He stared at Colin insistently. "He's just trying to be cute, something completely inappropriate in this situation."

Colin leaned over the table, leering at the both of us. "Ohh, come on now, Barry. You weren't so self-righteous the other night at the club! Nikki, you should have heard the things your attorney shared with me. Quite an item, you two were! Hell, the stories he told me about the Jacuzzi you guys used prom night kept me warm the last two nights! Who needs fantasies when you've got real-life escapades to picture?"

"*What* have you done?!" I didn't feel calm anymore, but somehow I managed to sound that way. Even though I could hear Colin's giggles and Hamm's violent whispers, I was no longer conscious of anyone other than Barry. "Barry, tell me he's making this up. Tell me he found out about prom night from anyone but you."

"Gentlemen, please excuse us." Barry's lower lip was bleeding, he'd bitten down so hard. As Colin gleefully slammed the door shut behind him, Barry stood and slapped his hips loudly. "Damn!"

"Damn what, Barry? Because you got caught dirtying your own client's reputation? What the hell did you tell him?" I was sounding like a broken record, but I didn't care. I was in the throes of raw, confused emotion.

"Nikki, you're not an attorney, are you? Ask around sometime, and you'll find that very few lawsuits, especially civil disputes, are settled or decided on the basis of merit. Just like with anything else in life, success is based on whom you know. And in this case, I know Colin's family." He strolled to the window and slid his hands into his pockets. "His father was one of my dad's first investment-banking clients. My dad has helped double that old fool's fortune! I had to get some mileage out of that."

"What does that have to do with you cozying up to my damn harasser?"

"Nikki, listen to me. You and I both knew your odds of success in court were tenuous at best."

"English, Barry."

He shook a hand at me. "Girl, you know damn well what *tenuous* means. In court, the odds of a jury finding for you were very low. Not to mention this fool would have pulled every trick in the book to trash your reputation. I mean it—I did some digging and came across a case of a suit filed by some secretary here four years ago. By the time Colin dragged out every boyfriend this girl had, he had her looking like Madonna. I wouldn't let him do that to you, Nikki."

"So what exactly *did* you do instead?"

Barry had obviously convinced himself that he was in the right. Sliding his glasses back on, he smiled weakly. "It was simple, really. Took him out for drinks, behind Hamm's back, of course, and let him tell me his life story. Dumb S.O.B. just overflowed with damaging information—nothing that would really hold up in court, but enough to make him realize it's in his best interest to settle. Anyway, he kept going on and on about you, and asking how I knew you . . ."

"Which, quite logically, led to your disclosing every possible detail about my sex life?"

"Nikki," Barry said, exhaling loudly, "I did what I had to do. I saw an opportunity to bond with the man, and I did. And it paid off—he and I hammered out this agreement that night." He held up the paper like a college diploma. "If I'd kept my mouth shut about us, you wouldn't have this man on the verge of offering you a payout and a guaranteed job for two years."

"Barry—" I stopped myself, pacing the room as a rush of anger coursed through me. Moments like these forced me to support gun control; as well balanced as I like to think I am, I know that if I packed heat on a regular basis, actions like Barry's would leave me no choice but to bust a cap in his ass.

"Barry, how could you betray me again?" *Damn*, I thought as I felt a warm tear bleed out of my right eye. I was *not* going back into the past. I was not going to let Barry drive me batty again. I'd come too far. "Is this really how you practice law? Do the ends really justify the means for you?"

"Nikki." Barry stepped all up into my personal space. His broad chest was half an inch from my chin. He reached to place his hands on my face. "Look, just let me—"

"No!" I pushed him away with near-violent force. "I don't need your kind of help! I will not let you destroy me again, Barry Roberts, you understand? I deserve better!"

I threw my purse over my shoulder and bolted for the door. I flung it open and shut it before Barry could catch up to me. "Nikki, call me!" I heard him say from behind me, a surprisingly desperate plea in his voice. "We'll work this out!"

We wouldn't work it out, I knew that much. I raced to the bathroom on my office floor, had a good cry, and told Sylvia to hold my calls for the rest of the day. Then I got to work calling attorneys.

Barry Roberts, once again, was fired.

* * *

BY THE TIME I hopped into Leslie's black BMW coupe five hours later, I was looking to put my trials behind me for a few. That didn't mean I wasn't willing to wallow in my funk a bit, though. As Leslie sped away from the curb outside my building and hooked her way onto Lake Shore Drive, I slid Chico DeBarge's *Long Time No See* compact disc into her player. Leslie grinned. "Thought you didn't like those pretty boys, girl? You never gave El and the family props back when they were big."

"That was then, this is now. Chico is no Eldra, he's a *hard* man. That's what I like. Plus, he tells it like it is." I fast-forwarded to "Iggin' Me," a bluesy rant about a brother whose woman left him for another.

"See," I said, "the pain of betrayal. A song of anger. That's what I know about. This song could have been written for me." I settled back into the leather interior of the BMW. Even as I let Chico's words soothe my soul, I felt my mind drift back to more pleasant days. For some reason, my troubles with Barry and Jomo had me longing for those days a few weeks ago, when I had Mitchell Stone around.

Before he flipped out on me at Luigi's, Mitchell was turning into the best male friend I'd ever had. He and I had conversations like I'd never had with a guy. Mitchell could really bare his soul when he wanted to. He talked openly about his struggles, his fears, his insecurities. He even admitted that he wondered if he was living up to the hopes and dreams his parents had for him. Looking at Mitchell's family from the outside, I'd always assumed his life was so perfect compared with mine; his father the prestigious journalist, his mother the business executive, his debutante big sister, and his big brother the football star and local celebrity. It was clear that Mitchell loved his family, but I could see how he compared himself with them, and he didn't seem to think he measured up. Every time the subject of romance came up, I noticed he always tied it into his desire to have a wife and kids; it was like he was incomplete without it. It was real obvious that Mitchell's failures at the game of love had damaged his pride. Personally, I thought he was mistaking marriage and parenthood for manhood. My own father was proof that there's really no connection between those two concepts. Maybe that's one reason I was less concerned with starting a family than someone like Mitchell was.

But I did believe in love, so I was sympathetic to Mitchell's pain. The more I thought about it as Leslie and I sped down Lake Shore, the more I wished I'd been a little lighter with my touch that night at Luigi's. Here Mitchell was feeling like a failure because he can't get a woman, even when there's a black-male shortage, and I added to the parade of sisters who passed him by. Maybe he had a right to be hurt.

Leslie pulled me out of my secret thoughts a minute later. "Hello, Miss Thang?"

I blinked a few times and realized we were almost there. We were headed for the Museum of Science and Industry, the site of this month's Black Network happy hour. Everyone from the National Association of Black MBA's to the National Society of Black Engineers cosponsors these meetings; they're the hottest ticket on the black side of Chicago. Angie and I routinely hit these happy hours in search of husband material, while Leslie always came purely for networking purposes. She'd already found two new vendors for Leslie's House of Style at the last two socials.

Leslie reached over and snatched my sunglasses off my face. "Okay, Mary J. Blige. We have business to attend to. Time for you to come out of that funk. We gotta get up in here and find Angie."

I climbed out of Leslie's ride and made the trek up to the main entrance. Brothers and sisters of every hue, from their twenties to their sixties, snaked their way up the front steps. It was a really good turnout. In times like these, it was easier to clear my head of my legal trials. That situation would be dealt with; I'd get back to looking for a new attorney, and possibly a new job, tomorrow. For now I was determined to enjoy myself.

As Leslie and I stepped into the lobby, we waved and nodded at various acquaintances, enemies, rivals, and former friends. The lights were dimmed, almost as if the place was lit only by candles. The pleasant scent of hors d'oeuvres and fine wine hung in the air, explained by the army of black-suited waiters running to and fro with loaded platters. A live jazz band was tearing it up in the far right corner.

I was preparing for an onslaught from a few fine, horny brothers when Tony Gooden, my old MLK classmate, sidled up alongside me.

"Nikki Coleman. Living proof that there is a God. Not only does he create such an awesome work, he preserves it for years. You haven't lost a step since MLK." He leaned in close and tipped his wineglass my way.

Just what I needed, this little punk with an oversized ego. Tony was a sharp brother, no two ways about it. Anyone serving as top aide to the mayor of Chicago, at twenty-eight, was hot shit. But that didn't make him sexy, at least not in my book. Word was Tony got around, but that did nothing for me. He had tried to pull me for as long as I could remember, but he was just going to have to accept the facts: I'm one goal he will never achieve.

Tony hadn't given in to reality yet. He bent my ear for what felt like hours, pausing every now and then to schmooze with one friend or another.

"Representative Harmon, how are you, sir!"

"Mrs. Washington, what a fine suit you're wearing this evening!"

"Judge Wilson, what's going on?"

"Andy Bailey! Chicago's finest stockbroker! Come bend my ear!"

Tony was in perpetual motion, constantly seeking new targets for his political charms. He wouldn't even let Leslie escape when she tiptoed by with a couple of AKA sorors I recognized from last month's social. He took Leslie's right hand like a gentleman caller and lifted it to his lips. "They broke the mold when they made the Forbes women." His eyes twinkled as he released his grip and ogled the AKAs. "And the company you keep, Leslie . . ."

We endured Tony's antics for another fifteen minutes before escaping toward the back corner, where Angie was standing in front of the band with a fine hunk of a man. The brother was a bit on the short side, probably no more than five feet ten, but he was built like solid rock. He was wearing a suit that looked like the ones my mother used to buy for the boys at her community center. A good "church"

suit, with no frills or accommodation to style. I found myself forgiv-
ing the suit, though, as I took in his sculpted pecs and the wavy tex-
ture of his fade.

Angie, resplendent as ever in a red skirt that complemented her
ebony complexion, stepped forward with a big ol' grin on her face.
"Ladies, I want you to meet Jamal Watkins. He's an intern at the *Tribune.*" Her smirk confirmed exactly what I was thinking. This was the
guy Angie had been hiding from us. She'd have some explaining to
do later tonight.

Leslie took the lead in welcoming Angie's friend. "Hi, Jamal." She
stood back and eyed the poor boy like a biological specimen.

I tried to play Good Cop. "What department are you working in at
the *Tribune?*" I wanted to ask him the real question on my mind: *Are
you curling my girlfriend's toes?*

Jamal flashed a crooked smile. "I'm interning in the printing office. You know, helping set up the presses and whatnot." He shook his
head in a streetwise manner that automatically identified him as
"from the hood."

I could feel Leslie's frown, so I tried to toss the boy a bone. "Well,
uh, where are you in school?" I wanted to tell Jamal to be very careful what answer he gave me; it would determine whether Leslie and
I viewed him as a blue-collar plaything or a potential Good Man.

Chomping on what appeared to be a wad of Trident, Jamal tugged
at his tie, which was a bit too wide to be stylish. "Well, you know, I'm
in school at Chicago State, at least I will be next fall. I kinda been in
and out, you know."

"*Chicago State.* Strike two." Leslie's whisper was barely audible
over the band's ruckus. I shushed her as Angie and Jamal turned to
appreciate each other for a minute.

Jamal waved at someone behind us. "Hey, I see one of my boys
over there. S'cuse me, ladies, I'll be back." As he stepped off, he slid
a hand across Angie's back, a move that said more than a thousand
words.

Leslie wagged a finger. "Ooh, ooh, messin' with jailbait, unedu-
cated jailbait at that. Bad girl." We all cracked up. Personally, Jamal

was not exactly news to me. I knew Angie had to be seeing somebody, and after what Bruce did to her, who could blame her for taking a comparatively safe route: someone young enough to be in awe of her, poor enough that she'll never depend on him, and hard enough to carry his weight in the sack. Maybe I needed to check out some of the interns at Empire.

"Nikki!" Leslie started tapping on my shoulder like a wild woman. "Look who just waltzed in!"

I turned to see Mitchell Stone walk through the main entrance, flanked by two sisters who were known to be regulars at the Black Network socials. Carmelita Hodge and Chante Banks were both un- employed women who believed in being "kept." These hoochies were always the first on the dance floor, and they were two of the biggest clotheshorses I'd ever seen. With their six-inch nails, blue contact lenses, and weave-heavy hairdos, they were long on style, short on substance. Most of the men at these things take them home eventually. But tonight they were jocking Mitchell of all people!

What was a Nice Boy like Mitchell doing with Carmelita and Chante? I had to admit, he was looking good. His fade was tight, and his maroon suit was straight out of *Ebony Man*. I tried not to stare as I watched him share some animated story with his little harem. Carmelita and Chante were laughing like Mitchell was Martin Lawrence or something. Seeing him like that pricked something in me; I didn't understand why he was with them. Surely he couldn't be messing with one of them?

Angie's ignorant ass insisted on calling Mitchell over. "Mitchell! Over here, it's Angie!"

"Angie, Leslie," Mitchell said as he stepped over and hugged my two friends, "how are my fine MLK sisters doing this evening?"

As I noticed he was ignoring me, I couldn't help but sniff his Polo cologne. This was new. The Mitchell Stone I knew always smelled like Dial soap.

I couldn't resist. I put my right hand on my hip and cocked my head his way. "Oh, so I'm invisible now?" I was a mature woman and all, but there was no need for Mitchell to play like he didn't see me.

He wrapped his arms around Carmelita and Chante before responding. "Nikki, how are you?" His formal tone was more of an insult than ignoring me would have been.

I decided I didn't have to take this. I'd had a crappy enough day without Mitchell Stone, of all people, trying to show out on me. "I'll be over there with Martavius and Bill when you all are ready to go," I said to Angie and Leslie. As I turned to walk over to the center of the atrium, Carmelita broke away and grabbed hold of my arm.

"Hey, girl," she said, a phony smile plastered on her makeup-caked face. "What you been up to, Nikki? You still making that big money at Empire Records?"

"I think I make the big money *for* them, Carmelita. I'll never make the big money until I'm working for myself. How about you, girl? What are you up to?"

"Oh, girl, I don't know. You know my divorce from Victor finally went through last year?"

I'd heard about the divorce. I'd also heard the marriage ended because Carmelita's fifty-three-year-old husband found her in bed with his twenty-year-old son. "Yeah, I heard."

"Well, anyway, I got just what I wanted from that fool, you know? A fat settlement, girl. I am taken care of for life. I just got to decide how to spend my days now. I can travel when I want, do whatever I want. It's a great feeling."

"I'll bet." I turned to head toward my other group of friends. If I lingered any longer, people might start thinking I was cool with Carmelita.

Carmelita, unfortunately, wasn't finished yet. She plopped her hands on her hips and moved closer to me. "Girl, let me tell you about another great feeling I had last night." She paused and smiled wickedly. "Mitchell Stone."

I felt every crease in my forehead as I stared at her wide-eyed. "Mitchell? What about him?"

Carmelita touched my shoulder lightly and eyed me conspiratorially. "Between you and me, right?"

As if that had ever been true for anything this fool has said. But I played along. "Okay, sure."

"I took that boy over to my place last night and he took care of some *business*. You MLK folk been holdin' out on a sister! I always heard Mitchell was a straight-arrow, conservative guy. He's an animal, girl—an animal. I guess you never know, huh?"

She'd thrown me for a complete loop this time. I knew she'd never been discreet, but damn. "Look, Carmelita, none of this is really my business. Why don't you tell someone who cares."

"Shoot, I'd tell Chante, but she was the one who tipped me off to him in the first place. You MLK folk are a wild bunch, if you keep that boy on the down low." As the band whipped into a Jonathan Butler number, Carmelita shook her hips and looked off toward Mitchell and Chante. "Well, that's my song. I gotta go. See you girl." With that, she shimmied off to join her friends on the dance floor.

I didn't know why, but as I watched Mitchell dancing with Chante in his arms, I couldn't stop the thought: *He could do better.* Suddenly I was ready to go home. This day had me so confused, I decided it was time to have Jomo make a house call to clear it out of my head. Had the world gone completely crazy?

CHAPTER 9

MILOS AND MISSY

Late May

MITCHELL

t's been a long day. This being a Dog thing is more tiring than I'd imagined. Spending every moment planning a way to get some ass takes up a lot of brain cells. It's already screwing with my performance at work. I couldn't get through the day without being harassed by Tony's trifling behind.

The first time he called me was right before lunch. "Mitchell, are you doing what you're supposed to be doing?"

"Tony, I'm trying to complete my analysis of the quarterly financial statements. If I don't have this ready to review with Stephon in twenty minutes, I'll never get on his good side."

"Yeah, I know you're sweating the brother so you can try to get a real job over there. But right now, my friend, you've got some homework to apply. How many numbers you get so far today?"

I wasn't being a good student. "Tony, are you calling me from your office?"

"What the hell does that have to do with anything? For your info, I'm down at McCormick Center, helping the mayor touch up the speech he's giving in a few minutes. I'm using one of the flip phones."

Tapping violently on my keyboard, I cradled the phone between my right shoulder and my ear. "So you're using public money to interrogate me about my social life? I'm thinking this would make a good story for the *Tribune*."

"You'd never prove anything, Mitchell. My boss is a black Bill Clinton—he could do Monica Lewinsky every which way but loose, in his own office, and walk away clean. He sure ain't worried about no phone scandal. Now answer my question."

I was speaking through clenched teeth now. "I got two numbers today, okay? A girl who works downstairs in the gift shop—"

"Oh, Mitchell. You don't really think I can give you credit for that?"

"Hold up, Tony. This girl's fine. She may not be any more than twenty, but she's bangin', man. A couple weeks ago, I'd never even have thought of stepping to her."

"All right, whatever. Who's the other?"

"A receptionist on Empire Records' main floor. Short, tan, and toned, like Jada Pinkett. I've made small talk with Regina for the last year but never took the leap to get the digits. I got 'em today!"

"And that's it?"

I stopped typing and gripped the phone with my right hand. "Tony, I'm hanging up."

"All right, all right—look, it's just I'm seeing a disturbing pattern here, Mitchell. A receptionist and a girl in a gift shop? You wouldn't have given a flying fig if both those girls told you to step off. You're choosing easy targets, my boy, and that just won't do. We got to get you some thicker skin, so you can handle rejection." He paused suddenly. "I'm gonna have to bring in an outside consultant. You just be good and ready to learn some more when we meet tonight."

"Yeah, I know. Giordano's in Lincoln Park, at seven-thirty. I'll be there with bells on. Now get off this phone and earn my damn tax dollars!" Slamming the phone back into its station, I asked myself again if my attempted transformation was worth it. What was I think-ing, giving an egomaniac like Tony free rein over my life?

Not to mention that I was still suffering from mixed emotions over my first foray into Doghood. Hanging at the Black Network social with Tony's friends Carmelita and Chante *was* fun. I really got a kick out of Nikki Coleman's reaction. If I didn't know any better, I'd think Tony's strategy was already working. The girl looked straight-up jeal-ous. I guess Nikki was further proof of the universal axiom: women don't want a man until he's with someone else.

Yeah, Friday would have been good clean fun, except for the sur-prise stunt Tony pulled. Apparently he not only paid Carmelita to fill Nikki's head with lies about my sexual prowess, he also coaxed Chante into offering me some. We hadn't even made it off the dance floor Friday night before she was pawing me. Before Chante pulled me outside to my car, pressed me against her warm flesh, and looked at me with baby brown eyes that called my name, I hadn't really planned on getting buck wild this weekend. I'd figured the task of building my public reputation would be work enough. But when Chante told me to take her home and show her what I could do for her, well, how could I resist? She wasn't the most virtuous woman, but at least she had no kids and supposedly no STDs, as she was quick to point out. Besides, it had been over two years since I'd been with anyone other than Tasha. The prospect had been too good to pass up.

I don't really know that I was all that great, but Chante didn't have any complaints. Except for an awkward moment when I realized that the shoe polish in my hair had seeped into one of her pillows, every-thing was cool. Chante got up early on Saturday, fixed me breakfast, and got me into a deep conversation about where we each saw our lives heading. It was kind of weird; Tasha's the only other friend I've slept with, but I almost felt like Chante and I could have the same kind of thing. But I need another female friend like I need a hole in my head, so I told Chante a little fable about calling her sometime and skipped out before things got too serious.

Saturday night was a little more low-key. Tony set me up with

April Bird, some model who's a friend of his live-in love, Juanita. We double-dated with Tony and Juanita, going to see *Dreamgirls* before hitting a couple of nightclubs downtown. Tony told me that in order to complete my study regimen he would have to see my natural charms in action, preferably with a woman stunning enough to test my limits. He did a fine job choosing April, who looked like Halle Berry with longer hair. Equipped only with my own inept rapping abilities, I failed miserably in gaining April's interest. By the time we hit the last club, I didn't even care that she wound up dancing and then going home with some brother who looked like Wesley Snipes. Clearly, I didn't measure up. I guess that's why Tony was trying to challenge me like he was.

Anyway, by the time Monday morning rolled around I'd been ready to focus on my job and do some work. After getting Tony off my back, I spent the afternoon haggling over Evans Entertainment's financial statements with my boss, CEO Stephon Evans himself. Even that meeting wound up being tainted by the issue of Doghood.

This was a particularly bad quarter for the label financially, so Stephon responded to my analysis with every profanity in the book. "Shitty, piece-of-crap record company!" Leaning over his desk, he narrowed his eyes like a snake and flipped through my charts. As usual, I sat there patiently twiddling my thumbs, waiting for him to say or ask something that made sense. Every employee at Evans who lasted longer than six months knew this was how Stephon worked. With him, conversations are not A says, B responds, A says, B responds. Stephon is kind of in his own world; he has to take time to go through every emotion before he can really talk to you. It's just how he is.

I sucked some air through the small gap in my teeth and waited for him to finish his tirade. Finally he leaned back into the deep leather cushion of his chair and folded his hands calmly. "These numbers are ugly. You hear me, UGLY! Are you *sure* they're right? How did we wind up two hundred thousand dollars under our sales forecast? And how"—he held up a palm as I tried to answer—"did we wind up with a negative cash position? Those assholes upstairs at Empire are looking for an excuse to jack me up, Mitch. I can't have this shit much longer."

"Sir, I understand. As I mentioned on the summary page—"

"Mitch, how many times I gotta tell you, I ain't even thirty-five yet! The name is Stephon, not sir!"

Never mind the fact that he'd been calling me Mitch since the beginning of time. I thought only white guys shortened folks' names without their permission. "All right, sir, I got you. What I'm saying is, the problem is twofold. That sales miss is due to the fact that the projections we got from New York and L.A. record stores were too high. Those *Wall Street Journal* articles about the slowdown in the record industry's sales have got everybody skittish. A lot of stores even tried to return some of the Milos and Saucy Sheryl product they ordered."

"*Shiiit.*" Stephon shifted his tall, lanky frame and ran a hand through his heavily processed hairdo. His eyes were black with disgust. "Why am I just now hearing this? My top artists are getting dissed by our retailers?"

Even though I was annoyed, I tried to pretend Stephon had a right to be shocked. "Our distributors are no better." *If you ever stopped and listened to your vice presidents, you'd know all this,* I thought. I like Stephon, I really do, but the man has no head for business. No one has a better hold on the pulse of the precious eighteen-to-thirty-five age demographic that Evans's artists sell millions of records to, but Stephon is out of his league when it comes to managing a company.

He shook his head wearily. "Well, I guess I can expect another beat-down from Mr. Lee and his Board of Assholes upstairs. How should I take it, Mitch, struggling like a man, or with my pants down and prostrate?"

"Sir, look, I really don't know—"

"Mitch, there's no need for you to talk anymore. You've served your purpose, and I get the message. My company is going down the toilet."

I knew this man needed help. "Sir—Stephon, the real issue you need to face is your relationship with our distributors. You asked about the negative cash position? The reason for that is we're moving most of our product through these national guys whom Empire set us up with. That means the majority of distributors we work with are buying from every Empire division. Guess who's always last to get paid?"

Stephon lurched forward in his seat. "What are you saying? We're gettin' pushed to the back of the line? Don't these MF's know who I am?"

"To be honest, the people who pay us don't know and couldn't care less. These are accountants, Stephon, people who pay only when they feel they have to." I was ready to go into everything. I'd been monitoring these problems for months and funneling them to Tom Carter, our chief financial officer. Somehow he never managed to hip Stephon to them.

I was still educating Stephon when his secretary's throaty voice filled his intercom. "Stephon, Missy is on line three for you."

Stephon clicked his teeth loudly. "What the hell, put her through, Beverly." He placed a finger on the intercom. "Excuse me a minute, Mitch."

As Stephon lifted his finger from the intercom, a woman's shriek made the hairs on my neck stand at attention. "Stephon, where the hell were you last night? Your daughters woke up this morning bawling their eyes out! You should be ashamed of yourself!"

It was like I was no longer in the room. Stephon ran a hand over the creases in his brow. "Missy, are you alone? The girls there?"

"Yeah, I'm alone, fool! Now are you gonna explain yourself, or are you gonna trip on me?"

Stephon glared at the intercom as if it were a living human being. "Look here, woman, how many times have I told you not to call and disrespect me at my place of bidness! You wanna be out on the street tomorrow, that can be arranged. I'll boot you out and take the girls, when the court finds you got no way to support them!"

"I got alimony, nigga! You ever heard of common-law marriage—"

"Missy, please! You really think I'm that ass-backwards? I had my legal eagles make sure my assets were safe from you a long time ago. Why you think I have three other legal residences, besides the estate? We break up tomorrow, I owe you jack!"

I fidgeted in my chair as Missy's shrieks turned into sobs. "Damn you, Stephon, you promised. You said you just needed another year and then we'd be a for-real couple. No more groupies, singers, or hoochies! Why are you stepping out on me again? What did I do?"

Suddenly Stephon wanted to drag me into his mess. "Missy, don't even play that. I gave you what you wanted—money, three beautiful children, and a phat crib. In return you gave me the only thing I wanted—that beautiful body. That's *all* we brothers want, ain't it, Mitch?"

I tried to wave my boss off with a mild shrug. "Oh, man, I really don't think—"

"Ah, come on, Player, be real with me here." Stephon was starting to have some fun. "Even a stiff accountant like you knows that women want men like me, right? It's a deal as old as time itself— women take their men's material wealth, in return for giving the man the freedom to do his own thang. Missy, have you *ever* had a man be faithful to you? Tell me that!" Stephon winked at me like we were best friends.

Missy was whimpering now. "Just 'cause all other men are Dogs don't mean you always got to be one, Stephon. Why don't you come home early today, baby, so we can talk?"

Stephon reached for the intercom again. "How's this, babe? I'll call you when I'm leaving out. I can't make you no promises, though."

"You know what, I don't care anymore! Your sorry ass can work all night for all I care! You wanna know something, Stephon? I *got* an answer for your little question!"

"Oh, really, what is that?"

"I *got* a man who's faithful to me. Your boy Milos. You always wondered how he turns away all them groupies. Well, guess who he's been saving his good stuff for?"

I swear a vein in Stephon's right temple popped straight out the side of his head. "Missy, if you're sayin' what I think you are, you're on dangerous fuckin' ground!"

"Well, I guess we're speaking the same language then!"

I took that as my cue. As Stephon rose from his seat and began shaking the intercom violently, I eased out of my chair and made a beeline for the door. Dogs and their women—it was not always a pretty sight.

When I become a Dog, I promised myself as I shut the door behind me, *I'll never treat my women like that.* At least I hoped I wouldn't.

CHAPTER 10

THE RULES

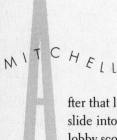

A fter that little scene in Stephon's office, I was relieved to slide into Giordano's a few hours later. As I stood in the lobby scoping for a sight of Tony, I felt a stinging slap on my back.

"Stoney! What up, Boyeee!" My wanna-be friend Trey Benton took me in an enthusiastic headlock, causing the two white couples nearest us to stare in disgust. Trey's desire to be down often gets this type of reaction.

I shrugged him off me before slapping him on the back in response. "What's happening, baby. What brings you up in Giordano's this fine evening?"

Dressed head to toe in Chicago Bulls gear, Trey leaned his six-foot-two, 220-pound frame against the hostess's podium. The young white girl stepped back a full two feet in horror. "I'm here for you, baby, I'm here for you."

"What?" I tracked back to that night at O'Dell's restaurant. I was pretty sure I hadn't told Trey that I wanted him to be my instructor. I'd chosen Tony. So why was the Great White Hope here?

Trey clapped me on the shoulders. "Tony didn't tell you? I'm the consultant. Hey, look, here he is now."

Tony walked up to us, his charcoal-black jacket draped over the arm of his white oxford. "What's up, fellas. Mitchell, I see you've met your consulting instructor."

"Look, no offense, Trey, but I'm feeling a bit out of the loop here. What are you doing, Tony?"

"Come on, lighten up." Tony put an arm around my shoulder as the hostess timidly led us to a table near the center of the restaurant. "This is business, Mitchell, remember that. You can't take this stuff too personally. I'm looking out for your interests. It's simple, really. You, my friend, are a failure with women because you're unwilling to make a fool out of yourself. Look at the diversity of the Dog population: Bobby Brown, Robert De Niro, Bill Clinton, Marv Albert, Eddie Murphy, any of the Kennedys—I could go on. You look at a cross section like that, and I'll guarantee you one thing: very few of them got to where they are with women by being proud. Look at Marv Albert—you think he was shy about telling women he liked to dress up in their clothing and be spanked? I think not!" Tony paused as we pulled our chairs out from the table. "Mitchell, women give it up to the men who ask for it. It's that simple. They may not pay you any mind every time—hell, they may hurt your feelings for a long, long time. But I'm living proof, they'll break eventually. Sooner or later, their amusement at your effort turns to flattery. They feel special, seeing a man make such an ass out of himself."

I looked up from my menu long enough to respond. "What's this got to do with Trey?"

"Trey is the ultimate example of a man with no pride. This man could be practicing dentistry with his father and be a member of the white establishment right now, if he had just done what his parents told him. Instead, what is he doing?" Tony paused. I don't think he had any more idea than I did about what Trey did with his time all day. About all we were sure of was that he was living with his parents and making noises about going back to college again. "This man has completely alienated himself from polite society, in order to pull every fine black woman he can get his hands on. Trey, when's the last time anybody other than a young honey complimented you on your scraggly beard and your ghetto gear?"

Trey smiled widely. "Like I care what anyone other than the honeys think. I ain't got to impress nobody else."

Tony looked at me and pointed a finger at Trey. "See, a complete lack of regard for what others think of him. It's a key to success with women, my brother. You can learn a lot from this man."

Trey smoothed his bushy beard with his fingertips and took a long chug of ice water. "You need to hear this man out, Stoney. I ain't no expert on women or nothing, but I think I know what makes them respond physically. I just figured, all the times you helped me out back in school at MLK, I could finally repay you by helpin' you get some real action. 'Cause, man, I gotta tell you, at the end of even the worst day, there's nothing like knowing you got some good poontang waiting for you."

The absurdity of my experiment was clear to me by now, but I was in too deep to get out. I'd be ridiculed if I backed out. "I'm touched, Trey, really. But given your record of making babies, I think I'll pass on the birth control portion of your lessons. I have that area pretty well handled."

By the time our salads arrived, Tony was ready to get to the meat of the night's class. "Mitchell, I'm gonna give you an overview of the course. These are the central elements most Dogs have in common. These are the qualities you'll have to develop if you're ever gonna get anywhere with the ladies. Trey looked these over this morning after I faxed them to him, so he helped me sharpen the list."

I accepted the leather portfolio with the mayor's letterhead and opened to the first page. Listed there was Tony's official list:

THE (DOG'S) RULES:

1. *All Dogs must have some distinguishing physical characteristic.*
   This is not limited to being tall, well built, or facially handsome, though any of these will help. For those lacking all of these, this deficit can be compensated for with a distinctive wardrobe, a

strategically placed earring or two, a good haircut, or a well-groomed beard.

2. *All Dogs must be men who are not easily tamed by women.* They must challenge a woman at every step of the relationship, always making her feel they are one step from giving her their complete commitment. For instance, the Dogs' women will always wonder if they are sleeping with someone else, spending money on illegal pursuits, or keeping some traumatic secret from them. This elusive quality is publicly labeled as a negative, but in truth it keeps women coming back in hope of a final victory.

3. *All Dogs must be able to use the art of conversation to their advantage.* Dogs know how to size up a female target based on the following characteristics: age, hairstyle, quality of clothing worn (as well as the amount of it), and environment. It comes down to a strong, animalistic sense of perception. The Dog instantly determines the woman's needs and adjusts his rap accordingly.

4. *All Dogs must have murky, complicated lives matched with a mysterious past.* Theo Huxtable would get very little ass in real life, because he is from a clean-cut, professional family with no apparent trauma or division. Even Dogs from middle- and upper-class backgrounds know enough to add some element of danger to their reputation. Examples of activities that increase a Dog's desirability include successful recovery from drug or alcohol addiction, spending at least one year in prison, and being accused of domestic abuse (any such charge should be completely unfounded, of course). It should be stressed that many desirable sisters will not stand for any of these activities in the present tense; they are desirable only as ribbons of one's past struggles.

5. *All Dogs must have other women and children already vying for their attention.* No woman wants a man who is not already in demand. Women are not quite as shallow as men when it comes to appearances; how else, then, are they to judge a man's worth, if

not by how many other women want him? Every Dog worth his salt will always have either a steady (and stupid) girlfriend or a long-suffering wife. The prospect of being "the other woman" is too intoxicating for some women to resist. In addition, a Dog's pulling ratio always increases in proportion to the number of illegitimate children he has. Most Dogs will have at least three children by two mothers. Anything less means you have some seeds to plant.

6. *Dogs of today must be adept users of technology.* Not even the most astute Player can carry on with multiple partners without the efficient use of pagers, call forwarding, cellular phones, and CallNotes. Note: Any beginning student who currently keeps an answering machine in his home must stop reading NOW and discard this relic of the eighties. In-home answering machines are invitations to trouble, especially when a Dog is entertaining one of his conquests. CallNotes services, which record the Dog's messages and keep them in a private depository for retrieval at his convenience, are the only way to go.

Disclaimer: *It should be noted that attainment of the above characteristics cannot be promised to guarantee success with any one specific lady. As quiet as it is kept, there are plenty of levelheaded sisters who are turned off by the aforementioned traits.*

I smiled to myself as I completed the list and began to attack my salad. "Tony, you are out of your mind. You go through all that and then tell me this may not even work?"

Tony waved his fork at me impatiently. "Mitchell, it's a standard product-liability clause. I can't pull the honeys for you, brother. That's all I'm trying to keep you mindful of. You are gonna have to do this yourself."

"Hey, your pep talks have worked, okay? I'm down for the plan. I do have a few questions, though." I leaned over the list again. "Either of you guys ever thought about why women like these things in men? I mean, I'm not disputing that a lot of this is true. I just don't understand why. My parents always taught me that women wanted to be respected first and foremost."

As Trey chuckled orange soda through his nose, Tony leaned back in his seat and crossed his legs in a classic businessman pose. "That's because you were raised by Mike and Carol Brady, man. Those of us who grew up in good old-fashioned dysfunctional homes learned the ugly truth about human nature a *long* time ago."

As I watched Tony's eyes break contact for the first time that night, I couldn't help but recall the night I learned his parents were splitting up. It was two weeks after our graduation from MLK. He and I had grabbed up Tasha and Tony's latest squeeze for a trek to Grad Night at Kings Island Park in Cincinnati. My cousins Allan and Adam Stone, who lived in Cincinnati, had talked me into celebrating their graduation with them, and I'd brought Tony and Tasha along for company. Although it had been the last time Tony and I hung out, it had been a cool weekend; the only annoying thing was the fact that he and his girl kept Tasha and me up all night with their sex matches (Tasha and I had been platonic at the time). Everything had gone smoothly until we dropped the ladies off that Sunday evening. As we pulled off from Tasha's house, I'd prepared to head to his parents' house.

"Hold up, man," Tony said. "I need you to drop me someplace else."

Grinning, I'd shoved him as I slowed down to get directions for where we were headed. "You sly dog, you. Getting your groove on all weekend wasn't enough, you going to see another hook-up now? You're unbelievable."

Tony just grumbled and got real quiet. By the time we got to the gated condominium a few miles from MLK High, I realized something was up. "Yo, isn't that your father's ride? Whose place is this, man?"

Tony kicked my passenger-side door open and clapped me on the shoulder. "Thanks for the ride. Had a good time."

"Tony," I said, laughing innocently, "what's up? Whose place is this?"

One leg out the door, Tony paused suddenly and stared at me. His face showed no sign of emotion. "My parents got divorced this spring, Mitchell. The whole deal became official right before graduation. Now my father's living here. Peace out." Tony was out of the car and through the gate of the condo before I could untangle my tongue.

It wasn't like I hadn't known the Goodens had a wobbly union. Dr. Gooden was a known stud, reliving his days as a college-aged tomcat with various secretaries, employees, even some of the students at his college, rumor had it. But I'd already seen enough by then to assume that the Goodens were simply one of those couples who had made the deal made between many Dogs and their women: just be good to me and keep the other women out of sight. Word had it that Mrs. Gooden's self-esteem had finally driven her to void the deal. Tony, however, never filled in the missing pieces for me. I'll never understand why it's so hard for us brothers to open up.

Now Tony reached over the table and snapped his fingers at me. "Mitchell, come on, what was your question? You don't understand why women don't want a Nice Guy?"

I took a sip of Pepsi before continuing. "All I'm saying is, black women are some of the most talented, warm, giving, precious creatures to walk the earth. To come through slavery, a time when they were separated from their men and raped by white owners; to come through Reconstruction and the great migrations to the North, when they and their men were free in name only; and to come through the industrial age into the 1960s, when they stood with their men and insisted on civil rights, the sisters have always been about business. So why don't more of them insist on what's good for them when it comes to their love lives?"

Trey stopped eyeing the Latina waitress at the next table long enough to respond. Pounding his Bulls starter jacket, he thumped his chest loudly. "Stoney, I had a feeling you might ask that. I been reading a book that sheds light on the subject." To my amazement, the Great White Hope pulled a pair of wire-rimmed glasses from his pocket. A second later he pulled a copy of Naomi Wolf's *Promiscuities* out of his leather satchel and laid it open on the table. "You see, my good man," he said, speaking in the stuffy Gold Coast accent his father was famous for using, "Ms. Wolf talks about how the sexist attitudes of this country have unfairly skewed the sexual experiences of most women, be they white, black, yellow, or red. It seems"—he rested his chin in his hands and narrowed his eyes—"it seems that most women are taught from an early age that sexuality is a taboo subject. It's treated like something they should keep hidden under a bushel, if you'll pardon the pun. For instance, how many teenage women do you think are encouraged to masturbate, as a way of getting in touch with their bodies?"

I tried to contain the laughter welling up within. "Let's see . . . there would be Joycelyn Elders's daughters, and then there would be—nobody."

"My point exactly. In most families, the father pats the teen son on the back and tells him to go plant a high hard one, carrying on the family legacy. What do he and the mother tell their teen daughter, though? Stay away from boys—they're bad! Or if they do let them date, it's with every restriction in the book. As Naomi says, all this does is heighten the female's interest in her sexual feelings. And on top of that, she starts to view her sexuality as this dark, hidden thing that can't see the light of day. Now tell me, is it any wonder most young women wind up associating sexuality with something forbidden and dangerous? Who's she gonna seek out when she's ready to unleash this forbidden energy—a dude who reminds her of her daddy, or a brother who's dangerous and forbidden himself? This paves the way for the insensitive, wild Dog who steals her virginity and makes her mad at the world. According to Naomi, America's prudish morals drive millions of girls into powerless, unsatisfying first sexual experiences."

Tony shook his head. "A shame."

Trey grinned. "Except for the fact that a bad first experience only lowers the woman's expectations, thus setting the stage for all the future Dogs in her life. No wonder it's a Player's world out there."

"A Player's world, huh?" Our waitress, Bobbie, an Indian honey dip with flawless features, leaned into our conversation. "I don't know if I'm welcome in this conversation."

Being around my instructors was starting to change me. Without realizing it, I leaned into Bobbie's ear. "Bobbie, *you* are most definitely welcome. What's your pleasure? We're easy to please."

Frowning playfully, she locked her eyes onto her notepad. "Well, I think I'm here to serve you guys. *Food*, that is. What will you have?"

After we flirted our way through our pizza order, Tony steered the conversation back to the previous topic. "I have another theory on why Dogs get over. Good old-fashioned racism, at least the residual effects of past racism."

I pounded the table. "Tony, be real! I've heard racism used as a straw man for plenty of things, but male-female relationships? Come on, man, relationships are screwed up because of the people involved in them, not some external force like racism!"

Trey, who majored in African-American studies at Howard for three years before dropping out, shook his head in support of Tony. "The man has a point, Mitch. Stop and think about the lives of black families after the Emancipation Proclamation, especially those in the South. Most people were really still living under slave conditions, the name was just changed to 'servant' or 'sharecropper.' And these people in the late nineteenth century were former slaves or direct descendants of slaves. You know how many stable, two-parent homes there were in those days?"

I frowned at the Great White Hope. "I was a business major in school, Trey. If you're gonna school me, just go ahead." *Something is very wrong here*, I told myself. It was time to start some self-study of my people's history; having Trey tell me about my own people made no sense.

"Well, the truth is that many Negroes back in the day believed in marriage, as a result of the Christian faith that pulled them through the horrors of slavery. But many found that marriage was more easily idealized than lived out. Most of the men had never had the opportunity to learn about commitment. They were often used as black bucks for the purpose of mating, before being shipped off to another plantation. Often they never even got to know their many lovers and children. Can you imagine the hell that was, walking around knowing you had kids and lovers out there but you'd never see them again?"

Tony stopped making eyes at a sister across the aisle long enough to add his two cents. "Well, I don't know how that feels, though I suspect I might have slipped a few soldiers past the gate over the years. But I still have no kids that I *know* of, thank God. Not that I don't respect a Father Abraham like you, Trey."

Trey and I both laughed as he continued. "No shame in my game, y'all, I love all five of my kids and I couldn't imagine not being in their lives. That's why I think the effects of slavery screwed up the black male-female relationship so much. With the economic, racial, and spiritual forces he had pressing on him, the Negro male did well to keep puttin' one foot in front of the other. I think that's when black women began cutting them slack in some areas, you know, as long as they took care of the most important things in life."

Suddenly Trey was making sense to me. "You know, now that you mention it, I have an example in my own family. My great-grandfather on my mom's side, J. Henry, was a walking mystery. The way I understand it, he was a former slave who had to work three jobs, almost around the clock, to support his wife and six children. In return for providing them with a roof, food, and clothing, they say he required only two things: free weekends and the summers to himself. He would disappear during those times and do God knows what— some say he gambled, some say he whored, others even say he had a second family hidden away down in Alabama. Regardless of what he did, though, the man is a legend in our family; he took care of his kids and his wife, and eventually built the first of the family's businesses."

"That's exactly what I'm talkin' about!" Trey almost leaped out of his seat. "Don't you get it, Stoney? Being a Dog is almost your duty, man! It's what women want and what they expect! And you can do this without sacrificing your reputation as a good man. Remember, it's a difference between being good and being dull!"

Pleased with our intellectual dissection of women's motives and needs, we dug into our spinach pizza and continued our classroom discussion. Tony treated himself to some entertainment at my expense, needling me for my failure to impress April Bird on our double date. Trey tripped off my exploits with Chante and unloaded some of the frustrations of being a single father with children by four different women. Before I knew it, we had finished our feast and were back on the street.

Buttoning my London Fog windbreaker as a shield against the winds blowing off the lake, I waved at my partners and headed toward my Accord. "You brothers take it easy!"

"Ah-ah!" Tony blocked my path. Trey stood behind him, his arms crossed mischievously. "My brother, have you forgotten that I have to give you a homework assignment? You've got to thicken that skin, Mitchell. It's time for you to get dissed, in some major ways. I want you to spend this next week doing everything possible to get women to reject your advances. You should be approaching five sure misses every day. It's the only way you'll ever be able to strike at a moment's notice. You've got to wipe out any fear instinct, any pride."

Snorting a little too loudly, I stepped to my right to make an end run around my instructors. I was tired. "Okay, sure. I'll keep you posted."

"You sure will." Tony whipped a miniature cassette recorder from the pocket of his jacket. "You're going to wear this every time you step to someone. This recorder is electronically wired to my cell phone's voice mail. Any conversation you record on here will automatically dump into my voice mail. Every day, I expect to pick up five messages in which I hear you either getting dissed or lucking out and getting some digits." He thrust the device at my chest. "Can I trust you to do your work, Mitchell?"

I snapped it from him and headed toward the car. "Who do you think I am, fool? I taught *you* how to study back at MLK, you know better than to question me. I'll take care of it!"

As I trudged to the curb, I could hear Trey and Tony slapping hands. Whether they realized it or not, they were officially mocking me now. As I slid into the Accord, the last sound I heard was Trey's ringing shout. "Don't worry, Boyeee, we'll get you some Nikki Coleman booty, before it's all over!"

If only it were that simple, I thought, *I wouldn't be in this mess to begin with.*

CHAPTER 11

LOOKING FOR MR. DO RIGHT

Late May

s I stepped onto the elevator in the lobby of the MCI Building this afternoon, I tried to focus on what I needed to do. I was not going to let my last conversation with Barry steal my sanity. At least not any more than it already had.

Barry actually had the nerve to show up outside my apartment Tuesday night. I hadn't returned any of his messages from Saturday, Sunday, or Monday. He must have gone looking for me at work on Monday, judging from the first question he hit me with when I opened the door.

"Where the hell have you been?" His arms were full of red roses. Before I could stop it, my mind flashed back to the way he used to sprinkle rose petals on the bed in his parents' pool house. "I called your assistant all day yesterday and today. She kept saying you weren't available." He shifted his weight from one leg to the other. "Nikki, will you let me in, please?"

Dressed only in a long T-shirt and a pair of stretch pants, I looked at him like he was out of his mind. "Why would I let you in, so you can steal the last ounce of my self-respect? Anything you got to say to me, you say it from where you are."

He eased the roses into my right hand, pausing to make sure I wouldn't toss them onto the floor. "Look, I know I screwed up, Nikki. I should have consulted you before I told Colin about our business. But I'm worried about you, girl. Why weren't you at work these past two days?"

I rolled my eyes and shook my head. I hadn't gone into work because I had given up on Empire Records. I was damned if I did, and damned if I didn't. If I went ahead and settled with that asshole Colin now, I'd be selling my self-respect and pride out for the almighty dollar. If I pressed ahead with the suit, well, I'd have had to be Pollyanna to think that would mean anything less than the end of my career in the music business. Who was going to hire a black woman who'd had the nerve to sue someone as well known as Colin Lee? Record executives across the country would know my name long before I walked into their personnel offices. Barry's ignorant ass had me teetering on the brink of unemployment and depression.

I don't know if this just hadn't hit home with me before then, but for some reason I lost it with him right then and there. "Barry, if you don't get out of my doorway right now, I will go find a sharp appliance and kill you! You do understand I'm not exaggerating, don't you?"

Barry stepped back several feet and threw his hands up. "All right, all right, I see I'm not the one to talk to you about everything that's going on." He reached into his pocket and pulled out a business card. I took the opportunity to drop the roses and grind them into the hardwood floor of my foyer. I was pretty sure I could clean the stains out later.

Trying to act as if the stomping of his roses didn't hurt, Barry kept his eyes on the floor as he handed me the business card. "You know Marvin Stone, right? Seems like I heard you were even dating his brother Mitchell for a while—" Barry pulled up, probably because I shot him a look that could kill. "Anyway, Marvin and I aren't really boys or anything, but we've stayed in touch since our MLK days, and there is no better attorney I know of. You may have to compete for his attention some, 'cause he's always in demand by talk shows and groups looking for motivational speakers. But if he agrees to take your case, he'll do you right."

Having Mitchell Stone's brother represent me? Something about that didn't quite sit right. "Barry, if I decide to even get another damn lawyer, I may give him a call. Bye."

As I gripped my doorknob, Barry began pleading frantically. "Nikki, I already talked to Marvin he says he's down with representing you. He's waiting for your call and look at it this way you won't have to worry about Marvin pulling any dumb stuff, he's a real clean-cut religious type. Really believe me I think you should call him and—" He was still yammering on as I shut the door and made sure it was a snug fit.

AFTER TAKING THE rest of the week off, I went ahead and called Marvin. I think I would have called anyway, but what finally pushed me to do it was the realization that he couldn't do me any worse than Barry had. Besides, I figured with his local celebrity profile, Marvin might add some credibility to my case. Not to mention the chance that I might get some scoop on what was happening with Mitchell these days. I still hadn't quite gotten over that night at First Fridays with Carmelita. If Mitchell Stone was sleeping with women like Carmelita Hodge, he must be trading in his Good Man card for a Player's Edition. I knew either way it was none of my business, but for some reason I was disappointed in him. Maybe I wasn't one of them, but there were women out there who needed straitlaced men like Mitchell Stone.

So after spending the rest of the week eating Ben & Jerry's and rice cakes and watching every trifling talk show under the sun, I cleaned myself up and went to Marvin's office at the MCI Building. When Marvin walked out into the waiting room to greet me, I almost forgot why I was there in the first place. He looked so much like Mitchell it was unsettling, but at the same time he was just so much better-looking. Aside from his additional inches of height and the rippling muscles beneath his oxford, it was hard to pin down the difference between him and Mitchell. But somehow, Mitchell is Boy Next-Door, while Marvin is Hunk. Today he was wearing a chalky gray pinstripe suit and a graciously appointed power tie. Hard to believe a man like that spends his free time bragging about the fact that he never gets any sex.

Sittting back in his office, Marvin rocked in his leather swivel chair and gave me his take on the case. "Nikki, from what I've read in the files and based on my discussions with Barry, I think you have an open-and-shut case that is only made complex by matters of race and privilege. For that reason, I feel confident that I'm the right attorney for you."

The assured, peaceful tone of his voice made me straighten my back and sit up in my seat. "Why do you say that?"

Marvin began chewing on a pen cap and smiled at me. "Well, Nikki, let's just say that my firm here, Wilder & Thorpe, has a distinguished history representing various parties in sexual-harassment and discrimination lawsuits. The only thing is, normally we're defending the bigoted White Anglo-Saxon Protestant males who perpetrate these crimes. In return for getting them off or helping to rationalize what they've done, they line our pockets with all the corporate law work we could ever need, and then some."

I was picking up on Marvin's hint. "So your firm is known for defending harassers. And that would make it all the more jarring for you to represent me."

"Most definitely. I can guarantee every judge in town will be shocked to see my name on this docket. Their first thought will be, if Wilder & Thorpe let Marvin Stone sue a corporate harasser, this case must be for real. Colin Lee will start shoveling cash your way before you can count to three."

Marvin's last sentence reminded me of my real problem. "Marvin, I can't make do with a settlement now. This asshole—" I froze, realizing I'd just cussed in front of a devout Christian. "This, uh, piece of trash has humiliated me in ways that can't be paid off. It's time to make a point here."

Marvin stopped rocking and turned to face me head-on. He planted his elbows on the desk. "Nikki, let me help you out here. I'm offering you a pretty good deal. What I'm talking about here, going against the grain of my firm by representing you, this is no small matter. The only reason I could even take your case is because my firm needs me as token black and token celebrity. Do you know that over half of our new clients ask to have me on their account? Everybody wants a piece of Marvin Stone. Now I don't say that to pump myself up; it's all about my Lord and Savior. I'm blessed to have these opportunities, but I'm careful with how I use them. But I want to help you out as a fellow MLK alumnus, and as a friend of my brother."

Oh, no. What had Mitchell told him about me? "Oh, so you know Mitchell and I are friends?" I lied a little by using the present tense. Marvin probably knew the truth anyway.

"I know you guys graduated at the top of the same class, and I know Mitchell thinks you're a great lady. He has a lot of respect for you, and that's enough for me."

I crossed my legs again and folded my hands in my lap. "Well, I appreciate your offer, Marvin, but I'm not going to back down. I want to take this all the way to court. If you're going to be my attorney, you will be bound to pursue that."

A cloud moved over Marvin's face suddenly. "You're a very determined woman, Nikki. All you sisters really think you can do it for yourselves, don't you? Don't you believe in leaving anything for the brothers to do?"

"What's that supposed to mean?" This suddenly felt like it was getting personal.

"All I'm saying is, if I tell you it's best to take a settlement, you might want to trust me. I am the attorney here."

I tousled my hair and eyed Marvin suspiciously. "So if I don't go along with your every decision, I'm suddenly just another ungrateful sister. Okay, fine." It was looking like I was going to have to hire a sister lawyer. Marvin Stone was turning out to be just another variation of a male asshole. Why did men continue to do nothing but disappoint me? Ever since my own father all but rejected me in order to keep his wife happy, I'd given other brothers the chance to fill his shoes. Barry, Jomo, and the nameless six or seven other men I'd been with. Every time, all I wanted was a little assurance; a little validation that *yes, Nikki, you're okay. You're what I want, what I need.* And they always said those things, too, until they got what they wanted. From there, it was always downhill.

I realized as I looked at Marvin that my success in school and on the job had always made up for the lack of approval from the men in my life. Or at least I thought it had. Now Colin Lee had taken the one thing in my life that gave me value and trashed it. I was not going to let anyone tell me how far to press this lawsuit. If Marvin Stone thought he was going to call every shot here, it was time for us to part ways already. Next candidate, please.

I got up from my chair. "Marvin, I'm leaving before you do or say something *else* we'll both regret. You have twenty-four hours to let me know if you'll represent me and take this case as far as I say to take it. If you won't do it, I'll find someone who will. Bye."

Marvin stroked his chin before rising and shaking my hand with a warm and comforting grip. "Everyone's entitled to their own opinion, Ms. Coleman. I will be in touch."

I huffed out of Marvin's office, but I was out of self-righteous steam by the time I got back out on the street. Something about his reaction to my challenge wasn't right. I had challenged his manhood, questioned his legal authority, and he had reacted like I'd brought him tea and cookies. The man had something different, something special, lurking beneath that Tyson Beckford build and that Denzel face. Something that Mitchell, in his own way, shared. Something I had yet to see in Barry, Jomo, or the various what's-their-names I'd passed time with in recent years. As I hopped a bus back to Lincoln Park, I could feel myself growing curious about both of the Stone men.

I might have been able to distract myself with thoughts about the Stones for the rest of the day, if Gene Coleman, my father, hadn't

been waiting for me in the lobby of my building. Seeing him standing there by the bellhop's station felt like a kick in the gut. I froze
right where I was, just inside the main entrance. Before I could will
my feet to move and take me back out the front door, he saw me.

"Hey, there she is!" Dressed in a plaid sport shirt and beige khakis,
Gene looked a little cleaner than I remembered seeing him a couple
years back, the last time we'd met in person. His pants were hanging
off his six-foot-three frame as if he had lost too much weight recently,
and his face was thinner through the cheeks than I recalled. He
looked old, but his eyes were still full of the misguided fire that I recognized all too well.

After dropping a few dollars into the bellhop's hand, Gene ambled
over to me like he was greeting an old friend. "Hi, Nikki. I thought
we should talk." Before he even reached me, his eyes started to shift
nervously. He was losing his enthusiasm at seeing me, and I knew immediately this was not a friendly visit. "I figured your recent message
deserved a direct response."

With everything going on in my life, I think I had blocked out "the
message." Now it all came back. It had been the night when I first
learned about his little pension fund, the one he was supposed to use
to help Mama out. Jomo had just left my apartment for the night, and
as usual I had found that an hour's worth of pleasure couldn't mask
my pain. Before I knew what I was doing, I was dialing my father's
number and leaving a message on his home voice mail: *Gene, this is
Nikki. I'm gonna tell you this one time and one time only, and I hope
your wife is listening in on this, too. I am going to help simplify your
life. You've never wanted to admit to fathering me in the first place, and
Jennifer's been in denial, too. Not to mention my so-called sisters. But
one thing is sure, Gene, you screwed my mother and made me! So you
owe her! It's not her fault her neighborhood's gone crazy! Every day
there's another carjacking or mugging! God, Gene, how long do you
think she has before she becomes a direct victim or an innocent by-
stander?! I'm making you a deal now—you give her the money she
needs to move out of Rosewood, and I will pretend you are not my father. I will never ask for one red cent again, I will never tell another soul*

that we're related, and I'll never, ever come around your house! Okay?
Because if you don't accept this deal, you will be sorry! I expect you to
keep your promise by the end of June! Don't make me call here again.

I felt myself shrinking back a little at the memory. Every word had
been true, but that didn't make it right. My mama raised me better
than that. Now I didn't know what kind of reaction to expect from
Gene.

"Your message was hard on my heart, Nikki." He stopped trying to
speak, as a violent cough wracked his bony chest. "Nikki, look, can
we talk, please? I ain't hear to preach at you, I just want you to think
about showing me and my family some respect."

"Respect?" What in hell was this? He was going to teach *me* some
manners? "Oh, please, Gene, teach your daughter about respect.
Let's see, what example should I use to learn your idea of respect?
The one where you slept with my mother and then denied fathering
me for three years? Or maybe the one where you act like I don't exist,
so much so that your own brothers and sisters sometimes forget they
have a third niece." I felt my eyes blur with tears. "I'm not doing this
here, and I'm damn sure not having you up in my apartment. Just
leave me alone."

Gene looked at me with eyes that begged for approval. "How about
a walk, then?"

It was a beautiful day, full of blue skies and sun. The chirps of birds
struggled against the blare of car horns and diesel trucks and the scut-
tle of worker bees crowding the sidewalks. I let the odd combination
of noises wash over me as Gene struggled to match my pace. "Have
you ever even thought about my side of the story in all this?"

"Oh, Gene, please, I've heard your story from all your brothers and
sisters. You know, the ones who are always running my mother down
and saying she was a whore who messed with you just to get pregnant,
even though she wanted to raise her child alone? Trust me, I've heard
your story more times than I care to count."

As we neared the Lincoln Park Zoo, my father sighed. "Nikki, did
it occur to you that I didn't marry your mother for one reason and one
reason only? I was already married to someone else! I'm gonna be
honest with you, I thought long and hard about leaving Jennifer. Our

marriage was in a rough spot, and she'd had affairs herself. And I thought I loved your mother, I really did. But you wanna know what? She wouldn't have me."

"I'll applaud her on that."

"I understand you would. Matter of fact, she was right, Nikki. She told me that I didn't know what I wanted, and that she had no reason to think I'd be a good husband. And she was right. It took three more years of AA meetings, a touch of church, and some counseling to make me a useful husband and father to Jennifer and the girls."

"So you weren't exactly a good catch. What's your point?"

He grabbed my shoulders and stopped walking. "Don't you see, you didn't get the most raw deal, Nikki. If I'd been in your life, it might have been more complicated than it was with me out of the picture. Besides, I think I deserve a little respect for sticking it out with my wife. And I think that means nasty messages like that mess you pulled aren't fair."

He was making a little bit of sense to me, but I couldn't even think about letting him off that easy. "Excuses, excuses, Gene. If you don't mind, I'd like to go home now."

"Nikki." He gripped my shoulder again, rooting me in place. "I will give you the money for your mother. It's probably best for her and me if we don't haggle directly over money matters." He took out a standard-sized envelope with my name scrawled on it. "I'd like to make you the point man on this. This check should cover a portion of your mother's expenses toward a new home. If she needs more, let me know. My pension funds are close to being tapped out, but I may be able to take out a loan or something."

I was too surprised to answer. This was coming a little too easily. "Okay, what's the catch?"

My father cleared his throat and started to walk in the direction of my apartment. "Well, I may not agree with your methods, but that message knocked some sense into me. I had no idea how much you hated me. I guess I figured by now you'd gotten over your disappointment in me. Hell, by the time I was your age, I'd forgotten my daddy ever existed.

"I just hope you can remember this gesture as proof that I—" He

stopped suddenly and stared off into space. "Never mind. Look, I—"
He was interrupted again by a long, hacking cough. I almost felt sorry
for him. "Look, I better go." He reached out to touch my hair. Sliding my eyes away from him, I let him fiddle with one of my split ends.
"Bye, Nikki."

Stepping back and watching him wobble off, I fought conflicting
emotions. On one hand, I was concerned. Something about my father's weight loss and his clumsy gait made me uneasy. But more immediate was my disappointment at the absence of a phrase I hadn't
heard from any man in far too long: *I love you.*

CHAPTER 12

THICK SKIN

MITCHELL

t's been almost a week since Tony told me to go out and collect as many rejections as possible. And like I told him, I'm living up to my rep as MLK's valedictorian by taking his assignment to the next level. In this last week, I've been laughed at, ignored, cussed out, slapped, and read from A to Z by women of all hues, heights, races, and socioeconomic classes. And I haven't limited my exploits to women I considered beneath me, like Regina the receptionist or the girl who works in the gift shop.

Last night I had the perfect opportunity to rub shoulders with the finest sisters in Chicago, which is saying something. Stephon Evans flew Milos back into town for a party celebrating the fact that his debut CD, *A Real Man*, hit the double-platinum mark. That was Stephon's stated reason, at least. I knew from our little meeting that Stephon was probably plotting some way to get Milos back for sleeping with his woman, Missy.

Apparently it was common knowledge that Milos had

been stamping Missy's bankbook for several months now, as I realized when I shared Missy's boasts about Milos with a couple of my colleagues. Anyway, Stephon's reaction made it clear that he had been the only brother other than me who had been clueless about the affair. The man was a walking double standard: he could freak whomever he wanted, but how dare Missy think she could do the same?

I didn't really see Stephon hurting Milos physically. We all knew that Evans Entertainment needed Milos worse than the new Motown needs Brian McKnight. Hell, Milos could sleep with every one of Stephon's favorite tricks and Stephon would probably still take a bullet for him. All the same, we also knew Stephon was no chump, so we figured he had something in store.

But whatever it was, he kept it under wraps the night of the party. All grudges and rumors were laid aside for that night, as everyone gathered at Harambee, a cavernous clubhouse that Stephon owns with a couple of guys from the Bulls. In attendance was anyone who's anyone in the twenty- to thirtysomething black community; competing record execs, singers, actors, pro athletes, local news personalities, and a sprinkling of doctors, lawyers, and investment bankers.

Personally, I was in rare form. In addition to my orders to collect rejections, Tony had insisted that I also apply Rule #1 and affect some sort of distinguished walk. He and I had argued so much over this point that I revoked my offer to get him a ticket to the party. He had insisted that I try a bowlegged gait, a suggestion I found ridiculous. After that we'd played around with several other methods: the Pimp Slow Roll, the George Jefferson Wattle, the *Sanford and Son* Shuffle, and the Billy Dee Glide. None of them worked for me. For that night, I decided to just go with an exaggerated version of my own walk, an amiable, slow-paced gait in which I slowly raise one foot and swing the opposite arm. Unfortunately, the Mitchell Stone Roll lacks the rhythm or brutality that Tony says most women like to see in brothers. I figured I'd try to compensate for this tonight by swinging my arms widely. If nothing else, it might make me look more arrogant, like I owned the personal space of everyone around me. That had to snag a few ladies' eyes, right?

A half hour into the party, I had downed a couple of Budweisers, made some small talk with Stephon and a couple of other executives, and vibed off Milos's CD with Regina, the receptionist. By that time, I realized I was letting the night get away from me without collecting my daily rejections. I needed to make my moves on some of the finest women, so I decided to start with the throng of groupies surrounding Milos's table. The crowd of women in skimpy skirts, low-cut shirts, and see-through tops made it impossible to even glimpse the star and his handlers. But I didn't care about seeing Milos.

Standing near the back was this chocolate-colored honey with Asian features. She was one of those exotically beautiful women who most of us brothers react to with false indifference. You know, the ones where we sit back and slap hands with our boys and say, "Damn, she fine." Then we just sit there and theorize on how jacked up in the head she is, all because we're too freaked out by her beauty to take a step in her direction. I don't think I had ever even held a conversation with a woman this fine. I usually figure there's no point; she won't want me for her boyfriend, and I damn sure couldn't be satisfied being her "friend." As I stood half an inch from this woman, though, my Dog training began to kick in. It was time for some thangs to change.

I reached forward and tapped her on the shoulder, but she just kept pawing those in front of her to catch a glimpse of Milos. I tapped again. After four more taps, she whirled around and glared at me like I stole something. "What?"

"My, aren't we articulate," I said. "Excuse me, sister, but would you like to dance?"

She tossed a hand through her wavy curls and had a good laugh. "Yeah, right."

Before I could respond, she waded back into the crowd around Milos's table. As I toyed with how to respond, I looked down at my outfit. Was it my clothing? Hell, I was wearing my favorite Tommy Hilfiger suit. I checked my fingernails. Clean, not that she even looked at me long enough to see them. I did the breath test. I knew I wasn't the best judge, but all I smelled was the Certs I'd popped a minute earlier. I even ran a hand across my forehead, to make sure that my latest dollop of shoe polish hadn't started to melt into my eyes. Finally, I glanced over at the wall-length mirror behind the bar. No, I hadn't turned into an ogre in the short time since the party started.

What the hell was her problem? I said to myself. Before I could finish wallowing in pity, I felt my cell phone vibrate in my pocket. Walking back toward the men's room, I flipped the phone open. "This is Mitchell."

"My boy!" It was Tony. "You must be at that party now, huh? How many rejections have you collected?"

"I've only just begun. You shoulda seen the way this last sister dissed me, it was *cold*. I just don't understand what's so bad about me, that a woman like that would dis me so bad. I mean, she acted like there was no chance in hell of her considering me!"

"Mitchell, listen." Tony paused, then I heard him say, "Juanita, babe, give me a minute here. I'm almost ready. Can't a brother have a minute to rap to his boy? Look, man, I've gotta take Juanita to a ball for the mayor's office tonight, but I wanted to remind you to have the 'eye of the tiger.' This is just the thing you need, to get that thin skin of yours good and callous. Face it, man! Very few brothers today have the candy store of dating that the media says we do! Unless you look like Shemar Moore, have the pocketbook of Michael Jordan, and the charisma of Eddie Murphy, you will not land most of these sisters!" He paused again. "Oh, Juanita, you know I'm not talking about you, shut up! Look, man, getting kicked to the curb tonight will make approaching a woman of substance like Nikki Coleman that much easier. Trust me here. I gotta go."

"All right, later." I flipped the phone shut and swung my way back into the crowd. Deciding to get straight to the point with the rest of the groupies, I introduced myself and immediately asked them to dance. In every case, they would either shoo me off or make conversation long enough to come up with an excuse why they couldn't dance right now. Once I had struck out with twelve of them, I felt that callus start to develop. I had nothing to lose.

That's when I spied a petite beauty at the bar. This sister looked like she was about business. She was wearing a crème-colored, double-breasted business suit that made me guess she worked at an investment bank or a consulting firm. And she was alone! No cloying sisters seated around her, ready to run down the first brother who stepped to her. I figured she must be without a date, too, and I saw no rings on her left hand. This was the type of sister I always felt pressured to step to—someone attainable but so ideal that I felt like my whole future depended on the quality of my rap. I mean, a sister like this could be my future wife and the mother of my children. It was hard not to feel pressure in a situation like that; to think that a wrong word or gesture could rob me of the woman I was meant to spend the rest of my life with. I don't know why I always had so much performance anxiety over approaching women; no test, exam, or presentation ever unnerved me in the same way.

I reminded myself again that the brother who used to quake in his boots was the old Mitchell Stone. I was in the midst of a transformation, and I had to act like it. Swiping another beer off the tray of the next waiter who came along, I swung my way over to the bar. I plopped onto the seat next to the mystery lady and tipped my head her way. "How are you this evening?"

The sister kept her eyes on her Long Island iced tea and smirked to herself. "Oh, I'm all right."

I decided to play things straight for as long as I could. "Hi, I'm Mitchell." I offered her my hand, which she took without bothering to make eye contact. "I work for Evans Entertainment. What brings you out to the party tonight?"

The woman looked at me with her big baby browns and recrossed her legs so that she was facing me. "My name is Valerie Simmons. I'm here at the invitation of a girlfriend."

I smiled. That was probably a cover line. Most of the women invited to these gigs were the playthings of Stephon, the artists, or the many black VIPs who came out to these deals. I tried to figure out who really invited her. "So, are you enjoying yourself?"

"Oh," Valerie sighed, "it's okay, I guess. When is that Milos gonna get his bony ass up onstage and do some numbers for us? That is why we're here, isn't it?"

I leaned against the bar, enjoying the flow of the conversation. It wasn't getting me anywhere, but I could throw out a line to raise the stakes at any minute. "I don't know what's up with Milos. Boy sells a couple million CDs and thinks he's too big to perform for the folk that made him."

Valerie wasn't having it. "You do work for Evans Entertainment, don't you? Can't you get the show on the road? Or was that all just a line?"

I took another swig of my beer and set the bottle on the counter. "Well, a woman as fine as you would make a brother feel he had to lie about his occupation to measure up. But I'm for real, I do work for Evans."

"He work for Evans all right!" I jumped at the sound of the loud-ass voice. Whoever it was sounded like he was standing on my heels. He had obviously been eavesdropping on our conversation for the last few seconds, and I was pissed. I figured it was time to add to my Dog repertoire by starting a fight, or at least jumping bad enough to make this fool think I was up to one. I turned around to set it off and was immediately disappointed. The husky voice actually belonged to Saucy Sheryl, Evans's number-two artist and the top female rapper on the scene. She was standing there with a smug grin on her face, with her arms crossed and a Bulls cap neatly tucked on top of her dreadlocks.

I couldn't hide my annoyance, despite the fact she was accompanied by two of her silent bodyguards. "Great, Saucy Sheryl herself. Can't you see the lady and I are having a conversation?"

Sheryl laughed loudly and placed a hand on Valerie's shoulder. "Val, is this accountant tryin' to push up on you? Dang, you make even the most square brother hot for it!"

I knew my chemistry with Valerie was slipping away, but I couldn't give up without a fight. "Sheryl, how many times have I told you, I am not an accountant! I am a financial analyst."

Valerie smiled and looked at Sheryl knowingly. "And what exactly is the difference?"

"An accountant counts money and records transactions in the accounting records," I insisted. "A financial analyst is a manager, ladies!

I get the financial statements after the accountants prepare them, okay? Then I sit down with Stephon himself and figure out if Evans is as profitable as we need to be, and how we adjust our strategy accordingly. I'm not some bookkeeper!"

Sheryl started picking at her leather vest. "Riveting, Mitchell, riveting."

"Hold up, I'll give you an example. Sheryl, remember the bonus you got a couple months back?"

She stopped playing with her clothes long enough to frown at me. "What about it?"

"Well, you have me to thank for that. My research on distributors helped Evans save several hundred thousand dollars, by firing those that weren't performing and hiring the new ones who got your CDs into four record chains that weren't carrying you before! I helped you make money! Now, what would you call someone who can help you do that?"

Sheryl shook her head and laughed. "An accountant!"

I don't know why I even tried going down that road with her. Ever since I rejected her advances last spring, when she cornered me in my office and said she wanted to know what it was like to "do it" with a CPA, she hasn't given me one ounce of respect. Her next sentence told me I could forget about Valerie.

"Valerie here is my attorney, my cat. She's based in Atlanta, but I always fly her in when big events like this be going on. She knows business better than I do, but even I know you ain't nothin' but a bean counter, Stone. Give it up."

I don't know exactly what came over me, but I think I decided to get myself another taste of rejection before Sheryl handed it to me. Ignoring her bodyguards, I bolted from my seat, eased Sheryl out of my way, and embraced Valerie like she was the last woman on the earth. I bent her over the bar and planted a warm kiss on her, the type I learned from Tasha years ago. I don't know how long it lasted; I'd guess five seconds, but Valerie's minty throat tasted so good, it felt like an eternity. Eternity ended when Sheryl yanked me back and Valerie slapped me a good one.

Valerie was clearly flustered. "Who the hell do you think you are?! I have a fiancé and a young child at home!"

What would a Dog say in a situation like this? I took a shot. "What's that got to do with me? I didn't know what you were or weren't when I walked over here! I saw something I liked, and I went for it!" I stepped back and placed my hands on my hips. "Damn, excuse me, sister!"

Valerie got up from the bar and stood between Sheryl's body-guards. I was guessing the only reason they hadn't killed me yet was the fact that Stephon had wandered over to us by then.

"Weeeeell, what have we here?" Stephon hoisted a half-empty wineglass my way as Valerie collected herself and Sheryl eyed me like a Rottweiler. "Is that CPA Stone gettin' his groove on? You go, boy! Hanging around me will get you some respect with the ladies eventually!" He drained his glass before sweeping his eyes over each of us again. He seemed to suddenly realize that I was not the most popular brother in the room. "Mitch, get out on that dance floor and help one of those girls work her moneymaker! I need to talk business with Saucy and her lawyer!" He slapped me on my back and winked as I rose from the stool. "Wouldn't have known you had it in ya!"

As I heard Valerie and Sheryl cursing my name to Stephon, I continued through the crowd. I don't know if Tony had expected this or not, but my latest rejection looked like it was going to help establish my new reputation. For the rest of the night, I noticed more and more women returning my glances. Many of them even approached me and dragged me out on the dance floor. Most of them admitted to being curious about why Saucy Sheryl was running me down and saying I deserved to get my ass kicked. These women were intrigued, and they were throwing phone numbers at me so fast, I had to work hard the rest of the night to find women who would reject me. Don't worry, I did find some. By the time I left that night, my skin was good and thick.

But I didn't go home alone. Regina, the receptionist, hung all over me the last hour of the party, so much so that I had to take her home. We'd basically done the nasty with our clothes on out on the dance floor anyway. As usual, I couldn't take her back to my place for fear of offending Marvin the Monk, so we got a room at the Congress Hotel. Regina was no shrinking violet; we did everything I've ever done with Tasha that night, and some of the more freaky stuff I did in my one-night stand in college with that Monisse girl. By the time morning rolled around, we both wound up calling in sick to work. Not surprisingly, no one was there to take our calls. It was common knowledge that everyone at Evans Entertainment called in sick the day after Stephon's biggest parties.

I got my first chance to exercise Dog Rule #6 (*Dogs must be adept users of the latest communications technology*) at 10:32 that morning. After trying out a new position on the windowsill, Regina collapsed on top of me and sighed. "This is really nice, Mitchell." She winked. "What say we play hooky the rest of the day? I could get used to you."

What? My recently planted Dog alarm went off loud and clear at that one. Regina was nice and cute, but I had a long way to go before I'd be thinking about "getting used" to anybody. Maybe Nikki could have turned my head with a statement like that, but anybody else could forget it.

After kissing Regina on the cheek and wrapping myself up in my new silk Player's bathrobe, I slid into the bathroom, shut the door, and pulled out my trusty cell phone. I dialed Tony's number at the office. No answer. Damn! I tried Trey's lazy ass, at his parents' house. No answer there, either. The boy was probably already out knocking the first of many boots for the day. I leaned against the door and looked at myself in the mirror before resigning myself to my next-best option. With a big old frown on my face, I dialed Marvin's number.

My brother proved to be as predictable as always. "Mitchell, you want me to call you back at some strange number? Where are you? What is this about?"

"Marvin, why do you have to ask so many questions? Will you just do your little brother a favor?"

"Mitchell, you and I need to talk. Do you even spend nights here at the apartment anymore? I really think you're biting off more than you can chew with this Dog business."

I put a hand to my forehead. "Marvin, I called you for a favor, not a counseling session."

"Are you using protection?"

I raised my voice at that one, so much that I was afraid Regina might hear me. "Man, please. Mitchell Stone never goes swimming without his shower cap."

Marvin grunted. "Look, I got a client coming by in a few minutes. I'm gonna play along with your trifling behind this one time, just to show I can be a good sport. But you have to promise me something."

"What?"

"You have to sleep at home one night this weekend and rap with me about women, marriage, the whole deal. Maybe we can help open each other's eyes."

I squinted in confusion. Marvin never really talked about stuff like that, at least not since he and Angela got divorced. "Uh, okay. Look, here's the number."

Five minutes later I let Regina answer my cell phone while I got ready to hop in the shower. Even from inside the bathroom, I could hear Marvin enjoying his role, shouting like a madman.

"Mitchell!" Regina ran to the doorway of the bathroom, the phone cradled in her right hand. "It's your boss, Tom! He sounds pissed that you're not at the office!"

Feigning concern, I wrapped a towel around my waist and took the phone. Pretending I was again starring in the eighth-grade production of *Our Town*, I winced, sighed, and hee-hawed my way through a performance that convinced Regina I was being called into the office. I was out of the hotel and back at my place by noon. Arriving home produced a new pleasure—I actually had some voice-mail messages. Three of the women I met at Milos's party had called, and they sounded eager to hook up. I was on my way!

The last message threw me for a bit of a loop, though. "Mitchell," the smooth, rich voice said, "this is Aunt Rhonda calling. Your mother wanted me to call and hip you to a seminar I'm holding in Chicago tomorrow night. I think you know the young man who owns the restaurant where we're meeting—O'Dells's Chicken & Waffles? I was invited to speak there by the Ebony Singles Organization. I'll be reading from my book and leading some discussions about the romance problems among people of your generation. I'd love it if you and Marvin could come by. I'll call you Friday night when I get into your parents' house. God bless."

I smirked at the thought of attending a relationship seminar where my mother's youngest sister would be the speaker. Aunt Rhonda is a highly respected sociologist and counselor, and this book, *What's Love Got to With It: The Divide Between Young Brothers and Sisters*, is a best-seller just like her previous two titles. That said, I didn't really think I could enjoy an experience that mixed sexual politics with family business. Although I was starting to see some promise in my transformation into a Ladies' Man, I wasn't exactly proud of the things I was doing, and I certainly couldn't talk about them in front of Aunt Rhonda. It was time to start planning some alternate activity for Saturday.

Still drained from my workout with Regina, I melted into the living room couch and put on some ESPN to serve as my nap soundtrack. One minute a sports announcer was droning on about the latest rumor about Michael Jordan's marriage, and the next I was floating on a placid river of sleep. My troubles melted away. As I felt myself surrender into the couch, though, I realized I was not alone. Seated across from me, in a smoky haze, was Tamara Shaw. At least I had heard that was her name. She was a girl I'd first met in passing at a party on Howard's campus, sophomore year. I had hit the party with some of my fellow baseball teammates at Georgetown. Like any brothers with good sense, we had traipsed over to Howard regularly to scope the finest honeys in town. We had also perfected the art of "blending in." The only Georgetown men who got dap on Howard's campus were Alonzo Mourning and his fellow basketball sensations.

I never learned much about Tamara; her major, year, hometown, and career aspirations will always be a mystery to me. All I know is she was beautiful, in that undeniable way that held my attention even when I tried to look away. I wanted to talk to her, I really did. There were even a few times over the years, at dances or parties, when she would be alone, looking for all the world like she was waiting for me to sweep her off her feet. I don't know why I could never bring myself to step to her. It wasn't like I was completely lacking in experience, even then. I was seeing Tasha during summer and holiday breaks, and I had a lengthy relationship with a classmate, Carmen, during junior year. It didn't matter when it came to Tamara, though; I choked every time I crossed her path.

Maybe that's why Tamara continues to visit me in my dreams (or nightmares) every now and then. That afternoon on my couch, she just sat there, a glowing testimony to what might have been if I had taken control of my love life years ago, instead of letting it just happen to me. Maybe then I wouldn't be driven to model myself after men like Tony and Trey, men I had once pitied for their immaturity and insecurity. Maybe I wouldn't be driven to force-feed a kiss on an engaged mother and deceive a trusting girl with a bogus phone call from my own brother.

The sting of sweat in my right eye brought me back to reality. I shot forward and almost fell off the couch. Stumbling to my feet, I trudged into the kitchen. I yanked the refrigerator door open and pulled out a cold bottle of Evian. As I chugged, I stomped my conscience down into the far recesses of my mind. It was precisely because I would never know what I missed with Tamara that I owed it to myself to make this Dog thing work. I slammed the Evian onto the counter and replayed that fateful night with Nikki as my final motivation. *Like it's my fault nobody wants your dull ass!* Those were Nikki's exact words.

I leaned against the counter and clapped my hands enthusiastically. I had nothing to be down in the mouth about. All I was betraying, finally, was a dull and listless persona that turned women off and made me consistently unhappy. I was changing things, thank God, and there was no need to turn back. Sooner or later, I was going to land me a Nikki Coleman. I started to feel so cocky and assured, by the time this morning rolled around, I'd made up my mind: I was going to my aunt's seminar. A nationally renowned speaker on relationships hosts a reception on that very topic? O'Dell's would be crawling with eligible honeys. And I, Mitchell Stone the Puppy Dog, am growing into just what they need. Wild horses couldn't keep me away.

CHAPTER 13

WHY MUST WE BE LIKE THAT?

May 30

don't know how I let Leslie and Angie drag me out tonight. I'm all for supporting O'Dell's restaurant, but I've never been too impressed with these relationship seminars. I read Rhonda Watts's *What's Love Got to Do With It?* and enjoyed it, but it didn't exactly change my life. You know, it was one of those books where you sit on your couch going, "Mmm-hmm" and "Say that" the whole time you read it. Then you finish it, put it back on your bookshelf, and keep right on doing the stupid shit that made you buy the book in the first place. I have no reason to think this little seminar of Dr. Watts's is going to do any more for me than her book. But Leslie and Angie whined and cried until I agreed to come out of sheer aggravation.

Walking into O'Dell's was like entering a mini-MLK High class reunion. I can never get over seeing O'Dell's wife, Lyssa, and their litter of kids. I know we're not babies anymore, but watching Lyssa herd those kids around the kitchen is almost depressing. She reminds me of my own mother. O'Dell and Lyssa, of course, were just the start. Members of every MLK clique were in attendance tonight—the jocks, the dealers, the nerds, the potheads, the preps, and the buppies. I guess that's why I wasn't exactly surprised to see Mitchell Stone over by the bar. He was chilling on a stool next to Tony Gooden and Trey Benton, who Leslie claims he's been hanging out with lately. I didn't know what he was up to, but something was definitely different about Mr. Stone. What I haven't figured out is whether I like it or not. I have to admit, though, I was almost flattered that he bothered to speak to me as I walked past the bar.

"Nikki, what's up? Can my boys and I hook you ladies up with some drinks?" Mitchell smiled innocently, but there was something about the slackness in his jaw and the twinkle in his eyes that sent a different message altogether.

As I slowed my stride long enough to consider his offer, the lights overhead began to flicker on and off. That was O'Dell's signal that showtime was near. Leslie pinched the back of my blouse and smiled back at Mitchell and Tony. "Sorry, boys, we better get to our seats before the show begins. See you later."

MITCHELL

As Leslie led Nikki and Angie to a table near the back of the main room, Trey massaged his beard and stared at the back of Leslie's wide load. "Damn, I guess we lost out 'cause we have dicks, fellas!"

Tony slapped Trey a high five. "Hey, now, don't go talkin' about the girl for doing what a girl's gotta do! Were *you* gonna take that whale into your bed?"

As their laughter died down, I took another swig of beer. I was more upset than Trey or Tony could imagine about what had happened. Dog or no Dog, I really wanted to rekindle my friendship with Nikki. Sure, I told her that night at Luigi's that I had no intention on being a "friend with a dick," but I'm wondering now if I really meant it. The rumor mill at work has been running over with news of her legal battle. Everybody says her career at Empire Records, and probably in the music industry altogether, is as good as dead. If that's true, it's a real shame. A woman of Nikki's intelligence, beauty, and charm should have the right to work in any industry she desires. And after spending four years rubbing shoulders with music artists, writers, and producers, going to work for your average Fortune 500 company will probably bore the hell out of her. I know Marvin is going to get her some legal and financial vindication; he's the best. But that won't be enough to fix her career troubles. I guess I figure in times like these, she can use all the friends she can get. That's why I was trying to reach out. Why did she let Leslie keep her from accepting my offer?

My thoughts were interrupted by a slap on my back. Tony was eyeing me like a schoolyard bully preparing for the kill. "Boy, if I didn't know any better, I'd think your ass was sitting there bumming about Nikki. I better be wrong."

I grabbed my beer and stood up. "Now why would I be thinking about any one woman, Tony? No Player ever lets that happen."

"You're damn right. You need to be like me, planning your night. After I roll up out of here, I'm making a pit stop at that girl Becky's apartment; she's been begging me for a tune-up all week. After that, I'm having a private workout with that aerobics instructor I met at Bally's last week. That reminds me, I'm running low on condoms. Oh, well, one more trip!"

I started to lead the fellas toward a table in the middle of the room, one of the last empty ones left. My aunt had packed the place out. "Well, Tony," I said, "enjoy these times while you can. We both know Juanita's going to stop traveling so much, once you guys get married. Then your days of Dogging will be over."

As we pulled our chairs out from the table and sat, Trey and Tony howled in laughter. I cowered in my seat, hoping they wouldn't draw my aunt's scorn. She was sitting up on the wooden stage, separated from us only by a microphone stand and a metal lectern. "Shut up, fools," I said over the faint din of the crowd surrounding us. "What is so funny?"

Trey leaned in close so I could hear him clearly. "Stoney, you really think Tony's gonna marry Juanita? What rock did you crawl out from under?"

I looked at Tony.

Tony smiled. "I forgot to share one Dog rule with you, because you have no need for it yet. Sometimes, a Dog meets that woman who does everything for him he ever wanted—great sex, great looks, a hefty income. However, no woman can ever make a Player forsake all others. That means when he wants to keep a woman around, he has to debase himself by at least dangling the fruit of a marriage proposal. You think a woman like Juanita would have moved in with me if I'd said I want to keep screwing around indefinitely? Hell, no! That left me no option!"

"So you're just stringing her along? Hasn't she nailed you down on a date yet?"

"Oh, let's just say that's been an exercise in creativity. First I told her we should set a date two years out. That would give me time to see where my political career goes, and give her time to get established as a model. Then she insisted on next fall. I played her game and agreed to a November time frame. Then I threw that shit out of whack by telling her I plan to go to grad school starting at the end of the mayor's term, next year."

"So you have no date set?"

"Oh, she's still trying to pressure me, doc, but she's getting the stiff arm. It's easy, man. I just promise that we'll sit down and agree on a date *next month*. Next month comes and goes, and if she thinks to ask again, I throw her off with a good lay and a few new outfits. Never fails."

Before I could poke holes in my boy's faulty logic, O'Dell's raspy voice demanded our attention. He was standing in front of the mike onstage, his wide girth blocking my aunt's view of the audience. "Ladies and gentlemen, brothers and sisters, O'Dell's is pleased tonight to present the first in our Distinguished Speaker Series. Dr. Rhonda Watts is a nationally renowned author and speaker on black love. In this tumultous day and age," O'Dell said, almost tripping over the big word, "brothers and sisters need to learn what it is that separates us. Dr. Watts is here to start us on that road. Put your hands together for our sister, Dr. Rhonda Watts!"

As O'Dell rumbled his way offstage, Aunt Rhonda stepped to the microphone. I was reminded again how much she resembles my mother. Add fifteen pounds, take out the braids, and replace my aunt's smooth voice with a self-righteous shriek, and you have my dear mama. After catching my eye and sending me a quick wink, Aunt Rhonda welcomed her audience.

"It is really a pleasure to see so many *clean*, young, good-looking, and enthusiastic black folk in one place! Give yourselves a hand, people!" She smiled warmly as we applauded. "I must admit I am most impressed with the turnout of men I see in the room. Would all you handsome brothers in the room please stand?" Her eyes flickered as she applauded the men, even though I did see her do a double take at Trey, who was standing next to me with his chest puffed out. "Now I'd like the sisters to stand!"

After this little pep rally, Aunt Rhonda got down to business. She broke down her assessment of the divide between sisters and brothers today, in terms everyone could understand. She had obviously perfected the art of cutting her academic theories into chunks that we laymen could handle. She was so good, when she wound down her lecture thirty minutes later, everyone was still on the edge of their seats.

"So you understand, my research has shown that the three pillars of black men and women's problems with each other are unrealistic expectations, displacement of black rage, and confusion over the roles we're meant to play." She stepped back and took a seat on her stool. "There's only one problem with my academic analysis, brothers and sisters. It won't hit home as long as it sounds like theories coming from some expert. I want you to see how these issues resurface again and again in your own lives. And that is the purpose of the rest of this evening. What I'm going to ask of you will require courage, and it will require honesty. There are probably two hundred of you here tonight. I'm going to make a guess that at least half of you have been intimate with someone in this room." She smiled wickedly as a wave of nervous laughter swept the room. "I think I hit a nerve. But that is the point. If tonight you will step forward and level with those of us in this room, I will make a guarantee that I will ask everyone in here to make: What is said here tonight stays here. No running back to tell people's business or start rumors, okay?"

"Yeah, right!" a skeptic shouted from the back corner. Everybody cracked up.

"Look, we're all grown folk here. And let's be real. I'm looking around, most of you are twenty-five or older. You're probably here because you're seriously interested in getting into a meaningful relationship." It was obvious that my aunt didn't know Tony or Trey very well. "So let's all behave. We have microphones stationed throughout the room for those who are willing to take part. Now, what sister would like to tell us what she thinks we want from our men?"

N I K
K I

I wanted to snatch Leslie and put her back into her seat when she got up to answer Rhonda Watts's question. First of all, I can't help but be embarrassed by Leslie sometimes. Everyone seems to know by now that she "plays for the other team," but she still insists on drawing attention to herself, doing silly mess like this. As usual, tonight was nothing but a thing for Leslie—she knows she's got all the Benjamins she could ever need, so she figures she has nothing to fear from anybody. It must be nice.

"My name is Leslie Forbes," she said. As some of the guys around us hooted softly and more than a few females rolled their eyes, Leslie bit her lower lip and looked right into Dr. Watts's eyes. "Doctor, my rep precedes me, as you may notice. Let's just say I'm a sister who's decided to deal with the black-male shortage in my own way. But that doesn't mean I don't know what my sisters want from the brothers."

Dr. Watts melted into her stool and crossed her arms loosely. "And what is it you think your sisters want, Leslie?"

"It's quite simple, really. Women want the things that very few men can provide—loyalty, emotional support, responsibility, self-control, and protection. That's it Dr. Watts. So many experts say women who go to great lengths to snag a man are wrong, but when you consider all we're hoping for, who can blame the sisters who make fools of themselves?"

Dr. Watts smiled. "Leslie, you just said something very telling. You think it's impossible for a man to be loyal, supportive, responsible, self-controlled, and protective? Why do you say that?"

"Come on, Dr. Watts. You know all the statistics. Men are conquering predators by nature, so they can never be loyal or self-controlled with respect to their bodies. They'll always be hunting the next victim. So right out of the box, we sisters learn we'll never get what we want from these brothers. From there we have to choose between taking what we can get or taking alternative measures."

That line set the men off something serious. More than a few brothers jumped out of their seats and began shouting in defense of all men. Dr. Watts wasn't having it.

"Men, now please, we must behave like grown folk here. Leslie has the floor now. You'll get your turn. Leslie, let's not even argue the point of fidelity right now. Let's talk about this idea of men who are supportive and protective of their women. Is that something you've ever experienced in your dating relationships?"

Leslie began tapping her right foot, a sign she was losing patience with the good doctor. "Doctor, I can't really say I've had a dating relationship with a man. Most of the men I was with were too busy trying to pick my pocket to think about my needs."

"So you're saying you wanted a man who would tend to your needs? What needs, exactly?"

"I don't know, maybe a little affirmation here and there might be nice. Though I don't know if men are even capable of that."

Dr. Watts sounded like she was ready to shrink some heads, Leslie's specifically. "Have you ever had a male who provided you with affirmation, like a father or grandfather?"

I heard Leslie mumble, under her breath. "Well, I don't really think my father ever thought much about my feelings. He was most concerned with his wallet and his image, in that order. So I guess

I learned to live without male affirmation. Why would I need it now?"

As everyone began to kick Leslie's comments around some, I tugged at her sleeve. "Girl, sit your tired ass down *now*." I didn't like this. My girl was starting to air her business for all the world to see, and I didn't want to get dragged in with her. So what if her father never read her bedtime stories or told her how great she was? I barely knew my father, and I've never stayed up nights worrying about being "affirmed" by Gene Coleman. Leslie was about to let Dr. Watts turn this into an episode of Ricki Lake.

A dark-skinned brother with a bald head stepped up to a microphone near the stage. "Dr. Watts," he said when he was acknowledged, "I'd like to hear more from Leslie about the types of affirmation and support we brothers are supposed to give women."

Dr. Watts frowned. "Why does this interest you?"

"Well, to be frank, I think sisters' expectations of what we men can provide are unrealistic. Brothers are catching hell out here today. We still can't catch cabs or step into elevators without scaring the mess out of white folk. We keep lagging behind the sisters and all other races because so many of us can't even get considered for the best jobs. And on top of that, we got plenty of sisters now bragging about the fact they don't even need us! How're we supposed to give you sisters *anything*, with all that going on?"

All us sisters knew how to react to that one—it didn't even take a thought. The room filled with shouts of "Tired, tired!" "Typical!" and "Next!"

Leslie crossed her arms and leaned into her microphone. "Well, Doc, we can go home now. This brother just proved my point. Men are too self-absorbed to even think about what we sisters go through— if they're not obsessing over their perceived oppression, they're worrying that they haven't bedded enough women for the month. They're too focused on satisfying their love jones to even think about keeping up with the Joneses, making money, and giving their women a comfortable life. That's why so many of us figure we don't need them."

MITCHELL

I really hadn't planned on taking part in this little forum. With my own aunt leading things, I had decided not to call attention to myself. However, Leslie's slander of all men was a bit too much to take. As the dark-skinned brother near the front calmly defended his remarks, I rose from my seat and smiled awkwardly at my aunt. I had my eye on a microphone a couple tables to our left. Before I could take my first step, I felt Tony's hand on my shoulder.

"Mitchell, what are you doing?"

I turned and whispered to him without returning to my seat. "I'm not letting her get away with this crap, Tony. Somebody's got to speak up here."

"Are you out your mind? Face it, man, you can't win here. You'll either piss off some honey you might have a shot with or make yourself look like a square if you're too sincere. Sit your ass down!"

I took a deep sigh. My instructor was treading on my nerves again. It was time for some independence. I ignored Tony's hissing and strode to the microphone. The brother at the other mike had finished speaking, and my aunt was eyeing me reluctantly. "He won't like my disclosing this, but I should announce the handsome young man at the microphone is my nephew. Mitchell, what did you want to share?"

I slid my hands into my pants pockets and tried to look nonchalant. "Yes, Dr. Watts, I'd like to respond to this indictment of black men. As a college-educated, drug-free, childless male with a good job, I'd like everyone to remember there are quite a few good men out here. Men who would be more than happy to give you ladies affirmation, support, protection, and loyalty, *if you'd let us.*"

My aunt gave me a knowing glance. "If they'd let you, huh? Exactly what do you mean by that, Mitchell?"

"Well, I seem to know more than a few brothers out there who have everything that you sisters claim to want, at least when you're on Oprah, Ricki, Jerry, or Sally. Men with mortgages, jobs, good health, and monogamous intentions. Unfortunately, these brothers all have one thing in common: they can't get anywhere with you sisters, because you're holding out for God Knows Who." Feeling my oats, I let my chest swell as the ladies flooded me with catcalls. "Oh, come on now, I know what you sisters really want, what you really talk about behind the scenes. We men ain't stupid. When I was in junior high, I saw how my older sister evaluated the brothers who stepped to her. Whenever I would eavesdrop on the conversations she and her girl-friends had, they would rate guys based on "the system." The system asked three simple questions: Question one was, is he fine? *Fine* usu-ally meant he had to be well-built and/or tall, have good hair and eyes of some color other than brown, and facial features like Denzel. Anyone who didn't measure up was automatically marked down. Question two: can he work it? If the brother didn't have a reputation for being skilled at knocking boots, it was on to the next applicant. Question three: is he rolling? If he didn't have a nice ride and money to hook her up with a regular supply of gifts, the brother was cut from the squad—"

I was cut off by a fine honey-colored sister who had taken Leslie's place. "Oh, so you gonna get on us women for doing the same thing you men do? You gonna tell me you would date a woman who was unattractive, bad in bed, and broke? Brother, please!"

I shifted my feet and smirked at the sister. "Sistah, did you hear me claim to be a saint? That's the difference between men and women. Men admit to what we are: either we're Dogs or we're Nice Guys. Personally, I used to be a Nice Guy, before I realized that ain't what you sisters really want. But either way, all men admit up front that we want a sister who's pretty, sensual, and has something to offer. But when we can't find that special someone, you won't hear us crying about some black-female shortage! No, we own up to facts—we ei-ther don't want what's out there, if we're Dogs, or we admit we're not what the sisters want, if we're the Nice Guy. You sisters, on the other hand, say one thing and do another. I'll bet if I polled this room, no woman would admit to wanting a cheating man. But I'll bet most of you are with a man who's cheating on you right now! Why is that?" My question was drowned out by catty shrieks from the ladies and hearty laughter from the brothers, including Tony and Trey. Confident that I'd raised enough hell for the night, I bopped back to my seat.

N I K
K I

An hour into the seminar, things were getting nasty. Dr. Watts was a smooth moderator, but even she looked a little surprised at the heated give-and-take going on. I was wondering if she was going to turn Mitchell over her knee later for getting us women so fired up. Angie was getting into the act, shouting into her microphone after a brother laughed at her for dating younger men.

"You're darn right I date younger and poorer men, if that's what it takes for me to have some quality male companionship! Why should I sit at home with my vibrator, just because the brothers with degrees think they can have fifteen women at once?"

A heavyset guy in a flashy silk shirt smiled at Angie from across the room. "Sister, the problem is that you're a rare one to date younger or blue-collar brothers. A lot of you would sooner cross over to another race!"

Angie stuck a hand into the air. "Hold up, don't even try to go there on my sisters! If brothers spent one day walking in our shoes, I bet you'd stop blaming us for seeming confused! Most of us are growing up in homes where our daddies did our moms wrong. Where do you think we learned to be skeptical of you all? And as for being independent-minded, my own mother showed me by example that you have to support yourself. Otherwise, you'll always be hanging by a thread, praying that your man won't decide to take up with someone else."

Dr. Watts checked her watch before jumping in. "Angie has a point, men. Black women are traditionally reared to watch out for Number One and to be self-reliant. I'll be honest, my own mother was known to warn us girls that men are no good. Many of us have to meet the right man before we can allow men to be what we want them to be."

The heavy brother waved his arms energetically. "Dr. Watts, how is that our problem? I mean, I could sit here and tell you that my mother's bullying and scolding made me very protective of my privacy and freedom. Shoot, I used to be so determined to keep women out of my business, I would see several at one time just to give myself an excuse to be shady. But see, I realize now that was wrong. I can't let my mother's mistakes poison my relationships today. And today I'm in my first serious relationship ever."

Everyone clapped in unison on that one. As the applause died down, Dr. Watts stood up again. "Well, I want to say this has been an eye-opener for me, and hopefully for everyone here. I want to make a proposition to all of you. I will be back through Chicago at this same time in two months. O'Dell's has invited me to hold Part Two of this seminar at that time, if you all are interested." She paused and batted her eyelashes playfully. "Well, are you?"

"Yes!" The room shook with shouts of assurance. I couldn't help but shake my head with the crowd. The night had been different, that was for sure. People were sharing more candidly than I'd ever seen a roomful of strangers our age do. It almost made me feel like there was hope for meaningful communication between brothers and sisters.

By the time Angie, Leslie, and I gathered up our Coaches and jackets, we were surrounded by male admirers. Several of the brothers actually seemed to be most interested in Leslie, trying to engage her in conversation on the topics she'd raised earlier. I was considering giving a well-sculpted brother with a blond fade my number when I felt a tap on my shoulder.

It was Mitchell. "Ms. Coleman, it's still early. Thought I might follow the spirit of the evening and atone for our standoff at Luigi's."

I crossed my arms and narrowed my eyes. What was he up to?

MITCHELL

As I waited on Nikki's response, I felt a faint stirring in my chest. Not the uncontrolled nervousness that used to overtake me in these situations, just a slight elevation in emotion. By now, my body count of sexual conquests had grown from four to fifteen, a sum that would still be considered paltry by most Dogs. But it represented a huge proportional increase for me, and I'd been feeling every bit of it. Yet here I was, a newly minted Dog, waiting with bated breath for one woman's approval. I told myself I didn't really care if Nikki gave me a chance to work my newly developed charms or not; rejection was the occasional price of being an active Ladies' Man. I imagine I might have convinced myself of that, if Nikki's answer had been any different.

She hugged Leslie and Angie and accepted a business card from the blond-haired Gold's Gym reject before turning to me. "I guess there's nothing better to do. Fine, Mitchell. Let's do this."

CHAPTER 14

LOVE?

Early June

NIKKI

t finally happened today. I guess sometimes you can run from the truth, but you'll never hide from it. For the past year that I've been seeing Jomo, I have worked very carefully to keep him away from my mother. Or should I say I've worked to keep Mama away from Jomo? This might sound simple to some, but for me it's been one big covert operation. Sometimes I feel like Jamie Bond, the female 007.

I had passed another afternoon with Jomo, one of those two-hour escapades where a girl can lose herself in a man's embrace and pretend the cold, hard world outside doesn't exist. While he was showering afterward, I shot forward in my bed when I remembered Mama was due to drop by at three o'clock. Great. It was 2:52!

I didn't give in to reality right away. Hopping into an old pair of yellow sweats and throwing a Bears cap on my head, I ran around like a cheating husband, searching the apartment and the sundeck for any evidence of Jomo.

I picked up, swept, sprayed some Lime Lysol everywhere to kill the smell of love, and tossed Jomo's funky jeans and T-shirt into the bathroom, just as he emerged from the shower. I was yelling at him to hurry his ass up and get out when my mother turned her key in the door.

"Nikki! You home?" As I ran out to the living room, my mother floated through the doorway and removed her sunglasses. "Baby, you look a mess! Did you forget I was coming over?"

I scratched at the baby naps peeking out from beneath my cap. "Uh, I overslept some, Mama."

Mama reached up and hugged me tight. "My baby's tired. This lawsuit is really draining you, I know. You just have to be strong with all this, Nikki. From what you've told me about how little Marvin Stone is handling that case, it's going to work out."

"I know, Mama, I know." I was hugging her back and looking over my shoulder at the same time.

As we separated, I cringed when I heard Jomo's voice. "My God, Nikki! This beautiful woman must be your mother. The resemblance is uncanny!"

It felt like time stood still for a moment. I was standing between my overprotective mother and my "thing to do." It had been a while since Mama and I had argued about the men in my life, but I knew we were due for another installment now.

My mother unwrapped the silk scarf around her neck and put her hands on her hips. "Hmph. And you would be?" She knew damn well who he was. Or did she think I was sleeping with *two* six-foot-four, dark-skinned, dreadlocked brothers?

"Jomo Hayes, ma'am." He was the perfect gentleman, taking Mama's hand and pecking it respectfully. "It is my sincere pleasure to meet you. You have raised a fine woman here."

"I'm sure you would know." My mother frowned and looked right through Jomo's hulking frame to me. "Nikki, we need to talk about some family business. Should I come back later?"

Before the tension could get any thicker, Jomo pecked me on the cheek. "No need for that, ma'am. I'm on my way out."

I breathed a sigh of relief and followed Jomo toward the door. There was only one problem; Mama was blocking it. She had hands on hips again. "Before you leave, young man—Jomo—I feel the need to educate you on something."

Jomo had obviously been confronted by disapproving mothers before. He smirked at both of us and crossed his arms. "What would that be, Ms. Taylor?"

"Jomo, I realize my daughter is a very grown woman. And more important, you ain't talkin' to no prude here. I got knocked up with this child when I was twenty years old, and her father wasn't exactly my first."

I already knew all this, but I still yelled, "Mama!"

She put her hand up to cut me off. "Jomo, I realize you're a fine, strong man with the sex drive of a Mack truck. It's in your nature to punch in to as many time clocks as you can. And I'm not here to argue with your right to do so. But it's time you realize that my daughter deserves to be treated in a special way."

Jomo took another step toward the door and waved his hands innocently. "Ms. Taylor, believe me, I know Nikki is—"

"Don't interrupt me, young man. You've probably enjoyed the fact that Nikki doesn't have a protective father waiting in the wings to kick your tail if you ever do her wrong. Well, I'm here to tell you, Big Mama packs a punch, too. I've broken up fights between strapping teenage males more than once, so don't think I'd hesitate to get in your ass."

Feeling like a first-grader who's been embarrassed in front of her classmates, I stepped in front of Mama. "Why are you doing this? Jomo's never done anything to me that I didn't approve first. Leave him alone, okay?"

Mama put a hand to her forehead and began to massage it. She waved a hand back toward the door. "Go on, Jomo. Just remember what I said, boy."

Unfazed, Jomo leaned over and pecked her on the cheek. "I got you, ma'am, I got you." We could hear his hearty laughter from the time the door shut behind him until he got onto the elevator.

I stalked into the kitchen and put on a pot of coffee. "Mama, why did you show out like that? This has got to stop!"

Perched on the edge of my Thomasville couch, Mama kicked off her shoes and kept rubbing at her forehead. "Nikki, a mother is entitled to react emotionally on occasion. You can blame yourself for that bit of unpleasantness. I told you a long time ago, I'm completely open to a 'don't ask, don't tell' policy where your sex life is concerned."

"Mama, I'm only human. Okay? One time I forget to have Jomo out before you show up, and that gives you an excuse to go psycho on him?"

Mama stared at me over the kitchen island, where I was slapping the wooden countertop. "You're right, I'm going psycho on the wrong person. Let me guess, Jomo didn't even initiate this booty call, did he?"

I tried to take a long beat on that one. As I stood over the coffeemaker, I let her jibe sink in. *No, she didn't.* I licked my lips and waited for my forehead to stop burning. "Look, I'm sorry, but that question's out of bounds. That's my business."

"Yours, and Jomo's."

"Dammit, Mama!" I almost knocked over the coffeemaker in frustration. "What do you want from me? Why do you have to ride me about Jomo so much?"

I must have been so blind with rage that I didn't see Mama walking over to the kitchen. She was tugging at my elbow by the time she replied. "Nikki, look at me." Her eyes were moist with that "good cry" warning. "Haven't I been pretty good about staying out of your love life?"

I sniffed and looked over her shoulder. "You weren't gonna preach at me, that's for sure. We both know I have yet to live up to your romantic record."

We shared a good laugh before she responded. "You're right, I was quite the Hot Mama before I had you, and even for a few years after that. So I always promised myself I would not be like your grandmother. Nikki, I can't tell you how much it screwed with my head when that woman sent us kids to church every Sunday morning so she could sleep with the neighbors' husbands. We used to have a running bet on Sundays. We'd place odds whether Mama had gotten knocked up with another brother or sister for us on that day. It was a mess."

It still tripped me out to think my Gram used to sell it for extra money. "She was doing what she thought she had to, Mama."

"That didn't give her the right to send mixed messages, baby. She never let me go on my first date while I lived at home. You know what that did, don't you? Drove me out into the streets that much faster, to learn the facts from men twice my age. Nikki, by the time I had you, if nothing else I had figured out that a sheltered, repressed child grows into an irresponsible, reckless adult. So I've never tried to shield you. But you really make it hard on me with this Jomo character."

"Mama, why?"

"Honey, what does he do for you, besides scratching your itch?"

"I don't know."

Mama poured me a mug of coffee and flavored it with Irish-mint cream and two Equals, just like I like. "Baby, in this age of AIDS, if you're gonna be sleeping with somebody, I think you oughtta know why. Let's be honest here. Some of this has to do with your father."

"We're all products of our environment," I said, shrugging, "or lack thereof."

"Well, maybe you should consider how Gene's presence in your life relates to your choice in men."

"Mama, I don't have time to be psychoanalyzed. How's your house-hunting going?"

She took a sip from her coffee mug. "All right, I'll let you change the subject, but I want you to think hard before you invite that Rastafarian around here again. As for house hunting, I may do a condo instead. Gene dropped me an extra check in the mail."

My mouth dropped open. I knew he sounded sincere when we had our argument a couple weeks ago, but I hadn't expected Gene to go beyond the call of duty and give Mama more money.

Mama filled the space while I sputtered in shock. "He's acting like a man on a mission. He even offered to help with my moving costs. What did you do to him, Nikki? This is not the Gene Coleman I knew."

I leaned against the counter, my mind racing. For some reason, I kept going back to that day in Lincoln Park, when Gene had coughed his way through an attempted explanation of his failures as a father. "Mama, do you think Gene's ill? Did he look okay to you?"

"Well, he's looked better, if that's what you mean. But he seemed like he was getting around all right. You sound like a concerned child. I don't know if that's good or not."

"Don't worry, he gets nothing where I'm concerned. All we did to help you out was a business transaction, pure and simple. So when are you moving out?"

Mama walked to the sink and began rinsing her mug. "I've got my eye on a development out in Chicago Heights. I'm moving out at the end of July."

As I clapped my hands in approval and kissed my mother, I glanced at the gold-plated clock above the sink. "Shoot! I need to clean up soon." I decided to toy with her. "I have a date to freshen up for."

Mama crossed her arms. "Jomo again?"

I took off the cap and tousled my hair wildly. "No, with someone you might actually approve of. Mitchell Stone."

"Little Marvin Stone's baby brother?" Despite the fact that Mitchell was MLK class valedictorian and a starter on the basketball team, my mother has never been able to remember him as anyone other than Marvin's little brother. "Well, there's a breath of fresh air. I don't know the Stones personally, but people speak highly of the parents. Mr. Stone rubs elbows with all the VIP's of black journalism — John H. Johnson, Earl Graves, Susan Taylor. And, you know Mrs. Stone is a soror — Skee Wee!"

"I know, Mama. They're regular black Kennedys. The perfect family to marry into." She can deny it until the day she dies, but my mother has always burdened me with her desire to see me "marry well." I know she believes that would finally make up for her disappointments in finding the right man. But after what Barry took me through, I decided that was a mantle I wouldn't carry. Couldn't she let a girl date a guy without inspecting his damn gene pool right away?

Mama rubbed me on the back and bulleted toward my bedroom, straight for the walk-in closet. "Well, for a date with a Stone, we must have the right outfit. Let me point you in the right direction, baby."

That took an hour. After letting Mama steer me into a slinky silk-chiffon tunic with matching drawstring pants, I whipped out the hot iron and refreshed my hairdo. Once Mama left, I had time to relax on my couch and catch some Zs before Mitchell showed up.

Even though I was still a little wary of him after our blowup at Luigi's, I had put that behind me by the time we got to the Starbucks coffeehouse near Hyde Park. I hadn't been quite sure what Mitchell wanted when he suggested we go out, but it seemed like he just wanted to talk. Something was up, though. As he sat across from me in a short-sleeve silk shirt with a pair of khakis, I knew something was different about my friend Mitchell Stone. Somehow he didn't feel like the same self-conscious, decent everyman who tried so hard to impress me a few months ago. It was like he'd been replaced by a slightly evil twin. He kept leaning in close, complimenting me on my perfume, and demanding my eye contact instead of searching for it tentatively. As we swapped gossip about the goings-on at Empire, I even noticed the way he swayed in his seat, a refreshing change from the stiff posture he used to have. I couldn't help but wonder where the change came from. Over cinnamon lattes, he entertained me with his story about Stephon Evans's love life. When I stopped laughing, I reached over and put a hand on top of his. "Mitchell," I said, "you never gave me an explanation last week, mister. When are you going to answer my question?"

MITCHELL

Even though it had been a week since Nikki let me drive her home from Aunt Rhonda's seminar, I knew exactly what she was talking about. Nikki Coleman wanted to know if I was seeing someone. Yes!!! My plan was working; she was officially intrigued. She had tried to pussyfoot around the issue during the whole ride home last week. By now, of course, I had learned to play hard-to-get. It was time to implement Dog Rule #4: *All Dogs must be mysterious, with murky and complicated lives.*

I drained my latte cup and smiled mischievously. "Nikki, you don't want to live in my world. It's dangerous in here."

Predictably, she crooked her neck and glued her eyes to mine. "I'm a big girl, Mitchell. What's so dangerous about the world of an accountant?"

Oh, Lord, not this crap again. These bean-counter jokes were getting tired, even from the woman of my dreams. "Financial analyst, Nikki. I ain't no accountant. You ever thought maybe there's a lot about me that you don't know?"

She blinked her eyes innocently. "Things I don't know, such as?"

"Oh, nothing." I bit my lip and considered my next step. I didn't want to scare her off. I decided to push one more time, since I'd piqued her curiosity.

She was chomping at the bit now. "What, Mitchell? What's this 'nothing' you won't tell me about?"

Bingo! "Just a few crazy women, is all. I tell you, you sleep with some of these women and they think they can put your stuff on lockdown. You know Carmelita Hodge?"

"Um, yeah, I've crossed her path a few times." Nikki's eyes darted toward the floor for a brief second. I knew she was recalling Carmelita's little fables about my romantic prowess. The two-hundred-dollar payoff Tony gave Carmelita to tell those stories was the best investment I've made in a long time.

I continued my little fable. "Well, you know I did the old one-night stand with her a few weeks back, and she's been riding a brother ever since! Constant voice-mail messages, pages, she even followed me on a couple of dates with other women! Can you believe that?"

Nikki started to drum the tabletop with her fingers. I swear, I could see the light going off in her head. *Mitchell Stone just might be a real man after all.* "So," she said, "you don't want to see Carmelita anymore?"

I shook my head wearily. "Please, I barely have time to see the women I *want* to see. I've had it with Carmelita. I never promised her anything more than one night, you know. Where's the disrespect in that? We had a deal, plain and simple. One night of passion, nothing more and nothing less. She's just going to have to recognize."

"Are one-night stands the norm for you now?" Nikki's eyes flickered with concern. I was touched.

It was time to pull up before I ruined things. Tony had warned me I'd be walking a very fine line. I clasped my hands in front of me and stared deep into her eyes. "You know what? There really is no norm for me these days. I'm just trying to find myself, Nikki. It's taken me a while to come to grips with some things in my past, and I guess I'm trying to deal with it all at once."

Nikki looked thoroughly curious. Was this all it took to get a woman interested? Acting like a basket case? "These things in your past," Nikki asked, "do you feel comfortable discussing them?"

I decided to solidify Rule #4 and find out more about Nikki's life. "You don't want to hear my stories. You have enough on your mind. I should probably wait until I know more about a couple situations before I tell you any more." I knew that would leave her wondering. Now I was ready to hear about hers. "Anyway, since my brother won't tell me anything about the progress of your lawsuit, how goes that?"

"Now, that's a long, ugly story. I gave you the history last week. Right now Marvin is doing a wonderful job. I don't think Colin Lee or the legal eagles at Empire Records know what to think of your brother. He's got them running to his office with new settlement offers every day, even though he's building a strong enough case for trial."

"So do you want to go to trial?" As much as I respected Marvin's legal savvy, I had a feeling Nikki was best off settling.

"I think I'll know when Empire stops making settlement offers. Right now, I figure it's worth it to hear each one. They just might come up with a price to which I can't say no."

I smiled. "Shoot, it wouldn't take much for me. But I understand if you feel the need to go to trial out of principle. Marvin told me about the stunt Barry pulled on you. If that isn't proof of how cavalier we men can be about sexual harassment, I don't know what is."

Nikki crossed her arms and shuddered slightly as a group of customers swarmed through the door, letting in a torrent of cool air from the lakefront. "You're right, Barry is like a lot of brothers who don't think sexism is in the same league with racism. You don't know how thankful I am that I've never been harassed on the job by a black man! Talk about a damned-if-you-do, damned-if-you-don't situation!"

I decided to speak from the heart for a minute. "It shouldn't have to be that way. Any time a man disrespects a woman, he should pay for it, regardless of the color of his skin. Not to say I believe every claim of sexual harassment is valid, though. A lot of women like to have it both ways. How many cases have there been of women who sleep with a man, and then sue for harassment after they break up with him?"

"Well, I know what," Nikki replied. "I'm not one of those women. No woman should have her job endangered because her boss finds her attractive. And one way or the other, I want that message sent."

A few minutes later we left Starbucks and rolled out to the lakefront. We threw on light jackets and went for a walk along Lake Shore. Nikki told me about her plans to set up her own promotions company. She seemed confident that she could snag a couple of her key Empire artists as clients. As beautiful as Nikki is, I found her determination and confidence almost as arousing as her physical glamour. Seeing the spunk in her stride as we continued down the beach, I slapped my hand back from her tempting frame. I didn't want to screw this up. When I got with Nikki Coleman, it was going to count. Everything had to be just right.

N I K
K I

Around ten o'clock we reached Mitchell's Accord, which was parked near a grove of trees a few feet from the shore. In just a few hours, it felt like we were bonding in a way I hadn't experienced in far too long. But something still felt odd. I blocked Mitchell's path as he tried to open the passenger-side door. "Are you sure there's not something you're keeping from me, Mr. Stone?"

He frowned at me and shook his head playfully. "Come again?"

"I guess I'm confused, Mitchell. I know we agreed last week that our Date from Hell is as good as forgotten, but I still have a clear image of you demanding two things from me that night: honesty and commitment."

He stepped back and let the arms of his jacket hang at his side. "Hold up, Nikki—I never asked for a commitment from you."

"I don't mean commitment in the technical sense. I mean you wanted me to give you an answer about whether or not I could exclusively date you. You didn't want to know if you could screw me, Mitchell; you wanted to know if I could see myself in a serious relationship with you. So why are you acting like *commitment* is a bad word now? These girls you're talking about—do you feel anything for them?"

Mitchell looked totally confused, like I was speaking another language. "I-I didn't know you cared, Nikki."

"Well, it's just, I don't know. I guess I always saw you as the type who would be married with rugrats by now. You *do* know the girls at MLK secretly voted you 'Best Husband Material,' don't you?"

Mitchell's face flushed. "Boy, I'd forgotten that one. No wonder I could never get laid back then. Well, you got it, Nikki, I peaked at the age of seventeen, as MLK's valedictorian. My single status is just another symbol of how little I've accomplished since then."

I looked at Mitchell in confusion. "What are you talking about? Boy, you earned a degree from Georgetown, you have a high-profile job with one of the largest black record labels in the country, and you're a young black male living in Hyde Park. Seems to me you're doing okay for yourself!"

Mitchell clenched his fists and turned back toward the water, looking like he wished he could jump in and swim into another world. "All that sounds good, but it ignores reality."

"Ignores reality? How?"

"Nikki, I don't know about you, but I grew up with the American Dream. That means my folks raised me to be a bigger success than they are. Better marriage, more impressive career, bigger house, more successful children, the whole nine. And I think it's safe to say, right now I don't exactly measure up."

Mitchell had me with this one. I don't know that I ever thought in terms of outdoing either Mama or Gene, but it struck me that my income was already greater than what the two of them make together. I didn't mention this to Mitchell, of course. I let him stay where he was, with his back to me. He seemed content with that. He even continued talking to himself.

"Nikki, when my father was my age, he had a precious two-year-old daughter, had been married for three years, and was awaiting the birth of his first son. He and my mother had just moved into their first house, a ranch in Oak Park. And Pops had just been signed to the editorial staff of *Ebony*. What have I done by comparison? I live in an apartment with a brother so confused about love and romance, he hasn't been in a woman's pants for over a year. I'm so far away from getting married it's not funny, and I can't even fathom being responsible enough to raise a child. It's like I'm a teenager in a man's body." He raised his left hand before I could move to him. "I know, I know, poor spoiled Mitchell, yammering on about problems a lot of folk would kill to have. Forget I said anything."

"Nothing to be ashamed of," I said, sliding next to him and keeping my eyes on the water. "I think you're selling yourself short, though. One thing my mama's always insisted on, my life is a precious, unique experience. I bet your parents feel the same way. You're not supposed to be their clone, Mitchell."

He didn't look at me, but the crinkles in his cheeks and the glimmer in his eye said plenty. "There you go making sense on me."

As we climbed into the Accord and jetted back down Lake Shore, I looked at the night lights bouncing off Lake Michigan and decided to change the topic. After the week I'd had, Mitchell's sudden confession was too much for me to match. If I had let the floodgates open around my problems, he'd have thought I was a basket case. I decided to let the night end peacefully. But I think we both realized there are layers to each other that will have to be peeled eventually, if we're ever going to be more than friends. That thought alone, though, was a little startling. *Mitchell Stone, more than a friend?*

When Mitchell walked me to my door, I turned and grabbed the knob, toying with whether or not to invite him in. My head told me there was no way I should get intimate with a guy who just a few weeks ago was friend material. The scary thing was, this time my heart was telling me something else. For Mitchell Stone, no less. What was I going to do?

Before I could decide, I felt Mitchell's hand on my shoulder. His touch was startling. He hadn't said a word yet, but the energy that coursed through his veins and into my shoulder said more than a thousand words. He wanted me as bad as I wanted him.

I could smell his Cool Water cologne and minty TicTac breath as he whispered in my ear. "Here's to honesty and, maybe someday, commitment." He wrapped his fingers around my waist and pulled me close. Without thinking or analyzing, I found myself turning into gooey fudge as I looked into the deep pools of Mitchell's eyes. Soon our bodies were merging, our lips were melding. *What is this?* Love, lust, passion, hope, and contentment flooded my soul in one combined, rejuvenating surge.

As I pulled him inside and let the door slam, I knew one thing for certain. For better or worse, my friendship with Mitchell Stone would never be quite the same.

We crossed my apartment threshold still kissing, lips entwined, feet entangled, his confident hands grasping my hips in surprisingly gentle fashion.

I hadn't turned on the apartment lights yet or even activated the stereo in my front room, so we stayed closeted in darkness, the only sounds the creaking of my cherry-wood floorboards and the whiz of traffic below. I think I heard ninety cars pass before we came up for air.

"I ... don't believe I'm finally here." Still holding my hips as if they were life preservers in the middle of the sea, Mitchell leaned into me and looked straight into my eyes. Touched, instinctively realizing that I, Nikki C., was not just another trick in his book, I shut him up by recapturing his tongue in my mouth and slowly tasting his minty gums. TicTacs are a wonderful thing.

Our clothes started to fall by the wayside. He shrugged his way out of his jacket without pulling his lips from mine; I kicked off my low heels while massaging his firm buttocks.

Pulling him across my Persian rug toward the bedroom, I stopped and placed a finger over his lips. "We need music. Let me get the Luther."

Do you know he had the nerve to frown? "Luther?"

"You have a problem with Luther Vandross?"

His grip on my hips loosened. "I didn't say that."

"You hesitated. I want you to be happy with whatever we play, Mitchell. What's wrong with Luther?"

"Look, I'm not ruining a mood by going through your CD collection. . . ."

"I suppose you'd rather play some whiny Prince or somethin'?" I heard an unwelcome note of irritation in my tone.

The next thing I knew, I was being swept off my feet. This fool literally had me in his arms! As Mitchell grunted softly and got his balance, I felt the tension drain anew. "You sure you can handle this?" I asked.

"Trust me," he said as he carried me into the bedroom and set me down on my sky blue comforter. "The music can take care of itself."

After flicking on the banker's lamp by the bed, I leaned over and clicked on my nightstand radio, a futuristic alarm clock with a funky digital face. If Mitchell wanted simple, he'd get simple. He wanted 103.1—eighties hits, but I put a hand over his mouth and kept the dial moving to WNUA. The room filled with the graceful jazz of Rachelle Farrell.

"You have beautiful furniture," he said, as if he'd never peeked his head inside on one of our earlier dates. "Very contemporary." He eyed me with simmering desire as he ran a hand along the polished

wood of my bed frame and took a seat next to me. "Is this an oak finish? I love the way the bed sits so close to the ground."

My only response was to yank him on top of me.

By the time we were both naked and under the covers, I had my
head buried in Mitchell's chest hair, inhaling his Cool Water again
and circling his hardening nipples with my lips. We'd been at it so
long, I'd already had more foreplay than in my last three encounters
with Jomo.

But something was wrong.

It had been fifteen months, two weeks, and three days since I had
taken a new man into my bed. When I realized Jomo wasn't serious,
I locked away the goods for anyone but him. He'd already hurt me, so
what more damage could he do?

Now I was trapped in this bedroom, my heart beating fast and my
spot growing soft, ready to take another man into my innermost
place. I looked down at Mitchell and saw every man in my history,
poised over my willing body on those first nights: Jamal, Duane,
Freddy, Barry, Bill, J.T., Lawrence, Mikembi, finally Jomo. I could
still recall each one's touch, the gleam in his eye, the whispers of
love, lust, or reassurance. *Where were those fuckers now?* And where
would this one be a few months from now?

"Nik . . . you okay?" Mitchell's question startled me, and I realized
I'd let go of him and pulled back from kissing his chest. "W-we can
stop right now," he said, starting to rise. "Let's just—"

I can't even try to explain, but that was all I needed. The doubts
crept from my brow and rolled off my shoulders like beads of sweat. I
smiled at Mitchell and leaned over him, delivering another deep
kiss. "I'm ready for you," I huffed. I was ready to reach for the nightstand, where Jomo's stash of condoms would be the perfect backup if
Mitchell had come unprepared.

"Not yet," he said, flipping me against the mattress and focusing
his attention between my legs. One thing was sure, he wasn't here
just to get in and jet. His eyes focused on my spot with careful intent.
He used his right forefingers to circle my outline, time and again,
clockwise then counterclockwise, until my aching was almost un-

bearable. Before I knew it he'd hit the jackpot, and of course it was all over then. I tried not to call his name, but as the rivers of pleasure washed over me I heard somebody saying, "Mitchell" loud and clear.

At last I straddled my new lover and took every inch of him inside my wetness, teasing and hopping until his breathing sped up and his eyes begged me for mercy. He'd had long enough, though. I widened the arc of my hips and shifted more weight onto his thighs as he began to buck and seize, his romantic cool finally wearing off. He is still a man. When he came, he held on to my hips for dear life and alternated between calling my name and thanking God.

As we lay panting in each other's arms, awash in sweat, cologne, and incense oil, I wondered if Mitchell was thinking the same thing I was.

Please. Don't hurt me.

CHAPTER 15

ASKING FOR TROUBLE

MITCHELL

left Nikki's place this morning with a big-ass smile on my face. It was kind of embarrassing, actually. I had to roll out of there before my cheesy grins gave her the wrong impression. After all, it was good, but I knew better than to think it really meant anything. Six weeks ago I wouldn't have said this, but I've learned that sex is nothing more than a business transaction between two consenting adults. I barely remember the names of three of my partners last week, although they sure had me calling out those names at one time or another. It amazes me how quickly I remove these girls from my mind, once I've dropped my load.

Not that I'll forget Nikki, or last night, anytime soon. Last night perfectly fit that song by Joe, "The Love Scene." Everything seemed to unfold according to a script. Granted, I'm sure Nikki's been with men more experienced than me, but I got the impression we clicked just fine. Our romance was a swim in a heated indoor pool—comforting, warm, splashy, even a little messy. I have to admit, I would do well to have an experience like that every time I lie down.

My sexual adventures prior to becoming a Ladies' Man were a bit erratic compared with my time with Nikki. Sex with my girl Tasha has always been like a relaxing Sunday drive—no pressure, just a touch of heat, plenty of relaxation, a great vehicle for tension release. She's always had the effect of a penetrating massage taking my mind off reality and transporting me into an alternate reality.

Then there was my only real girlfriend from college, Carmen. She made me appreciate Tasha all the more. The woman was incapable of enjoying sex. She had a competitive streak a mile long, and unfortunately this was true in the bedroom more than anywhere else. The youngest of several fine sisters, she had some hangup about being the least attractive because she was shorter and a bit heavier than the rest. That was my theory, at least. I never brought it up, for fear she'd stab me to death with one of her Number 2 pencils.

Doing the do with Carmen was a full time J.O.B., and not in the good sense. She paid so much attention to detail it was ridiculous. "No, not here, there! Down there! This way, that way! Do it now! Faster! Thrust harder!" I still can't recall a time she asked about my needs. Of course, mine were pretty simple back then; as long as I got my release when all was said and done, I was good to go.

Last night with Nikki, though, took me back to the only one-night stand I experienced before attaining Dog status. Monisse was this athletic, honey-colored Sharon Stone that I met at the Ritz club in D.C. my senior year. I don't know what I was on that night, but somehow I talked this girl into coming back to my dorm room, and it was on like Donkey Kong. My little dorm cot saw action that night it hadn't seen before and probably hasn't seen since. The woman was a Six Flags roller-coaster ride—a mind-blowing, overheated, out-of-body-type of experience that had me doing and saying things I never thought I was capable of. With Nikki, though, there were aspects of both Monisse and Tasha. The white-hot passion that I felt for Monisse, offset by the calm sensation that bonds me with Tasha.

I guess my thoughts about my night with Nikki were plastered on my face when I pulled into the lot of Bally's gym. I had left Nikki's place at 7 A.M. so I could run home, throw on my workout clothes, and meet Marvin, Trey, and Tony for our Saturday-morning workout. Marvin and I used to work out together, but since I've been in training, I've spent more time at the gym with Tony and Trey. I hadn't even made it out of the car before Trey burst out of the front door of the club.

"Stoney! What's up, Boyeee! You lookin' a little light-headed to me, like a man got some late-night lovin'? Who was the lucky victim?" By now he was leaning so hard against the driver's side of my Accord, I was afraid he was going to leave a dent in my roof.

"Trey, would you let me get out of my own car, please?" I shoved him aside and slammed the door shut once I was out.

He stroked his beard and eyed me suspiciously. "Oh, so you're gonna leave me hanging about last night, are you? Let me hip you to something, Stoney. Marvin already told me you had a date with Nikki Coleman last night, *and* that you didn't come home."

"What the—" I looked around the asphalt lot for my brother the traitor.

Trey chuckled as we headed for the front door. The sun was finally peeking into view, and our jibes were almost drowned out by the tweets and chirps of birds overhead. "So my question for you, Stoney, is just how good of a Dog are you? Did you pass the ultimate test, already?"

I held the door open for my trifling friend. "What exactly are you asking me?"

Trey cut his eyes at me as we handed our driver's licenses to a plain white girl at the front counter. "Brotha, I mean, did you get in those panties?"

Pursing my lips as the girl stared at us in disgust, I took my license back and made a beeline for the locker room. Nikki deserved more respect than this.

Trey was in hot pursuit of the truth, almost stepping on the heels of my Nikes as we entered the musty locker room. "Don't go silent on me, boy!" It was time for me to remind Trey that not even he had any business calling a black man "boy."

"Stoney, come on now, you got to give it up. You can't be goin' soft on us now."

"Maybe he's not as much of a Dog as he thinks!" Marvin's voice was unmistakable. I looked across the room to see him standing beside the last row of lockers. He was ready to hit the floor, dressed in black Speedos and an OSU jersey.

I shook my finger at him as I stormed past and cracked a locker open. "You know you're not right, Marvin. Why don't you grow up?"

Marvin winked at Trey before walking over to my locker. "Come on now, Big Willie. What do you care about spreading a good woman's business around, in a locker room, no less? You sound like you want to treat Nikki with respect. Doesn't that violate one of those Dog rules?"

The words that came out of my mouth were really just meant to shut Marvin up, although I should have known they'd cause more trouble. "Is that a challenge, bro'? Because I don't play that Nice Guy stuff no more. Y'all want me to say it, fine! I pulled Nikki Coleman last night, and it was damn good! Happy?"

Trey almost hit the ceiling, he jumped so high. "Oh, shit! Did you hear that, Marvin? Your brother already passed Go and collected his two hundred dollars! You weren't supposed to knock that for a while now!" While Marvin stood there with his hands on his hips and I slowly removed my sweats, Trey took a beat before going on. "This is *very* interesting. Excuse me for a minute." He stepped over to his locker, ran his combination, and removed a cell phone. In seconds he had Tony on the phone. In three more minutes he had spread the word and gotten Tony's take on what my next steps should be.

"Well," he said as he hung up, "Tony's not going to be joining us this morning. He's taking his mother to breakfast. Apparently she's pissed about his plans to marry Juanita."

"What," Marvin said, "is she saying Tony's not ready for marriage? What a shock that would be."

Trey eyed my brother up and down. Watching these two interact was quite an experience. They were the same height and roughly the same build, but that's where the similarity ended. Trey was a proud pleasure seeker, Marvin the insistent monk. Ordinarily they would never cross paths, if not for their connection through me. Their mutual dislike was getting harder to sweep aside.

"You trying to talk about my boy, Marv?" Trey's eyes flashed.

"Look, Trey, unlike my brother, I'm proud of my full name. You will call me Marvin. Not Stoney, not Marv, not Big M. Don't make me tell you again."

Trey helped himself to some of Marvin's personal space. "You got a problem with me, Marvin? 'Cause I'm just a man trying to help your brother be all he can be, where the women are concerned. Somebody's got to do it; you obviously don't know much about that area."

Shaking my head, I slid between my brother and my friend, not knowing what to say.

Marvin backed up a few feet and raised his voice. "You know what, Trey?" he said, not caring that several heads throughout the room were turning our way. "You're nothing but a fraud. A big wanna-be fraud. You need Jesus just like everyone else. Just because you don't realize it yet doesn't mean you can mock me."

"What the hell am I supposed to think, man?" Trey's voice was shaking now. I couldn't tell if it was from conviction or fear. He had to know Marvin could take him. "People do talk, you know. Your personal life, or lack of one ain't none of my business. But I ain't gonna let you sit in judgment of me and my boys, just 'cause you're unhappy with your life."

Marvin grabbed his workout towel. "This conversation is getting nowhere. I'm going out on the floor, before I have to put my size thirteens up somebody's butt. Trey, I'll be praying for you. You, too, little brother."

I grabbed my brother's arm as he breezed toward the locker-room exit. "Marvin, hey, don't take it so seriously. Trey's just full of hot air."

As he neared the exit, Marvin slowed his pace. Smiling at me, he shrugged off my grip. "Mitchell, you've had enough Bible training to remember the verse about 'the way that seemeth right to a man, that leadeth to destruction'? Take a step back, man, and ask yourself if you really wanna end up like your trainers. Is this what you want?"

I couldn't quite lift my eyes from the floor as I responded. "Marvin, look, I don't know. I just don't know. What should I do, end up like you?"

Marvin clicked his teeth and took another step out the door. "One thing I have every night is peace. Can you say the same thing?" He had barely finished the sentence before he was out the door.

Trey didn't waste any time trying to clean things up. "My bad, man," he said as he slapped me on the back, "let's hit the floor."

Forty minutes into our StairMaster workout, Trey insisted on taking me to the woodshed over Nikki. "Tony and I agree that what you did was a no-no, Stoney!" He was shouting over the blare of New Edition's "Hit Me Off." "What were you thinking, sleeping with a woman you could actually care about? That woman will clip your Dog hairs like Delilah sheared Sampson bald!"

Pumping up and down to burn off my baby gut, I looked over at Trey wearily. "Trey, I didn't plan this."

"Well, a seasoned Dog never does. I'm just impressed you caught on so quick."

"You don't get it. I still have to work for most of my victims. But with Nikki, it was just natural. I mean, I admit, when I first asked her out last weekend, I did have romantic motives, but they were long-term. What happened last night was like a bomb that just explodes without warning. I don't think either of us saw it coming."

Trey gripped the control panel of his StairMaster and grunted loudly. "Well, it doesn't matter how it happened. You are not to let that happen again, young man, not until you've bedded several more honeys. We can't have you fallin' in love and wasting your talents this quick."

"Trey, come on—"

Trey stopped pumping suddenly and stared me down. "Stoney, look, I'm dead serious. I'm gonna have to treat you like the Secret Service should have treated Clinton, to save him from Monica Lewinsky. You're now officially on a leash. You are not to go within fifty feet of Nikki Coleman, until you cement your identity as a Dog. Are we clear?"

I jumped off my StairMaster and flung my towel at him. "Go to hell. I'll see who I want." I started muttering to myself. *Boy's out his damn mind.*

I might have ended my training right there, if not for what crossed my field of vision as I headed away. This woman on the NordicTrack was too much—a vision in aqua spandex, which outlined a ripe bosom and a washboard waistline. She was my favorite height, about five feet ten. Tall for a woman, like Nikki, but short enough to look up to me. I was falling in lust, moment by moment.

Trey walked up and put a hand on my shoulder. "So, Mr. Self-Righteous is scopin', huh? You sure you wanna do that, Mitchell? Nikki might get pissed at you!" He was like a playground bully now. "Step aside, young man, I'm going in. Let a real Player show you how it's done."

Trey's arrow hit its mark. My pride got the best of me. "Hold up, Trey, you don't need this one. You got enough mouths to feed as it is."

"All right, I'll let you step to her. But first you got to catch her eye with some moves. Let's go hit the free weights."

We walked past Marvin, who was pressing three hundred pounds like it was Styrofoam, and settled in at a bench across the way from Aqua Woman. Throwing on my lifting gloves, I leaned back onto the bench and gritted my teeth as Trey loaded two hundred pounds' worth of weight onto the bar. This was a little more than I usually started with, but I knew I needed to start high, so I could finish around three hundred and maybe catch this girl's eye. Tony and Trey had taught me a while ago that Rule #1 was all too true: *Dogs must carry themselves in a manner that communicates sexual prowess and confidence.*

As I sweated and grunted my way through my first set of reps, Trey stood over me and coached. "Push that bar out, Stoney! Push it! Arch your back, dammit! Thrust those hips! Pretend you're makin' love to your woman!"

Trey's coaching took me straight back to the one misguided season I spent as a football player, junior year at MLK. I went out for the team hoping to show up all the idiots who claimed basketball and baseball players didn't have as much heart as football jocks. I'd figured my natural speed and conditioning from the other sports would make me a competitive defensive back. Wrong! Despite a football camp and hours of practice, I had two left feet out on that field. For that reason and others, every practice and every game was an exercise in humiliation.

Most annoying of all was the experience of having my on-field performance used as an indicator of my sexual prowess. Everything we did, whether it was agility exercises ("Move the legs, twist those hips like you do when you're deep in your woman!") or weight lifting ("Push that weight out with the same force you knock your girlfriend out the bed!"), was tied into screwin'. And the people making the most lewd remarks were usually the coaches. No wonder so many of those jocks treated women like trash.

I'll never forget the way my friend Juan Menafee got played, at a practice one stormy afternoon in October. A chunky, cherubic offensive lineman, he failed to put a block on his man for the third time in a row. Coach Haggart, a tall, bearded man who was rumored to be a church deacon, blew his whistle and threw his hat onto the ground, then proceeded to stomp the mess out of it. "Menafee!" He shouted as he charged right at Juan. "Come here, boy." Coach hissed the words out. "Damn!"

We all froze, those on the field and those like me who remained forever trapped on the sidelines. Haggart was good for halting practice every now and then, for the sole purpose of humiliating a screwup, even someone like Juan who was a starting player. However, what he had in store for Juan was new, at least compared with what I had seen that season.

He yanked Juan's helmet off and stared into the boy's sweaty, downcast eyes. "Menafee," he said, "have you ever had a woman? So much as a piece?"

I'm sure some of the nearby residents thought we were having a pep rally that night. Haggart's crack had everybody rolling in the grass, whooping it up like we were at an Eddie Murphy concert. Juan was a great guy, but he didn't exactly have a reputation with the ladies.

His spirit as broken as any self-respecting teen's would be, Juan had locked eyes with the grass beneath him. "Uh, hell yeah, Coach!" It was more of a whimper than a yell.

Haggart shoved Juan back into the grass and tossed his helmet at him. "Bullshit, boy, I'll bet you ain't even seen first base! You need to learn some rhythm, Menafee. Damn! When you come up to that line, you got to be able to dance back and forth, and block these oncoming motherfuckers! If you can't do that, keep your ass off the field till you get you some ass!"

Poor Juan had done the only thing he could—turned around on the next play and played like his life depended it. I suppose Haggart got what he wanted, but he got it at the price of Juan's pride.

I never forgot that lesson, though. I knew everyone in the club was using my physical fitness as an indicator of my abilities in the sack. I had to perform, and perform well, in order to impress Aqua Woman. So I came with all the drama as I completed rep after rep, hoping that Aqua Woman was paying attention. I was on my tenth rep of 250 pounds when Trey suddenly yanked the bar off of me.

"What are you doing, Trey? I got this!" I was pissed. What was he trying to do, make me look weak?

Clanging the bar back into place, Trey leaned over, flooding me with his stale breath. "Yo, man, your target is about to get away! You better catch her before she hits the women's room!"

I stood and inhaled suddenly when I saw Aqua Woman heading for the women's dressing room. She was getting away! I felt like I was back at Georgetown again, watching yet another beautiful woman walk by, before I could fix my mouth to make a play. I felt like stopping right there and singing Jodeci's "Come and Talk to Me."

But there was no need for that now; I had learned my lessons well. It was time to pull out a big gun. Asking Trey to stall my target, I raced down the stairs to the basement, where I knew my goddaughter, Maya, was taking part in the kids' fitness class. Tasha was an instructor of a step-aerobics class on Saturday mornings, and she always has Maya in those classes. It wasn't uncommon for me to bring Maya upstairs to the main floor on occasion; she always got a kick out of being around grown folks. Today, though, I was going to need a little favor from my goddaughter.

I had trained her for the past two weeks in case an opportunity presented itself. She didn't disappoint me. The little angel hopped right up to Aqua Woman as she headed for the locker room. "Hello, ma'am."

Aqua Woman reached behind her neck and unfastened the wrap that had pinned back her mane of spongy curls. Mmm, good. "Hi there, honey. What's your name?"

"Maya," my goddaughter giggled. "What's yours?"

"My name is Gina. Maya, that's a beautiful name. Are you named after anyone?"

"It's my grandma's name."

"Oh, that's nice. Can I help you with something?"

"Well, it's not me. You can help my daddy, though."

I had heard just enough to know it was time to pounce. Acting as if I had just climbed the stairs, I turned the corner and grabbed Maya playfully by the hand. "Maya, ha-ha, come on now. What did Daddy tell you about bothering strangers at the health club?"

As Aqua Woman watched me suspiciously, Maya squirmed like a bona fide actress. "But Daddy, I just wanted you to get to meet her."

"Meet me?" Aqua Woman, I mean Gina, looked pleasantly surprised. A slight smile tugged at her mouth as she addressed me. "Did you set this up, *Daddy*?"

I waved my hands innocently. "I might have made a comment that you were pretty. You'll have to excuse me." It was time to move in. "Uh, Maya, why don't you go back downstairs. Daddy will meet you down there." I patted her on the head and kissed her cheek.

"Okay, Unca . . . Daddy." She scampered off as I prayed Gina didn't catch her stumble.

She didn't. In fact, she was looking downright flattered. "It's not every day I have little girls put up to hitting on me."

"So, do I win points for originality?"

"You might, if your adorable little girl's mother isn't in your life."

My, she was making this almost too easy. I would later learn why. "For the record, I am very single. Or should I say, I'm between relationships right now. Things with Maya's mother didn't, uh, end well."

That, I told myself, *should be vague enough to make a brother look mysterious.*

Gina crossed her arms and smiled. Her cheeks folded up with two adorable dimples. "A long story, huh?"

"A long story I'd be happy to share over dinner sometime."

She looked at me with narrowed eyes, but she was still smiling. "Do you always work out here?"

"Yeah, I'm somewhat of a regular. You're new, aren't you?"

"I've been coming here for a week or so. I have to admit, you're the most respectful of the guys who've hit on me. Would you be a gentleman if I agreed to go out with you?"

I tried to make my smile as sinister as possible. "I don't know how to act any other way."

Gina and I bantered for the next twenty minutes. I used every bit of my training to seize on everything she said, asking questions that kept her talking and made me look like a good listener. Gina was a Chicago-area native but had just recently relocated to Hyde Park, after spending her high school and college years in Arizona. She was interested in getting back into some local social circles, which I of course offered to help with. I was enjoying this. Gina reminded me of Nia Long with longer hair, and it turned out she was a young thing: twenty-three. She was a nurse but spent her free time singing and dancing in community theater. Needless to say, a sly mention of my employment at Evans Entertainment secured me the digits. This one was going to be child's play, once I casually revealed that Maya was really my "play" daughter. No need dragging that charade out.

By the time I sent Gina on her way, Marvin and Trey were both bugging me to finish up my workout so we could go to breakfast. Tony had called to say he could meet us at Shoney's and get an update on my overall progress. Not surprisingly, Marvin decided to pass, saying he needed to do some more work on Nikki's case. I waved him off and hopped into my car, ready to follow Trey over to Shoney's. Nine A.M., and as Ice Cube would say, this was already shaping up to be quite a good day.

CHAPTER 16

CHOICES

June 11

NIKKI was dreaming about Mitchell when the phone woke me this morning. As I groped for the receiver and sat up in my bed, I squinted at the clock on my nightstand. Who was calling me at 5 A.M.? I knew something was up when Mama started talking before I could say hello.

"Nikki, you need to get up and get dressed, baby."

I wiped a piece of butter from my eye and steadied myself. Something was up, but it sounded like Mama was all right. "Mama, what's wrong?"

"Nikki," she sighed, "Gene had a heart attack late last night. Jennifer came home last night to find him slumped over the table. He'd been hosting a group of his friends for a card game, and it looks like the booze and smokes caught up to him."

I hustled out of bed as years of resentment melted like snowflakes. "My God, is he, is he okay?" I could feel my throat tighten. My breath was coming in short gasps.

Mama's voice became urgent. "Nikki," she said, "don't

go getting out of sorts. He's been in the hospital all night, he just got out of surgery. Jennifer just called and told me."

I collapsed back onto the bed. I didn't know why, but the fact that he was alive was comforting. "Well, should I . . . should I . . . Mama, what should I do?"

"Baby, I can't tell you what you should do. Gene may not be a great man. He may not be a good man. But he is your father."

I flicked on my nightstand lamp and shuffled into my house shoes. "If he's okay, maybe I should just let it be. I can just imagine who all is down at the hospital."

Mama took a beat. "I won't tell you what to do. But I will say this. If you go, I think it would be for your benefit, not Gene's. Don't think you'd be doing him any favors. You should go for your own needs. Only you know if you need to see him before he dies."

"Mama, what are you saying?"

"Baby, he may come through this fine, he may not. Just think about how you'd feel if you never see him again. The choice is yours. You want me to come over and drive you to St. Luke's?"

"No," I said, yawning. "You go back to bed. You need your rest more than I do. I'll call you later this morning. I'm going to go see him."

As I rushed through the motions of showering, curling my hair, and choosing a low-maintenance outfit, my mind filled with memories of my father. I started to wonder what life would be like without Gene Coleman. I knew for me it really wouldn't affect my daily routine; I tried to think of him as rarely as possible, and we did well if our paths crossed once a year, during Christmas. But like it or not, he is the man who made me. I guess it's that fact, if nothing else, that kept me moving until I arrived at St. Luke's.

The waiting area on Gene's hallway was filled with Coleman kin. Tisha and Tia, my half-sisters, were camped on the end of the first row of cushioned chairs. Tia, the big baby girl who got every bit of Gene's six-foot-plus height, was sprawled across her chair, snoring like a foghorn. Tisha, who was born exactly one year before I was, sat with her arms crossed, staring into space. Even a family crisis wasn't going to unite us. The fool looked right through me as I walked up on her. I was about to force her to give me the lowdown on Gene's condition when Jennifer burst out of her seat near the back of the room.

"Nikki!" She shouted like we were best friends and came at me so fast I was afraid she'd trample me. Jennifer was a good thirty pounds heavier than when I last saw her. I accepted her eager hug and stepped back to get a better look at her. She looked as frantic as could be expected; hair just barely curled and running wild, eyes red and bugged out, face full of wrinkles that were probably hidden from view on her better days.

"Your father is doing better, praise God," Jennifer said as she steered me to a seat across from my sisters. "I've been telling him for years to get his act together. I hope he'll listen to me now." She paused as a tear oozed out of one eye. "The doctor says his heart is stabilized again, but they're going to keep him under observation until they've run a battery of tests. They're also concerned because he's diabetic."

I shook my head and looked at the floor. I was so uncomfortable. Here everyone was, crying and carrying on over a man who for me has personified irresponsibility and disappointment. Why was I here?

Jennifer patted me on the shoulder as she got up to tend to Tia's two little boys, who were tearing up the hospital furniture. "Do you want to speak to the doctors, to get a little more information on how Gene's doing?"

I tried not to frown. "No, that won't be necessary. I trust you to keep me up on things. Thanks, though." I was *not* going to play the self-righteous child over Gene, interrogating the doctor like some border guard. Being here was enough.

I spent the next thirty minutes staring blankly at Tisha, who finally got to talking after we both grew tired of the staring contest. We traded a bunch of empty small talk, until I accidentally mentioned my lawsuit. After that, Tisha was on me like white on rice.

"Ooh, girl, are you for real? Men can be such animals! It don't make no damn sense."

I rested my head against the back of my chair and sighed. Tisha's self-righteous outrage wasn't going to do anything for my problems. "Yeah, girl, it's a mess. I'm hanging in there, though, that's all I can do, you know?"

"What are you doing for work in the meantime?"

"Hoping I can do something on my own. I have a meeting scheduled later today with a potential client, actually."

"Who?"

I asked myself if I should share this with a sister who's never once bothered to call or write me. What the hell, I decided. If a family crisis couldn't break a little ice between estranged sisters, what could? "You know James Martin of the Martins?"

Tisha's eyes bugged out. She sucked air through the large gap in her front teeth. "James Martin! You gonna work with him? Man, I got, like, four of he and his family's CDs! They were the bomb back when we was in high school!"

I crossed my arms and smiled at my sister. She was really impressed. I didn't know why. I'd told her before, at Christmas gatherings over the last few years, that I worked at Empire Records with various music stars. I guess she never understood how Big Willie I was.

Tisha smiled shyly and leaned across the aisle until I could smell the Hostess Ho Ho's on her breath. "Not to push up on you, sis, but maybe you could introduce me to James Martin sometime? You know, like when your label throws a party for him or something? You know I used to hang out with some of his band members? I even had a short thing going with one of his drummers while I was at Chicago State."

I tried to look like I cared. What was it we Coleman women had about dating musicians? I was hoping Tisha had never dated Jomo or any of his cronies. I knew she had dropped out of Chicago State after wasting too much time in the streets, but I was pretty sure she had gotten out of that scene before Jomo arrived in Chicago. I didn't feel like comparing notes with her about how much of a jerk he was.

By seven-thirty there had been no further news from the doctors. I decided it was time to get up and stretch my legs. After finishing the rounds of the waiting room and receiving some "sugar" and hugs from another nameless uncle, cousin, and aunt, I wound my way down to the cafeteria for a breakfast of Diet Pepsi and a wrinkled bagel. After knocking off my meal, I went to the pay phone by the waiting room and checked my voice mail. I had two new messages: one from Barry, one from Jomo. My two angels. Somehow Jomo had called earlier and then harassed my mother into telling him about Gene's heart attack. He went on and on about how he wanted to be there for me, that I should call him ASAP. Barry's message was more to the point.

Nikki, I need to know how the lawsuit is going. Are you doing all right for money? If there's anything you need, please let me know.

What did this joker want? I decided right then and there that I was not going to return Barry Roberts's phone call, ever. My life was too screwed up as it was, without getting back into the web of a married man who had already betrayed me twice. I may not be a genius at the game of love, but I know fire when I see it.

I had hung up the phone and turned back toward the waiting area when Gina Tatum damn near ran me over. I was glad that I recognized her right off; otherwise there might have been a catfight up in that hospital hallway. Gina stepped back just before we collided and planted her hands on her shapely hips. She was styling in a turquoise matte-jersey ankle-length dress, showing off every inch of her figure. At eight in the morning, the girl was already Superfly.

For a minute Gina and I stared each other down warily—she was probably as startled to see me as I was to see her. Looking at Gina for me is sort of like looking in a mirror. We share the same five-ten height, similar cocoa-brown complexions, and athletic, long-legged builds. Our personalities, however, are nothing alike. Gina's younger than me in years and in maturity. I knew she'd been out West for a few years trying to make it in TV and film before attending nursing school in Oakland. I had heard she was moving back to Chicago, but it wasn't until now that I knew she had hit town.

As we both stood there with arms crossed, Gina ran her eyes up and down my faded khakis, denim shirt, and suede loafers and sniffed in smug satisfaction. I knew she was comparing my getup to hers. "Nikki, what's up, little cousin?"

"Don't even try it, Gina. How you been?" I smiled as fake a smile as I've ever worn, raging at Gina's little crack. There wasn't an ounce of shared blood between us; we just had the bad fortune to be two kids whose parents had always been close friends. When I was a sophomore at MLK and Gina was a seventh-grader, our mothers had enrolled us in the same summer basketball camp, meaning we had to spend time in each other's presence. Gina's never forgotten how strangers we met that summer always thought she was the older one. It wasn't like she was cuter; the only reason brothers thought that was 'cause the minute she hit puberty her trifling mother let her wear heavy makeup, a weave, and shirts with plunging necklines. With a no-nonsense mama like Ebony Taylor, how could I compete with that?

Gina and I walked slowly toward the waiting area. I tried to hint at how her latest hospitalization for depression went. "So, you're feeling all better these days?"

Gina cut her eyes at me defensively. "I'm just fine." She stopped suddenly and turned to face me again. "For the record, Nikki, for all the gossip, my act is together now, okay? I haven't needed treatment for two years now, and I'm a fully licensed resident nurse. I showed up for my shift when I heard about your father being in here. I wanted to give my best regards."

I decided not to ask if she was still stalking guys the way she did Dwayne Pearson, the man whose complaints got her admitted to the first hospital. "Okay, Gina, okay. I didn't mean to pry. Look, if there's anything I can do for you—"

"Just let the past be the past, how's that?"

As I froze in place at Gina's snap, she walked into the waiting room and brought it to life. Despite the fact that she was no relation, she'd attended school with some of my cousins and was cooler with them than I was. As I stood there and listened to the whoops, hollers, and hugs, I compared Gina's reception to mine. There was no contest; being an illegitimate child in the Coleman family carried a price. I would never be viewed in the same way as Tisha, Tia, or even a wanna-be like Gina. I was family, but in that sort of fringe way reserved for black sheep.

Right there, in the middle of that hallway, the person I wanted to talk to was Mitchell. I knew why. After all the recent nights I'd spent with Jomo, I had told him next to nothing about my lawsuit or my recent run-in with Gene. Jomo was really little more than a tool; I was admitting that to myself more and more each day.

Who would have thought one night with Mitchell would have given me the chance to talk to a man about my life? That was a good night, no doubt. Mitchell wasn't in Jomo's department when it came to length and width, but he was no slouch. He was also more conservative than Jomo—reasonably skilled, but still a little reserved. No rapid pumping or Tarzan yells from this one. But he knew what he was doing, all the same. He lasted for two hours and three condoms!

More than the lovemaking was the afterglow. There we were, in each other's arms, and Mitchell was the one who asked *me* how I was handling things! I don't know if it was the way he asked or just my need to talk to someone new, but I told him everything, from my fear about starting my own business to my history of anger with Gene. He didn't even say that much; he sat back, listened, and shared a few thoughtful responses.

Nikki, if your father's as bad as he sounds, he'd said, *you're living proof people are influenced more by environment than by genetics. Don't give him the power to pull you down.*

Tapping my foot and leaning against the paisley wallpaper of the hallway, I bit my lip. Mitchell was right; my reflections on the Colemans' mistreatment of me were giving them power they did not deserve. I slipped into the waiting room to grab up my things and slinked out before anyone bothered to notice. I figured I could call back every few hours for news about Gene's condition. I could only endure so much "family time."

* * *

FOUR HOURS AFTER I broke out of St. Luke's, Leslie and I walked into the Signature Room in the John Hancock Center. A top-floor restaurant surrounded on all sides by glass, the room offers a view unlike any other, and today was a great day for it. The early clouds had lifted, allowing the sun to sing brightly against a rich palette of blue sky. I'd eaten here a few times before on Empire's tab, but this would have definitely been out of my price range today if not for Leslie. The Signature Room was her idea of the perfect place to woo my first client, James Martin.

James was waiting for us, just inside the lobby. The hostess, a reed-thin woman wearing a silk outfit that looked too expensive for a working woman, was flirting with him. It's no wonder; washed-up or not, James Martin is a Dish. He looks at least a decade younger than his thirty-seven years, and judging by his buff build, he must hit the gym hard every day. He's adjusted well to near middle age, too, chopping off the S-curled mound he was once known for and growing a rich beard that fits his squared jaw and chiseled features nicely.

James walked up to us and crossed his arms over his three-piece tailored suit, one that looked to be of Italian design. Even though we last met on the day Colin first harassed me, I had forgotten how much shorter he is in person; he was barely my height. "Nikki, I remember you," he said, taking my hand, "and you must be Leslie." He smiled at Leslie and took her right hand in both of his. "I think when I last saw you, you were all of five years old! I'll always be in your father's debt." Apparently James hadn't forgotten that Leslie's father used to own the label that put out his family's first album, *Funky Rhythm*.

Leslie actually blushed at James's comment, a surprising twist considering she usually hates to be reminded about how great her father was. "*Funky Rhythm* was going to be a classic record on one label or another, Mr. Martin. My father was no saint—he just had the business sense to know you were going to blow up."

James smiled as the hostess led us to a table with one of the best views. Between Leslie and James's clout, I guess we couldn't miss. "Ladies, please call me James. Mr. Martin sounds too mature."

I accepted my menu from the hostess and crossed my legs, business-style. "Well, James, it would be my pleasure to keep things less for-mal."

The next twenty minutes involved the science that I had perfected in my career at Empire, before Colin ripped it to shreds. Leslie and I traded small talk with James about everything we could dream up to build a rapport, that sister-brother kinship I knew I'd need to land him as a client. We knocked him over with our analysis of the Cubs' and Sox's odds of making it to the playoffs, as well as our opinions of the latest draft picks made by the Bears. We knew, of course, that James was a legendary attendee at all of these sporting events. When sports was exhausted, we talked about his family and his children, oohing and ahhing at how well adjusted they sounded for an enter-tainment family. We even stroked his ego with some platonic flirting about how well he kept himself up. He handled it all like a pro, giv-ing and taking stories and wisecracks without showing any ulterior motive, like trying to sweet-talk me into a trip to a local hotel.

By the time our entrées arrived, Leslie signaled with her eyes that the coast should be clear for my pitch. I decided to be a little more blunt than I used to be when representing Empire. I was too desper-ate to be proud. "James, are you happy with the state of your career today?"

He adjusted his napkin on his lap and reached for his fork. "Who is ever happy with their artistic career, Nikki? That's a two-pronged question, anyway. First, am I happy with the artistic quality of my music? Second, am I happy with the reception I'm getting from the people, am I selling records?" He paused and began to slice into his orange roughy. Leslie and I waited patiently, playing with our salads. "I'll answer your question like this. I'm very upset that I can no longer trust my past collaborators. Most of the cats I came up with, they're still writing stuff that's tailor-made for the adult R&B Quiet Storm. You know—stuff that sounds like the Temptations, O'Jays, Whispers, what you kids would call 'the old folk.' Well, I'm not that old yet. I know anyone over twenty-five is a geezer in the eyes of the kids run-ning the business today, but James Martin is not going into senior-citizenhood gently."

I took a swig of water to help clear my throat. James was playing right into my strategy. "So you're tired of being matched with old-school, traditional R&B beats?"

James frowned and swept his eyes over Leslie's and mine. "You got me, young sister. The Martins were never about going with the flow! Nobody had ever heard a sound quite like ours when we hit the scene. And I don't want to settle for being conventional anymore. But I can't do it on my own."

"What you're saying," I said, "is you need a lifeline to some of the younger players in the market?"

"Hell yes, that's what I'm saying."

Leslie smiled sweetly at James. "James, I've seen you on the *Soul Train* Awards, laughing it up with Maxwell, D'Angelo, and Kenny Lattimore. Why don't you bring some of them in to work with you?"

James swallowed a bite of roughy before responding. "You think I haven't hung out with some of these kids, told 'em how I like the things they're doing? They all talk a good game about respecting me—hell, most of 'em have paid me royalties to sample some of my old hits, but not a one has ever asked me to appear on remakes of my own damn songs! It's a cold market out there today."

I moved in for the kill. "I think this is where I can help. If you don't ask these guys to help you out, the fact is that they won't offer. Let's be honest. You haven't charted a single in *Billboard*'s R&B Top 40 since 1996. You haven't had a gold album since *On My Own*. That's a long time! And as tight as money is in the industry today, an up-and-coming artist has to be concerned for self! They can't work with too many old-heads as gestures of charity, they've gotta work with the ones who are still hot enough to help their careers—the Ron Isleys, the Gladys Knights, the Barry Whites. The point is, James, these artists who could help authenticate your sound with some new flavors, they're going to have to be courted. Who are you most interested in working with?"

James leaned forward and looked deep into my eyes. "Well, I would think you would already have a good idea of who I should be working with. You do want my business, don't you?"

I took his hint. "Well, personally, I'd like to see someone who could anchor the grit of your falsetto with some hearty retro soul. Not a style as sparse as Erykah Badu, mind you, but someone who can evoke the seventies funk that inspired you while bringing you into the new millennium. I'll tell you my top choices: Milos, D'Angelo, and Raphael Saadiq of Tony! Toni! Toné!"

My heart leapt as James's face spread wide in a cheesy grin. "Those are exactly the cats I see myself with! I don't suppose you know how to convince them to work with little old me?"

I finished a bite of grilled halibut. After detailing my connections with all three stars, I reached into my leather portfolio and handed James the ten-page business plan I'd spent the last week slaving over. "If you read this plan, you'll see that I've analyzed every piece of music you've touched—all eight Martin Family albums and both of your solo CDs, along with your brother Michael's solo project. I've identified specific songs that are similar to D'Angelo, Raphael, and Milos's work. It's a clear and concise argument for how well you'd fit with these guys. I can do this, James. Would you like to give me a chance?"

Watching his eyes light up, I could feel myself swelling. I was on my way! I'd land James Martin as my client, get him paired with the right collaborators and record company, and show Empire Records that they couldn't keep me from succeeding in this industry. Finally, a ray of hope was breaking through my cloudy skies.

I moved in for the close. "So when should I call you to make some formal arrangements? I'd like to get on the horn and start tracking these guys down for you right away."

James picked up his glass of Chardonnay and eyed the sunlight that glanced off of it. "Just one more question before we start talking money, Nikki. I need a guarantee that I can safely work with someone in your position."

What? I could feel my face growing hot. I licked my lips, hoping I was misunderstanding him. Deciding not to ask for clarification, I allowed my silence, amplified by Leslie's, to make the point obvious.

Grinning sheepishly, James leaned back in his chair and crossed his legs. "I hear the rumors. This suit you've got against Empire sounds like serious business. Colin Lee himself called me last week to suggest I steer clear of you, even suggested I could get into legal trouble if I worked with you, since our first contact was on Empire's behalf."

I shushed Leslie, who was about to rise out of her seat. "Mr. Martin, I don't understand what you're saying. I never signed a covenant not to compete, if that's what you're worried about. I'm starting a freelance business because my career at Empire is in a challenging phase. Trust me, Colin Lee and Empire would have no rights over you in court."

James shook his head in concern. "I wish it was that simple. You gotta understand, I'm in no position to be linked with somebody who's pissed off a major record company."

"Pissed off a record company? What?" Leslie jumped out of her seat. "Do you know how ridiculous you sound?"

Feeling the heat of stares from nearby patrons, I grabbed Leslie by the hand. "Leslie, sit down. *Please.*" She obeyed my command, and I tried to look as pleasant as I could, despite the fact that my mouth was caking up with the taste of cotton. This couldn't be happening. "James, if you don't want to work with me, just say so."

He waved his hands in proclaimed innocence. "Hey, hey, look, I'm not trying to cause trouble, sister. I just need some assurance that you're going to smooth things over with your employer. Colin tells me they've been throwing you settlement offers left and right! Why don't you accept one? Think how much easier it'll be to work for me, and others, when you have this nastiness behind you."

"What?" I finally gave in to reality. "You didn't come here out of interest in my services, did you? Empire sent you to push my buttons and get me to settle!" I walked over to James and stared him down. As he stared back, sweat building up on his forehead, I crossed my arms. "We can sit here and make a scene all day as far as I'm concerned, Mr. Martin. Otherwise, you need to answer my question!"

"Sister," he said, scooting back from the table, "this meeting's over. I don't need your services. But you really should accept that offer! Hell, I wish my deal with Empire was that good!" With that, James Martin sniffed, straightened his tie, and headed for the lobby.

* * *

THE NEXT THING I knew it was nine in the evening, and I didn't have one clue what I'd been doing since lunch. I remembered shedding some tears, after Leslie and I huffed out of the Signature Room. I saw I had six bags from Saks Fifth Avenue, so Leslie must have treated me to a shopping spree to take my mind off the experience. She even liquored me up a little bit when we got back, probably thinking that would dull the pain, the reality of the fact that my career in music management was as good as over.

She was wrong.

CHAPTER 17

FINAL EXAM

Early July

MITCHELL

t's eight o'clock on a Saturday night, and small puddles of
sweat are starting to clog my underarms. I sure am glad I
put on an extra layer of Right Guard before I left the crib.
We'll be at Nikki's in a few minutes, and I've got to get it
together before then. Tonight all my training comes to a
head.

Seated across from me in the Lincoln limousine he
rented for the evening, Tony is patting Juanita on the lap
as she barks instructions to her agent on the cell phone.
The woman's in her own world, and with Trey and Cassie,
his latest baby's mama, steaming up the windows in the
third compartment, Tony and I might as well be alone.
Tony glances out the window at the ripples of Lake
Michigan as we hurtle down Lake Shore toward Lincoln
Park. "My boy Mitchell Stone. Do you realize what
tonight represents?"

I try not to fiddle with my hands, even though my re-
flection in the mirror over Tony's head shows that my

bow tie is crooked. I'll get it later. I can't let Tony pressure me. I've got to treat tonight the way I treated big exams and projects in college. I know I've done my homework; my sexual-conquest count is up to twenty-eight, and it could be higher if I wanted it to be. Fortunately, though, I've kind of settled into a comfort zone, splitting my time between two women: Nikki and the mysterious Gina.

As Tony reminds me every day, I know I'm on dangerous ground with Nikki. If I really thought I had a prayer of keeping her, I'd throw away my shiny new black book and all the related hoochies tonight. But history's taught me too many cruel lessons to allow me to be that naïve. Odds are, the minute I trade in my Player's card and try to become Mr. Do Right for Nikki, she'll run back into the arms of a true Dog like Barry Roberts or that jerk Jomo Hayes.

Nikki doesn't think I know about Jomo. She's not completely covert, of course; she mentioned something the last few times about having a male "friend" who she couldn't really talk to. I know good and well she's talking about Jomo. The brother's obviously not very discreet; I heard about the fact that he was making house calls to Nikki last year, from one of the receptionists at Evans Entertainment. Now, I'm not suggesting the brother's an empty vessel, but let's just say it's clear Nikki's not with him for what's between his ears. Sometimes it amazes me that sisters can act so self-righteous about men who are Dogs, when they'll be the first to use a guy sexually when they get the chance. It's clearly a practice Nikki believes in, so I'm not relinquishing my Doggish safety blanket until I'm convinced she's outgrown her indulgences.

Tony starts snapping his fingers in my face, as Juanita continues yapping into her cell phone. "Mitchell," he says, "come back to earth, bro. You do understand that if you pass the test tonight, you'll be on third base of your Dog course? Graduation's right around the corner!"

I cross the arms of my tailored tux, an expensive gift I bought myself after I bagged my twentieth victim. "Explain it to me one more time, Player."

"It's simple. Tonight you will be called on to implement every one of the Dog rules in a challenging setting. The mayor only throws this charity ball once a year; everyone who's anyone, regardless of race or religion, will be there at the Hyatt tonight. Your challenge will be to juggle your lovely date, several of your past victims, and a surprise guest on whom you will work your new charms."

"That's a lot to accomplish in four hours, Tony. Who exactly are these past victims?" I hope he didn't invite just anybody; some of the girls I'd kicked out of my bed had taken the experience better than others.

Tony smiles. "Revealing who it is would ruin the surprise, partner. Just rest assured, if you make it through tonight, you're on your way!"

I thump my chest proudly. "Bet. I do this, I can go back to being myself once I land the right honey."

Tony reaches out and grabs my wrist. He locks eyes with me, looking deadly serious. "Mitchell, let me warn you again. Don't think your Dog abilities can be dropped like a bad habit and then reacquired. You'll get rusty, real quick. You have a responsibility to maximize your skills! Every honey you can pull, you must pull! You start slacking off and focusing on a woman like Nikki, you're gonna end up whipped and rejected when a real Dog catches her eye! Understand?"

I'm still trying to convince myself Tony's right when I step into the lobby of Nikki's apartment building. Checking my look in the mirror, a good look if I do say so myself, I head to the desk to have her buzzed. She was supposed to meet me in the lobby. Where is she?

"Evening, Mr. Stone."

I turn at the sound of Nikki's voice and fight to keep my tongue from hitting the floor. She's dolled up in a form-fitting black evening gown that accentuates every asset she has, in tasteful but proud fashion. *How did I end up here?* Back in the day at MLK High, a date with Nikki Coleman for me was as much a possibility as a weekend getaway with Janet Jackson. As I look into Nikki's eyes and remember the tender night we shared twenty-four hours ago, I feel the Dog in me lower a steel cage around my heart. As we lock arms and head toward the limo, I wonder: is it the Dog moving to protect my heart, or is it my bruised, often rejected inner child? Somehow, I don't really think it matters.

By the time we arrive at the Hyatt, I've blocked these types of distinctions from my mind. We all pile out of the limo and follow Tony into the central ballroom, where councilmen, CEOs, bankers, physicians, attorneys, and fresh-faced wanna-bes like us clog the marble floors. For the first half hour, we all huddle behind Tony and nosh on caviar, salmon, and finger sandwiches while our boy schmoozes everyone who crosses his path.

After we get in the obligatory meet-and-greet with the mayor and the rest of Tony's staff, he pulls me aside and knocks me over with his champagne-laden breath. "Time to make your break. You've gotta circulate so you can run across some very special guests. Not to mention," he says while checking his Rolex, "you got someone to meet outside the main ballroom at nine o'clock. You miss that appointment, you've failed for the night. Got me?"

I'm still glaring at Tony when Trey suddenly bursts into our midst with Cassie, Nikki, and Juanita in tow. "Yo, Mitchell, Nikki don't believe I know some of the *major* players on the hip-hop scene! I keep trying to tell her I know a lot of entertainment attorneys and shit! You don't mind if we take her around, help her network?"

Nikki looks at me with sweetly begging eyes. "You mind?"

I'm flattered; this doesn't feel like an empty question. Nikki really cares about what I think. Not that it really matters right now. Nikki and I are both pawns tonight. I shrug. "Don't let me stand in the way of progress. See ya." Nikki and company head into the thick of the main ballroom; Tony steers me out to the atrium, where a crowd is chugging drinks and vibing off a salsa band.

I haven't made two steps before Leah Harmon is standing on my toes. A short honey dip with a natural cut, Leah is a one-night stand I met at the Hot Spot last month. Personally, I was a bit embarrassed by our encounter; you see, Leah didn't quite pass my sniff test—she didn't have B.O. exactly, just an odd cheesy scent that curdled my stomach. I happen to be very particular about smells, something I used to blame on my lack of dating. Most of the time I can screen women for B.O. before things get too physical, but Leah had fooled me up until the last minute. By the time I decided I couldn't deal, though, we were already buck naked on her couch. So I did what I came to do, quickly, and scampered out. I could have done without running into Leah again.

"Hey, stranger," Leah drawls in her Valley Girl accent. "Check you out, running with the VIPs! What's been up?" She plants her right foot against the floor and grabs a highball from a passing waiter. "You don't know how to call a woman back, Mitchell?"

Impressed she remembers my name, I decide to try to keep Leah happy with me. Even if I don't want her, as a Dog I should be able to have that option. I step all up into her personal space and hold my breath as best I can without making it obvious. "Was that you? Leah, was that you?"

"What are you talking about, Mitchell?"

I lean closer and touch her lightly on the shoulders. "About a month ago, a woman came to me in my dreams and gave me the best night of my life. It was so unbelievable, I just knew I had imagined the whole thing. You mean that night was real?"

She playfully smacks my cheek and blushes. "Boy, you are a silly one. Get outta here." She turns toward the ballroom, looking ready to get her groove on. Pivoting one last time, though, she faces me with teasing eyes. "I'm gonna give this to you one more time," she says, slipping me a business card. "If I don't hear from you this time, I'm taking it personal." She blows me a kiss. "Bye, Mitchell."

As I take the card, I look out of the corner of my eye and catch Tony spying on me. The brother is actually allowing my misadventures to distract him from a conversation with Oprah Winfrey! I take advantage, though, waving the card in his face and mouthing, "One down!"

By the time nine o'clock rolls around, I've survived encounters with three more partners, including Regina from work and Heather, the Pamela Lee look-alike Tony suggested I get out of my system.

Every black man wants to put it to at least one white woman before he settles down with a sister, was his exact quote. *It's a natural impulse, Mitchell. Who gets used as the symbol of desire, the symbol of*

beauty in this society? The blond bombshell, that's who. And we broth-
ers are only human. You get bombarded by images of Barbies day in
and day out from age five, you got no choice but to associate manhood
with the acquiring of a white woman. Even if only for one night, it's an
experience we all need to have.

Whether it was Heather, Regina, or the third girl, whose name I
can't remember, I'm just glad to have plowed my way through them
without having Nikki cross our path. She knows I'm not seeing her
exclusively—hell, that's probably the only reason she's seeing me in
the first place—but she's too classy to have to be subjected to other
women. What I can't figure right now is who I'm supposed to be
meeting in the atrium at nine.

Standing here by the water fountain, I feel my eyes narrow in on a
vision in a black strapless gown made of airy silk. My immediate admiration is quickly turning to recognition, though. Tamara Shaw!
The woman I lusted after, to no avail, for four years while I was in
D.C. The same woman who visits my dreams every few weeks, to
taunt me for failing to step to her. This woman is one big regret as far
as I'm concerned. Now she's just a few feet away, a few feet out of the
new Mitchell Stone's reach. Shit! I look around frantically, until I
lock in on Tony's smug grin. He knows he has me with this one. Why
did I tell him about Tamara that first night we met for training, and
worse yet, why did I mention I had heard she was relocating to the
area? The word had been she was joining the Chicago district attorney's office. It must have been child's play for Tony to find her. What
was I thinking?

My feet are still rooted to the floor when I hear Nikki yell my
name. I turn and engage her and Trey in some conversation as they
share all the contacts they're making. It does my heart good to see the
wide smile on Nikki's face as she tells me about the VIPs she's meeting. She's finally getting over that nastiness with James Martin. I keep
telling her, she's going to triumph over this Empire mess. Maybe
tonight, combined with Marvin's success in getting a trial date scheduled for next month, is convincing her that things are going to work
out.

Once I build up my nerve, I let Trey conveniently whisk Nikki and the other women off again. As I head over to Tamara, who's convers-ing with an older gentleman wearing a sharp double-breasted tux, I feel about as sophisticated as I did the first night Tasha taught me the facts of life. I can barely walk in a straight line, my heart is thudding, and my shins feel so tight I must look like a robot. This sucks.

Tamara looks up when I extend my hand. "Hello, have we met?" She's shaking her head in that "I don't really care" way most women used to greet me, in my Nice Guy days.

Afraid my voice will flutter like a schoolgirl, I work my diaphragm good and push out a phlegm-clearing grunt before responding. "Uh, you attended Howard for college, didn't you?"

Tamara glances at the older man beside her, seemingly apologiz-ing for my inconvenient presence. "Yes, I did graduate from Howard. Are you an H.U. alum? I don't recognize you. Who did you know while you were there?"

I feel myself shrugging, in that self-deprecating way that the nerdy characters in movies do when they're under pressure. *Damn!* "I, uh, graduated from Georgetown actually. But I used to see you around a lot at parties and clubs, I think. Didn't you hang out with Susan Quinn and Michelle Tillmon?" Susan and Michelle were pretty plain next to Tamara; I had buddied up to them several times through the years, always hoping they would give me an "in" to Tamara. So much for that!

Tamara shifts her weight from the left leg to the right. "Yeah, Susan and Michelle were my girls. I haven't talked to them in a while." She looks ready to send me on my way. "What did you say your name was again?" I can tell her next words will be "Nice meeting you."

Feeling three feet tall, I let my shoulders slouch and prepare to crawl off. "I'm Mitchell Stone, Chicago native."

"A native, huh? Have you been here since you graduated from G'town?"

"Yes, I work at Evans Entertainment, as a financial analyst." The way Tamara's losing interest in me, I might as well use my real title. *Accountant.* This is a lost cause either way.

Suddenly the older gentleman surges forward and grips my hand.

He demands my eyes as he gives my hand a vigorous shake. "You're working at Evans, huh? How do you like it there?"

Feeling my eyes narrow, I keep staring into the brother's cocoa pupils. "It's not a bad way to make a living, surrounded by music stars, writers, and producers. I'm not where I want to be paywise of course, but I could be doing worse."

My new friend, who is a couple inches shorter than me, releases my hand and crosses his arms over a rotund belly. "What I really meant was," he growls through what look to be freshly capped teeth, "do you think the management of Evans, and Empire Records, has its act together? You're a businessman, you should have an opinion about the job they're doing."

This cat is no joke! I mirror him, crossing my arms and taking the opportunity to ignore Tamara. She wasn't about to give a brother play anyway. "I could keep you here all night with opinions, brother. The bottom line is Empire Records has an aging artist roster, no creative spine with which to find the real talent of tomorrow, and horrendous money-management skills. But you didn't hear that from me!"

Now the brother's sliding a gold-tinted business card into my hand. "My young brother," he says, grinning, "my name is Chauncey Wells. I have a few business interests scattered across the country. I'm here in town for the charity ball because the mayor has asked me to take an interest in Chicago's economic development."

As Tamara slips her eyes over me to check my reaction, I try to keep a poker face. I'm rapping with Chauncey Wells! I know all about this man's "business interests." My father has done three profiles on him in *Ebony*, *USA Today*, and *Emerge*. Wells has even broken into the very exclusive Forbes 400 list of the richest Americans. His businesses rule the *Black Enterprise* 100's lists. Between his investment-banking firm, his fast-food franchises, and his million-dollar motor-manufacturing business, the brother is strapped. What's he got his eye on Empire for?

Wells's raucous laughter snaps me out of my trance. "Look here, young brother, hold on to that card. I'm not at liberty to go into detail, but things may be changing around your place of work." He claps me on the back and grabs a highball from another waitress. I can see he's ready to move to the next crowd; no need to name-drop my father to him right now. I have the brother's card! "Well, Mr. Stone, Tamara, you kids enjoy yourself! I'm gonna go find my little woman!"

As I cross my hands behind my back and watch Wells strut off, I realize Tamara is still standing next to me. She's eyeing me with what looks like friendliness, stroking the inside rim of her champagne glass. "So, you work with Stephon Evans and Milos?"

This isn't exactly how I thought I would catch her interest, but I'll take it. I step closer to her and sniff with just enough pomp to convince her that I'm an arrogant jerk. Might turn her on. "Yes, well, you know, I help Stephon make money. I kick it in his office all the time, you know. He and I talk about *everything*. But you didn't hear that from me."

Tamara tilts her head back enough to send a stream of minty-fresh breath into my burning nostrils. "You know, Mitchell, I'm new in town. Does Evans sponsor much in the way of parties, happy hours, you know, where I could meet some people in entertainment?"

This woman is definitely passing my sniff test. Her scent reminds me of freshly sliced oranges. I don't know if this is some new perfume or if she's just got it like that, but I'm in love. It's time to turn on the charms, full steam ahead. How can I shroud myself in enough mystery to reel this woman in? "Well, Evans Entertainment hosts parties at local clubs all the time, in connection with artist tours and new releases. I usually take a date, you know. Though lately the challenge has been who to take—but you don't want to hear about that."

"What do you mean?"

Now I'm outperforming Cuba Gooding himself. "Well, you see, my little boy's mother is having a hard time letting go of me. The boy's three years old next week, and she still thinks our breakup is temporary, you know what I mean? I think she's finally getting the picture, though. My last girlfriend set her straight."

Tamara smiles wickedly. "Are you really that good, that it takes a sister three years to get you out of her system?" *She's intrigued!* I tell myself triumphantly. *It's on!*

Applying Rule #1, I fully relax my body. The tightness in my chest and knees is gone, and I'm officially chillin', sending Tamara a non-verbal message about how fit and flexible my body is. "Well, I'm not one to brag, you know—"

Tamara and I keep rolling with each other's flow until I feel hot breath tickling the hairs on my neck. "Uh, excuse me, what do we have here?" The voice is full of accusation, betrayal, and more than a few threats. I know it's Gina before I even turn around.

I point aimlessly from one woman to the other, trying to keep from getting embarrassed. "Er, uh, Tamara Shaw, meet Gina Tatum."

Gina slips her left hand around my waist and uses her right to pinch the hell out of my right cheek. *Oww!* "Hi, Tamara," she hisses through clenched teeth. "How do you and Mitchell know each other?"

Tamara's face is loaded with muffled amusement. I'm convinced I had a shot with her, but it's over now. She's ready to pull up stakes and let another Player take his best shot. "We crossed paths back in D.C., in college," she replies. She and Gina exchange that wordless look only black women have perfected. The glare, the arch of the back, the twist of the neck that says, *Bitch!* Unaccustomed to these types of confrontations, I do my best to slink out of the line of fire. I can't help but exhale like Terry McMillan when Tamara ends the game of chicken. "Mitchell, it was nice meeting you. Maybe I'll see you out on the town sometime. Bye!"

Watching Tamara's hips shimmer away beneath that silk gown, I almost forget that Gina's staring me down. I want to yell to Tamara, "You can't leave without surrendering the digits! Please!"

Gina silences that notion. "Mitchell, you have some explaining to do."

I don't even have to look at her to know her arms are crossed. "Gina, baby, what are you talking about?"

"I'm talking about the fact that Gina Tatum doesn't believe in man-sharing, that's what. We've had our fun for a few weeks, mister, but eventually you're going to have to slow down if you want this. Are you game or not?"

"What?" I look at Gina like she's lost her mind. I know she's not trying to call me out in the midst of the damn charity ball, and I'm wondering if this sister has all the pieces to her puzzle. I put my hands on my hips and look around for Tony. Predictably, he's standing near the water fountain flanked by two bubbly staffers from the mayor's office, a big smile on his face as he laughs at me. I tell myself I'm gonna kick that boy's skinny tail before this course is through.

What do I tell Gina, as she stands in front of me with arms crossed and lips frowning? Gina's no Nikki, but she does come with some advantages. She's the most athletic woman I've been with, meaning I never know what to expect each time. Her years as a balance-beam gymnast have not gone to waste. On top of that, the girl is very funny, saucy, adventuresome, and, most important, easy to please. I don't think Gina's been treated well by most of the men in her life; she melts when I do so much as cook her a steak or open a door for her. She's still too young for me, though. This relationship is the type my boy Tony grew up on—shallow, freaky, and deceitful. And look where it's gotten him! He's about to marry Juanita, a woman so fine that foreign dignitaries and senators are drooling over her tonight.

As Gina strokes my chin with her slender fingers, I decide to give her a month. I don't need many more sexual conquests, anyway, so I figure I can get freaky sex out of my system with Gina on the one hand and build a potential relationship with Nikki at the same time. This should work, especially given how discreet Gina is. She doesn't want anyone to know about her personal life, so I know she won't blab to anyone who could get word back to Nikki. I lean in close to her and smile. "All right, you snared me. It's you and me, kid." I sneak a quick peck onto her lips.

Gina grabs me by the collar. "Look, I agreed we could come to this thing separately, but I am not going to sleep alone tonight. Let's get a cab, now!" Her tone is clear: *take me!*

Using my mental powers to try to stop the sudden bulge that's forming in my slacks, I step back from her. I wanted to spend the night with Nikki! Now what do I do? "How's this for a deal? You know I came here with my boy Tony, right? Why don't you go ahead and take a cab, and I'll meet you at home when I get out of here?"

Gina's next words cement my decision about who to spend the night with. "You have until one o'clock, Mitchell. You show up after that, and you get nothing but the missionary position tonight!"

After dreaming up some good lies about why I need to stay behind, I send Gina on her way out the main entrance. Already I know how this night is going to end. I'm going to spend the next two hours (until shortly before one o'clock) spinning Nikki around the dance floor, enjoying the life I hope will one day be mine. After Tony's limo drops Nikki off, I'll have him and Trey drop me at Gina's, where I'll spend the rest of the night having empty, acrobatic sex. Such is the life of the Player, I suppose; balancing the women who move your heart with those who feed your jones. I guess this beats my old routine of going home alone, but there's no denying: This could get old real quick.

CHAPTER 18

COMING TO TERMS

Mid-July

NIKKI

aint or no saint, Marvin Stone is a lion in the courtroom. I couldn't help but stare in awe as he approached Judge Beam's bench this afternoon. The judge was obviously impressed; he sat nodding his bald dome the whole time Marvin made his argument. Marvin ran everything down, from the depositions taken from five women who had been fired from Empire after Colin propositioned them to the records he obtained from the Betty Ford Clinic showing that Colin had checked in for three visits there in as many years.

Jack Hamm, Colin's attorney, held a game face throughout the whole proceeding, but even someone of his experience couldn't keep from sweating as Marvin piled one embarrassing fact on top of another. His only defense seemed to be the fact that I had no corroborating eyewitness. Marvin, of course, was quick to remind Hamm that the publicity of a trial would cost more than a wisely offered settlement. By the time Judge Beam denied Hamm's motion to dismiss and pronounced an opening trial date for early August, it was all I could do to keep from jumping into Marvin's arms as we floated out into the hallway. Maybe my career in music was over, but I was not going to go quietly, not where Empire Records was concerned. Payback was going to be a mother!

I was so souped up I invited Marvin out for lunch to celebrate. We left the courthouse and took a bus over to State Street, where he suggested we hit his favorite Chinese restaurant, Lucky Chow. Although the name was a little spooky, I walked in behind him and tried not to admire the width of his rippling shoulders.

"Two, please." Marvin smiled at the thin teenage girl manning the podium near the entrance. She smiled broadly, revealing two crooked front teeth that offset her pretty, angular face. Her lack of composure and the smart twinkle in her eyes made me figure she was the owner's daughter. She looked nothing like the usual zombies who populated these types of joints, and she didn't seem to have a care in the world.

We walked past what looked like a statue of a little sumo wrestler and took a seat in front of a grove of waist-high plastic plants. I leaned back in my chair and smoothed my business suit. I was wearing a knee-high number like the ones the girls on *Ally McBeal* wear when they go to court. I looked across at Marvin; in the dim light of the restaurant, he reminded me more than ever of Mitchell. I tried to tell myself not to bring him up, though.

As a waiter set cups of hot tea in front of us, Marvin smiled and looked at me curiously. "You seem awfully happy, Nikki. Is all this joy due to the way things went back in the courtroom?"

I felt my internal alarm go off. "Why, Marvin, of course it's about the way the lawsuit is going. Sure, my career is in the toilet, but I'll get some money out of the deal, right?"

Marvin took a sip of his tea and said, "The lawsuit will take care of itself. As I've said before, I think you need to take the next settlement offer they come with. You realize they'll be nearing three hundred thousand?"

I frowned at him. "They can offer the moon, Marvin, I'm still taking this all the way. Someone's going to pay for my loss of livelihood.

I can't even get a washout like James Martin to work with me now. I'm not going down alone!"

Marvin raised a hand in self-defense. "All right, sister, take it easy. I'm officially backing off. Let's talk about something more pleasant. Like your feelings for my baby brother."

I huffed and rolled my eyes. "I have *no* idea what you're talking about."

He leaned forward in his seat and lowered his voice, his eyes dancing like sparks in a fire. "Nikki, I'd like to take my attorney hat off now and speak as a potential brother-in-law."

"Oh, please!"

"Look, I'm halfway serious. Come on, I do have caller-ID, you know. More than one morning recently, Mitchell has called me from your apartment. You telling me you kids are just playing checkers those nights he spends over there?"

I shook my head and smiled in astonishment. "Marvin, no you didn't!" I laughed hard. *So he acknowledges that others have sex lives, even if he doesn't,* I thought.

"Nikki," Marvin said, laughing, "I think you are the best woman Mitchell has had in his life in a long time. That boy has been unlucky in love. It's so refreshing to see a catch like you digging him. I'm serious!" he said as I covered the chuckle escaping my mouth. "You guys seem good for each other. You're just doing one thing wrong."

I twisted my neck at that one. "And what am I doing wrong, in your humble opinion?"

Marvin grinned. "You need to save him from himself. Tie him down."

"Meaning what?"

He squinted in concern. "Uh, what's your impression of your relationship with Mitchell? Is it exclusive?"

"It's two consenting adults having a tender, good time. We haven't defined it any further than that."

Marvin leaned back as the waiter brought his plate of hot braised chicken and my egg rolls. "Well, I'd like to see it defined. Mitchell has too many girls on his plate."

I paused with an egg roll inches from my mouth. "Marvin, do you really want me to hear this?"

"Nikki," Marvin said, "you really think I would expect you to be freaked out by a guy who has other women in his life? Have you ever dated a man who *didn't* have other women around?"

I bit my lip and slid the egg roll back onto the plate. "Who are you to judge me like that?" The next words flooded out before I could stop them. "That's bullshit. Who are you to judge me like that? You don't know me that well." I shook a finger in his face.

Marvin finished his first bite of chicken and rice before dabbing at his mouth with a napkin. "Hey, look," he said, "don't take it personal. We all have our own weaknesses. How's this, to show I'm not here to judge you? My personal life has been a shambles since May 11, 1998. Know why?"

Caught off guard by Marvin's sudden departure from the present, I bit into my egg roll and cocked my head.

"When I joined church and accepted Jesus as a teenager," he said, "I was taught that the Bible forbade sex before marriage. And I didn't just accept it blindly. I studied Scriptures carefully, even argued over various interpretations with my parents and friends. Whether I liked it or not, though, the answer remained clear: no fooling around before marriage. I could see all the problems it caused long before most of my boys in high school did. The minute any of them got busy, women ceased to be anything more than vehicles to them. They acted like animals. Personally, I was having none of that. I pledged to only date women who would respect my desire to wait for marriage."

I couldn't keep a cheesy grin from splitting my face, regardless of how hard I tried. "Marvin, how did someone as fine as you keep it in your pants all those years?"

Marvin shook his head. "I'm a rational human being, Nikki, I always was. I made my decision, and I stuck with it. I was prepared to be dateless, until I met Angela. She was my perfect complement; beautiful, smart, saved, and pure."

I washed down my first egg roll with a shot of Slice. "So why wasn't that enough to save your marriage?"

Marvin looked like he regretted he'd started the whole thing. I almost felt sorry for him as he stroked his forehead and continued in a low, somber tone. "You get to know Mitchell well enough, you're going to hear this anyway. I just ask you to keep it confidential. Can I trust you?"

I scrunched my brow in confusion. "Sure."

Marvin placed his hands in his lap and glared at his half-eaten plate of chicken and rice. "I divorced my wife because she was unfaithful to me in our second year of marriage. I filed the papers a few weeks after I learned 'our' son had been fathered by someone else."

I opened my mouth to respond, but nothing came out.

"You see," Marvin continued, "I went off on a self-righteous tear. The betrayal, so early in our marriage, was just too much. I don't think I heard one word Angela said to me after I got the blood-test results."

Something finally came out. "I am so sorry."

"Don't be. About a year ago, I finally looked back at what really happened. I was never home. The first years of our marriage, I was in law school. Chicago's curriculum was grueling, I was student-body president, treasurer for the local Young Republicans, doing speaking engagements for Christian youth ministries . . . I guess I figured Angela should just feel lucky I made it home every night."

"What was she doing all the time you were gone?"

"She helped her father run his church, leading a bunch of ministries and things like that. But I left her sitting at home a lot. I *did* set aside Saturday nights for romance, though."

I twisted my mouth into a frown. "Once a *week*?"

He shook his head from side to side. "Maybe I wasn't as eager about the bedroom as I should have been. I was no champ in the sack. I expected to make my wife's toes curl like some porn star, right off the bat. I was Marvin Stone! But I was a novice at how to put a smile on my wife's face. Maybe my pride was a little wounded."

I crossed my legs and leaned back in my chair. "So you did what most guys would do when something doesn't work. You pulled away."

Marvin nodded. "Sex wasn't really the main problem, though, it was just a symptom. I'd spent so much time running from physical intimacy that I neglected the art of emotional intimacy. My schedule was crazy, I was so tired when I was home I couldn't give my wife what she needed in any form. I'll never be able to deny . . ." Marvin broke away from my gaze and hissed hot air through his nostrils. "No denying I may have driven her away."

Watching this strapping, successful man bare his soul, I was almost moved to tears. I tried to nonchalantly ease a packet of Kleenex out of my Coach bag. "You, uh, you haven't tried to reconcile with her, now that you see things more clearly?"

Marvin returned to his plate of food. "She's been seeing someone new lately. We have kept up the friendship, though, mainly because I've agreed to continue on as Marvin III's father, until we feel he's old enough to know about his biological dad."

"Where is the dad?"

"He's a semipro basketball player, traveling the world and too unstable to be around for now. So I'm filling in, I guess."

I was *so* glad I'd found the Kleenex by then. I mashed one against each eye as the tears began to flow. *Damn you, Marvin*, I thought. *Why do you have to be such a saint?* This man could take responsibility for a child who was not his, but my own father could barely claim me? The betrayal, disappointment, and envy that had bubbled beneath the surface for too long started to flow right there, at a round table in the Lucky Chow restaurant. A voice inside my head was crying, in an adolescent whine. In Gene Coleman, I would never have a real daddy, at least not in the way a daughter should.

Squinting at my tears, Marvin looked like a new father holding a baby who'd just crapped his Pampers. "Uh, Nikki, are you all right? Look, I was trying to make you feel better."

Sniffing and straightening in my seat, I steeled my nerves. Through a haze of tears, I blinked as sweetly as I could. "Yes," I said, clearing my throat. "What did all that have to do with Mitchell and the other men in my life?"

His eyes brightening as I started to sober up, Marvin smiled at me tentatively. "Well, the point was really to get you distracted, so you'd forget my crack about you dating men who have other women. You were pretty pissed!" We had a good laugh at that one, finished our plates, finally, and washed it all down with another pot of hot tea.

By the time I got out of there, it was almost four o'clock, and I knew I had to go by the hospital to see Gene. It had been almost two weeks since I had seen him, after he had gone home to rest up for his next operation. He was back at St. Luke's now, awaiting a bypass surgery. Everyone was saying his odds were good, but they were also pressuring me to see him before he went under the knife.

I guess it was my near breakdown while talking with Marvin that gave me that extra motivation to go see my father. I decided it was time to officially deal with my "father hunger." There was no way Gene was ever going to fill that need, whether he lived another month or another century, but I figured I had to face the void. Maybe I couldn't control him, but I could control my reaction to him. And maybe the best reaction in this case would be to treat him like I'd want to be treated.

He was asleep when I got to his room. As I sat by his bed watching the liquid in his IV and flipping the remote on his TV, I took time to reflect on the new me. Now that I'm back home and looking over the day (for that matter, these past few months), I'm starting to see some of the patterns in my life more clearly. Regardless of how this lawsuit affects my career, I'll land on my feet professionally, I know that. Where I've let this father hunger get me is in my personal life. The empty screws with Jomo, the clinging to needy pretty boys like Barry, all of those things grew out of my dissatisfaction with the man who should have been most important in my life. Well, no more.

Fate has finally opened my eyes to a wonderful man who's not what I used to think I wanted. As a man, Mitchell has more on the ball than Barry or Jomo ever will. I know he's still sowing some oats, but given my past, I can't afford to judge him for that. He's not a Dog; he's just like a sheltered kid who's loose in a candy store for the first time. His sweet tooth will rot soon enough, and he'll be ready to make the same proposition to me that he made months ago, the night when I naïvely broke his heart. This time, when he asks me to be his lady, the only breaking sound will be the box springs on my bed. This girl is ready to take herself off the market.

CHAPTER 19

UNPLANNED PARENTHOOD

Late July

MITCHELL

T he condom broke at 3:03 this morning. It's not fair; a Player was just minding his business. Of course that business was an unplanned rendezvous with Gina. We were standing up in my kitchen, enjoying the fact that Marvin's square behind was out of town on business. Gina and I both had gotten tired of pounding away on the waterbed in her loft apartment near Wrigley Field, and the hotel game was getting too risky; I'm trying not to be spotted in public with anyone other than Nikki these days. So when Marvin told me last week that he'd be in Dallas all week for a conference, I knew it was going to be on. I was planning to dump Gina by month's end, so I figured this would be my chance to take things to one more level before severing our ties.

Because I'd been busy all week at work, Gina wasn't seeing much of me during waking hours. The woman was a machine, though. It didn't matter if I came home at seven in the evening or at midnight, she was a primed pump waiting for my attention the moment I crossed the threshold. And considering the innovative cut of the silk teddies and other lingerie she was sporting every night, I was an easy mark.

This morning we'd been in the midst of our second round when I felt a slight tear developing right near the head of my ribbed Trojan. Before I became a Dog, my sexual activity had been infrequent enough that I was shielded from the odds; I've heard that one condom out of seventy-five can tear at that most inopportune moment. I'd heard stories of it happening to some of my boys, of course, but I never figured it would be a problem for me. Shoot, in my Nice Guy days, there were nights I prayed it *would* be a problem for me.

Anyway, the moment I felt the tear, everything began to happen in slow motion. It was like being in a car accident; seconds feel like hours as you careen toward another car or into a brick wall. I was gripping Gina's hips and holding on for dear life, and even as my mind warned me of the danger, my body continued forward in search of that trusty love explosion. Even as I continued to put a hump into my back and pressed Gina against the Formica counter, I tried to warn her. "I need to get out!" I knew she wasn't on the pill. This could be serious!

Gina was surprisingly unimpressed with our dilemma. I could swear she actually smiled as she groped at my ears for traction. Her eyes shone like bright lights as she continued to bob up and down. "Shut up, Mitchell! Shut up and keep working!"

I don't know if I enjoyed the remaining seconds or not. It was like a hazy nightmare, but I'd be lying to say it didn't feel good. Before I knew it, I was spent, broken condom and all. I set Gina onto the countertop and stumbled back as I surveyed the damage. The condom, that supposed iron shield, protector of the Stone Jewels, was ripped down the middle like Saran Wrap. As the endorphins that had flooded my brain began to subside, reality set in. I couldn't even try to be cool.

"Oh, damn, oh no!" I tripped and fell hard against the refrigerator handle, nearly puncturing my rear end. Steadying myself, I slid down onto the linoleum floor and hiked my boxer shorts back up over my manhood. What had I just done?

I looked up to see Gina flopping around like a black Pollyanna. "Oh, Mitchell, that was wonderful!" Naked as a jaybird, she put her hands on her shapely hips. "Babe, you realize we just shared *fluids*? I think that is so romantic." She picked up her lace panties and shimmied into them before starting what looked like a ghetto version of a ballerina dance. I sat there watching her and wondered what was going on. My mother's words were echoing in my head: *Mitchell, I can't tell you how to handle women, and I sure can't stop you from havin' sex. But promise your mama this much; you won't sleep with a woman without getting to know her first. You don't have to love her, or want to get married to her. But you need to at least know and respect her.*

I had by and large heeded my mother's advice through the years, except for that fling with Monisse. These last couple months, though, I'd lowered my standards a bit. And sitting there on the floor, I was looking at a perfect example of what lowered standards get you.

"I'm hungry," Gina was saying. She had slipped back into her pink Frederick's of Hollywood two-piece and was standing over the stove. "I'm gonna make an omelet. You got any beer?"

I put my head in my hands. "Gina, do you realize what just happened? More important, what could happen?"

She slapped her right hip with a hand and looked at me with a fat frown on her face. "What is your problem, Mitchell? You worried I'm gonna get pregnant?"

"Uh, well, unless there's something you're not telling me, it is a concern, right?"

Gina was shouting now, as she rumbled through the cabinet underneath the stove. "I don't consider conceiving an innocent life to be a concern. I'm almost twenty-four. The average woman has her first child before age twenty-five, you know."

My face was cracked like a walnut. "What?"

Gina found a no-stick frying pan and slammed it onto the counter before walking over to me. "You're blocking the refrigerator, mister. Raise up."

Too stupefied to do otherwise, I struggled to my feet and let Gina open the fridge door. As she pulled out eggs, Parkay margarine, and a half gallon of 2-percent milk, I crossed my arms and shook my head. I had to be imagining this conversation. "Look, you told me you weren't on the pill for medical reasons. Now you're saying you *wanted* to get pregnant?"

Gina turned the right front burner of the stove on and sliced up some Parkay. "*Wanted* is a strong term. But if it happens, it happens."

The hell it does, I thought. I'd never be down with abortion, but that moment was the closest I'd ever come to switching my view. I did *not* want to have a baby by this woman. *How did I end up here?* Sliding into a funk, I told Gina I wasn't hungry and trudged into the living room. I shoved Marvin's Bibles and our pile of *Ebony* magazines aside so I could prop my feet on the coffee table while I melted into the couch. I knew I was making a bigger deal of this than I needed to right now, but my mind was filling with every worst-case scenario in the book. Gina was free to have a baby when and where she wanted, but I didn't want to be responsible for it.

I was starting to question her state of mind, anyway. The girl was getting a little possessive. The last three weeks, every night I spent with her turned into a sleepover. She had actually blocked her apartment door several times, forbidding me to leave before the sun rose. On top of her clinging ways, she was a bit too secret-agent. I knew why I was keeping things on the down low: Nikki. What I didn't know was why Gina, who acted like I was God's gift, was so secretive. She had sworn me to silence, forbidding me to even tell anyone that we were seeing each other. She said that she had some family and friends in the area that she didn't get along with, and she wanted to keep them out of her business. Ordinarily I'd have been suspicious of her claims, but given that I viewed her as nothing more than a diversion, what did I care? Well, now I cared. I cared so much I had to raise up from the couch and puke my guts into my toilet, while Gina hummed to herself and put the finishing touches on a monster omelet.

By eight o'clock, when I dragged myself into my office, my head was still heavy with worry. I felt myself rooting for the defeat of the wayward sperm that escaped the ruptured condom. *Die, you little soldiers, die!* As I laid my briefcase down and wiped a fresh splotch of Gina's lipstick off the wrinkled collar of my white oxford dress shirt, I noticed a Post-it stuck on my monitor. I recognized Stephon's chicken scratch immediately. The Man Himself was summoning me.

Stephon's secretary ushered me into his office, where I came face-to-face with a unique spectacle. Milos, our star artist, was crumpled into the shiny black leather couch lining the west wall. His slender frame was draped in a shiny silk shirt and a baggy pair of plaid slacks that hung off him like meat off a tender rib bone. He could have been posing for an album cover, if not for the fact that his high-yellow face was marred by black puffs of skin underneath each eye, and his fleshy lips were oozing rivers of blood. I froze in the doorway at the sight, feeling both embarrassed and repulsed. The boy was a mess. If not for the way his frizzy mane of hair shadowed his face, the damage would have probably been even more obvious.

Stephon reclined in his desk chair, bobbing up and down like he didn't have a care in the world. He'd gotten his mound of S-curls trimmed into a short fade and was dressed like he'd just come off the golf course with Tiger Woods. I realized then that he wasn't even paying us any mind. He was holding a conversation on the speakerphone with what sounded like a young child. "Daddy, when you coming home?" The voice sounded like it belonged to a nine- or ten-year-old at best.

Stephon winked at me and motioned for me to take a seat. "Honey, what did I tell you? I'll be back home tonight."

"But are you going to be here all week? Mommy says you can't always spend every night in the house with us. Why that?"

As I stayed frozen in place and Milos gazed at me with bloodshot eyes, Stephon looked at us both and shook his head. "Look, hon, let me call you at lunch. Okay?"

"Awright. I love you, Daddy."

Stephon hung up the phone and stared at the ceiling for a minute. Finally, after I had gone ahead and taken a seat across from the desk, he smiled. "Mitch," he said, "I need your expertise."

I reached for my notepad. "What do you need, Stephon?" I was ready to dig into some financial analysis now. Anything to get my mind off of whatever was happening inside Gina's uterus.

"You can put that away," Stephon said, shrugging. "Mitch, you ever thought about getting married?"

I laughed, louder than I'd planned to. "Uh, no, Stephon. At least not for a while now. Why would you ask?"

He stood and stared me down as he crossed his arms. "I'm asking because I'm starting some wedding preparations, that's why."

I laughed again, thinking this was a joke. "Okay, Stephon, tell me something I can believe."

He strolled around his desk, clapped me on the shoulders, and made his way over to Milos, who stiffened as Stephon approached. "Mitch, see Milos here? You know what happened between my Missy and Milos, don't you? How they were gettin' busy behind my back? Well, I thought it through and decided that Milos needed to be taught a lesson." He reached forward and cupped Milos's chin in his right hand. "See that piece of handiwork? I screwed up that pretty face good, didn't I?"

I shrugged. "Yeah, so?"

"The point, Mitch, is that kicking Milos's ass didn't heal my pain. I realized my pain was over the fact that Missy messed with someone else. I could have lost her, man! That's when I realized I need this woman in my life! And now that I've realized the truth, man, I'm acting on it right away!"

I straightened in my chair and rubbed my eyes. The world was going freaking crazy. Here I was, the ultimate Nice Guy, just a heartbeat away from being a Baby Daddy, and Stephon Evans, Player Extraordinaire, was getting married!

Stephon wasn't quite done basking in his newfound glory. "Mitch, man, I've been sexually faithful to Missy for the last month! It is just so refreshing, brother! My life is changed. I'm reading Iyanla Vanzant and Dennis Kimbro every morning, and I ain't watching those trifling BET videos no more. Except the ones made by my artists, of course. I'm able to think so much more clearly. It's such a load off not to be plannin' my next stick and move on a new woman, you know?

Now I see what you Nice Guys always saw! Life is best when you're just yourself, right?"

"Right," I said, hoping this would shut him up so I could get out of there. I pointed tentatively at Milos. "He needs medical attention."

Stephon placed a hand on Milos's shoulder again. "He's fine. They're all flesh wounds, I made sure of it. He'll heal up by next week and be ready to hit *Soul Train*, Letterman, and Leno. I wouldn't mess with my meal ticket, Mitch!" Stephon's grin was so goofy-looking, I started wondering what illegal substance he was on. I decided to play along.

By ten o'clock, I had agreed to serve as Stephon's informal adviser for the wedding ceremony, despite the fact that I had never walked the aisle of a church or city hall. Apparently I was one of the few brothers Stephon knew who wasn't a straight-up Player, Dog, or Ladies' Man. He seemed to think I could give *him* tips on how to stay faithful to Missy and be a good role model for his kids. It was funny.

As I returned to my office, I laughed out loud. It had been a long time since any man had envied my love life, or lack thereof. The funny thing was, Stephon was asking me for advice about a way of life that was becoming increasingly foreign to me. My screwup with Gina that morning had been a wake-up call that I was officially a Dog now. I decided there was no need for Stephon to know about my transformation, though; even if I wasn't a Nice Guy anymore, I could still teach him how to be one. I had twenty-eight years of experience at it, after all.

Shortly after lunch, I was bopping my head to my *Commodores' Ultimate Collection* CD when my phone rang. I paused "Slippery When Wet" and hit the speaker button so I could keep typing the memo I was working on. "This is Mitchell Stone."

The female voice, familiar to me as any, stabbed me in the chest. "You low-down, dirty alley cat! Are you out of your mind?!" There was no mistaking; it was Tasha, my former best friend and lover.

Relieved only to the extent that it was anyone other than Gina calling, I whipped around and grabbed the receiver. My office door was shut, but Tasha was yelling so loud, I was sure someone out in the hallway would hear. "Hey, hey, now! What's up? Why you tripping?"

Tasha's sweet voice had a touch of gravel to it. "Oh, no reason. I just called to tell you that you are officially banned from my house and from my life. You've gone too far, Mitchell."

I sputtered into the phone, shaking my head in disbelief. I knew Tasha was never in support of my transformation into a Dog; she'd made it clear I could forget our friendship and our occasional nights of intimacy as long as I was whoring around. Still, we had stayed in contact through these last three months, talking on the phone and hanging out at the gym some. I tried to calm down, hoping I could calm her down as well. "Tasha, just start from the top. *What* did I do?"

"Do you want to tell me why you're using my daughter to meet women?"

Without thinking, I slapped the mess out of my forehead and fell back into my chair. *She wasn't supposed to know about that!* Maya and I had agreed that the role she played in my come-ons to Gina and several other victims at the health club would be our little secret. I slapped my forehead again. *You fool, five-year-olds don't know nothin' about keeping secrets!* It was time to beg.

"Tasha, look, it was all quite innocent, really. Maya kind of happened to be walking with me in the gym one day, and a woman asked if she was mine. She was so caught up in how cute Maya was, I knew I could score some points. I couldn't help myself—"

"Mitchell, stop. Stop it right now. As far as I know you've never lied to me before, but you're damn sure trying to now. I don't care how much of an amateur Dog you are now, I can see right through you. You ought to be ashamed!"

I paced my marble floor and fought off the sweat beads forming on my forehead. I didn't have time for this. "Tasha, I'm sorry. Really, I never meant to use Maya. She's my goddaughter, and you know I'd never hurt her."

"She *was* your goddaughter. I'm assigning that privilege to someone else."

"Oh, come on!" This wasn't even right! The day was quickly going from bad to bizarre to worse. "Tasha, can we be real? I think this is about us! Are you sure you're not upset that I decided to be a Dog, instead of trying to make a move on you?"

Tasha's voice rose a pitch. "What? Don't flatter yourself, Mitchell! We had an agreement to be there for each other but we always agreed it was no-strings and it wasn't about romantic love."

"Some nights you could have fooled me."

"Please, Negro, every night with you was a charity project, as far as I was concerned."

This conversation had officially gone off the tracks. "Tasha, if I could have had my way, long ago, we'd have been real lovers. Sometimes I look at Maya and wish she was my daughter, thinking maybe that would have helped bond us romantically. But you know and I know that friends were always what we were meant to be. You always wanted someone more Doggish than me, and I always wanted someone I had to work harder for."

"Someone like Nikki Coleman."

I smiled at the mention of Nikki's name. I remembered I was supposed to call her this afternoon, to cement our plans to do the symphony tonight. "If you must bring up specific names, yes, someone like Nikki."

Tasha sighed deeply. "Look, I'm still pissed about what you pulled with Maya. Don't call me, I'll call you, eventually. But you're right, Mitchell, we were never meant to be more than friends. I just hate to see you ruining one of the few good men out there. I'm serious about this much—I hope you get yourself straight before Nikki finds you out. You two would be cute together."

I cheesed like I was sitting in front of a professional photographer. "Thanks, Tasha. Look, call me sometime, okay?"

"I will. Hey, I should probably warn you. I was so pissed when Maya first told me about your little stunt, I called your mom to complain. She may be getting on you about it. Bye now."

I set the phone down and turned back to my desk. *She called Moms, huh?* I started counting down time on my right hand. "One, two, three, four—"

The phone rang and I picked up nonchalantly. "Mom!"

She paused, taken off guard by my clairvoyance. "Uh, yes, it's me. How did you know?"

"Oh, I just had a sense my mommy was worried about me."

"Look, son, I'm not here to preach at you. But Tasha mentioned what you've been up to, going to any lengths to meet women. Mitchell, I've kept my mouth shut, at your father's insistence, but you should know Tasha's not the only one spreading your business around. I had *three* sorors ask me about you at this month's AKA meeting! All of them think you're dating their daughter, or were at some point! How many different holes are you plugging around town, boy?" My mother is a churchgoing woman, but when she wants to talk the language of the street, she embraces it with true grit.

I fingered one sideburn and took a deep sigh. "Mom, you're on forbidden territory."

"I knew I should have made your father call."

"Maybe he realizes I'm a man who can make his own decisions."

The sudden catch in my mother's voice snapped me out of my smart-ass mood. "I, I just wish my children could be happy." Her speech slowed suddenly, and her words were heavy with grief. She sounded like she was testifying at a church revival. "Mitchell, I look at you and Marvin and I just don't understand. What did we do wrong? Why couldn't Marvin make his marriage work? Why can't you find a woman who appreciates you and lets you start a family of your own?" She almost sounded like she was weeping now. "What did we do wrong, Mitchell?"

I almost collapsed into my desk. I wasn't used to these types of emotional shows from my mother. She was always big about appearances, and grieving over two healthy children didn't make for the most attractive appearance. Caught off guard, I leaned forward and spoke in a hushed tone. "Mom, there's nothing you did wrong. Times have changed, that's all. A lot of women in this day and age have seen all the successes of the female baby boomers and decided they can have everything: the job, the house, the luxury car, then the perfect husband."

My mother sniffed. "Hmph."

"And I do mean perfect. A man has to have it all to compete for some of these women. They want more than ladies of your generation asked for, Mom. I think a lot of them aren't even pressed about ever getting married.

"Well, I think you're a bit cynical, Mitchell. I know you boys will meet the right women soon enough. So please, stop this crazy lifestyle. Live right."

I'm no fool, so I put up with my mother for the next ten minutes as she lectured me from the Bible and insisted I give church one more chance. She was so sure that a thundering sermon from Pastor Willis would knock some sense into me. Not only did I agree to go, I also decided to invite Nikki. I figured it would give my mom some more hope, seeing me with a prime catch like Nikki. Plus, my mishap with Gina had convinced me all the more that it was time to lock things down with Nikki and get out of the game. Now if I could just let Gina go with the right touch of class. . . .

When I got home, my answering service was loaded with messages. As I loosened my tie and pulled my shirttail out of my pants, I flopped down on the couch and let the messages play over the speakerphone. Every message but one was from Gina. The canned female voice announced each message dutifully, and I cringed at every one. I wanted to literally melt into the couch.

"Message one, at nine-fifteen A.M.: *Mitchell, this is Gina. Hey, I'm starting my shift at the hospital. Guess who I'm thinking about? This morning was beautiful! Who knows what might come of it?*

"Message two, at ten-fifteen A.M.: *Mitchell, this is Gina. I would have called you at work, but I know you don't like to be interrupted. I just wanted you to know, I told my friend Judy about you. She thinks you are so special! She says we'd probably make great parents if we are pregnant. Isn't that sweet? Love you! Bye!*

"Message three, at three-fifteen P.M.: *Mitchell, this is Gina. I am so hot right now, I could scream. I want to re-create this morning as soon as I get off work! I should be home by six, so you be oiled and ready! Love you — Daddy!*

"Message four, at five-oh-three P.M.: *Hey, Mitchell, it's Nikki. I got your message about the symphony. I'm definitely down, we haven't seen enough of each other this week. My father's out of the hospital now, so my weekend's wide open. Let's hook up!*

Thank God! I headed back to my bedroom and pictured myself decked out in my favorite chalk pinstriped suit. I was ready for Nikki, as soon as I figured out how to get rid of Gina when she showed up. It wasn't going to be easy.

CHAPTER 20

SERIOUS BUSINESS

NIKKI

Something really funny is going on, because today was the second time I stepped foot in Trinity Methodist, Mitchell's church, in the past three months. Normally I do well if I attend an Easter service each year. But I can't exactly say that the Holy Ghost lured me out to God's house this morning. I was surprised and flattered when Mitchell invited me to attend church with his family. I decided to take it as a sign that he was looking to get serious. I already knew he didn't introduce just anybody to his mother; Marvin had told me that Tasha Parker is the only girl Mitchell's ever brought home.

The service was okay, nothing out of the ordinary. What was interesting was the family dynamics among the Stones. Mr. and Mrs. Stone tried to act nonchalant, but I could tell they were scoping me out as well as my girl Angie, who I brought along for Marvin's benefit. They were sizing us up something fierce, probably wondering how many men we've been with, how many babies we can have, and whether our family trees are full of winners or losers.

We all sat in one long wooden pew, shifting uncomfortably as the senior choir treated us to one wooden selection after another. They really seemed like a nice group of people, and I even recognized some of my second cousins in the choir. But they were doing no favors to the hymns they selected this morning. More than once Mitchell and I relied on the mountainous hats of the ladies in front of us, grinning and whispering about the sour notes in confidence that no one could see us. In between their selections and the obligatory offering and announcements portions of the service, Mitchell and I broke every rule of church etiquette, trading gossip about what was happening at Empire, my lawsuit, and of course Gene's health.

The one thing other than the sermon that caught our attention was when a heavyset man with a head of gray-flecked hair and a dazzling navy blue suit took to the pulpit. Pastor Willis had introduced him as Chauncey Wells. Mitchell almost jumped out of his seat. He whispered that this Wells had major bank. I got a hint of what he meant when the brother began to speak.

"Brothers and sisters in Christ," Wells said, gripping the podium like a veteran preacher, "I just want you to know there is at least one businessman in this town now who knows where his help comes from." The congregation whooped and hollered at his clichéd phrase. Church folk will take any excuse to go off.

"Brothers and sisters," Wells said, running a meaty hand over his silk tie, "I wanted you, the sister church of my church back in Atlanta, to hear this first. On Friday, I officially filed a hostile takeover bid for the largest entertainment company headquartered in middle America. If the Lord blesses, I will be the majority shareholder and chairman of Empire Records in the near future."

The church exploded as if Jesus himself had come back. As women in flowery hats swayed back and forth and a couple of goofy-looking brothers cut a step in the aisles, I couldn't stop from smiling wide myself. *A brother might end up owning Empire Records!* Twenty, even ten years ago this would have seemed impossible. But in the new millennium, brothers and sisters are doing it for themselves. As down as I get sometimes about my work situation and life in general, it's hard not to be optimistic when you see barrier-breakers like Reginald Lewis, Oprah, Robert Johnson of BET, and Chauncey Wells accomplishing things that were taboo for blacks when my mother was coming up. Black isn't just beautiful, it's bad!

By the time service let out, we were ready to go. Imagine my surprise at seeing Gina Tatum, though, as we neared the back of the cavernous sanctuary. She was sitting in a back pew by herself, with her arms crossed and much attitude written all over her face. I had never known Gina to be a churchgoer, but then, neither was I. I smiled at her, thinking maybe she was turning over a new leaf. She did look cute, in her olive pantsuit and white silk blouse. Deciding to be the mature, pleasant one, I turned around to tap Mitchell on the shoulder and do introductions, but he had darted off. Gina's eyes seemed to follow him as he strode toward the front of the sanctuary, where his parents were still besieged by friends and well-wishers. I couldn't help but wonder, *why did he rush off like that?*

Gina smiled at me like a cat with a canary hanging out of its mouth. "Who's your friend, Nikki?" It was more of a challenge than a question.

I smiled at her in confusion. "Oh, that's Mitchell. I'll introduce you when he comes back over."

Gina kept her arms crossed but held my gaze. "So, you're a member here?" I could barely make out what she was saying, because she was biting her lower lip with a vengeance. My lip hurt just watching her.

"No, Mitchell invited me. He and I are old friends from high school. Lately we've been going out, too."

Gina smirked. "He looks really *nice*. I didn't think you went for those types."

Nice. She said it like it was a dirty word. I shook my head and decided to let that mess fly right over my head. Maybe I could be embarrassed out of dating a certain type of guy in high school, but life had taught me too much to pay Gina's foolishness any mind. "He's a great catch, that's for sure. I don't know where things are going with him, but I'll give it a chance."

I could have sworn Gina rubbed her little washboard stomach before responding. "Well, Nikki," she said, "just remember all that glitters ain't gold. I gotta go."

I still don't know what she was talking about. It's frightening to think Mama once expected me to be friends with that heifer.

MITCHELL

I admit, I didn't face adversity with much courage today. When I saw Gina, I wanted to run out of the church screaming like Damon Wayans when he did "Men on Film" on *In Living Color*. I took one look at the eye contact between Nikki and Gina and knew they were acquainted somehow. My Dog training flashed across the recesses of my mind, just in time.

Mitchell, Tony had said, *if you're ever stuck out in public with two of your women, remember that there is no shame in fleeing, if it will head off a confrontation. Now, once you're found out, a true Dog has no choice but to stand his ground and tell both women to kiss his ass if they don't like it. But if you can slip away before each woman realizes the other knows you, DO IT! When in doubt, live to fight (and plot) another day.*

I showed no shame and implemented Tony's advice to the letter. I pivoted away from Gina and dove into the crowd surrounding my parents, leaving Nikki on her own. Everyone was on their tip, mainly because of my father's rare appearance. Despite the fact that Dad proudly disdains all religious institutions, Pastor Willis and the church members still ride his jock. On top of the usual hangers-on, Chauncey Wells had broken away from his own crowd of admirers to make small talk. As I suspected, Wells and my father had already met several times over the years, through their mutual friend John H. Johnson, the publisher of *Ebony* magazine. Wells recognized me from our meeting at the mayor's ball. He shook my hand and said he hoped to be signing my checks soon. I stretched our conversation out until I saw Gina walk out the front door of the sanctuary.

I emerged from the crowd as Nikki walked up to me with Marvin and Angie trailing behind. Marvin had a look in his eyes I hadn't seen in a long, long time: lust. Apparently Angie was awakening his sleeping beast. They were carrying on like old friends already, dropping names and arguing over their completely opposite political views. Nikki and I egged them on for a few minutes, then Nikki leaned close to me and bathed me with her sweet breath. "Are you ready to get out of here?"

"But of course." She had read my mind; we were supposed to go out to dinner with everybody else, but Nikki and I needed some quality time. I told my folks I'd catch up with them later in the evening and escorted Nikki out to the parking lot. As I got into the driver's seat of my car, I smiled at her and said, "So what would you like to do?"

Nikki kicked off her high heels and leaned back in her seat. "Well, I'm not hungry yet. Why don't we go for a drive? We could, you know, talk."

Talk? I wasn't so sure this was good. Usually when a woman wants to *talk*, it means she wants to talk about something her man did wrong. *She's going to ask about Gina, I know it.*

We were headed east on Highway 80 when she went there. "Hey, I was going to introduce you to somebody today. You disappeared on me all of a sudden. Where'd you go?"

I hugged the road with my eyes. I'm no fool, I know eyes are the windows to the soul. "I, uh, got called over to meet Chauncey Wells. You know my parents, always networking."

Nikki smiled. At least it felt like she did. I wasn't daring to make eye contact with her until we got past the subject of Gina. The horrible reality was sinking in. Tens of thousands of black women in Chicagoland, and these two were acquainted.

Nikki placed a tender hand on my shoulder. "Mitchell, do you remember a nasty little conversation we had, back in early May?"

I smiled despite myself. "You mean one that ended with a glass of ice water in my face? Yeah, that's still in my memory bank."

"Well, I thought it was time I gave you a meaningful answer to your question."

Nikki's words finally tore my eyes from the road, so much so that I swerved immediately to keep from running off onto the shoulder. My heart slammed against the walls of my chest. I thought of several smooth responses, but all that came out was, "A-and?"

I could hear Nikki turn in her seat, so that she was looking right at me. "Mitchell, I'm tired."

N I K
  K I

I was into my best-actress mode now. Not that I wasn't about to be truthful with Mitchell. I was pretty much ready to bare my soul to this man. But I was shaking inside, as if I was riding the Beast roller coaster at Kings Island. My challenge was to keep from looking that way. I kept my voice smooth and steady, and looked as deep into Mitchell's eyes as he would allow. You see, I realized right then that every man I'd ever put my trust in had ultimately found a way to disappoint me. So this was no light-hearted leap I was taking.

"Mitchell, I'm tired. I'm tired because I've been playing games with men my entire life. You want to know who taught me the first game I learned to play? My father ignored me so much when I was a child that I felt I had to earn his attention. I mean, I was six years old when he first introduced me to my half-sisters, and you know the greeting I got? They pulled at my hair and attacked me like two professional wrestlers. By the time my father pulled them off me, he raced me back to my mother's house and said this proved he was right. *See, Ebony, I told you there's no way I can bring her around my family. I'll visit when I can, but that's the best I can do.*" As Mitchell slowed the car down and started to glance at me with concern, I kept my eyes locked on him.

"Mitchell, I don't think I'll ever get back the piece of my soul that I lost that day. My father all but told me I wasn't a part of his family."

Mitchell frowned. "What a jerk!"

"That's not the point. I actually thought I could turn my father around, if I just gave him what he wanted. I figured he must want a perfect child, right? Someone better than my half-sisters. I knew

Tisha and Tia weren't the brightest lights in the bunch, and I was always cuter than they were, so I played those talents to the max. I worked in the evenings at the local mall as soon as I was old enough, earning money to buy myself all the fly-girl outfits when we were in junior high and high school."

Mitchell smiled. "You did always look good back at MLK."

"I was fly, and I was always on top of the books. I busted out every class, got a full ride to U. Chicago, and took as many club offices as I could grab up. But you know what ? None of it mattered to good old Gene Coleman. I held out hope as late as ninth grade, when I invited him to take me to a banquet for an essay contest I won. You think he ever showed up?"

Mitchell shook his head. "Nikki, I'm so sorry. I don't know what to say."

"You don't have to say anything. Just know that after that, I gave up on my father, but I decided to give other guys a chance to take his place. From there, I was ripe prey for someone like Lowball Spencer and all the other men who've clogged my life since. What I'm saying, Mitchell, is I'm finally tired of that. Back in May, when you asked me what I felt for you, I didn't really think about it."

Mitchell cut his eyes at me. "You want to explain that one?"

"I guess I had already downgraded you to friend status."

"From our days in MLK, or because of the way our dates had gone?"

"Some of both, probably. You know I did always think you were cute back in high school. Had you ever thought about stepping to me then?"

"When would I have done that, Nikki? At any given moment, you were either wrapped up with Barry, or you had every superjock and drug dealer–type jockeying for your attention. I knew I couldn't compete."

I finally decided to ask a question that had haunted me for the past two months. "Mitchell, for the record, if you'd stepped to me at the right time, I would have considered it. But when you look at all the time we spent side by side in classes, National Honor Society meetings, and student government, how could I view you as anything more than a friend? You never made yourself known." I inhaled slightly and asked, "Have you ever really competed for a woman's attention, Mitchell? Do you always scare off just because other guys are in the picture?"

Grimacing as if I'd just pinched him, Mitchell flashed his wide eyes at me before returning to the road. "Nikki, you wanna hear about a time I competed for a woman's attention? When I was in the third grade, I had a bit of a bedwetting problem. Don't laugh," he said as I giggled, "it wasn't funny to a little eight-year-old kid. I was the best student in class, the teacher's pet, and I was one of only three blacks in Julienne Elementary. The only black girl, Kathy Billings, was in my class. She was my first crush. You know, back before we even knew what sex was about, unlike the elementary school kids today. All I knew was Kathy made my heart beat just a bit faster than anyone else I'd ever met. So I did what any boy would do: I tormented her. You know, stealing her books during recess, tossing spitballs at her in the hallway, and calling her dirty names like Butt-sniffer."

"You charmer, you."

"Anyway, one day we were doing show-and-tell in class. I had just chased Kathy around the playground during recess, and she had scared the mess out of me. She had stopped right in the middle of the blacktop lot outside and let me run smack into her. Then she grabbed my head like some brothers grab a watermelon and pulled me close. I swear she tried to suck my face completely off. She even had the nerve to slip me the tongue! By the time I stumbled away from her, it was time for class. And I had to go first for show-and-tell!

"Anyway, I get up there, trying to talk about my copy of my father's biography of Andrew Young, and all I could do was think of Kathy's kiss, and how funny it made me feel. I don't quite know why what happened next did, I just know it happened. I was talking and felt a warm rush of liquid cascading down my right pant leg. I just kept talking. I guess I was in denial about what was happening. In seconds, of course, my classmates' whispers turned to rolling-on-the-floor laughter. My teacher, Ms. Patterson, was so embarrassed for me she flung herself over me and dragged me out into the hallway. She really looked out for me; I cleaned up in the rest room and got sent home for the day. But ask if I ever lived that down."

I looked at Mitchell and smiled at his honesty, his transparency. Even back at MLK, I would never have guessed he'd suffered an embarrassment like this. I couldn't imagine he'd ever shared this story with anyone else. "Mitchell, that sounds horrible."

He shrugged. "I think after that, I realized that women were the one area I'd never be able to control. You know, as a Stone, I was bred for success. And success in the classroom, on the playing field, all that came much easier to me. But Kathy taught me that I couldn't trust myself to be in control around women. Since that day, I think I've tried to play it safe, so I wouldn't be hurt or embarassed like that, ever again."

I stared at him with concern. "But you've dated, I know you have. You went out with that Tasha girl in high school, right? And I know you had a steady at Georgetown. Nobody else?"

He laughed as we took an exit off Highway 80, nearing our old MLK stomping grounds. "That's about it. Nikki, the success I've had with women has been unintentional. Tasha came after *me*. Carmen came after *me*. The nameless basketball groupies who I dated in high school came after *me*. The few times I did the chasing ended like that night with you a few months ago. Except that I meekly accepted my fate with all the others; you were the first one I stood up to."

"Let's make a deal," I said, sliding a hand on top of one of his. "Why don't we take our eyes off everyone else, in the past and present, and see what we think about each other?" I was kind of dancing around what I wanted to say: *Let's get serious.*

MITCHELL

I prayed Nikki was saying what I thought she was saying. "Are you saying you'd like to view this as a relationship, Nikki?"

She looked at me with warmth seeping from her eyes. "Yes. *I'm* not seeing anyone else right now, and I'm willing to keep it that way, until we decide how serious this might be. What about you?"

It wasn't her fault, but Nikki was in danger of ruining the mood. I planned my words very carefully. The slightest hesitation, the smallest stutter, could give me away. I was not going to disappoint Nikki in the way Gene Coleman, Barry Roberts, and Jomo Hayes had. "Nikki, I am willing to make you my number-one priority. How's that?"

"Pull the car over," she teased as we rolled up to the football field by MLK's red brick building. "I'd like to celebrate this moment."

I exhaled, came to a complete stop, and cupped her silky smooth chin in my right hand. As we embraced and dove into a long, heated kiss, I thanked God for his mercy. My evasive answer got me over. Sure, I was being a little deceitful, but my heart was in the right place. I was ready to toss my still-shiny black book. It was clear that Nikki trusted me, and I decided right there to live up to that trust.

I would do it, too. As soon as I resolved the Gina situation.

CHAPTER 21

UGLY WAYS

Mid-August

NIKKI

still can't believe it. Here my life had been going so much better for this past month. Mitchell and I have spent the better part of our nonwork hours together; he even keeps a couple of suits and a few pairs of jeans at my place. We're definitely not shopping for rings anytime soon, but we are enjoying each other's company. It's so refreshing to be with someone who's my intellectual equal, who's handsome and sexy enough to keep me excited and witty enough to keep me a little off balance. I can't figure out how much of the charm I see in Mitchell was always there and how much of it is new. I know he dated around a bit for the few months before we hooked up, but I figure most of what I see was always there. It's amazing how easily I overlooked a gem like him back at MLK, in favor of flashy lumps of coal like Lowball Spencer and Barry.

Anyway, between the daily walks in the park and the weekends away with Mitchell, along with my temporary gig as a manager for Imagination, a local female R&B group, life has been much improved. I've even developed a civil relationship with my father. Gene seems to have recovered well from his heart surgery, although he always complains that Jennifer won't let him get out and do anything.

The last time I stopped by, he was in good spirits, but he kept tripping. "Nikki, look, you need to come and get me out in the midst of some sunshine. Jennifer's acting up, trying to treat me like a prisoner. I can't eat anything with a drop of fat or cholesterol, and God forbid I even look at a bottle."

I had shaken my head and laughed at him as he fumed on the plaid wool couch in his living room. A Cubs game was blaring on the TV. "I'm serious," he continued. "Can't you at least run out and get me some smokes?"

I cut my eyes at him and asked, "Gene, what have you done for me lately?" It was a harmless joke as I recall, an attempt to avoid the fact that I had no intention of helping him ruin his health again. That was when I realized that Gene's illness and other recent events had affected our relationship, seemingly for the better. Gene even surprised me when I left that night; he squeezed my arm and smiled shyly. "Hey, for the record, I ain't no fool. I know your mama didn't force you to come see me in the hospital or drop by the house like this. I can't say I'll ever be worthy of you, Nikki, but you need to know this: your coming by meant more than anybody else's visits." He hugged me, smothering me with the smell of Right Guard, and sent me on my embarrassed way. It wasn't exactly *I love you*, but it was more than I'd ever expected.

With things working out with Mitchell and improving with Gene, something had to give. I guess that's why Judge Beam decided to throw out my lawsuit against Empire Records this morning. He didn't exactly throw it out, so much as he threw us a curve Marvin never saw coming. After reviewing all the evidence gathered for trial, he remanded the case to a third-party mediator, saying that he believed it was in both of our interests to come to a settlement. Marvin argued strenuously on my behalf, so much so he was almost held in contempt.

The judge, unfortunately, wasn't having it. I was so pissed I couldn't even talk to Marvin. He tried to tell me that this mediator has a reputation for being fair, that we could probably get a cushy settlement. His assurances fell on deaf ears, though. All I could do was glare at Colin's smug, freckled face as he and his attorneys gathered up their briefcases. One look at the evil twinkle in his eyes, and I knew it was over; maybe Empire would give me good money to go away, but there was no way I was getting back into the music industry now.

I shrugged off Marvin's attempts to console me and caught the bus home. After debating whether to call Mitchell and torture him at work with my pain, I decided to hit Mama up first. She was off for the day and agreed to come pick me up and take me back to her new condo in Chicago Heights.

When I saw her Buick roll up to the curb outside my apartment, I smiled despite myself. I was going to enjoy the afternoon with my mother and let her tell me everything would be all right. Then I would let Mitchell encourage me and love the pain away, all night. I had my little routine set in my mind as I walked to Mama's idling car. My plans changed the minute I opened the passenger-side door.

Mama had the radio tuned to 103.5 FM, which was oozing Kenny Lattimore's "For You." I felt like just relaxing to Kenny's smooth, reassuring crooning, but Mama was full of excitement about her condo's features and about her latest "mission."

"Nikki, I forgot to mention on the phone," she said as she pulled away from the curb, "that Gina Tatum called me this morning, probably at Shirley's insistence."

Oh, God. I sighed to myself. Here went my mama the Super Social Worker, trying to save every stray and wayward child that crossed her path. Mama's had a soft spot for Gina's janky butt since we learned that Gina's father abused her when she was little. Personally, I believe there comes a point when you have to stop blaming all your faults on things in the past. If you don't cut that out eventually, you'll become a lifelong guest on Ricki Lake or Jerry Springer. But my mother has a much softer and more naïve heart. "So," I said, trying to feign interest, "what's Gina's latest drama?"

"Well," Mama said with a sigh, "the girl done gone and got herself pregnant. Or should I say, let some Dog impregnate her."

"Whoa!" I tried not to snap my neck too quickly at that one. Gina was pregnant? That was a scary thought. I nodded soberly and said, "That's serious business."

"She's not the first young woman to have an unplanned pregnancy, and she won't be the last. I told her she has my unconditional support and I'll be there to help her learn the maternal skills."

"She know who the father is?"

Mama smiled absentmindedly. "We didn't get into that."

I decided to keep my lip zipped. Dogs were all I'd ever known Gina to date. I was sure glad that with Mitchell I was officially leaving Dogs, Players, et cetera in my romantic past. I had no need for them now.

"Well," Mama said, "Gina will grow as a result of this experience. Now, how about you and me have some fun? We've got some things to celebrate, some things to mourn, and some things to prepare for. Are you in the mood for lunch at Fuddruckers? I just love their strawberry shakes!"

I put both hands on my forehead and began to massage like there was no tomorrow. My time with Mama felt a little tainted by the news about Gina. Mitchell was going to have to make up for quite a bit when I got back home.

MITCHELL

Trey, Tony, and I were locked away in my office. It had been six hours since Gina called with the news of her expected bundle of joy. After I'd picked myself up off the floor, I'd been too tongue-tied to cast any doubt on whether or not I was the father. All I knew for sure was that I hadn't slept with Gina in over a month, since my Trojan turned into swiss cheese. I had been up-front with her since then, letting her know I couldn't see us being serious and saying I needed "space." Unfortunately, she was swearing she was roughly six weeks along, which placed her conception smack-dab in the middle of the time that we were getting busy like clockwork. Getting screwed was going to screw up my entire life, if this child was mine.

I had attempted to calm Gina down by taking her to lunch earlier in the day. While we ate at a Wall Street deli, I apparently went too far when I asked if she'd been seeing anyone else recently. All that got me was a screaming Gina who hurled a plastic fork at me and then yelled all the way back to the Empire tower. On top of that, she damn near turned violent when we got back to my office.

Tony, Trey, and I were now seated amidst the carnage Gina had left in her wake. My computer monitor was still resting headfirst on the carpet underneath my desk, after Gina gave it a karate chop that sent it hurtling from its desktop perch. My family portraits with my folks, Marvin, and Deniece were strewn about the office. My picture of Tasha and Maya lay cracked on the floor, having dropped there after Gina slammed the office door shut with the force of a gale wind. My potted plants, the fake ones as well as the genuine articles, lay in disarray in the far corner. On top of everything else, the place had the smell of a woman scorned—an unsettling mixture of feminine sweetness and desperate perspiration.

Realizing just how far gone Gina was, I had called Tony and Trey, who dropped what they were doing and came over immediately. Now Tony leaned back against a broken wooden chair and surveyed the damage to the office. "Damn, cuz," he said, "you're in deep with this one. Mitchell, how did you manage to knock up a psycho, in just three months of Dogdom?"

Fuming in my desk chair, I glared at my friend. "Apparently my instructor left out a few key lessons along the way, *Tony*. You got me into this situation, man. Now you've got to get me out."

Trey fiddled with the Blow Pop in his mouth and walked over to me. "Stoney, chill out now. You think you're dealin' with something we've never handled? There's all sorts of avenues you can take here."

I put my right hand in Trey's face, Martin Lawrence–style. "Hold up, Trey. I don't want to hear any more of your stupid-ass theories. I have a major problem here! I want solutions, nothing more, nothing less."

Tony shook his head confidently. "All right, here's the deal. Based on what you've said about how flaky this Gina is, she's most likely the type of sister who's looking to snag a brother by any means necessary. We all know for some women that includes getting pregnant on purpose. She's thinking that you'll fold like a house of cards the minute you believe she's having your baby."

I crossed my arms defiantly. "Well, I don't care what she thinks, I'd never marry someone just because they had my baby. I'm all for family values, but I'd have to be a fool to get tied down to someone I knew wasn't right for me."

"Mitchell," Tony interrupted, "you're missing the point. Even if this girl is pregnant, you're probably not the father. You haven't spent every night with this girl, have you?"

"No," I said, "we would see each other maybe two times a week, at best."

"Bingo!" Tony said. "That, my friend, is the beginning of circumstantial evidence that there are other potential fathers out there. Now all you have to do is exploit that possibility to the fullest."

I shrugged. "What do you mean?"

"He means," Trey said, " that you've got to find some other fellas who've hit that in the last few weeks. Until blood tests can be taken, those brothers will be your best friends."

"How would I do this?"

Trey grinned and bit into his Blow Pop. "Bro, it's really quite simple. You'll need to find an excuse to get back into Gina's place and get a copy of her personal phone book. From there, it's just a matter of calling each name and gettin' some good info. All it takes is that one gossipy girlfriend of hers, or a loose-lipped boyfriend. Then you confront her with the fact you know she's been seeing other guys, and tell her you won't hear anything more until the baby's born and a conclusive blood test can be taken!"

I crossed my arms and frowned. "You sound like you've done this before, Trey."

Tony chuckled. "You think Trey claims five kids 'cause that's all he's been *accused* of fathering?"

"Mitchell," Trey said with a face full of sincerity, "I love my kids as much as I do because I *know* they are mine. See, it might be different if I was a punk and just said okay every time a skeezer fingered me as Daddy. But I always apply my system, and separate the wheat from the chaff. It's the only way, man, 'cause trust me: when they do turn out to be your kids, nothing else matters. You'll learn to love them like you've never loved before."

For a moment I felt my stomach settle as Trey waxed eloquent about the joys of fatherhood. Then reality hit me. "This all sounds good, but what if it doesn't work? How else can I at least keep Gina out of my hair, and out of Nikki's hair, until paternity can be proven one way or the other?"

Tony walked over to my desk, stepping around the computer monitor. "Well, there is one other option. You could do the old pay-off; give her money to go away. I'm not so sure that would work in this case, though."

Trey smacked his lips as he bit into the chewy center of his Blow Pop. "Stoney, you're gonna have to trust me and Tony. Why don't I make a sacrifice to help advance the plan?"

"What are you talking about?" I was a little scared by the wide grin on Trey's face.

"Why don't I seduce this Gina and get her to take me home? Then I can make off with her phone book, hell, maybe I can even grab up her diary, if she keeps one. Then we'll set up shop this weekend at your crib and call folks until we have enough dirt to get her to back off."

Tony stood, checked his watch, and clapped his hands loudly. "Brilliant! Look, I've got to make a meeting with the superintendent of schools. Trey, get a list of Gina's hangouts from Mitchell and track her down tonight! We'll all hook up at Mitchell's Saturday morning to go into action!"

"Tony," I said, "I don't think this is the best way—"

"It's already been decided," Trey said as he headed for the door with Tony. "Just call my voice mail and leave the names of Gina's hangouts. In the meantime, I'll ask around and find out what I can on her. Mitchell, it's on!" With that, my two instructors breezed out the doorway and left me seated alone in the wreckage.

I sat there and wondered if I could live with myself if I went along with Tony and Trey's plan to manipulate Gina. Three months ago, I would have thrown them out of my office for such a ridiculous idea. But times had changed. I was a Dog now, and I'd created quite the pile of doo-doo. I was in love with Nikki but trapped by Gina. I felt for Gina, I really did, but my months of hard work were not going to be in vain. I had Nikki now, and losing her was not an option.

Inhaling deeply and holding my nose, I searched my memory banks for Gina's hangouts and did the only thing I could do. I reached for the phone and dialed the numbers for Trey's voice mail. Like it or not, Trey had been right. It was On.

CHAPTER 22

MY HERO

Late August

NIKKI

decided to bring my girls with me this morning. I was not going to make a deal with the devil without having Leslie and Angie's back. As the three of us climbed into Angie's maroon Camry (we had spent the night at Angie's crib in Woodbridge), the sun was shining and the air was heavy with humid heat. I, of course, was dressed for the occasion. I had my hair pulled up into a ball and covered with a crème-colored silk scarf. In my black Ray-Bans and crème pantsuit, I figured I was looking like Mary J. Blige in her "Not Gon' Cry" video. I'd been through too much in the last months to sweat this anymore. I was going to end this nightmare today, one way or the other. Marvin had been secretive about today's meeting but had promised that Empire would make an offer I couldn't refuse. I knew that was technically impossible—how do you compensate someone for a loss of dignity?—but I was going to hear it out. I had other things in my life to tend to.

Scooting into traffic on the Dan Ryan Expressway,

Angie flicked on *The Tom Joyner Morning Show* and began cracking up at Tom, J. Anthony, and Sybil's latest antics. I appreciated what she was doing, trying to distract me from the fact that I was minutes away from writing the epitaph of my career in the music business. Who would hire me after this mess? It just wasn't fair. Feeling a tear seep from my right eye, I was glad I'd kept my sunglasses on.

From her spot in the backseat, Leslie seemed to sense my mood. "So Nikki, tell me about your latest adventures with Mitchell. He puttin' a ring on that finger yet?"

"No," I chortled, "he knows better than to try to pull anything like that. Nikki Coleman is not trying to be anybody's wife, anytime soon."

Angie cut her eyes at me as she flashed a middle finger at the driver behind us. He was still leaning on his horn thirty seconds after Angie jumped into his lane. "Nikki, are you mad? Here you finally wake up and appreciate good husband material like Mitchell, and now you talk like you're just in it for a good time?"

Forgetting my anxiety, I whipped off my Ray-Bans and snapped my neck in her direction. "Did you hear me say that, Angie? All I said is I know better than to think I'm ready to marry *anybody* right now. Hell, I'm enjoying having a functional relationship for the first time. Will you let me get that down pat first?"

Angie chuckled. "Sorry if I jumped the gun, girlfriend. I just happen to think we've got ourselves two good men, and I'm trying not to let Mr. Marvin Stone get away."

"Well," I said, "just remember Marvin isn't baggage-free himself. Give him some time to get used to being in a relationship before you rush him anytime soon."

Angie smiled wickedly. "Oh, I know a little about waiting now. Marvin's teaching me how to be *very* patient."

Leslie poked her head into the front seat. "What? Girl, are you saying what I think you're saying? Marvin ain't spankin' that ass?"

Flicking her wrist in Leslie's face, Angie laughed louder than the rest of us. "Pull up while you still can, Leslie. Marvin happens to have very impressive reasons for abstaining from sex, and I would never stand in the way of them. Besides, it's not like I haven't gone without for a while anyway."

"Hmmph," I said, "what about that hard-body boy Jamal you were with back in May?"

"Oh," Angie said, looking sheepish, "Jamal was about *maintenance*, girls. Marvin is about *romance*. I can do without having my toes curled for a while. Marvin is so bright, so passionate about his political and religious beliefs, and he knows some of everybody. He makes love to my mind."

"That's probably all he knows how to do," Leslie cracked.

I couldn't help myself. I turned to look at my girl and said, "You're a fine one to talk, Leslie."

She leaned back against her seat. "What's that supposed to mean, Miss Thing?"

"Well," I said, "doesn't seeing the success that Angie and I are having with men inspire you? You know, make you think about trying out things on the other side of the fence again?"

Angie wrinkled her nose like she was smelling spoiled cheese. "Nikki, don't."

Leslie leaned forward in her seat and started speaking in clipped, measured tones. "No, Angie. Let's do have this discussion. Nikki, do you have a problem with my being a lesbian?"

As a burning sensation spiked my heart, I turned back toward the windshield. "That's a ridiculous question, Leslie. You're not a lesbian."

"Yes, I am." Leslie's words were weighted with more sincerity, more pain than I'd ever heard in her voice. "So what do you have to say about that?"

I continued to watch the cars on either side of us. *How much longer before we get to the downtown Loop?* I wondered. "Leslie," I squeaked, "what you do in the bedroom is your business. I haven't made the smartest choices in that area myself."

"What?" Leslie whispered. "You're equating my lifestyle with your foolish taste in men? You know what you're saying, don't you? That I won't be as 'good' as you and Angie until I have an acceptable *man* in my bed! It ain't like Mitchell is squeaky clean these days, anyway. Who made you judge and jury over my love life?"

I pleaded with Leslie, stretching my eyes wide as I turned to face her. "Leslie, don't start this politically correct argument with me, please! I admit, I don't like seeing you lead a homosexual lifestyle. I just don't get it. Girl, I know all your sob stories. I know how many fools didn't appreciate you, and I know how much more tender, sympathetic, and supportive women can be! But dammit, when all's said and done, they still can't bring home the bacon!"

My ending jibe worked. We all howled in laughter until Leslie shushed us again. "Look, you gets no argument from me about the differences between brothers and sisters. And not that it's anybody's business, but my sexuality isn't exactly etched in stone. Maybe one day I'll meet that man who sweeps me off my feet. Right now, though, that ain't happening. So I hope you two can accept that."

Angie reached back and slapped fists with Leslie. "You my girl, Leslie, regardless of who you bed with. Just don't tell Marvin!"

We all tittered again as Leslie's and my eyes met in Angie's rearview mirror. I didn't slap hands with her, but the message was clear: *we're girls, no matter what.*

We were all still giddy from our car ride when we stepped off the elevator onto the thirty-sixth floor of Empire Records' headquarters. I was a little surprised that we were meeting with Colin and his lawyers on the main executive floor. All the top brass worked on this floor, which was off-limits to the rest of us peons. Even now it took five minutes for the receptionist to locate my name, get clearance to admit me, and buzz me through the towering oak doors that separated the floor from the lobby. After accepting hugs and prayers from my girls, I followed a tall white boy in a navy jacket and gray pants through the doors. We walked across a plush Oriental carpet until we came to a huge conference room. Marvin was seated inside at a rectangular glass table, across from Colin and Jack Hamm. Everyone was extremely tight-lipped; Marvin barely made eye contact with me as I took the cushioned seat next to him. His eyes were dancing with something, though; I just couldn't tell if it was desperation, amusement, or fear.

I had barely taken my seat and composed myself when the heavy-set little man who spoke at Mitchell's church barreled into the conference room. I remembered Chauncey Wells immediately. He was dressed in an impeccable beige pinstriped suit with matching handkerchief, silk tie, and loud gold cuff links. Strutting like George Jefferson, he bopped his way past Marvin and me and took a seat directly across from Colin. Before his chunky little bottom had hit the seat, he began talking with the same preacherly cadence he'd used at church that Sunday.

"Ms. Coleman, Attorney Stone, let me formally introduce myself. My name is Chauncey Wells, and effective noon today, I will be the majority shareholder and chairman of Empire Records." He winked as if he had just told a harmless joke. "I'm here to close the book on the nasty situation here."

As Marvin fiddled with his hands, I looked from Wells to Colin and his attorney and back. Colin and Jack Hamm were staring at the table like scolded children whose father was apologizing to their schoolteacher.

Hope sprang up in my heart as Wells crossed his legs and put his arms behind his head. "Ms. Coleman, I'll be announcing this deal along with Mr. Lee's father at a press conference today, but I thought you might want to know ahead of the time. I figure after the amount of time you've suffered as a result of Colin's immature antics, you needed some good news." He shot out of his chair and began to make a lap around the table, eyeing the paintings of dead white men that lined the walls.

"Ms. Coleman, if we had time, I could keep you here all day with tales about my beloved mother. She lives with my wife and me on our Atlanta estate, but that woman worked the first half of her life cleaning houses to support me. And when I think of the way some of the rich, stuffy white men who she worked for treated her"—he cast a chilling glare at Colin and Jack Hamm, making them shrink even deeper into their seats—"Well, let's just say I've come a long way since the days I used to see my mother mistreated, and I vowed that when I had the power, I'd never again stand by and see one of my sisters disrespected." Wells stopped pacing and stood between my chair and Marvin's.

"Now that Empire Records is under new management, sexual harassment is going to be a thing of the past. The Good Ol' Boys Club will be replaced by the Down Brothers and Sisters Club. We will be an equal-opportunity employer in word *and* deed. And I'm going to use this case as an example.

"I am offering you the following: three hundred thousand dollars' compensation for the emotional and financial damage you've suffered; a public apology, both in the form of a press conference and a memo signed by company officials, and finally, I am offering to restore you to your prior position, at an increased salary of ninety thousand dollars."

I tried not to smile too brightly. Could this really be happening? "I, I don't know . . . will my salary be increased because I'll be at a higher level of management?"

Mr. Wells popped Marvin on the shoulder playfully and grinned at me. "My, you are a pistol. You want a promotion, too! Well, you best believe if I offer you a raise, it's because I'm expecting even more work. Your new title would be junior vice president of promotions. Are you interested?"

Hell, yes, I'm interested, I thought. Smiling from ear to ear, I tried to be cool as I tapped Marvin on the shoulder.

Taking his cue, Marvin stood, smoothed his suit jacket, and shook Wells's hand vigorously. "Mr. Wells, thank you for your personal involvement. Nikki and I will discuss your offer and get back to you as soon as possible."

Wells groped at his beard and nodded slowly. "Well, the offer's good until midnight tonight. I didn't get where I am by being a patient man, Marvin. Your father can tell you that."

I couldn't help myself. I darted around Marvin and extended a hand to Mr. Wells before I knew what I was doing. "Mr. Wells, I can't tell you how much this means. To see you come in and make this right"—I looked triumphantly at Colin and Jack Hamm, who were slowly gathering up their things like mourners leaving a funeral—"to see a brother come in and set things right, this is the stuff our people dream of. I *will* get back to you, today."

"I'll be waiting," Wells said. "Now you two clear out of here. This place is gonna be a zoo for a while. Besides, Ms. Coleman, I expect to see you in here first thing next Monday."

I smiled before turning and following Marvin out into the lobby. I grabbed at his elbow playfully as we neared the elevator. "Mitchell is gonna flip when I tell him about this! I knew Wells was trying to buy Empire, but who really thought he even had a chance, and who could have known he'd buy it so quick? Mitchell will be in shock!"

As we stepped onto the elevator, Marvin sniffed. "Uh, I don't think so, Nikki."

"What do you mean?" I asked.

Marvin leveled his eyes at me and smiled. "Who do you think hipped Wells to your lawsuit in the first place?"

CHAPTER 23

REVERSAL OF A DOG

MITCHELL

t was six-thirty on a Tuesday night, and Trey was driving his black '99 Ford Mustang down Michigan Avenue like he was Bo or Luke Duke. It had been a while since I'd ridden anywhere with this fool, so I gripped the passenger-side door desperately as we careened from one lane of traffic into another. As a cool evening wind whipped through the open windows, Trey yelled out an update on Operation Take Gina Out. He'd finally tracked her down at the Pines, her favorite club, the night before.

"She was an easy lay, yo," he said. "I mean, I chose not to hit that, given that she's technically one of your babes."

"*Was* one of my babes, Trey."

"Whatevah. Point is, I got her to take me home. After I convinced her to go change into something more comfortable, I rummaged in her bedroom and found a diary *and* a little black book! I gotta say, even I was impressed! This girl gets around!"

I was having a hard time hearing Trey over the roar of his engine. "Of course she's round, she's pregnant, fool!"

"No, I said—never mind! Anyway, dude, I hate to break it to you, but it looks like there's at least five other potential fathers of the bun in Gina's oven."

I heard that line loud and clear. An odd sensation came over me. Relief that I might not be the father made me feel twenty pounds lighter, but I couldn't shake a simultaneous blow to my pride as a Ladies' Man. *Gina played me,* I thought. I guess I'd never thought about it, but I actually think I'd figured that Gina wasn't seeing much of anybody else. By the time Trey got done detailing the dancer, the Chicago Bears fullback, the pediatrician, the painter, and the Chicago State professor, those notions were wiped clean. I'd been played by Gina, in exactly the same way I'd been playing the women in my life for the past three months. *Good Lord,* I thought, *is this what goes on in the Dating Game all the time?* Was this it, this tortured, deceitful dance between unfulfilled, confused souls who never showed their true selves or opened themselves up for examination? I wanted no part of this business anymore. Being a Dog had given me what I wanted in Nikki, and I was ready to cash my Player chips in and walk off into the sunset with my true love. I convinced myself that it was just a matter of time before I'd have Gina scared off, a notion Trey was supporting.

"Yeah, Stoney," he said as we pulled up to Tony's gated condominium, "we got her now. You're in the clear. Next time Gina comes calling, throw those dudes' names in her face, and tell her your name is Bennett and you ain't in it, until she gets a paternity test. I'll lay you money she'll be off your tip then, at least until the baby's born. By then you can have Nikki squared away, and even if you turn out to be the father, having fathered a kid nine months earlier will look a hell of a lot better than having knocked her up a few *weeks* ago."

"You ain't never lied," I said as we climbed out of the Mustang. *That wouldn't be so wrong,* I rationalized. Bottom line, I had no way of being sure Gina's baby was mine. Why risk my relationship with Nikki over something that might never materialize? Trey was right; it made sense to hold Gina at bay and lock things in with Nikki first. Now I just had to figure out how to keep Gina from bursting my bubble. I was counting on Tony to help me figure out some angles where that was concerned.

Trey and I walked into the lobby and nodded at the tall, bearded doorman, an older gentleman who had come to know us by name. He didn't even bother to make us wait while having Tony buzz us in. "Go on up," he said, smiling. "I'm not worried about regulars like you."

By the time we arrived at the door to Tony's condo, I was thinking the doorman should have checked on him first. It didn't exactly sound like a party was going down in there. Clangs, smacks, bangs, and smashes could be heard through the door, followed by muffled shouts that sounded every bit like Tony's obnoxious voice. While I stood there in confusion and looked up and down the hall for help, Trey ran a hand over his bald head and whispered to himself, "Frickin' deal." Before I knew what he was doing, he took two steps back, twirled 360 degrees, and unleashed a long-legged kick against Tony's wooden door, which cracked under the weight and creaked open.

"Tony!" Trey hopped across the threshhold like a ninja poised for battle. I stumbled through the doorway behind him, watching him with amazement as his eyes swept across the plush beige carpet on the floor and the Ansel Adams photographs that filled the walls of Tony's living room. "Tony, what the hell's going on in here? You trippin' again?"

"He's out of his mind!" Juanita, resplendent in an olive evening gown and decked out in sparkling gold jewelry, rushed out into the foyer. It was only when she paused to stare at us that I noticed the smudges in her mascara and the disarray of her silky hair. The sister was out of sorts. She stood in front of Trey and stared at the floor as she gasped out her words. "Trey, he needs help. I've always known it, and now he's proven it. I don't have to take this. Tell him I'm sending someone for my things tomorrow. If he knows what's good for him, he won't touch anything!" As she gathered up her gown to keep it from dragging on the floor, Juanita brushed against me and barreled toward the door. "Bye, Mitchell."

She flew out into the hallway as Tony emerged from the bedroom. The boy looked like hell. I guessed he hadn't shaved for a couple of days, and going by the musty smell leaping off him, he hadn't washed his ass either. This was not the Tony Gooden I knew. Something was up.

As Tony stared at Trey and me with the dazed eyes of a crack addict, I walked over to him, inhaled deeply, and fixed my eyes on his. "Tony, you all right? Something wrong with your folks or something?"

"Hmmph!" He looked right through me and ambled over to the wet bar in the far corner of the living room.

"Trey," I pleaded, "what's going on here?"

Trey sighed and fell into the L-shaped leather couch near the bar. "She left you again, didn't she, man? What reason was it this time?"

Tony poured himself a Scotch, screwed the cork back onto the bottle, and knocked the shot glass back. As he moved to refill it, he said, "Why you think, Trey?"

"Look here, Money," Trey said, as he stood and towered over Tony. "You ain't got to come at me like that. Every time she pulls this mess, who's had your back lately?"

Tony downed his second Scotch and slammed the glass against the bar. "I'm through with that woman. I deserve better than this shit. If she doesn't send someone for her stuff tomorrow, I'm tossing it over the balcony. I'm the top aide to the mayor of Chicago, dammit! I can have any woman I want! I'll be damned if I'll ever let Juanita play around on me again!"

I swallowed hard. "What? Juanita was messing around on you, too? You mean to tell me *you* were getting played, not the other way around?"

Tony stumbled out from behind the bar and swung his arms over his head. "Mitchell, you'll have to excuse me. You weren't supposed to see the underbelly of the Dog life. You see, after a while, playing the Game robs you of self-control. Juanita's been telling me for the last year to keep it in my pants, to be faithful. She thought it was a good idea for me to get used to being monogamous, before we got married."

I shook my head sarcastically. "Women and their crazy ideas."

"Anyway, man, I would last a few weeks at a time, but then I'd meet an irresistible piece. What can I say? Eventually, she got tired of it and started showing me how it felt to be played." Without warning, Tony's voice cracked as his chin slammed into his chest. "Damn, why'd she have to do that?"

The next few minutes were a trip. Tony took us through a play-by-play of the last few months with Juanita. Apparently her flirtations with other men, which she had started as a lesson to him, turned into full-blown affairs. Most of the men had been better-looking and richer than Tony, so it had just been a matter of time before one of them swept her off her feet for good. Trey and I let Tony vent about everything, from his regrets about cheating on Juanita to his anger at himself.

Apparently he felt he was weak for having fallen in love with Juanita. His father, a veteran Player, had taught him how to woo and conquer women, but he had warned Tony to keep his heart hidden from them. In Tony's mind, his father had been proven right every time he fell in love. Each time, he said, the women eventually left him for one reason or another, leaving his heart exposed and battered. Right there in his apartment, Tony swore he'd never experience such pain again.

Before we could talk some sense to him, there was a loud knock on the door. Trey went to the door and eased it open. Two middle-aged police officers in blue uniforms swept into the room.

"Had a report of a domestic incident here," said the heavyset one, through what sounded like four pieces of Bubblicious gum. He looked the three of us over, seeming unsure who to attack first. He finally noticed the tattered condition of Tony's white oxford and the wrinkles in his jeans. "Uh, are you Anthony Gooden?"

Tony approached the officer and held his hands up. "Don't shoot, Officer, my name ain't Rodney King."

"Officer," Trey said in the most respectful tone I'd ever heard him use, "you should know this man is deputy mayor of Chicago."

The thinner officer, a plucky little man with sprouts of hair sticking out from under his cap, frowned at Trey. "Don't tell us how to do our jobs, boy."

Trey blinked twice. "Boy?"

The officer walked over to him. "I said boy. What, you want a resisting-arrest charge or something?"

Trey just stared at the officer, eyes defiant.

I'd have to blame Trey's smart ass for our trip to the local police station. He and Tony were treated to a ride in the police car, and I, Mr. Calm, was allowed to meet them at the station. We didn't emerge from the jailhouse until a few minutes before eleven that night. Tony was the only one who spent any time behind bars, in a solitary cell while the officers put a scare into him. I think he learned his lesson; fortunately he hadn't laid a hand on Juanita, he had just tried to frighten her with another of his tirades. I think the intimidation of the officers, combined with Tony's political ambitions, helped him to see that even the hint of violence toward a woman was unacceptable.

As we stepped out into the cold night, Tony sucked in the fresh air and slapped Trey and me on our backs. "Good looking out, brothers. I promise not to put you through this crap again. Next time I fall in love, I'm taking it slow and easy. No more running from commitment, no more being afraid that a woman will control me. The right woman will let me be my own man without smothering me, right?"

I smiled as I thought of Nikki. "Yeah, Tony, I believe she will."

"Well, I mean it," Tony said as we climbed back into Trey's Mustang, which I'd driven over. "Thanks, brothers."

Two minutes later we were headed back to Tony's place. He was fast asleep in the backseat, and Trey and I were deep in thought. I didn't know what Trey was mulling over, but I knew what I was going to do. It was time to tell Nikki the truth and end my own games once and for all. I reached for Trey's car stereo and fast-forwarded Joe's *All That I Am* CD to "Don't Wanna Be a Player." At that moment, no song could have been more fitting.

CHAPTER 24

IF ONLY FOR ONE NIGHT

NIKKI

Jomo leered at me across our table like a man who just knew he was about to get some. I probably should have refused his lunch invitation today, but his begging had finally gotten to me. I felt so sorry for him, I even offered to pick up the tab as the waitress at Kwanzaa's brought our espressos.

"It's all right, Nikki," Jomo said through an outstretched grin. "I just deposited my first check for my work on Milos's *Unplugged* CD. Soon enough I'll be rolling like you!"

I waved him off with a shrug. "Jomo, please, I haven't even earned my first paycheck from Chauncey Wells yet."

Jomo's eyes sparkled with mischief as he fondled his coffee cup. "Ah, girl, you ain't worried about your paycheck, are you? I hear you already got hooked up with a big settlement check!"

I folded my hands in my lap and said, "Jomo, please, could you be a *little* discreet? If you must know, I am pretty well taken care of. But if I had to choose between the money and being able to go back to work, I'd take work any day."

Jomo shoved aside his cup and lunged for my right hand. "Nikki, I am so happy that everything worked out for you. You deserve all the happiness in the world."

I smiled and slipped my hand into my lap, where it was safe from his reach. "You're right that I've earned the happiness, Jomo. And I have a very special man to thank for it."

Jomo wrinkled his bushy eyebrows. "Oh, really? You mean that Wells guy?"

"No, Jomo, I mean the man who not only paved the way for Chauncey Wells to help me but who also showed me that a man can be romantic, sensitive, honest, and unselfish, all at the same time. But you wouldn't know anything about that, would you?"

As the waitress brought our check, Jomo clamped a hand over it and frowned at me like a spoiled child. "Nikki, why you makin' waves, girl? I thought we was having a nice lunch, and now you tryin' to bless me out?"

I narrowed my eyes. "Jomo, can we be honest with each other? *Really* honest?"

He smiled wide and leaned forward, sending silverware flying as he flopped his elbows onto the tablecloth. "Sure, girl. What?"

"How many other women are you seeing?"

"Nikki," he chuckled, "you don't want the answer to that question."

"No, Jomo, I do want the answer. You see, the problem is that I've been content to mess around with you regardless of how many other women you were seeing. I never viewed you as anything more than a Boy Toy. Didn't it ever hurt your pride that I didn't care who else you were seeing?"

Jomo shifted uneasily in his seat and tugged at the collar of his silk shirt. "Nikki, I don't judge people's morals. I figured you and I enjoyed each other's company, that was all that mattered. Look," he said, leaning forward again, "I'm not some animal, and neither are you. We have other problems and concerns, and those don't include a preoccupation with settling down or getting married. I don't know when I'll be at a point in my career to settle down. I figure I'll know when the time comes."

I relaxed and tapped Jomo's left hand. "But Jomo, you're already thirty-three. I know you're not exactly old yet, but do you wanna wake up at forty and realize you're still not ready for something serious?"

"I don't know," he said, shaking his head. "I just don't know, Nikki. I got bigger fish to fry."

"Well, I can't tell myself that anymore. I need love, no two ways about it. I've been through enough these past few months to realize I've let my career, my past, and my fear of pain keep me from romance for far too long. That's why I realize we can't see each other anymore. I've found someone else. Or should I say, I've rediscovered someone else."

Jomo bumped a foot against mine in a clumsy attempt at footsy. "You sure we couldn't still see each other on a part-time basis?"

I scooted my chair back from the table and chuckled. "Jomo, no means no. I can't trust myself around you."

He pulled out his wallet, withdrew a stack of twenties, and laid them on top of the check. "Nikki," he said as he rose to his feet, "I can take a hint. I'm fired, huh? You think I would have figured it out after you stopped returning my phone calls. You take it easy." He leaned over and pecked me on my cheek. Then Jomo Hayes turned and walked out of Kwanzaa's and out of my life. As always, he took every female eye in the room with him.

By the time I got home this afternoon, Mama was waiting for me. She was off work for the week, so I had invited her to crash at my pad the last couple of nights. When I walked in, she was curled up on my couch, watching a taped episode of *All My Children*. She stopped cheering for Erica Kane long enough to turn toward me and bathe me with a warm smile. "So, how's my working woman doing today?" She patted the couch cushion next to her. "Take a seat and fill your mama in."

Mama and I had a ball for the next hour as I recounted my day. My closure with Jomo was only one of several pieces of good news. My first week back at Empire Records was going unbelievably well. I was back in charge of Sylvia and the other promotions staff who reported to me before the lawsuit. We were designing some awesome campaigns for some of our proven acts, and despite how he dissed me, I was leading the charge on a new campaign for James Martin's new CD. The first few tracks he recorded sounded pretty tight, and with me behind him, he couldn't help but blow up. I didn't have to like him to make money off of him.

Before we knew it, Mama and I realized it was almost six o'clock. We scampered around the apartment trying to get me fly enough for my date with Mitchell. He was supposed to pick me up at seven. That hour before he arrived was a blur of ironing, curling, showering, spraying, and primping. Mama pulled one of her apple pies from the fridge and placed it on the kitchen counter just as the doorbell rang.

"That's my cue," she said as she gathered up her car keys and purse. "Now, you be a good girl!" She turned and opened the door wide. "Mitchell!"

As Mitchell swept through the door and made small talk with Mama, I stood in the foyer and admired my new man. Mitchell was looking more toned these days than ever, proof that he was working out to keep himself up for me. His hair was cut lower than usual, so low he almost looked bald. But it was all good; it gave him a Michael Jordan–type appeal. His goatee was meticulously groomed, and he was draped in a sharp gray-blue single-breasted suit that hugged his body like a model's. In that instant, I forgot all about every other man in my past. Mitchell looked good, and he was my man!

I had barely shut the door behind Mama when he took me in his arms and melted into me with a kiss that turned my knees to silk. "Nikki," he said when we finally came up for air, "I can't let the night get away without telling you what you mean to me. I've always loved you, I see that now. I wanted you back at MLK, I wanted you when our paths crossed again in the spring. I just didn't know how to take my feelings and turn them into reality." He loosened his hold on me and looked over my shoulder. "How I got up the nerve to come at you correct, well, that's a long story."

I smiled and put a finger against his lips. "Mitchell, you don't have to dredge up the past. Let's focus on the present."

"But I need to tell you—"

I caressed his chin and looked deep into his eyes. "Mitchell, you don't have to explain how we got to this point. Let's just be thankful that we've come this far. All this time, we were right under each other's noses." I pulled him close and sucked in the smell of his smoky cologne. I was convinced tonight was the first night of the rest of my life.

MITCHELL

I really wish Nikki had let me finish my thought before we left her apartment. I was going to tell her everything, in that very moment: Gina, the pregnancy, even the several women who still insist on calling me and acting ignorant because I loved 'em and left 'em. These last few weeks, I've been kicking one skeleton after the other into my closet, trying to stuff them in before Nikki sees any of them. Somehow I'd succeeded so far, but I was only so good at it.

I was ready to lay everything out and pray that Nikki would still choose to be with me, until she pulled me close again. Despite the fact that we'd made love several times by then, for some reason tonight felt like we were starting from scratch, in a good way. The rosy smell of her hair, the Obsession perfume that bathed her body, and the mintiness of her breath made me feel like a starving man who stumbles onto a four-course meal. By the time we unlocked our lips, my head was far too dizzy for me to remember my pledge to come clean. For the next several hours, I surrendered to the pure pleasure of being with her.

When I took her outside to my car, I surprised her with a bouquet of ten red roses. When I told her the quantity represented the number of weeks since we first made love, she almost fell out. We vibed off of my Jeffrey Osborne CD until we arrived at Chicago Place. Nikki couldn't believe it when I revealed that Luigi's Fine Dining, the site of our Date from Hell in May, was our destination. Over dinner, we laughed about how heated that night had been and compared our day at work. I tripped her out with details about Stephon Evans's wedding plans. Even Nikki couldn't believe Stephon is actually going through with marrying Missy. As she said, "if Stephon Evans can settle down, anything's possible."

When we finally walked arm in arm out of Luigi's, we went for another stroll out on the shores of Lake Michigan. It was hard to believe how far we had come since our last walk on the beach. We were no longer two cautious friends relating to each other; we were lovers, soul mates, reaching out to each other with complete selflessness. As we neared the car around midnight, I looked at Nikki and admitted what I'd been afraid to for several weeks: I was lucky beyond my wildest dreams.

In order to end the night on a unique note, we went to the Inter-Continental Hotel instead of going back to her place. Fortunately, Stephon had regular access to the presidential suite and let me use it gratis, so I got to look classy without breaking the bank. The place was sharp: deep antique carpets, high ceilings, two levels connected by a winding staircase, and a view to die for—Lake Michigan *and* Michigan Avenue. On top of all that, the staff had followed my instructions and lit vanilla-scented passion candles in the front room, bedroom, and main bath. Nikki was impressed, but like me, she was more interested in who she was with than she was in our surroundings.

After we disrobed and turned the lights low, we took up residence in the main bathroom's Jacuzzi. Nikki played footsy with me and ran her hands over the silk wrap atop her head. "So, are you looking forward to taking me to this party at Empire tomorrow?"

I was surprised we had gone so deep into the night without discussing the Empire party. Chauncey Wells was so determined to show his support for Nikki, as well as his disdain for sexual harassment, that he insisted on holding a formal welcome-back party in her honor. I didn't really think it was necessary, given the sweet financial package she got and the fact that she was already back at work. Truth was, I was uneasy about celebrating anything just yet.

I reached into the soapy bubbles of the warm water and massaged Nikki's right thigh. "Babe, I don't know if I can make the party tomorrow. You know, between this financial plan Stephon and I are presenting to Chauncey Wells and the final planning for his wedding, I don't think I'll have time—"

Nikki wasn't having it. She blew some bubbles from her mouth and clamped a hand against mine. "Mitchell," she cooed, "this is going to be a public acknowledgment of what I accomplished. It's a victory for women's rights at Empire Records. Of all people, I need you there." She smiled the most suggestive smile a woman has ever sent my way. *"Please?* I'll make it worth your while."

I reached for her, ready to guide her onto my stiff, eager staff. That's when it happened.

A voice whispered to me, from somewhere in the far right corner of the bathroom. *You haven't even told her everything,* it said. *You're just going to take her, while she's in the dark?*

"Baby?" Nikki's soft hand on my damp shoulder startled me, and I rustled the water as I met her gaze. She had slipped over to me while I searched the thistle of hanging plants in the corner for the source of the mysterious voice. Now she had grabbed hold of "Mitchell Junior" and was positioning herself over me. "I said I'd make it worth your while—"

I placed a tentative finger onto her warm, full lips. "Let me make it worth yours." Before she could resist, I sat her on my lap, placed her right calf on my left shoulder and held her left calf in my right hand. She lifted her face to me and we kissed violently as I teased the fingers of my left hand down her thighs, between her legs, out again, and back in. Building friction from one minute to the next, I plunged deeper and deeper into my lady, taking time to kiss and tease her full breasts as well. As the CD player we'd sat on the sink filled the air with Michael Jackson's "Lady in My Life," Nikki shuddered with pleasure and let me take control.

I brought her to climax twice before pulling her from the Jacuzzi, drying her with a terrycloth towel, and taking her to the bed for a full-body massage. I worked her from the smooth, rounded tips of her toes to her chocolate-colored, precious calves, to the sinewy tips of her knees, to the firmness of her taut thighs, to her athletic, bulb-shaped hips, to her flat, sweet-smelling waistline, to the beautiful, quivering hills of her chest, to the easy contours of her shoulders, and finally, to the flushed, warm skin of her beautiful face.

My nature still looming and almost painfully erect, I heeded the voice—it was still there, asking, *when will you tell her?*—and rolled off the bed, searching through my night bag, which sat on a loveseat in front of the bed.

"Mitchell," Nikki whimpered, "this is great, baby, but one thing's missing." She was getting her breath back. "That erection would be a terrible thing to waste," she chuckled.

I found what I was looking for, dropped the bag, and turned to face her. "Don't worry about me," I said, hoisting a glistening glass jar of honey. "Tonight is all about you."

"Ooh, baby," she whispered, biting her lower lip and eyeing the jar. She knew what was coming. We'd discussed using the body as a human plate before and agreed there was no better way to inspire a lover's creativity. "Get over here."

I went to my woman and began to drizzle her. I was prepared for a long night of pleasuring, and I was committed to making the pleasure all Nikki's. Until I could figure out how to tell her the full truth, I didn't deserve to invade her most private space. Hopefully she'd be too exhausted to realize the difference by the time I was done with her. If only that had stopped the voice.

When do you tell her?

CHAPTER 25

TOO LATE

Late August

MITCHELL

walked into the main conference room on Empire Records' executive floor and checked my watch. It was almost seven o'clock, time for Nikki's party to begin. I knew the hospitality suite down the hall was packed with guests, all of whom were starting the celebration early with the alcohol and other beverages stocked in Empire's wet bar. In a few minutes they'd be flooding into the conference room, ready to toast Nikki and eat from the spread Chauncey Wells had laid out. Servers dressed in rented tuxedoes rushed back and forth between the tables lining the far side of the room and the massive kitchen behind the back entrance. This was going to be quite a shindig, and I was determined to enjoy it. Nikki had earned it, and so had I.

I had finally arrived. I had passed all my final exams and been certified by Tony and Trey as a bona fide Dog, Ladies' Man, and Player. In the last three months, I had made up for considerable lost time, experiencing a wider range of women than most brothers see in three years. Best of all, my transformation had almost immediately paid off. Nikki was mine now, and I was definitely hers. I'd shredded my black book the night Trey and I got Tony out of jail, although Trey had insisted on keeping a few pages for himself. Whenever a past conquest called, I had taken the direct approach, apologizing for my behavior and explaining that I was now in a monogamous relationship. Most of the sisters had proven very cordial about the whole thing.

All except for Gina, that is. If she was to be believed, she was now almost two months' pregnant. Even though I had confronted her with evidence of her affairs with other men, she was clinging to the conviction that I was the father. By now, I had decided that the only mature response was to lie low and stay out of her way, until paternity could be proven or disproven once and for all. My only concern, in the meantime, was figuring out how to confess to Nikki. Even if I had been intent on continuing in my role as a Ladies' Man, I would have had to 'fess up; they clearly weren't close, but Nikki and Gina traveled in some of the same crowds. It was only a matter of time before Gina made good on her threats to tell Nikki about me.

As I reflected on my dilemma, Marvin burst into the room with a wide smile on his face. I could tell he was still high from seeing Angie, whom he was dating hot and heavy now. I knew she was in the hospitality suite with Nikki, her coworkers, and her family. I had slipped away for a minute to gather my thoughts before the festivities kicked off.

As he sauntered over to me, Marvin's smile faded. "You're looking a little down, baby brother. This is your woman's big night. What's up?"

"You know what's up," I said, as I headed back to the buffet table. "I'm trying to figure out when to tell Nikki about my little situation."

"What?" Marvin clamped a hand onto my right shoulder. "I thought we agreed you were going to tell her the whole story last night?"

I wrestled my way from my brother's grip and waved my hands innocently. "I tried, man. Last night was just too precious to ruin with that unpleasantness. I need more time."

Marvin narrowed his eyes at me. "Just do it. Trust me. You won't get away with this."

"Marvin, we just need to get through tonight. I'm taking Nikki out of town next weekend. We're going to Hilton Head. I can tell her everything then. She doesn't need that drama right now."

Marvin shook his head and ran a hand over the clean slope of his head. "Little brother, listen to me, you really need to—"

Marvin paused as Chauncey Wells himself bopped into the room. His blue oxford shirt was unbuttoned to the second button, and he had a full cocktail glass in each hand. "Gentlemen, let the games begin! I got a roomful of folk right behind me!"

As the room flooded with close to a hundred Empire employees, friends, and family members, I inhaled deeply and decided to put Marvin's frantic-ass warnings out of my head. There would be time to clear the slate with Nikki tomorrow. She deserved to have an unblemished night first.

Time flew as everyone made their first pass at the buffet table and stocked up on the buffalo wings, caviar, finger sandwiches, crackers, exotic cakes, and ice creams that lay before us. When Nikki made her entrance, flanked by Angie, Leslie, and her mother, I almost passed out with admiration. She was so beautiful, in her short-sleeved maroon pinstripe suit with matching kerchief and scarf. More important, her face was radiant with confidence and peace. I was so proud of her, seeing how far she had come and how much her trials had taught her. Now that I'd finally made her mine, I figured I was ready to learn some more lessons about life, with her at my side.

The champagne flowed and the food was devoured for what seemed like hours on end. Around nine-thirty I was enmeshed in a good-natured, drunken argument with Chauncey Wells, Stephon Evans, and Nikki. I had made the mistake of telling them that my aunt Rhonda was hosting her follow-up relationship seminar that weekend, a revelation that got them going on the topic of male-female relationships.

"The problem," Mr. Wells was saying, "is that these young folk today have put romance too far down on their list of priorities. Everyone wants to be rich NOW, to go as far as they can go in their career NOW, then get married. Nobody has faith in the future anymore. Hell, when I was eighteen, I met my wife and fell head over heels in love. Didn't have a pot to piss in or a window to throw it out of, but none of that mattered! I put a ring on her finger and started making babies, right then and there! We had an agreement—we'd never leave one another, but we'd always push each other to be all we could be." He waddled back a little bit and raised his hands to the sky. "See what my wife's pushing got me?"

Stephon put a finger to his chin and smiled. "You may have a point, Mr. Wells," he said, "but you got to understand times have changed from how they were when you was comin' up. You all didn't have the pressures we do. Shoot, these days, racism or no racism, there's no denying that your skin color alone can't keep you from ac- complishing anything in this country that you set your mind to! That's not how it was when you were a kid. And even though we have more opportunities, we also have higher expectations. How can we focus on romance first in this day and age?"

I was enjoying the battle enough to throw my two cents in when I felt an insistent tap on my shoulder. As a spike of fear numbed my chest, I turned to find Tony standing there. I had invited both him and Trey, but Trey had to skip out to take a paternity test, and Tony had said he didn't feel up to a public appearance these days. As I looked at the fresh lines of his fade and the sleek fit of his tailored, double-breasted suit, I figured he must be back in top form. I smiled and gripped him in a brisk handshake. "What's up, man? Glad to see you made it."

The frown on Tony's face stopped me in my tracks. "Mitchell, I'm not here for my health. Step out in the hallway with me, *now*."

I smiled as calmly as I could, excused myself, and followed Tony out into the lobby. He paused and fixed me with another pained frown before opening the massive doors that shut the lobby off from the elevators.

By the time I saw Gina twisting her neck and thrusting her right forefinger into the chest of the security guard outside the lobby, I had already accepted my fate. At least on a subconscious level. My surface-level response was loaded with denial. I strode over to Gina and stepped between her and the embattled security guard, an older white gentleman who apparently wasn't used to dealing with pissed-off sisters.

"Gina," I whispered, "what are you doing here?"

Gina crossed the arms of her cut-off silk T-shirt over her little protruding belly. "You know I'm a friend of Nikki's family, Mitchell, don't trip. Her mom invited me personally."

"But ma'am," the flustered little security guard squeaked, "your name ain't on this list of guests. I can't let you in without being on that list."

Gina clamped onto my right arm. "Is his name on this list?"

The guard shook his head in confusion. "Uh, yeah, that's why he was already inside. What does that have to do with anything?"

"I am carrying his baby," Gina said, "and that means I have a link to this man. If he's invited, so am I."

As I felt my brain shut down in the face of Gina's insanity, Tony slid between us and placed a tentative hand on her trembling shoulder. I could tell from his serious tone and the squint of his eyes that he was not treating Gina in the shallow, sexist manner he had perfected through the years. I hadn't seen such sincerity in Tony in years.

"Gina, can we talk? You really need to pull up. Would you look at what you're about to do? If you go in there, you will ruin a lovely evening for Nikki." He paused as Gina knocked his hand from her shoulder. "Look," he said, "this whole thing is really my fault. I taught Mitchell everything he knows. He was never meant to get mixed up with people as confused as you and me. Trust me, if he's the father of your child, he'll own up to it. In the meantime, why don't you let him and Nikki have a shot at happiness? God knows we all should get a shot at what they might have."

Gina ignored Tony's plea. "To hell with that!" Before Tony or the security guard could stop her, she flung the lobby door open and came face-to-face with Nikki, who stood there with her hands on her hips and a face of granite. Suddenly, I was more concerned for Gina's safety than my own.

NIKKI

I didn't survive relationships with Players like Barry Roberts and Jomo Hayes without developing a sixth sense that alerts me to men who are screwing around. At least I had it before I fell in love with Mitchell. When Gina flung that door open, I was ready to pull her inside, scold her, and get on with the evening. But the minute I saw Mitchell and Tony cowering there like I'd caught the two of *them* in bed together, I flashed back to that day at Mitchell's church when he vanished as soon as Gina showed up. Everything fell into place for me.

I swear the next few seconds unfolded so slow, they felt like hours. I tried to smile as sweetly as I could, even as I started to dance on the balls of my feet. "Gina, do you have to show your ass out in public, even at my party?"

She was too shocked to jump bad with me. She paused suddenly and looked between Mitchell and me like a child searching for a parent's guidance. That one pause alone was a knife through my heart. When Mitchell looked away from us, Gina turned back to me. The shaky, high pitch of her voice told me she was lying. "Hey, Nikki, I was just trippin' because of this guard here. He was illin', but Mitchell and Tony set him straight."

As the guard sat back down at his desk and started to do a crossword puzzle, I hissed out a response. "Oh, somebody set you straight all right, Gina. But I don't want to hear it from you. Mitchell, why is Gina here, and why are you up in the middle of this?" I wanted to slap myself as I threw my drowning lover one last raft. "What, did Tony get Gina pregnant?"

Mitchell looked like he'd been kicked in the stomach. His chest was heaving up and down, and his forehead was filling with sweat. "Tony, Gina, please go on inside," he said as he took a seat on the leather couch just outside the elevators.

When they were gone, I leaned against the doors and crossed my arms. "So?"

Mitchell looked up at me with desperate pleas in his eyes. He reminded me of Clinton in front of that bogus grand jury. "Nikki, I-I don't know what to tell you. There's no excuse."

"Oh, come on, Mitchell. I figured you had changed some since you started hanging with Tony, but I guess I underestimated you. You can do better than that. Come on, tell me how you really loved me and just viewed Gina, emotionally fragile fool that she is, as a sexual plaything. Tell me that it's not like you cheated on me. After all, you met her before we became serious, right? And the fact you never told me you could be the father of her child *and* acted like you didn't know her when she showed up at your church? Come on, you Dog, feed me a good line!" I no longer cared that the security guard, who kept stealing glances our way, was there. Or that the tears streaming down my face were ruining my mascara. "Come on, Mitchell! Surely you've learned by now how to fool a trusting girlfriend! Why would you be different from anyone else I've dated?"

"Nikki," Mitchell said as he rose from the couch and groped for words. "Nikki, I can explain." His voice started to flutter and took on a soprano pitch. "I'm not like the others. Just hear me out."

"No, thank you," I said, as I hit the down button for the elevator. My head was swimming, my stomach was curdling, and my knees were buckling. I took the only satisfaction I could from the panic that filled Mitchell's face.

"Nikki, wait. You got people here to help you celebrate, you can't—"

I reached out and grabbed Mitchell by the collar with a force that surprised me as much as it did him. "Don't you ever," I said through clenched teeth, "ever try to tell me what I can or can't do. Congratulations, Mitchell Stone," I said as the elevator door opened, "you just killed my last hope of believing in a man, you son of a bitch." As the door started to close, I released my grip on Mitchell's collar and threw myself into the elevator. The last thing I saw before the doors closed was Mitchell's choked, weeping face.

As the elevator raced for the first floor, I let every bit of betrayal, disillusionment, and resignation that welled up in me go free. "*Why?!*" I slammed a fist against the back of the elevator and slid to the floor, tears filling my eyes and plopping onto my suit, beading up against its fine fabric. My body refused to calm down, but in my mind I made a solemn vow: I had just suffered my last heartbreak.

No man was worth this.

CHAPTER 26

BACK AT THE SHACK

Mid-September

MITCHELL

thought long and hard before I climbed into my Accord and headed downtown to O'Dell's Chicken & Waffle Shack. Aunt Rhonda was hosting the follow-up to her *What's Love Got to Do with It?* seminar, and I couldn't resist going to see the fireworks, despite the fact that my own love life was a complete shambles.

As I cruised over to Tony's apartment, I looked at the clock on my dashboard. It was seven-thirty in the evening; we'd do well to make it to O'Dell's by eight. The seminar had started at seven, so we'd be fashionably late, just the way I wanted it.

When I rolled up to the curb, Tony and Trey were standing outside the main entrance, chilling. Trey was looking a little different these days. He was actually letting his blond head of curls grow back in, and he had shaved every bit of hair from his face, including his raggedy beard. It was kind of scary; he looked like that Justin Timberlake kid from N Sync. He was still the same old Trey, though. He bounced into the backseat as Tony climbed into the passenger seat. "Stoney, what's up, Boyeee! Let's move! You got work to do at O'Dell's!"

"Trey," Tony said as he turned toward the backseat, "shut the hell up. You and I are going along tonight for one reason only: to provide our brother moral support. We're the ones who got him in this situation in the first place."

Trey shifted in his seat and rolled his eyes at me in the rearview mirror. "Excuse me, partner. Stoney, what's the good word?"

I gritted my teeth and put the car into gear. "I don't know, man. I really don't know why I'm even going to this seminar." I shook my head and allowed myself to feel the aching sensation in my chest, a hurt that symbolized my longing for Nikki. I had spent the last few weeks living life like a zombie: going to work, going to the gym, coming home and tripping with Marvin, and going to bed. I hadn't returned so much as one call from a lady the whole time, and *sex* was a word that was becoming foreign to my vocabulary. Nikki wasn't returning my phone calls, and even her mother wouldn't put in a good word for me. As she told me on the phone, "Some women can only take so much, Mitchell. I believe you mean well, but I ain't the one who just had her heart stomped on. Nikki has to make the decision to speak to you herself."

Without Nikki in my life, there was no point searching for anyone else. Sure, I knew I'd get over her someday and hopefully figure out how to find someone else, but who knew how long that would take? The only good thing that had happened to me the last few weeks had been my agreement to start attending some church activities with Marvin. Now that I was without a social life again, he and I had made time to talk in depth about our respective problems. Seeing how far he had come since his divorce and his newfound ability to talk about what had led to it, I felt obligated to share some of my own mess. I guess the fact that Marvin and I stopped judging each other and started talking is what led to my agreeing to attend some prayer meetings and Bible studies with him. I was even starting to think about joining Trinity United and getting active in their singles ministry.

Considering how I'd fouled things up with Nikki, it was looking like I'd be single for quite some time.

By the time we rolled up to the parking lot of O'Dell's and hurried inside, a battle of the sexes was in full roll. Aunt Rhonda was moderating a discussion about what black men need and want from black women. She was perched onstage on the same wooden stool she used before, with her arms crossed and a weary smile on her face. "People, people, please calm down. I know we can all get sensitive at times, but we have to let this brother who has the floor finish his comment. Please quiet down."

As Tony, Trey, and I sauntered down the front steps and crossed through the bar, I inhaled suddenly when I heard the voice of the male speaker. As we came to the opening of the main room, I froze at the sight of Barry Roberts, Nikki's ex, standing at the microphone. I found myself hoping that she'd decided not to come tonight.

"Ms. Watts," Barry was saying from his spot near the front of the room, "I don't think we can talk realistically about the problems black women have finding mates without acknowledging what they've done to ruin more than a few honest, upstanding brothers." Barry shrugged and fondled the Polo emblem on his rugby shirt as the women in the crowd erupted again. "Noise won't intimidate me, ladies. I save captains of industry millions of dollars every year and sweet-talk juries on a daily basis. I can take the heat. Look, how can you deny the fact that every woman in this room would have wanted to get with me just a few months ago? I had everything—pretty-boy looks, a rich family, plenty of my own money and ambition, and I've always been a smooth talker.

"But you know what? Until a few weeks ago, I was the most selfish piece of work you've ever seen. I married my wife mainly because I got her pregnant in college. So when I grew tired of her a few years back, I started fooling around. I love our child, but I never transferred that love to my wife. I was all about myself. My wife was still willing to stay with me, and every other woman I knew offered to take me off her hands. That is, all except one." Barry paused all of a sudden and turned to the next table to smile lovingly at a fine sister who was seated next to Marvin and Angie. It was Nikki.

"One woman," Barry said as he locked eyes with *my* woman, "made it clear that she wouldn't continue to validate selfish behavior from the man in her life. Nikki, you told me in no uncertain terms that I could forget being in your life, as long as I was married and committed to someone else." He grinned slyly and put a hand into the pocket of his khaki slacks. "Nikki, I did it. I left my wife last week. Our separation is now official. I will always love my son and be in his life, but I had to be honest with myself: you're the only woman I've ever loved." A wave of awed silence washed over the room. This was turning real personal. Barry stretched an arm in Nikki's direction as she looked away in embarrassment. "We can have what we always should have had, Nikki. You know there's *nothing* I can't give you. Give me a chance?"

As the women in the crowd actually whispered sounds of encouragement, anger and embarrassment bubbled up inside me. Before I knew what I was doing, I looked Tony and Trey in the eye. They both clapped me on the shoulder and shoved me through the entryway. I stumbled down the steps and burst onto the stage and Aunt Rhonda stared at me as if I was a crazed fan. As our eyes met, family intuition took care of everything. Aunt Rhonda seemed to sense immediately that I needed her microphone, so I could jump in before Barry made a damn marriage proposal to Nikki. Without even trying to introduce me, she slid back from the mike and watched me expectantly.

As the room buzzed anxiously, I flashed a look at Marvin, who gave me a thumbs-up. That was all I needed. I gripped the mike with one hand and started to pace around the stage like a rock-and-roll singer. "Excuse me, people, but Barry's decision to get personal this evening leaves me no choice. You see, this man has just put the woman I love on the spot."

"Oh my Gawd!" A woman at a table near the back slapped hands with one of her girlfriends. "This is gonna be good!"

Playing her off, I looked right at Barry. "Barry, I should commend you, man. Your general point, that stuff about women encouraging men to be selfish Dogs, et cetera, that was all good. But you see, Barry, your problem is that you *are* a selfish Dog."

The group at Barry's table, a bunch of overdressed, overprimped buppies, huffed and heehawed. "Who is this loser?" I heard one of them say to the other.

Barry stayed at his microphone and eyed me like a fellow cat who had grabbed his favorite mouse. "Look, Mitchell—that is your name, isn't it?—you don't have to go and act black over this. I heard about the way you made a fool out of Nikki at that Empire party! Who are you to tell me what kind of man I am?"

"Who am I?" I chuckled and paced toward the left side of the stage. "Barry, I'm the honest, responsible brother who used to sit on the sidelines and hear treasures like Nikki complain about the BS you and your fellow Dogs put her through. I *used* to be that brother, that is." I paused and planted my hands against my hips. "He's right, brothers and sisters, I did embarrass Nikki recently. I'll tell you why. I wasn't proud of who I was. I felt unappreciated by Nikki and every other woman I'd tried to date, so I thought I'd try the Dog lifestyle on for size. All it got me was the pain of hurting the first woman I've ever had the opportunity to love."

My heart stopped as Nikki finally rose from her seat, crossed her arms over her suit jacket and looked from Barry to me and back. I swear, you could have heard the proverbial pin drop.

N I K
K I

Score another point for gun control. If I'd been packing that night, I would have plugged Barry first, then Mitchell. Then I would have dropped the gun on my table and walked out of O'Dell's with my head held high. I had second thoughts about attending tonight for fear of running into Mitchell, but damn, this was way beyond my worst nightmares!

The worst thing about the whole experience was the way each of these men affected me. Hearing Barry talk so personally and so lovingly fulfilled dreams I had clung to for more than a few years after we broke up. To see him drop the woman who stole him from me in the first place, and then proclaim his loyalty to me—I'd be lying to say it wasn't both satisfying and thrilling.

Seeing Mitchell bolt his way onstage and take Barry on was a double-edged sword as well. Every woman dreams of having a man who's so into you that he would go to any length to win your heart, and Mitchell's split-second decision to take over the stage was pretty impressive. As I stood there and eyed the both of them, my head struggled to tell my heart to shut up. The words of both men sounded nice, but I already knew they had both fallen down on the job.

I put a hand on my right hip and gathered my strength as Tony rushed over with a microphone in his hand. I grabbed the mike and started speaking. "Brothers and sisters, what you're seeing is two Dogs struggling to clean up their own crap. Cute, isn't it?" I tried to smile as the audience laughed. I think they appreciated my attempt to relieve the tension.

I looked at Barry first. "Barry, please sit down. You are an extraordinary man, but you are not for me. I hope you're sincere about cleaning up your life, but between your impending divorce, your responsibility to your child, and your record of disappointing me in every way possible, you have more baggage than I can handle." I hated to embarrass him like that, but I had to simplify things quickly. Barry looked at me with downcast eyes, gathered up his leather jacket, and headed for the door. He didn't even seem to care that the rest of his table mates ignored him and stayed rooted to their seats.

As the door slammed shut behind Barry, I put my hand on my hip, licked my lips, and nodded in Mitchell's direction. "Now, what, ladies, do you suggest I do with this one? Without getting too personal, let's just say he failed to disclose that he was seeing several other women while we were dating. I admit, we weren't exclusive, but I thought he was different. Now he says he can hang up his Dog-like ways and be loyal to me. What do you say, girls? Once a Dog, always a Dog?"

A petite girl who looked like she was still in college responded from a mike at the table next to mine. "Not to take up for the brother, but don't most guys go through a Dog phase at some point? I think they can settle down, once they've sowed their oats."

A heavyset sister in loud jewelry bolted to a mike in the far left-hand corner. "I don't think so! All brothers are captive to their sex drives. Any man who hasn't learned to control that by now will never change. Look at yourself, girl! You've obviously put up with this BS all your life. You deserve better. Send this fool packing!"

"Okay, okay," I said, waving the other three sisters who had hopped up back to their seats. "I guess there's no easy answer." I paused and looked at the wooden floor. I was too drained to continue airing my business in public. Over the last several weeks, I had already heard every argument for and against Mitchell, anyway. The only thing I knew was that I loved him, deeply, and even before he had shown up at O'Dell's, I knew he felt the same thing for me. Most of all, I knew beyond a shadow of a doubt that he was sincere about giving up his short-lived Dog ways in order to be the man I had always needed. I had a feeling about where things were headed, but there were still some very real questions to deal with, not the least of which would be the outcome of Gina's pregnancy.

Mitchell stood onstage looking ready to collapse from frustration and embarrassment, and as the room buzzed with anticipation of my comments I put my mike down and waltzed toward the stage. Even Mitchell's aunt Rhonda looked at me and mouthed, "Take it easy, now."

I climbed the steps and stood a few inches from Mitchell. His jean shirt was a little damp with perspiration, and even though he was smiling faintly, I could tell he was shaking inside. As he took my trembling hands in his, he said the words I had waited to hear for years, in a way that told me they were for real. "Nikki," he said loud enough for all to hear, "I love you."

As my head rang and the room filled with the weeping cries of the women and the skeptical catcalls of the men, I decided to let pure emotion guide me. I stood on my toes, slipped my hands around Mitchell's neck, and whispered into his right ear. "Mitchell, I love you, too. Call me sometime soon. Not tonight, not this week, but soon."

A smile spread wide on Mitchell's face, and he reared back to respond. I released my hands from his neck, smiled back, and slammed my right fist against his jaw. Too startled to catch himself, he stumbled back against his aunt's stool and slammed onto the floor. As the crowd burst into loud, joyful shrieks, I descended the stage, motioned for Leslie, Angie, and Marvin, and headed for the door. They say every Dog has his day, but Mitchell's wouldn't be today. He had earned the right to sweat a little.

I was through rewarding bad behavior.

December 21

he drive out to Chicago Heights felt like a cross-country road trip. By the time we neared the exit for Nikki's mom's condo, I was starting to question my judgment, even though Ebony had assured me that Nikki knew I was coming and everything was okay.

Fortunately I had Terry, my little "brother" from the Chicagoland Mentoring Project, with me for company. He and I had spent all afternoon downtown doing our Christmas shopping. Ordinarily I do my gift buying at the malls in Homewood, Calumet City, or toward Skokie, but Terry lives in the Robert Taylor Homes and had never seen the Christmas displays on Michigan Avenue or the Magnificent Mile. I had to let him take it all in at least once. He's twelve, so pretty soon he'll be too old to care about the Santa, Frosty, and Rudolph exhibits.

He's a perceptive kid, too. He eyed me skeptically as we came to a stop at the first red light. "You get sick from something we ate at the Navy Pier, Mr. Mitch? You got that look like my mama gets the first few months she's pregnant."

I decided to be as truthful with him as I could. Since laying down the Ladies' Man mantle months earlier, my radar for self-deceit had become sharper than ever. "I'm, uh, going to be fine, Terry. This lady that you're going to meet is just very special to me."

Terry chuckled and adjusted the fit of his Cubs baseball cap. "That mean you love her?"

"Yes, I do," I said as I zoomed through the intersection. "Someday you'll learn about that, hopefully in a better way than I did." I decided at that moment that whether or not I was about to become a father, I would at least help Terry through his teen years, hopefully in a way that would help him avoid the pathology of the Dog or Ladies' Man. In just three months we already had the easy rapport of a boy and his young uncle. At least something good had come of my exit from the dating scene.

When we pulled up to a space adjacent to Nikki's mom's condominium, I let Terry go to the trunk and retrieve the packages of gifts I'd purchased for her and Nikki. Surprising myself, I let a silent prayer cascade from my lips as I followed him to the front door. I really wanted them to appreciate the gifts, to understand I was here not to get something, but to truly give in a spirit appropriate to the sacred holiday. I guess that's why my heart was hammering was so loudly.

N I K
K I

"They're here," Mama said in a fluttery voice as I lay on the leather loveseat in her great room. I was right underneath the skylight, staring up at the snowflakes matting the glass and listening to Luther Vandross's Christmas CD. I had told myself I wouldn't let it affect my mood when Mitchell stopped over, but I had decided to stop being paranoid and play things by ear.

I stood up and straightened my sweater as I heard Mama flip the locks on her door and flood the room with a blast of chilled air. As she welcomed them in, I looked over and smiled as little Terry removed his galoshes and Mitchell shrugged out of his stylish three-quarters boots. He still knew how to look good.

We all sat in the great room and made small talk for half an hour or so, our attention focused on Terry and his exploits in school and on the basketball team. He was clearly a kid with a lot of promise, and I had confidence he was in good hands with Mr. Mitchell Stone.

"Terry, do you like sweet-potato pie?" Mama's question kind of came from nowhere, just as Terry was getting into a Bears game on television. "I've got that, three flavors of ice cream, and hot chocolate in the kitchen. Wanna join me?"

"You got a TV in there, too?"

"Yes." Mama crooked a finger in his direction and wiggled it. He looked at Mitchell for approval and made a beeline behind her in seconds.

As they disappeared, Mitchell looked around anxiously and seemed to slide a little further down the couch, away from me. I was still in the loveseat, but in his prior position on the couch our elbows had almost touched. "Nik, do you want to open your gift early? You don't have to, but I thought it would be nice."

I frowned. "I can wait." *Can you?* I thought. I wasn't buying him a gift, but I knew that wasn't what he was worried about. "Look," I said, "so you know, I heard about Gina."

Mitchell swallowed, looking stricken, and looked at Mama's spongy new carpet below. "I was going to tell you, but not tonight."

"Why?"

He shrugged. "Thought it would look too self-serving."

I bit my lower lip and looked at the floor myself. He was right. When I heard that Gina had moved back out to Los Angeles without informing anyone—Mama, her family members, or Mitchell—it just confirmed for me what a mistake Mitchell had made messing with her in the first place. "What exactly did she tell you about the baby?"

"That she knows in her heart it's not mine," he said, his voice catching. "She says she thinks she knows who the father is, but that it's not worth sorting through the possibilities. She doesn't want anything to do with any of us." He met my gaze, communicating more than just the words. "She thinks she can handle the baby on her own."

"So she is keeping it?"

"*Him*. Yes, she's keeping him."

I exhaled deeply and resisted the urge to draw Mitchell's head to my bosom. "Are you going to try something legally, maybe demand a paternity test?"

"Marvin's offered to help me investigate some channels, assuming we can ever find her. Look, can we change topics?"

"Yes." I sighed.

"How are we going to handle the wedding? This is scaring the mess out of me."

"You, too," I said, grinning. "I think my girl and your brother are nuts to be engaged after four months of dating. But I've never seen two people more in love than Marvin and Angie."

"Oh, they know what they're doing," Mitchell chuckled. "I just don't want the weekend to be too awkward for us."

"Mitchell," I said, "we've got four more months to prepare for that. Not to mention, we've been okay on the job, too."

He stood up and I felt my heart race.

"Nikki," he said, walking toward me, "I hear all that, but it's not that simple. I have to leave now before I make you uncomfortable."

I stood to face him and touched his shoulder, hoping to calm him. "I'm fine, Mitchell. What's wrong?"

"I know I messed up," he said, taking both my hands in his. "Just promise me that someday, sometime, you'll give me another chance. If you say that much, I'll wait as long as you need."

Seeing the sincere pain in his eyes, feeling his cool breath, and smelling the same scent and cologne that had driven me to heights of passion months ago, I slowly relived the previous months' horrible events. Learning about Gina, knocking Mitchell out in public, and retreating into seclusion. Who was I to judge a man who had tried to do right for so long, and changed up only because I had sent messages that I didn't respect that? I had said it all that night at O'Dell's.

My man was standing right in front of me, and I wasn't letting him get away.

"You know what?" I whispered above the CD and the muted television. "I'm going to wait and open my present on Christmas. But I want you to have yours early." With that, I reached up for his shoulders, let him wrap me in a careful, close embrace, and let a feeling of holiday warmth, cheer, and love flood over us.

Q: Was it difficult writing from a woman's point of view?

A: Maybe I should be concerned about this, but it wasn't as difficult as I had feared. Seriously, I developed Nikki's voice from observations of various women in my life. You pick up the nature of people's character, their thoughts, their speech mannerisms, through conversations and just spending time with them. Whether I was writing in Mitchell's voice or in Nikki's, I had to step outside of myself and let these characters speak on their own.

Q: What did you want to convey about male-female relationships in this novel?

A: I'd like people to think a little harder about the way we select our mates, lovers, or "baby-mamas." Mitchell goes to extremes to win Nikki's heart, but would he have ditched his "nice guy" persona if he hadn't received such discouraging messages from women in general?

Q: Do you think women really want bad boys?

A: There's no point generalizing, but I'd guess more than 50 percent of women do want a "bad boy," at least until they hit an age where they want a responsible breadwinner and father for their children. Men are stereotyped as fixating on looks and sex, but I think there are certain types of women who are fixated on men who bring excitement and danger to the table. It's probably those women who may later want a "reformed" Dog, but even then they like the challenge of taming him.

Q: How is this novel different from your first book, Between Brothers?

A: *Nice Guy* is definitely more irreverent than *Between Brothers*. It's a quicker read and focuses on two central characters. With *Between Brothers* I took readers into a more plot-driven, complex story line. I was also more concerned with offsetting negative images of the black male in that story. With *No More Mr. Nice Guy*, my goals were simpler.

Q: Was there a message you wanted to get across in this novel?

A: I'd like to hear from female readers whether they find Mitchell more interesting in his authentic "Nice Guy" persona or in his affected "Ladies' Man" mode. A lot of my good brothers out here love their black women, but feel like they can't win them over by being themselves.

Q: What is next for you?

A: Right now I'm working on two new manuscripts. One is a suspenseful love story entitled *The Power of Love*, and the other is a sequel to *No More Mr. Nice Guy*, currently titled *The Perfect Blend*, which focuses on Nikki and Mitchell but features O. J. "Sinister Minister" Peters from *Between Brothers* as a supporting character.

1. Mitchell's dissatisfaction with his life is caused, in part, by pressure to live up to the expectations of his successful family. How do his parents and brother, Marvin, influence his decisions? How hard is it to live with the pressure of expectations?

2. When Mitchell becomes a Player, juggling all his different women sometimes seems to be more trouble than it's worth. If he could do it over, would he make the same decision? If Nikki continued to reject him, would Mitchell still be a Player?

3. Frustrated by a lack of male attention, Leslie chooses to opt out of the dating game entirely and get her satisfaction elsewhere. Is she doing it just because there aren't any good men? Why doesn't Nikki accept her choice?

4. Although Nikki is friendly with Mitchell, it is only after he changes into a Dog that she thinks of him as someone who is more than a friend. Would Nikki have fallen in love with Mitchell if he hadn't become a Dog? Had she loved him before and not realized it?

5. Mitchell thinks he knows what kind of man women want. Is he proven right?

To print out copies of this or other Strivers Row reading group guides, visit us at www.atrandom.com/rgg.

6. Nikki's relationship with her father affects her expectations about the men in her life. What role does Gene play in Nikki's decisions about whom she dates? Is Nikki trying to find in others the love she missed with her father?

7. At their fateful dinner, Mitchell feels Nikki has been leading him on: she knew she would never date him seriously but still allowed him to wine and dine her. Is Mitchell right to tell Nikki she must pay for her meal when she rejects his advances? Does the fact that a man spends money on a woman obligate her to anything?

8. Do women want a man who is "bad" because they have been taught—as Trey claims—to think negatively of their sexuality? Do women prefer a "bad" man over a "good" one? Do women reward bad behavior?

9. Mitchell and Nikki want to find love, but neither truly understands what love is. Nikki associates it with betrayal and Mitchell sees love selfishly, as something he deserves. In the end, they both realize love is something more. How does this happen? What do they come to understand about love?

10. There is a good deal of game-playing between men and women in dating relationships. One reason Mitchell feels he needs to be a Player is because his honest approach puts him at a disadvantage when everyone else is playing a game. Does it pay to be honest in relationships? Are the games men and women play harmful?

11. Tony and Trey's relentless pursuit of women seems designed more to pad their egos rather than provide any real pleasure. Are they trying to compensate for insecurities? Why can't Tony stay faithful to his girlfriend?

C. KELLY ROBINSON is the author of the novel *Between Brothers*. He holds degrees from Howard University and Washington University in St. Louis and is also a former volunteer with Big Brothers Big Sisters, Mentor St. Louis, and Student Venture Ministries. A recipient of the 2001 National Communicative Disorders Award, he is working on his next novel and delivering motivational speeches to teens and young adults. He lives in Dayton, Ohio. Visit his website at www.ckellyrobinson.com or send him an e-mail at ckrob7071@aol.com.